FROM THE LIBRARY OF

The
Strawberry Girl

The Strawberry Girl

Helen Upshall

PIATKUS

First published in Great Britain in 1993 by
Judy Piatkus (Publishers) Ltd of
5 Windmill Street, London W1P 1HF

**The moral right of the author
has been asserted**

*A catalogue record for this book is available
from the British Library*

ISBN 0-7499-0150-0

Phototypeset in 11/12pt Linotron Times by
Computerset, Harmondsworth, Middlesex
Printed and bound in Great Britain by
Butler & Tanner Ltd, Frome and London

Kind acknowledgements to David Warwick
for his two books published by Ricktomes,
entitled: *BYGOME WICKHAM* and
MEON VALLEY MEMORIES which gave
me valuable insight into the life and times of
the people of the Wickham area at the turn
of the century

For Grace and Phil
with love and many thanks for
your help and inspiration

PROLOGUE
1899

Agnes Mead straightened herself from the back-breaking work of picking strawberries. She looked towards the west where the sun was hanging low in the June sky. Only another half hour or so and she could go home. As she savoured the balmy evening air, taking deep breaths to fill her tired lungs, she ran her hands gently over her belly. Home was a small brick house she shared with her husband, Dick, and their brood of five children. As if she didn't have enough to do caring for them all as well as thinking for them without the added burden of working until sunset. She was of medium height but much too thin. Never enough food to satisfy her own stomach after giving the others their fill, and never enough rest or sleep to prepare her body for the next day's toil. What had she done to deserve such a punishing life? she wondered.

A couple of crows chasing one another cawed excitedly as they made for the rookery in distant tall trees. The thickly wooded Forest of Bere, situated in the north-west and east of Hampshire, sheltered vast acres of fertile fields where strawberry growing had brought prosperity to the local community. The warm southern aspect created an ideal climate in and around Hundred Acres in Wickham where long, tidy rows of rich green foliage hid the ripened plump fruit growing in abundance.

More crows circled and swooped above Nessie's head. Spring and summer – a time for mating, time for rearing young. The blackness of the huge birds reminded her of Dick and she smiled to herself. When sober he was a bit of a lad, fond of horseplay, seldom serious. With his gypsy dark hair and fiery black eyes not unlike the rook who noisily chased after his mate. Nessie wasn't sure whether the rook had another side to his nature but Dick certainly did when he'd had too much to drink. He wasn't too clever at holding his liquor, and the after effects caused nothing but disruption in an otherwise happy

3

homestead. If he wasn't such a slave to the drink he'd be able to hold down a job, and if only he'd do an honest day's work to keep his wife and family there'd be no need for Nessie to be picking strawberries. No rent, no home. Dick had little pride.

It piqued Nessie that Jake Taylor, her one time suitor and Dick's rival, was the new rent collector. He was as embarrassed as she when she'd had to admit that she couldn't pay the rent but had quickly come up with the suggestion that she work in the estate fields in lieu. Nessie knew that Dick would be furious. She'd toyed with the idea of telling him in the hope that he would turn over a new leaf, but with his quick temper to consider she knew it would mean a beating instead. It was easier this way. As soon as he'd left for the inn in Wickham each weekday evening, Nessie could leave the children in the care of her younger sister, Beth, while she came out into the fields to work. Although she was weary she did find a small measure of peace here in God's sweet-scented air.

A wave of nausea swept over her. She passed a hand across her brow against the setting sun and gulped for air. The moment passed. Down on her haunches again. She must get on, payment was according to baskets filled. No time to feel hungry. If she earned enough and to spare Benjie needed new shoes. In solitude she could romance about all the things money might buy . . .

A shadow blotted out the sun momentarily and Nessie came back to reality. Not another fainting fit – the hand on her shoulder made her start, and she looked up to find Jake Taylor standing over her.

''Evening, Nessie,' he said in a voice which was just a mite too friendly.

'Hullo, Jake.' She found it difficult to meet his gaze. He was taller than Dick, his intense dark eyes revealing the strain of gypsy blood which most of the local families had inherited, being descendants of squatters who had lived, worked and moved about in the forest region for the past century.

'Working late again, I see.'

Nessie daren't glance up as she said with irritation: 'Got to earn the rent, as well you know.'

'There's another way you could earn it – a way we'd both enjoy much better.'

Nessie moved along the row of strawberry plants trying to put more distance between herself and Jake. He was as aware as she of how his handsome good looks could charm any woman. In their younger days she had almost fallen victim to his fatal charm, but Dick Mead had seen the danger signs and made sure he put his girl in the family way so that a shot-gun wedding was necessary. Jake had never forgiven

4

Dick for taking Nessie, and she could never look him in the eye for fear of seeing his blatant desire. He could still stir some feeling in her breast. She was, after all, only twenty-five, for all she had borne Dick five children over the past seven years.

Jake followed Nessie along the row. He bent down inches behind her.

'You know you always fancied me better 'n Dick Mead,' he said in a low voice. 'That scruff was too old for you, too vulgar and coarse with his rough habits. What sort of life can he ever give you when he spends every penny on drink? By the time you're thirty he'll have worn you out having babies.'

'Dick's only five years older than me, and I'm happy with my children,' Nessie replied defiantly.

'But I'm nearer your age and you would have been mine if that swine hadn't . . .'

'Don't dare speak ill of my Dick!' Nessie spat out at him over her shoulder. Just one glimpse of his narrowing covetous eyes gave her a warning which came too late. He was atop her with more savagery than Dick ever showed.

'Get off me, Jack Taylor,' she shouted, but her cries were lost amidst the screeches of the flock of rooks homeward bound in the pale pink sky.

She tried to fight him off but her wasting muscles were no match for his prime strength. In seconds her skirt was pulled off along with patched underwear and he entered her with no preliminary wooing. Her body was no stranger to abuse but this sudden, vicious attack made her retch before she fainted and went limp beneath Jake's bulk.

The faint was genuine, though if by orchestrating it she had hoped to put Jake off she was mistaken. As she revived it was to realise that the attack was far from over. He was demented, slapping her back to life, urging her frail body to respond to his demands, and when she didn't he pulled back only to plunge into her with renewed force, again and again, until with a hideous cry he lost control. Groans of lust changed to moans of pleasurable satisfaction which filled Nessie with total disgust. She turned her head to spew away the contents of her heaving stomach.

'That's how I want the rent paid, Nessie, my dear – but don't let's make such hard work of it next time. Be ready for me. Clean sheets in the bed when Dick goes off on his drinking binges,' he whispered in her ear. 'Your young sister will be glad of a copper or two to take the kids off your hands.'

'Dick'll kill you when he hears . . .'

Jake laughed. 'You know you'll never have the courage to tell him – he'd kill you first and ask questions afterwards.' He got up and turned from her, making towards the edge of the field to keep out of sight although thankfully there was no one else around. Laughter from other pickers in the next field had long since died away as dusk cloistered Hundred Acres.

Nessie didn't know how long she remained motionless on the ground. She moaned and wept from humiliation, hardly aware that her cries made an eerie sound across the fields. She tried to put the memory of Jake's laughter out of her mind. He had succeeded at last and now there would be no stopping him. There was a way, of course. She only had to tell Dick. But the force of his anger would be felt by her first. Nessie was so distraught that she didn't hear the soft thud of a horse's hooves approaching. Then a figure bent over her with concern.

'Why, Nessie, it's you – whatever's the matter?'

With great relief she recognised the voice of Doctor Grant. She struggled to get up, desperate to disguise the evidence, but swayed crazily and would have fallen if he hadn't caught her.

'Are you ill? Did you faint? Cyril Grant glanced down at her dishevelled state. 'Your clothes!' The truth dawned. 'My God!' he exclaimed. 'Jake Taylor? Was it Jake? I've just seen him going home. He was looking dishevelled. I . . .'

Nessie tried to pull away from the doctor with embarrassment but he steadied her. 'Nessie – was it Jake Taylor? Did he attack you?'

She shook her head, trying to pretend that it hadn't happened. She turned from the doctor, scooped up a handful of straw, and keeping her back to him, tried to clean herself down with it.

'Come along, my dear. That's no way to get clean. You need soap and water. On my horse and back to my house.'

'No! No, thanks. I must get home before Dick.'

'And you know you can't let him see you like this. Besides, he'll be at the inn for a couple more hours yet, and when he does leave it'll take him half the night to totter his way home. You shouldn't be working, let alone until this late, Nessie.'

'Someone has to pay the rent.'

'Ah! So that's what this is all about. Jake's suggestion?'

Nessie nodded. 'But Dick mustn't know.'

'He won't hear anything from me – now, up on Benedict. No!' He raised his hand against her protests. 'I know you're a proud woman, Nessie, but for once you'll do as you're told.'

They met no one until they reached Wickham Square and then Nessie slid to the ground and shot up an alleyway to wait by the side door to the doctor's surgery.

Cyril Grant unlocked the side door from inside and led Nessie into the consulting room. His mind was racing ahead in leaps and bounds.

6

He doubted that this poor young woman would survive many more pregnancies. Nessie was the eldest of eight children herself, but they had all been conceived with love. He supposed Dick loved her in his own simple way, but there had been plenty of evidence in the past that Nessie, and each of their five children, suffered from his drunken abuse.

'I'll go through and have a word with Doctor Serle to let him know how old Mr Andrews is. While I'm gone you have a good wash at the basin here. Then we'll talk about what's to be done.'

Nice scented soap, soft warm water . . . never did Nessie have such luxury to bathe herself in at home. She sighed, wondering how she was going to explain the bruises away. Dick wouldn't notice anyway, and if he did he'd think he was responsible. He regarded bruises as a measure of his prowess.

With trembling fingers she straightened her skirt and was rebuttoning her blouse when Cyril Grant knocked lightly before entering.

'Oh, you're dressed,' he said. 'Don't you think I ought to examine you? Make sure no damage has been done – I could give you something. You've enough of Dick's offspring.'

'It . . . it's all right, Doctor Grant, really.' Cyril Grant knew that Nessie was about ripe to conceive again, her youngest girl being just over a year old. 'Maybe it'll be all right – I don't want anything done – it wouldn't be natural – if it's meant to be –'

'But if it was a case of violent rape, Nessie. You may be injured. This is a special situation. You should try to rest for the next few days.'

'I'll try, Doctor, and thank you for helping me, though I'm sorry you had to come along just when you did.'

'It's a good thing I did. I ought to inform the authorities, you know. Rape is a punishable offence. Men like Jake Taylor shouldn't be allowed to get away with it.'

Nessie shook her head. 'You know my Dick, Doctor. If he ever finds out, he'll do his own punishing. Least said, soonest mended, I reckon. I'd best get off home now. Beth will be wondering where I am.'

Cyril wanted to drive her home in the pony and trap but she wouldn't hear of it. People might notice and gossip, she said. Dick would demand to know the reason.

After she'd crept away into the night the doctor paced up and down in the carpeted surgery, concerned for Nessie Mead and angry with Jake Taylor.

Nessie implored the God she'd been taught to believe in as a child to make her infertile. With each passing day the thought of having to

7

carry Jake's child filled her with dread. She couldn't understand why she conceived so easily when it was obvious she was not the healthiest woman in the world. Took after her mother she supposed, who'd reared eight children and grieved over two miscarriages. Nessie had enough on her plate without another mouth to feed, let alone the trying months of carrying an unwanted babe. It mustn't happen, it couldn't happen . . .

When Jake Taylor called each week for the rent Nessie did her best to keep him at bay. She'd give him the rent book and he'd sign it. Then: 'Did you say you wanted me to look at that sink?' Or: 'Nasty thunderstorm we had last night, Nessie. Your bedroom ceiling leaking again? Perhaps I ought to take a look.'

Nessie's younger sister Beth didn't care much for school so to be offered a few coppers to take the children off for an hour or two was enticement enough to stay away from lessons. She was a trouble-maker in class anyway so the teachers were glad when she didn't show up, and no one bothered to find out why she was absent so frequently.

'Take the children down to the bridge, Beth,' Jake said. 'Give your sister a break.' With a bewitching smile he handed the eleven-year-old girl some coins, and followed Nessie into the house.

'You'll have to stop this, Jake,' she said as soon as he'd locked the door. 'If Dick ever finds out he'll kill us both. Think what the scandal would do to your Lily and young Adam, for goodness sake,' she begged.

'No one's going to know. Let's have a look at that ceiling – from the comfort of your feather mattress.'

'No, Jake, I won't do it. Besides, you can't – I . . .'

'Can't? he interrupted. 'What's that supposed to mean? I'll soon show you that I can and will.' He laughed and caught at Nessie's slender waist, drawing her close and planting his mouth firmly over hers. She struggled against his clawing hands at her buttocks but he held her so tightly she couldn't escape, and already his loins were rubbing frantically against her stomach.

'D . . . don't think I can make it . . . up the stairs, Nessie,' he panted.

'No, you won't and you can't – because I'm pregnant.'

He gulped. Her words stunned him, then when he'd had time to digest them he grinned fiendishly.

'That's the best news I've had all day,' he said. 'No need to worry any more, Nessie my love. What's done is done. Now we can really enjoy ourselves. You realise what this means? I knew it wasn't me who couldn't father any more children. Now I know 'tis Lily's fault.'

'You don't understand,' Nessie protested. 'This baby is Dick's. I was already pregnant when you . . .'

8

He held her at arm's length, studying her expression. Then between gritted teeth he said: 'You lying bitch. Don't expect me to fall for that old trick. You can't cheat me that easily.' He grabbed her arm and pulled her behind him up the stairs.

'No, Jake, please,' she pleaded. 'I don't *want* to.'

'Since when did a woman have any right to choose? I'll make damned sure this child carries my mark, Nessie Mead. You should have been Nessie Taylor and well you know it. For years you've taunted me with your sweet smile, goading me on, asking, begging for it. Well, now you now how it is – and I'm going to have my fill.' He threw her on the bed and added with a leer. 'Or rather fill you to the brim.'

Jake was incensed with aggressive passion. Nessie regretted having voiced her wish that any infant she carried must be Dick's. She knew it wasn't true, indeed she wasn't even sure yet that she was with child except for a nagging feeling from past experience.

Of late when Dick came home from the inn, singing and shouting, waking everyone up with his: 'Where's me little woman? Come 'ere, me darlin, I needs you more an more,' eager to keep him quiet she helped him up the narrow stairs and into the front bedroom. He would flop heavily on to the feather mattress and allow Nessie to remove his boots and socks. Whereas once the drink had added to his virility, nowadays he was so sodden with it he was unable to reach his goal. By the next day his hangover was so bad that he no longer had the desire.

As she suffered Jake's torment she prayed again that she might escape becoming pregnant – but in her heart she knew it was too late.

When the strawberry season ended Nessie hoped Jake's visits would cease, but as the evenings drew in he took to calling as soon as Dick had left for the inn, when the children were in bed.

The period of morning sickness passed, and for a few brief weeks Nessie felt and looked better. She tried appealing to Jake.

'I reckon I've more 'n paid the rent,' she said. 'There's no need for you to come any more. You must understand that this baby isn't yours, it's Dick's. He isn't drinking as much now he knows we'll soon have another little one, so he'll like as not walk in and then there'll be trouble.'

Jake pushed his way inside and closed the door behind him.

'Rent's gone up, Nessie. You can't deny me now. You enjoy it as much as I do. It's even better when you put up a fight. That's always been the trouble with my Lily. Just lies there waiting for it all to end. What pleasure is there in that for a man?' He gathered her in his arms and kissed her almost tenderly. 'Don't worry about that drunken swine of a husband of yours. I can handle him – he's drinking himself to an early grave, and you know it.'

'I told you, he's not drinking so much these days. He's not as bad as you think and he's doing everything to help me.'

'And it's *my* baby – don't you forget that, Nessie. Keep me happy and I'll give you all the help you need.'

As she lay beneath him, her body responding in spite of her guilt and distaste, she couldn't help thinking how much easier her life might have been if she had married Jake Taylor.

By Christmas, though, Jake no longer found her appealing as she became bigger and much less energetic. His visits became infrequent as wintry weather turned Nessie's bedroom into an ice-box. He called only occasionally to collect his dues. She found her burden cumbersome, gaining strength at her expense. It kicked her viciously, sapping every ounce of nourishment from her so that she was obliged to remain in bed for the last few weeks.

As winter progressed the doctor was kept busy with the usual coughs and colds. Times had changed over the past fifty years in these parts from what he'd heard. The frost-bitten earth crunched beneath the horse's hoofs as he made his way from village to hamlet visiting the sick. It wasn't difficult to conjure up a picture of the hard-working forest inhabitants living in roughly made houses in the woods, making hoops and faggots, spars and hurdles. They'd lived and loved much to their own rules, hardy against the elements until the area had been enclosed by the Squire who wanted his park to look nice. After having a selected area of some sixty acres on another part of his estate cleared, two dozen houses in pairs were erected which he offered to the squatters with the added enticement of an acre of land with each at an incredibly cheap rent. This was the birth of Hundred Acres. Cyril wished he'd known it in the old days which many of his elderly patients loved to tell him about. They were the ones who hadn't welcomed change, but the younger generation reckoned they had come up in the world. They had benefited from their parents and grandparents hard toil to make the land as profitable as it was today. Not that there was much doing in the winter months when the ground was covered with frost or snow, usually after a blustery autumn when fallen leaves made their colourful carpet and trees fell as easily as matchsticks during a gale.

As he wound his way through the woods, avoiding branches of the broad oaks which had broken off, he recalled his senior partner telling him how things used to be in this area. He could almost smell the smoke which would have hung among the trees from the makeshift houses occupied by the squatters. Matt Serle had learned to keep a few scraps of food in his pocket to keep at bay the flea-bitten dogs which bared their teeth and barked furiously at his approach. In the summer the air was pungent with the smell of rotten vegetables mixed with sewage odours, and when the local women gave birth it was a miracle any of them survived in such squalid conditions.

Cyril smiled to himself as he thought of all the births he'd attended since his arrival here five years ago. Not so many though, since Minnie Fletcher considered confinements her responsibility and there was no one better. He only attended when things got difficult, as when Charlie Mead was born. Poor Nessie, just a slip of a girl at twenty-three, lying on a bed of linen smelling of windblown country fragrance in a room freshly whitewashed in spite of next to no income. Nessie's widowed mother assisted Minnie as Nessie continued to emit loud animal cries while the ten pound baby inside her struggled for delivery. After several hours, while he and Minnie sweated almost as much as Nessie, the screaming infant was safely delivered, his nose squashed, his large head covered with a mass of dark brown curly hair. Even his hands and feet seemed to belong to a child a year old, but at least he was a healthy boy even if it turned out he didn't have his full quota of intelligence. Nessie's fifth child, and third girl, had come easily enough, being barely seven pounds. She had a larger family than she could cope with, he thought now, while other women had trouble enough to conceive even one.

He was concerned for Nessie's health. At first she'd blossomed, but latterly she'd become rundown and listless. She didn't consult him often but if he was that way he sometimes called to make sure she was getting enough food and rest. They never mentioned that June evening. As far as anyone else knew, the child she was carrying was her husband's and Dick did appear to be more considerate towards her. But Cyril was disturbed by the rumours which had circulated back in the autumn that Jake Taylor was a frequent visitor to the Meads' house, and not only to collect rent. Nessie had seemed distressed at the time but could he have been wrong about violent rape? She had refused his offer of help and had recovered sufficiently to walk home. Was it possible that she had been a willing participant?

It was a dark, chill March night when someone banged noisily on the back door of the doctor's surgery. Cyril excused himself from his patient and knew at once something was wrong by the state of the midwife. Minnie's face was purple from over-exertion and she was puffing badly.

'You must come, Doctor, you must!' she said in a frightened whisper.

11

'Go round to the kitchen door, Minnie. I'll see you there.'

Cyril Grant endeavoured to keep calm as he completed his consultation, then instead of opening the waiting-room door to call in the next patient, went through to the back of the house and let Minnie into the kitchen.

''Tis Nessie Mead, Doctor,' she said urgently. 'Dick sent Benjie over for me at dawn. All last night and throughout today she's been screaming and wailing. But it's delivered, and it's all right. Small for Nessie – only about six pounds, I reckon. Remember her two boys were nearly ten each but they were easier to deliver than this one was. It was as if it didn't want to come into this world – and I'm not surprised!'

'Why?'

'It's got the strawberry mark on it,' Minnie said in a hushed voice. 'A great red patch on its forehead, real ugly, and a girl at that.'

Doctor and midwife stared at each other.

'I'll get over there as soon as surgery is finished,' Cyril said. 'Doctor Serle is unwell today so I'm on my own.'

Minnie hesitated. 'I'm worried, Doctor. Dick's going mad, threatening to kill it, but first he's off to the inn to drown his sorrows.'

'Leave him to me, Minnie.'

Cyril could hardly concentrate on the rest of his patients but he did his best then saddled Benedict and set off at a trot for the Meads' homestead. Benedict was no stranger to hurried trips across the landscape, and tonight, though bleak with a heavy frost, there was a good high moon to light the way across the fields. A short cut here and there and he made the journey in less than half the usual time. Benjie the eldest boy, aged seven, took the reins and secured the doctor's horse to a nearby tree.

'Time you were in bed, Benjie,' Cyril said kindly. 'No need to fret, your ma will be all right.' He lowered his head to climb the narrow staircase where Dick's voice could be heard cursing and swearing as he stomped around from bedroom to landing.

'Come on now, Dick,' Cyril said, 'you're not helping Nessie or the younger children.'

'And who's helping me, I'd like to know? Dear god in heaven have you ever seen such a freak? It must be a bastard – it can't be mine.' He threw his arms in the air, waving his large meaty hands in utter despair. 'Get rid of it, Doctor, or I'll put it out of its misery even if I need an extra drink or two to do it.'

'You'll have the extra drink or two in any case. Now calm yourself, Dick, until I've had a chance to look at the child. Birthmarks aren't that rare. Plenty of people have them even if they can't be seen.'

'But no child of mine has one,' Dick roared unreasonably. 'It isn't mine, I tell you, and it hadn't better be here when I get back.'

'Then don't bother coming back until you're sober,' Cyril answered angrily. He didn't often lose his temper but he didn't like the situation he found himself in. Dick Mead was quite capable of committing murder if driven – both mother and child could well be victims, and if he, the doctor, dared to tell the truth of the matter, Jake Taylor might also be added to the list.

Dick brushed past him as he tore off down the stairs and out into the night. Cyril went softly into the front bedroom where the first thing he saw by candlelight was Nessie's rich chestnut-coloured hair spread out over the pillow. Poor though they were, Nessie's house-keeping and cleanliness were a credit to her. Minnie Fletcher had done her job well and now the mother of the new infant was resting comfortably between clean white sheets and soft feather pillows covered in starched white pillowcases. Cyril knew that she was crying. He laid a gentle hand on the turned back sheet.

'Nessie, my dear, it's all right. The mark will most likely fade in time.'

'Have you seen it?' She half-turned. 'I can't bear to look at it. Dick's right – it mustn't live. I can't take any more.'

'But you must give it love and nourishment, or it'll die.'

'Then let it – I want nothing to do with it! Dick says it's hideous. It's a curse – a curse, I tell you. Take it away. Do whatever you must before Dick does. And he'll not do it humanely.'

'Nessie, there's no need for anyone to ever know what happened. It's our secret. It's your babe – you've given birth to it – it has the right to live and be brought up with the rest of your family.'

A floorboard creaked and Cyril turned in time to see someone move away from the door.

'Who's there? Benjie, is that you?' he called.

'It's my sister, I expect,' Nessie said in a tired voice. 'Beth, I thought you were making tea. Doctor Grant must have something warm before he goes home.'

It was several minutes before footsteps sounded outside and Nessie's younger sister entered carrying a small round tin tray. She avoided looking directly at Cyril. Had she heard any of their conversation? he wondered. For eleven years old she was tall and well-developed, her young breasts pushing forward against her jumper. Although the Waterstone family was such a large one they were highly respectable, but Beth had the hallmarks of a flighty piece.

'You're here to help your sister then?' he asked now.

'Ma's leg is too bad for her to come,' Beth said. 'I can look after Nessie and the children.'

13

'Good girl. I'm sure you'll do a good job, Beth.'

Cyril drank his tea before taking a look in the crib. Even he started at the sight of the small round head covered with the thick black hair so typical of the inhabitants of Hundred Acres. The left side of the face looked dark too – dark and ugly. Cyril lifted the small bundle from the crib and turned back the white knitted shawl, hardly able to believe what he saw. For once Dick Mead was right. The birthmark made the infant look grotesque.

'I'm sure the mark will fade in time. Probably by the time she's ten, if not sooner. It's the type that does disappear without trace eventually. Once you've started to feed her you'll love her like the others,' he hastened to assure his patient.

'No, Doctor, and you know why. That strawberry mark will always be a reminder, and if Dick ever finds out . . .'

'Who's going to tell him? Certainly not me – and I'm the only one who knows. Get some rest now, Nessie. Nurse Fletcher will be here first thing in the morning and I'll look in too. You'll feel better after a good night's sleep. That's what you need most now.'

But Nessie had no will to live, no love or instinct to feed her new baby or even look at it. She went into a deep depression, lying back against her pillow with her eyes closed, pleading with Nurse Fletcher not to draw back the faded and worn curtains. She refused visitors – she just wanted to die. Guilt was uppermost in her thoughts. Not that she could have prevented Jake Taylor from raping her, but she was filled with remorse because she had tried all manner of things to terminate the pregnancy – one she'd never intended to carry full term. This ugly child was her punishment and it was more than she could bear. The child didn't deserve to be marked and have to face a life of shame. The shame was hers, Nessie's. Dying would have been too good for her.

For the next day and night Dick Mead was missing. Some said he was too drunk to leave The King's Head, others said he was with another woman, but some time after midnight on the second day he turned up at the doctors' house, ranting and raving like a lunatic.

Cyril Grant went down to the door in his dressing-gown.

'For goodness' sake, Dick, do you want to get arrested? Get off home and look after Nessie and the children. She's gone into depression and needs you.'

'Depression, d'you say?' Dick roared. 'How the hell d'you think I feel helping to produce that . . . that . . . imbecile? It's got no right in my family so I'll not go home 'till it's been put down.'

'You can't know what you're saying, Dick. You know I can't take a life. It would be a criminal act.'

'You can do it painlessly – but I'll do it if I have to.'

Cyril Grant watched Dick shuffle away in the direction of Fareham. It was cruel to see a man so wretched with himself, and if the doctor hadn't known so much about him he'd have felt sorry for Dick Mead. His sympathy now wasn't so much for Nessie even but the poor child who hadn't asked to be conceived. He couldn't take its life. He knew of doctors and midwives who would, in pity for the child. What kind of future did it have? Dick would surely ill-treat it even if he could be persuaded to spare its life, and Nessie – what a mess? She believed this was a curse put on her for having a relationship with Jake Taylor.

Cyril didn't sleep well and was up early the next morning before any of the local people went to work. Out for a morning canter to all intents and purposes – a canter which took him to the midwife's cottage, Beech Cottage, set in a copse of the trees which in summer helped to keep the cottage cool. Cyril loved this spot and recalled reading about the famous sixteenth-century herbalist Gerard who had warned people against taking beech leaves into their houses in case they brought death. He remembered too that Joan of Arc had seen visions under a beech tree. Yet he knew that no forest tree had richer foliage than the beech, in autumn providing a pageant of colour in rich bronze-browns. He shrugged off his superstitions though admitted that at this moment he could well do with a vision of what to do. He should, of course, be sharing his dilemma with his senior partner but Matt Serle was going downhill rapidly. Cyril knew that very soon he would be holding the fort alone, but he would accept the challenge readily.

Minnie was already up and had seen him coming so the door was flung open. Ice-cold in temperature the cottage might be, even in summer, but it was a haven of warm friendliness like nowhere else in the whole district.

'What brings you here so early?' she asked, stoking up the fire she'd kept going all night. 'You're worried about Nessie Mead, I daresay?'

Cyril made himself comfortable by Minnie's hearth, and over an early morning cup of tea told her all he knew.

'I can't do what Dick says,' he said wearily. 'I'm just not made that way. There's no reason to put the child out of its misery when it's perfectly healthy in all other respects, and as far as I can tell will look as normal as any other child in a few years. But at the same time neither can I leave it to Dick's not-so-tender mercies, or even Nessie's come to that. The child is unwanted on more than one count.'

'She still refuses to look at it. I even held it to her breast but it wouldn't feed. I believe Dick may be right – it is a freak. We've both

15

seen unsightly children before but we don't have the right to decide their fate, do we?'

'Life can be hard and cruel for such children but what can *we* do?'

'Not much – except . . .'

'Except what, Minnie? If you've any ideas please speak up. I'm at my wit's end.'

'We-ell – I was in the New Forest visiting my sister last Sunday. As you know she's a midwife too and was rejoicing with a couple who've just had their first baby after waiting and wanting for several years. Phoebe Hunter is thirty-five and this would probably have been her last chance after being barren for so long. Now they've got a baby girl and are mighty grateful that she's arrived safely. Small but healthy.'

'What are you suggesting, Minnie? What's this couple in the New Forest got to do with my problem – or rather Nessie's?'

'I was just thinking, there's the Hunter couple rejoicing in the birth of their babe – a much wanted babe – and we've got one in the village that's unwanted.'

'Minnie, I can't imagine what you're suggesting but it sounds – interesting.'

'More'n interesting, Doctor. Who's to know that the Hunters didn't have twins? I met Phoebe only hours after Belinda was born. They were so happy. They're good Christian folk who would give Nessie's infant a much better chance in life than ever Dick and Nessie can. They live in an isolated cottage in the Forest, miles from anyone else. He's a master carpenter, and they're the kind of people who keep themselves to themselves. Ideal to take Nessie's babe.'

'Only they won't want it either when they see it,' Cyril said.

'You could be wrong there. They believe in fate and I think they'd see it as a special request from God, in thanks for at last having one of their own. Besides, they're the kind of intelligent couple who will understand that the mark will fade in time. What could be better than going to a family miles from gawping neighbours? The locals here won't ever get to see her, so what they don't know about they won't fret over.'

There was a long pause while Cyril thanked the beech trees for her timely vision. A vision which scared him as much as it did Minnie Fletcher.

'What could we tell Nessie and Dick though?' he mused. Then, with a click of his fingers, 'I know – the baby died naturally, of course.' He rushed round the small oak table and placed his hands excitedly on Minnie's shoulders. 'Is it feasible, Min? Dare we? Think of the child, and the good home it would be brought up in.'

'There'll be a few white lies to tell and a few forged papers to sign,' she reminded him.

16

'To save a child's life? Anything is worth that!' he declared. 'No one must ever find out – but then, by the time she grows up we shall be long gone. Retired or moved on. All we have to do now is to think of a way to get the baby to its new home before Dick Mead commits a crime.'

While Minnie hastened to visit her sister in her pony and trap, Doctor Grant paid a visit to the Meads' house. He felt duty bound to make one last effort to persuade Nessie to take her baby.

'What are you going to call her?' he asked.

There was no reply. Nessie remained facing the wall and refused to look at the doctor or the baby.

'Are you being fair, Nessie? Doesn't she have a right to your love, the same as the others?'

'No – I wanted no part of it. I'm weary of bringing up children, tired of being tired.'

'I'll do all I can to help you get on your feet again.'

'I don't feel as if I shall ever walk again. God is punishing me for what I've done.'

'But it wasn't your fault, my dear. You should have let me help you then – at least have Jake Taylor brought to justice.'

'I felt sorry for his wife and child, and I knew if Dick ever found out there'd be a murder. That would have been both our families having to live with disgrace of one kind or another. None of the children deserves that, and this one, even though I hate it, doesn't deserve the taunts of unkind people in the world. Better that it should die.'

Cyril Grant bent over the crib. 'Her breathing's not good,' he said, and it was true. It was in a poor state and if something wasn't done soon the baby surely would die of starvation.

'I'll be back later today to have another look but get Beth to see if she can get the child to feed from the bottle.'

He went away and had great difficulty in channelling his thoughts towards other people's ills. He was glad when it was dark and he could ride over to Beech Cottage where he found Minnie having a meal with her sister.

''Tis all arranged if the situation is the same, Doctor.'

'Worse, I'm afraid. The infant's breathing is shallow and if it doesn't get love and care in the next forty-eight hours, it really will die.'

'Then that's settled. The Hunters are overjoyed at having a twin sister for Belinda. They know nothing of the circumstances though and there's no need for them to. I'll visit Nessie as soon as I think Beth has gone home but before Dick gets back from the inn. A spot of ether will ensure that the babe doesn't suddenly cry out.'

17

Cyril Grant looked at the two middle-aged women with a worried frown.

'Is it going to work?'

'Like you said, to save a child's life it must work, and God help us.'

The small house was eerily quiet when Minnie drove up to the gate. It was after ten o'clock when most people were already in their beds. The front door was unlocked so she crept in and went up the stairs.

''Tis only me, Nessie dear.' She knew Nessie would know her voice and would trust her whatever she told her.

'Doctor Grant was worried about the babe. 'I'm sorry I haven't been in today but I had to visit my sister as she's not been well. Not easy when you live alone. Now, dearie, let's have a look – oh dear! Oh, my goodness, poor wee mite.'

She took out her handkerchief to feign distress but quickly placed the faintly-smelling ether pad over the babe's nose. There was no sound except for the faint rustling of sheets as Nessie turned over in the big bed.

'What's the matter?'

'I . . . I'm afraid 'tis gone, Nessie. And without being baptised or anything. I'm so sorry, my dear, but I have to tell you that even if I'd come before there was nothing I could have done for it.'

'See to it all, Nurse Fletcher. And before Dick gets home – if he ever does come home, that is.'

'Well, the doctor must attend, or perhaps I could take it straight to him now, to ease your heartbreak?'

'There's no heartbreak, Nurse. 'Tis better for it. May the Lord rest its tiny soul.' Her voice cracked and Minnie knew that Nessie was quietly weeping.

'I'll bring back its clothes after –'

'No need for any funeral, just do whatever they do with stillborn babies, and do it with its clothes on. I'm not going to want baby clothes any more.'

'Shall I ride over and fetch your ma or Beth?'

'No, they'll be in bed. There's no need for grieving for this one. 'Tis better off wherever it's gone.' Nessie snuggled down under the bedclothes. 'At least Dick will be satisfied now.'

Minnie Fletcher let herself out of the house after wrapping the infant up in two blankets. She laid it on the floor of the trap and set off for Doctor Grant's house. Together they finalised the conspiracy by forging a death certificate and then Minnie urged her pony at a good trot for Beech Cottage.

The deed was done. The cold night air brought the baby round and Minnie sat by the fire contentedly as the perfect rosebud mouth sucked eagerly from the bottle. At least the little one had a future with good parents, and Minnie would be able to follow her progress through her sister who was going to take her to her new home as soon as it was light.

Chapter One

'Strawberry girl . . . strawberry girl . . . strawberry girl . . .'

Seven-year-old Rachel Hunter covered her ears with her hands against the unkind taunts. Hot and on the verge of tears she ran for dear life. The boys quickly gained on her and the leader of the gang, Charlie Mead, grabbed and caught his prey with a shout of triumph.

'Pull 'er 'air back – 'ave a look,' he ordered his mates. 'She's a witch – she's got the mark of the strawberry on 'er.' They pulled and tugged at Rachel's hair, laughing and peering at the raised red patch which tainted her otherwise pretty white skin. 'Did yer ma 'ave a craving for strawberries when you was comin', Rachel Hunter?' Charlie squealed with glee. 'Reckon as 'ow she ate too many an' they came out on you.'

The other boys cheered him on but Rachel kicked backwards with her foot causing Charlie to loosen his hold. She managed to escape and ran and ran, on through the wood, the boys screaming and yelling after her. Her throat burned horribly and she began to cough as tears fell from hot, hurting eyes. She didn't see the tree root and suddenly went sprawling. The boys descended on her like a pack of hungry wolves.

She banged her head on the ground and both knees felt as if they were rubbed raw. The boys were pounding her back as they shrieked obscenities. She was sure they were going to strip her of every last item of clothing.

'Get off, you mongrels!' an angry voice bellowed through the giant oaks. A horse snorted, footsteps scuffled on the dry, parched earth, and when Rachel managed to scramble to her feet she saw most of the boys running away in all directions while Dr Grant held Charlie Mead fast in a stranglehold.

'What the devil d'you think you're up to?' Doctor Cyril Grant growled angrily.

'We . . . we was jest lookin' at 'er mark,' Charlie snivelled.

'And you'll be lucky if I don't put a mark on you, my lad.'

'I'll tell . . . my dad of you,' Charlie choked, his cheeks getting redder by the minute. Rachel began to feel a bit sorry for him as the doctor did seem to be exerting more pressure than was necessary. 'He's . . . bigger 'an you.'

'And when he's had a drink or two he's only fit for battering defenceless women,' Doctor Grant muttered. 'Be off home to Hundred Acres where you belong, boy. Don't let me see you molesting Rachel again.' He threw the boy to the ground with disgust.

Rachel was weeping desperately. Her throat was really painful, but she could bear that. The humiliation she had suffered from the boys making sport of her disfigurement was much worse. It was the school nurse's fault for remarking about the strawberry birthmark and bringing it to Charlie Mead's attention. It just wasn't fair, and on a day when her twin sister Belinda had to stay at home because she had measles.

'You all right, Rachel my dear?' Doctor Grant asked kindly.

Blood and tears mingled together as Rachel lifted her face for the doctor's scrutiny. He opened his bag and took out a piece of bandage to clean her. 'There, that's better. Can't have you going home to your mother looking as if you've quarrelled with the ground, now can we?'

He closed his bag, hitched it over his shoulder on its long leather strap, and then lifted Rachel up on the saddle before hoisting himself up behind her.

Rachel wasn't normally a cry baby but she had been very afraid of the boys and alarmed at the amount of blood which poured from her forehead.

'Good thing I came along at just the right time,' Doctor Grant said. 'I'm sorry Nurse Cull commented on your birthmark today. It was thoughtless of her. She won't mention it again, but as you get older, my dear, I'm afraid you'll come across people who might be unkind about it. You're a very brave girl, and I can assure you that it will fade in time. Don't worry about the bleeding, Rachel, it will soon stop.'

The horse, unused to carrying anyone other than its master, trotted along the bridlepath dutifully, occasionally tossing its head with a protesting snort and flick of its mane.

'Now that's enough of that, Benedict,' the doctor said. 'You're highly honoured to have a pretty young maiden riding on your back.'

Rachel thought she was the one who was highly honoured, and was very thankful that the doctor had intervened on her behalf and saved her from an unthinkable fate.

Rachel's mother, Phoebe Hunter, was standing at the garden gate, her hand shielding her eyes from the sun's glare as she stared in disbelief at the approaching horse and rider.

'Why, Doctor Grant,' she exclaimed, 'whatever are you doing with our Rachel?'

'It's all right, Mrs Hunter, no cause for alarm.' He pulled the horse in by the fence and hung the reins over the post before jumping down, Rachel in his arms. 'There we are, Rachel, safe and sound.'

She looked up at her mother, expecting a scolding for a dirty dress and grazed face and knees.

'Whatever happened to you, darling?' Phoebe asked with concern.

'She had a little altercation with some naughty boys.'

'But you haven't come all this way just to bring her home, Doctor?' Phoebe asked.

'No, I'm on my way to see Nurse Fletcher. She had a nasty fall last week, cutting her leg quite badly. The wound was ulcerated so I need to keep an eye on it. It's such a lovely day I decided to ride over there after my annual school visit.'

'Will you stop by for a glass of something, Doctor? A cup of tea, perhaps?'

'A cool drink would be most appreciated, Mrs Hunter.' He followed the small, wiry woman into the thatched cottage, lowering his head to avoid knocking himself out on the oak rafters. The rooms were small but cool, with an aromatic smell of freshly carved wood to titillate his nostrils. Wally Hunter, Phoebe's husband, was a master carpenter who had turned Calder Cottage into a showplace for his craftsmanship in just the few short months since they had come to live in Kingsmere. A round mahogany table stood in front of the latticed window, so highly polished you could almost see your face in it. Cyril Grant was surprised that Wally allowed his wife to put a bowl of roses on it though. He sat down in the dark oak rocker while Phoebe filled a tall tumbler with fizzy lemonade. She had sent Rachel outside into the garden to drink hers.

'So what's this all about then, Doctor Grant?'

Cyril sighed. 'I've been half expecting something like this to happen ever since Rachel started at Wickham School, Mrs Hunter,' he said sadly. 'Our nurse is not the most tactful of people and when she spotted the birthmark she remarked about it, and unfortunately Charlie Mead saw it too. He and his gang followed Rachel into the woods and were setting about her when I happened along. By the look of her throat when I examined her today she's in for measles any minute so I should keep her at home tomorrow. I s'pose I ought to have suggested it when Belinda went down with it, but I don't hold with children missing their education unless absolutely necessary.'

'Poor Rachel,' Phoebe said in a low voice. 'Life isn't going to be easy for her, is it?'

'We must guard against being over-protective. The birthmark will fade, God willing. Many I've seen have gone by the time the child reaches the age of five or six. Rachel seems to be one of the unlucky ones so we must do our best for her and be especially understanding. Meanwhile she has to face the world, I'm afraid.' Cyril Grant stood up, thanked Phoebe for the drink and returned outside to where Rachel was holding a bucket of water for Benedict to take a drink.

'There's a good girl, Rachel,' he said patting her head before he rode off to the other side of the wood to take the Waltham Chase road.

There was a cool, restful breeze through the trees and Cyril let his horse set a slow pace, glad of the peacefulness of the wood and the time to wonder if he had done right to allow Minnie Fletcher to find a new home for the unwanted, ugly baby seven years ago. His conscience had taken a knock today, seeing that young thug with Rachel beneath him on the ground, especially as he knew they were half-brother and sister, but he refused to allow his memory to torment him with what had happened on that fateful day nearly eight years ago in the strawberry field.

When he reached the cottage where the retired midwife lived, he tied Benedict to the beech tree.

'Hullo there, Minnie?' he called as he knocked on the back door.

'Come in, Doctor,' the seventy-three-year-old spinster invited. Any visitor knew by the tone of her voice that they were assured of a warm welcome. Minnie Fletcher was round as she was high with rosy red cheeks and a genuine sparkle in her soft blue-grey eyes. She was sitting on a sofa by the window.

'Glad to see you're keeping that leg up.'

''Tis good of you to come over all this way, Doctor. I'm sure there's no real need though. I can manage well enough.'

'I know that, Minnie. But to tell you the truth I needed to be out in the fresh air for a bit and there's nothing better than a ride through the woods. Made my school visit today. Lot of measles about – wonder the whole school isn't down with it.'

They chatted easily in the manner of old chums while Cyril examined the wound on Minnie's leg and as he redressed it he told her how unkind the school nurse had been to Rachel Hunter.

'Tactless woman,' he said. 'Too bossy, totally unsuitable to deal with children, and of all the children to pick on, it had to be little Rachel. Today of all days when Belinda's home from school with the measles. Charlie mead and his gang took full advantage of Rachel having to go through the woods by herself.'

'Did they hurt her?' Minnie asked, with concern.

'I think she was more scared than anything else. A few cuts and bruises. Bumped her head and grazed her birthmark which bled profusely. That frightened her. Now Charlie Mead and his gang know, everyone for miles around will know too but they'll soon forget. Mrs Hunter has made an excellent job of styling Rachel's hair so that the mark is barely noticeable in the normal way.' He sighed. 'Someone sooner or later would have noticed it, I suppose. Never did we imagine that the Hunters would up and move in this direction did we? Has fate cheated us, Minnie?'

''Tis only you and me knows what happened that night, and after all this time any rumours about Nessie Mead and Jake Taylor will have long been forgotten, let alone a baby that died.'

'I can hardly believe Rachel's the same child. She's bonny enough now and will grow up to be a fine-looking young woman. It's going to be hard on her though till the mark fades.

'Looks aren't everything. Rachel may well have the stronger character. Only time will tell who she really takes after.'

'I ask myself time and time again, Minnie – did we do right to let her live? Wouldn't it have been kinder to do as Dick Mead asked?'

'Kinder? For Rachel? Either way we have to live with our consciences. Nessie and Dick believe their infant died of natural causes, and heaven alone knows she was sickly enough and caused enough trouble for poor Agnes a'growing and a 'coming. But you took the Hippocratic Oath, and it wouldn't have been right to deny the infant the right to live. No, Doctor, I reckon we did what was right in the sight of God. She'll have a better life and upbringing with Phoebe and Wally than she ever would fightin' for survival with Nessie and Dick's brood.'

'I feel responsible, Minnie, and weighed down with guilt all over again since the Hunters moved to Kingsmere.'

'Reckon we're both responsible. I aided and abetted you, Doctor – but I'm getting old and past worrying. Have no fear, no one will ever hear a word from me,' Minnie assured him. 'Wally Hunter's made a name for himself so when Squire offered him regular work and a cottage as well, who could blame him for moving? There's four of them in the family, two of them growing girls to clothe and educate. Takes some doing these days, and they weren't to know they were bringing Rachel back to her roots.'

After Cyril had enjoyed a cup of tea with Minnie, he set off on the homeward route deep in thought. He just prayed that Dick Mead never found out that Jake had taken his wife or there'd be trouble. Everyone knew that Dick Mead was capable of murder, and Jake

25

Taylor probably deserved it. But the Meads and Taylors of this world didn't warrant much consideration. It was little Rachel Hunter he worried about. His conscience was always going to trouble him over this one, whatever comfort Minnie tried to give him. He'd never believed in superstitions yet here it was before his very eyes. Conceived by rape in a strawberry field. Born with a hideous strawberry mark. The mark of the devil if ever he'd seen it. Maybe it was time he moved on to a different district, but he doubted that he ever would as that would be a coward's way out. He felt responsible for all the people in the Meon Valley who depended on him and whom he had come to love over the years. They in turn showed him affection and respect which he valued. Now that Rachel was back in the area he felt he owed her his protection if nothing else. How she turned out and what she made of her life would convince him whether or not he'd done the right thing seven years ago.

Phoebe Hunter squeezed the cold water out of the piece of soft flannel and wiped it round Rachel's face.

'There,' she said gently, 'I do believe the fever has gone at last. Let's change your nightie and the sheets. You can lie in Mummy's bed, darling, while I make up a nice clean bed for you. Then I reckon you'll sleep 'till the cows come home.'

She lifted the little girl into her own place in the high double bed and set about stripping the truckle bed of the damp, smelly bed-linen.

'Must be all nice and clean when Doctor Grant comes to see you. He'll be pleased that your temperature's down, and I expect your cough will soon get better now.' Phoebe bundled the nightie, sheets and pillow case into a ball. 'You just lie there quietly while I get your dad's breakfast, then, when I've got these things into boil I'll come up and get you back in your own bed.'

Phoebe went down the narrow twisted staircase carefully, hurried to the outhouse where the brick copper stood empty, and had begun to fill it with buckets of water when a strong hand took one from her.

'I'll do that, Phoebe love,' Wally said. 'You've had no rest, hardly a wink of sleep for too many nights. I've put the kettle on and started my breakfast. I'll fill up with water and get the fire started.'

Phoebe grated slivers of household soap off a new bar and left her husband to set light to the cardboard and sticks under the copper. Soon, from the kitchen window she could see a thin streak of smoke coming from the small brick chimney. It was a dry, sunny morning and there was the promise of a long hot summer in the air.

It was still only six-thirty. She sat beside Wally as he ate his bacon and eggs, sipping her much needed cup of tea thoughtfully.

'Don't reckon Rachel will go back to school now 'til after the summer holidays,' she said. There was a tone of relief in her voice.

'No use being too protective, Phoebe. It's something she's going to have to get used to – people are bound to notice her mark and there's nothing we can do about it.'

'Thank God for measles, I say,' Phoebe said. 'Won't be so bad for her though if the two girls can stick together.'

'I never knew measles could be so bad,' Wally said. 'But then no two young'uns are ever the same. You can't expect the girls to be side by side all their lives, Phoebe. Belinda mustn't be made to feel she's Rachel's protector.'

Phoebe looked at Wally. They were divided over their loyalties. Wally favoured Belinda, Phoebe knew. Not that he ever showed favouritism where presents and such were concerned, but sometimes his expression revealed the love he felt for his own daughter, whereas for Rachel Phoebe suspected it was nothing but pity. So, she knew it was up to her.

'The girls are devoted to one another,' she said. 'They'll always look out for each other whatever happens, Charlie Mead or no Charlie Mead.'

'If it isn't Charlie, it may well be someone else. Children can be cruel.'

'Cruel one minute, loving the next. At least they'll go through school together, and Doctor Grant says that the mark will fade as time passes.'

Wally grunted. 'Reckon he doesn't know too much about it. No sign of any change as far as I can see.'

'But you don't see, Wally,' Phoebe said. 'I have to look at it every day when I wash her and brush her hair. It breaks my heart. It might have been Belinda, remember.'

Wally pushed back his chair and with a non-committal grunt went out of the back door and along the path to the privy. Phoebe had touched a raw nerve but he needed to be reminded occasionally of the need for consideration. After about ten minutes Wally came back, stood at the sink and washed his hands, then turned to Phoebe who was buttering bread for Belinda's breakfast and lunch box.

He pecked her cheek, and with his hand round her upper arm gently squeezed reassuringly.

'We won't let Rachel down,' he said softly. 'She's our responsibility and the girls will be treated the same. We knew it wouldn't be easy for her. I hadn't reckoned on trouble the minute she started at the new school, though.'

'It need not have happened but for that stupid school nurse. I've worked hard to train Rachel's hair to cover up the blemish, and it's been all right until now. I suppose the children she grew up with in the New Forest didn't pay any attention to it. She's too young to take this on her own shoulders, Wally. We've got to help her all we can. You know, watching her while she's been ill I've noticed how pretty she's getting. As long as that mark is covered up she'll be as bonny as any other child of her age. She's as dark as Belinda is fair, and yet Rachel has whiter, more delicate skin. Her eyes are so big and black too – shouldn't wonder if she isn't a real beauty when she gets to be a young woman,'

'Maybe you're right. Now I must be off. I'll be at the big house all day. Squire wants some work doing there. Cook'll give me dinner, I dare say, save me coming all the way home when it's so hot.'

Phoebe went to the garden gate and watched him walk off down the lane towards the river. The air was sultry, and she wasn't sorry to get back inside the cottage where it was cooler. She went quietly up the stairs to look in on Rachel. A mass of dark hair was spread out over the pillow – Phoebe's pillow – as if the child gained comfort from lying where her mother had lain a short while ago. Her small thin face was pale but her expression was more restful now in sleep. This was what she needed, rest and good food to build her up until she was strong and healthy again. Phoebe tiptoed to the bedside and smoothed the damp tendrils of hair away. Rachel was lying on her left side so that the strawberry mark wasn't visible. Yes, Phoebe thought, she has the makings of a fine young woman with good looks. Different in every way from Belinda who was the spitting image of herself at a similar age. It didn't seem likely that anyone would really be fooled into thinking the girls were twins. But then again, Wally was dark-haired with warm brown eyes. Folk would think Rachel took after him. Phoebe bent and kissed the soft cheek, then went across the small landing to the other bedroom.

'Belinda?' Phoebe shook the child gently. 'Time to get up, dear.'

Belinda rolled over, moaned, and then sat up abruptly.

'Is Rachel all right, Mummy?'

'Yes. She's asleep now, so don't make a noise when you come down. I think the fever has left her at last.'

'Will she soon be able to come back to school?'

'Not until after the summer holidays, I expect. She'll be weak for a while but she's on the mend. Doctor Grant's coming to see her today.'

Belinda pushed the single sheet away. The night had been too hot for any more bedding. She drew her knees up to her chin and looked at her mother with shining eyes. 'I'm *so* glad she's better,' she said with genuine earnestness. 'I couldn't bear not to have Rachel. We'll stay together always, Mummy. I wish I had a mark like her, then she wouldn't feel so bad, would she?'

'None of us is exactly alike, dear,' Phoebe said. 'Rachel's mark will fade in time. And mostly I think she forgets it's there.'

'It was horrid of that school nurse to remark about it,' Belinda said as she swung her legs over the side of the bed. 'And it would have to be Charlie Mead who saw it. He's such a hateful boy.'

'He hasn't been bothering you at school, has he?'

Belinda didn't answer at once. She sat on the floor to put her white socks on. 'No-oo, not much,' she said. 'I told his sisters, Susan and June, that he'd better not say another word to Rachel about it or I'd get my dad on to him.'

Phoebe helped Belinda with her bodice, petticoat and dress.

'Best not to take any notice of them, then Charlie and his friends will soon forget.'

Phoebe wasn't convinced but prayed that Rachel would soon be delivered from the scourge.

Charlie Mead sat at the breakfast table in the overcrowded kitchen of the little house in Hundred Acres and chewed noisily on his crust of bread. For once his father was sitting at the head of the long whitewood table. Dick Mead, a rough and ready labourer, was often sleeping off a night's drinking at this time and scarcely saw any of his five children.

'Shut your mouth when you're eating, Charlie,' Dick growled over his enamel mug full of strong black tea.

'How can I get the food in me mouth if it's shut?' the boy retorted.

'Don't answer your father back,' his mother scolded.

'Why shouldn't he? You do it often enough?' Dick said, looking up at his wife with a cheeky grin.

'You're not my father,' Nessie answered shortly.

Dick roared with coarse laughter. 'You can say that again. Else I'd be in clink for incest, eh?'

Nessie shot him an indignant glance and got on with serving the girl's their breakfast. It was a never-ending task, feeding the family, preparing lunch boxes, washing, ironing and mending, as well as cleaning for two hours a day at St Nicholas Church School.

Dick was in convivial mood. No money for drink so he'd spent the evening annoying his wife and eventually demanding his conjugal rights when the kids had gone to bed. He'd had her knickers off even before Charlie had left the room – just to make the boy see red. Nessie had managed to ward Dick off until she'd shut the door behind their son.

29

'You've no right, Dick. Behaving like that in front of the children. All the village must know what you're like.'

He had only laughed. 'Reckon they do. Come 'ere – let's have a feel . . .'

Nessie had long since lost any feelings of real desire. Yet in spite of the hardships of the past few years she still managed to retain a gentle prettiness about her which made many a man look twice in her direction.

'Got time for a quick frolic after the kids have left for school?' Dick said now, pinching her bottom as she refilled his mug.

'I've got to get to school to do my cleaning and I should think it's time you were off. If you're late again they'll be giving you the sack. 'Tis a busy time during the strawberry season.'

'Stop your nagging, woman. 'Tis only just seven. Plenty of time.'

Charlie suddenly started giggling in his babyish way.

'And what's so funny to you?' Dick shouted, waving his hand in a mock clout.

Charlie's expression changed instantly. He was never quite sure how to take his father. He glanced across at his mother.

'Rachel Hunter's got the mark of strawberries on her face,' he said. 'I saw it the day Nitty Norah came to school.'

Nessie cuffed him round the ear. 'Don't let me hear you speak like that about the nurse, Charlie. We may be poor but we don't have to be common.'

Dick looked at his great oaf of a son. Simple and yet not so simple.

'Hunter?' The name was unfamiliar. 'Is that the new people over at Kingsmere who've got two girls?' he asked.

Nessie turned to the old stone sink and began to stack the dishes.

'Got the strawberry mark, d'you say?' Dick asked Charlie.

'Yeah – she's ugly and I told her so. Told her, her ma must have eaten too many strawberries when she was coming. Told her she had the witches' mark on her.' Charlie nearly fell off the chair with laughter.

'And if you go on at her again, Belinda's going to get their dad on to you, so there,' his younger sister June said, sticking her tongue out rudely.

'I ain't afraid of 'im,' Charlie said.

'That's right, son. Don't you let no one boss you about.' Suddenly Dick stood up and lashed out at Charlie. 'But don't you mock someone with an affliction either or I'll have your hide.'

Charlie began to bawl. Nessie gripped the side of the sink. She hadn't heard about anyone in the district having a strawberry birthmark. Memories came rushing back. After seven years she had begun

30

to forget – forget that Jake Taylor had offered her a job in the strawberry fields to help pay the rent and then taken a mean advantage of her. One peep at the baby who came nine months later had been enough to remind her how it had been conceived. She could only look at it with undisguised hatred because its ugly stigma reminded her of Jake Taylor. She'd been brought up in a Christian home to defy superstitions. Yet there was no doubt that the innocent baby carried the brand of its father's sin. She felt a measure of guilt for hadn't she always felt an attraction to Jake Taylor? But she would never be unfaithful to Dick. It had been a stormy marriage because of his drinking problem, but five healthy children, who brought pleasure as well as a mountain of work, were compensation enough.

As she worked at the scullery sink the memory of that time eight years ago was torture. Her body had become a tool – for the child to sap her strength, for Jake and Dick to use at will. When the last weeks wearied her beyond endurance, Jake had grown impatient with her so left her alone to face the consequences. The confinement was long and more painful than all five previous births put together. Her health was poor afterwards and it was weeks before she was on her feet again.

Jake never bothered her after hearing that she had lost her baby. The following year, though, he made sure she got a job in the strawberry fields again to earn extra money, but she never ate another one.

Nessie sighed. Things were better these days. Since the strawberry growing had continued to prosper there was full-time work for Dick, when she could persuade him to take advantage of it, and as Nessie had no more unwanted pregnancies to contend with she became much healthier.

For two years now she had worked at the school, making sure that she kept her own wages to help feed and clothe all of them.

She still felt a degree of desolation at losing her baby, guilt too because she had felt no love or compassion for it – until it was gone. But, in the circumstances, she was just so thankful that the baby had died soon after birth.

Chapter Two

By the time Rachel and Belinda Hunter reached the age of eleven years, Rachel's birthmark was receding, but very slowly. Much too slowly for a lively, high-spirited young girl who asked for nothing more than to be as pretty as her twin sister.

Rachel stood by the window peering into a speckled old mirror, trying to assess the size of her mark.

'It won't go away by keeping on looking at it,' Belinda said. 'You're for ever looking at yourself, Rachel – as Daddy says, one day you'll see the devil.'

Rachel made a gruesome face. 'I *am* the devil,' she said in a low, menacing voice. The girls laughed as they curled up on the end of their bed to share secrets. 'Belinda, you just don't know how lucky you are,' Rachel said. 'Your hair is fair and wavy, and your eyes are the prettiest blue, like Mummy's.'

'And I wish I had dark curly hair and big brown eyes like you and Daddy,' Belinda said wistfully.

Rachel guessed that her sister only said these things to try to make her feel better. When they were out with their parents people always spoke first to Belinda as if Rachel wasn't even there. No one actually remarked on her blemish. Rachel almost wished they would, at least she would get some attention instead of being made to feel unworthy of notice.

At school it was different. Most of the children at the Church School in Wickham had got used to it by now, and it was only the older boys like Charlie Mead and his gang who took every opportunity to taunt her about it. But they were coming up to fourteen years old and would soon be leaving to start work.

Just before Easter when there was an air of excitement in anticipation of a few days' holiday, and Easter Eggs too, Rachel had to stay behind in class to finish a composition before she could go out to play.

32

It hadn't been a good day because Miss Davis was in a bad mood, and Rachel had been unable to concentrate. But now the teacher wanted to get to the staff room for her cup of tea so she took Rachel's exercise book away from her with a sigh.

'You'll have to do better than this, Rachel,' she scolded. 'You can do as well as your sister, you know you can, but you seem to waste so much time daydreaming. This work is poor. Untidy and dirty. You'd better wash your hands before you go outside for what's left of playtime.'

Rachel did as she was told and as she came out of the cloakroom she saw a group of boys in the hall. Needless to say it was Charlie Mead at the centre, standing on a stool and straining to reach a picture hanging on the wall. With a bright red crayon he was colouring in the side of the girl's face.

'Charlie Mead, you'll be for it now,' Rachel said in a loud voice.

The boys giggled. ''Tis you, Rachel Hunter,' Charlie mocked. 'See, the mark of a witch – the only one in Wickham School, I reckon.'

'I'm going to tell,' she said and ran off through the door.

Rachel wasn't a tell-tale but she did want to distance herself from such wanton vandalism as quickly as possible, knowing that the picture was quite valuable. The girl wasn't a bit like herself, she thought crossly. She was fair haired, red-lipped, standing beneath a tree in a poppy field, carrying a straw hat with blue ribbon round it. But now everyone would see the girl in the picture as Rachel, and Mr Stanley would be sure to think she had something to do with its mutilation.

To avoid suspicion she joined in with some other girls who were skipping but didn't have a chance to have a go before the bell went. They lined up and to everyone's surprise were led into the hall. Rachel wanted to die. The girl in the picture looked hideous, seemingly glaring down on the whole school accusingly. Rachel felt as if all eyes must be on her but when she glanced round no one appeared to have even noticed.

Mr Stanley the headmaster quickly changed all that, though. With a long cane in his hand he pointed to the picture and proceeded to lecture the whole school of one hundred and fifty children.

'No doubt the artist of this evil deed won't have the courage to stand up and admit to his crime, but I'll find him and when I do he will be made to suffer his punishment in front of you all.'

There was an ominous silence. Now, all heads turned from the picture to where Rachel was standing.

Mr Stanley rapped on his reading desk sharply to command attention.

'We should all have learnt during Scripture lessons that we do not mock the afflicted. If we do we are guilty of sin and will be punished.' He was a tall man with a mean-looking long thin nose with nostrils that were almost closed. His mouth appeared like a narrow stripe across his bony face, but when he parted his lips his voice echoed deep and hollow from a great cavern.

'Now, I want you all to hold out your hands in front of you, palms uppermost.' His tone was menacing and some of the younger children who thought they were about to be smacked unjustly started whimpering.

With long strides Mr Stanley walked briskly through the first two or three rows of children, hardly glancing at their small trembling hands.

'Lead these off to their classroom, Miss Davis,' he said in a softer tone. Then with more diligence, he went through each row examining every hand carefully.

There was some kind of skirmish in the back row before he reached it. Mr Stanley pushed his way through the frightened scholars and grabbed Charlie Mead by the collar of his well-worn jacket.

'I thought as much,' he growled.

Charlie was frantically wiping his hands down the side of his size-too-small trousers but the headmaster saw the evidence he needed. He pushed him to the front of the hall.

'You are a menace to this school, Mead,' he roared. 'Who are you to ridicule anyone else? You haven't got an inch of brain between your ears, lad. This picture, the Poppy Girl, was very valuable, given to the school by the members of Wickham Council many years ago on the accession to the throne of Queen Victoria.' Mr Stanley's face was becoming rather red as anger increased. He began tapping his palm with the cane as if impatient to mete out punishment. Charlie stood looking up at him with his usual stupid grin. He was no stranger to beatings everyone knew. Nothing the head master could do to him would match the abuse he had already suffered. Rachel was tall enough to look over the heads of the children in front of her. She could see Charlie's sister June, two years older than Rachel but several inches shorter, already weeping.

'Prepare yourself, boy, to be the laughing stock of Wickham. Remove your trousers.'

A gasp went up. Spankings were a common enough occurrence but never in a state of undress, and in front of the entire school. Charlie's expression changed only slightly as he paused then started to undo his buttons. Rachel could hardly bear to look. Time seemed suspended as Charlie shrugged his braces over his shoulders. Rachel couldn't stand any more. Some unbidden force urged her forward and on to the platform where she stood defiantly between Mr Stanley and Charlie.

'Don't do it, sir,' she begged. 'I know he did it because of my mark, but he doesn't understand. I . . . I can't help having a birthmark and Charlie can't help being soft in the head. He didn't know the picture was worth anything. He's always in trouble and it isn't fair.'

Mr Stanley looked down at Rachel in disbelief. He could scarcely believe what was happening. This poor girl with an unfortunate brand on her face was actually standing up for Charlie Mead who had caused her nothing but misery ever since the Hunter twins came to Wickham School.

'Rachel, child, don't you think he should be punished?'

'We-ell, yes, for damaging a good painting, sir. But beatings don't mean much to Charlie. I reckon he's had the sense knocked out of him already. Couldn't we just wash it off, Mr Stanley – sir?'

The headmaster's expression softened but he was obliged to ask: 'Did you have some part in this, Rachel Hunter?'

'No! Would I make fun of myself? Charlie's always made fun of me – but he can't help it, sir. The other boys egg him on.'

No child had ever seen Mr Stanley at a loss for words but he didn't seem to know what to do next.

'Apart from the aspect of Charlie's ridicule of you, Rachel, to have this crayon removed will cost a great deal of money and I doubt whether you or Charlie Mead has the wherewithal to pay for it.'

'Perhaps we could have a collection?' she suggested hesitantly.

Now Mr Stanley thought she was being facetious and pulled himself up to his full height. 'The punishment must fit the crime, Rachel Hunter, but since you plead so eloquently on behalf of Charlie Mead I will spare the feelings of the other children.' He glanced across at Miss Davis and the rest of the school was led away.

Rachel supposed she was in for a caning as well, but at least she had bought time for Charlie Mead. She walked sedately by Charlie's side as Mr Stanley urged them towards his study.

'Now, Charlie Mead, bend over.'

'No! No, please Mr Stanley – don't,' Rachel pleaded.

But the cane whizzed through the air and came to rest on Charlie's backside with a dull thud. Once, twice, three times . . .

Rachel had placed her hands over her ears, but suddenly she rushed between master and boy and took the force of the cane descending for the fourth time on the right side of her face.

Charlie waited, gritting his teeth to prevent himself crying out, and realised that the caning had been halted. He stood up and turned to see Rachel holding her cheek.

35

'You *never*!' he shouted at the headmaster.

'It . . . was an accident. Rachel, I'm sorry, my dear. I didn't mean to hit you – you of all people.' There was a tremor in his voice.

'Why? Because I'm already marked? Now I've got another one to match!' she shouted in order to stem the flow of tears. Her eyes smarted uncomfortable as Mr Stanley threw the cane down in disgust.

'Get out of here, Mead, before I do something I shall regret even more,' Mr Stanley ordered.

Charlie started for the door then stopped and looked at Rachel.

'You all right?'

She nodded.

'T'was your own fault for meddlin' – and don't you ever say I'm soft in the 'ead again or it'll be the worse for you. I 'aint no crybaby. I can take a beating better 'n you, soppy girl! Now look what you got for not minding your own business. All over some silly picture too.' He shuffled away, rubbing the seat of his pants.

'Oh dear, poor Rachel. I know you meant well, my dear, but I'm afraid Charlie doesn't have the sense to realise.'

'Caning's one thing, Mr Stanley, but not in front of the whole school.'

He sat down on his chair behind the large oak desk strewn with official-looking papers. For a second or two he closed his eyes then rubbed his hands over his face in agitation.

'Since when has your opinion been of importance in this school, may I ask?'

'I was only being what Vicar said we should be to those less fortunate than ourselves – compassionate.'

'And why do you think Charlie Mead deserves your compassion, Rachel?'

''Cos, whatever he says, we all know he's twopenneth short of a shilling, sir.' Rachel looked down at the handkerchief she was twisting between her fingers. 'I don't really know why I did it. I just did, sir.'

Mr Stanley pressed his fingertips together. 'You'd better let Miss Davis look at your cheek,' he said quietly and with deep regret.

'It'll be all right. I'll just go and wash it. I know you didn't mean to hit me, Mr Stanley.' Rachel walked towards the door then turned back. 'Will the picture be all right, sir? I mean, can it be cleaned? T'was only crayon.'

'Only crayon, Rachel,' he repeated patiently, 'but an oil painting shouldn't be defaced, and it can only be cleaned by an expert.'

'I don't think Charlie Mead will be able to pay for the damage – nor his dad.'

36

'There you may well be right, Rachel. Please return to your class. I must write a letter of explanation to your parents.'

At hometime when all the children gathered round Rachel, most in admiration of her courage, shocked too at her scored cheek, she began to worry what her parents were going to say, and once she and Belinda were alone to walk the last mile to Kingsmead she voiced her fear.

'They'll be cross, won't they?' she said.

'Whatever made you do it, Rachel?' Belinda asked wide-eyed.

'Don't know – that devil that's in me, I s'pose.'

'And for Charlie Mead of all people.'

'He won't be at school much longer, thank goodness.'

Phoebe Hunter's first words when the girls reached Calder Cottage were: 'What on earth have you done now, Rachel?'

'It's nothing,' she said, but dutifully handed over the letter Mr Stanley had entrusted her to deliver to her parents. It wasn't that she hadn't considered throwing it in the river on the way home, but Mr Stanley would see her parents at Church on Sunday and there was a risk he would mention it.

Belinda stood by her sister as the questioning continued until bedtime, and Phoebe did her best to explain that a girl of eleven was in no position to take matters into her own hands, let alone question the actions of the headmaster. Wally took himself out to his shed. Planing a nice piece of oak until it had a satin finish helped to take his mind off the cost of cleaning the picture in the school hall. He wasn't sure that he agreed with his wife that it was their duty to contribute but Phoebe was anxious to do the right thing.

After morning service on Easter Sunday, as the congregation assembled outside to meet and chat with friends from outlying villages, Nessie Mead, with June hanging on her arm, joined the small group where Phoebe and Wally were in conversation with George Cropper, the local lumberjack and his wife.

'Excuse me,' Nessie said, 'but I believe you're Mr and Mrs Hunter? I just want to say I'm sorry for what our Charlie did. It was unforgivable of him to poke fun at your daughter.' Nessie turned her attention to Rachel and Belinda and after a few seconds said with a smile: 'You aren't much like twins but at least with different coloured hair your mum can't get you mixed up.' She placed her hand on Rachel's arm in a friendly gesture. 'It was brave to stand up for him like you did, dear. He didn't deserve it. I hope your face is better now?'

'Children have high spirits,' Phoebe said. 'Especially after a long winter when they're kept in. They're all growing up so fast –'

37

'And it's time our Charlie was put to work, I reckon. I understand you've kindly offered to pay for the picture to be cleaned, but there'll be no need. I've asked Mr Stanley to deduct so much a week from my wages and as soon as Charlie begins to earn he'll have to pay me back. After all, it wasn't your fault – or Rachel's.' She stopped short of saying more. Didn't she know what a shock it was to have a child born with a disfigurement? She found herself staring intently at Rachel Hunter. The child's mark was hardly noticeable with her hair styled to cover the left-hand side of her forehead, and June had said that it was fading gradually. Belinda was such a pretty, delicate child in contrast to her sister who was taller with rich dark hair and eyes which had a fierce intensity about them.

Nessie's duties at the school were to clean before the children got there and after they'd gone home, so she wasn't familiar with many of them except the locals who came from Hundred Acres like herself. She knew the Hunter family hadn't been in Kingsmere more than a few years. Rumour had it that Wally Hunter thought he was a cut above the rest, having a good trade and Squire giving him work. That didn't mean that Nessie was going to allow him to pay their debts. She was far too proud for that. Nessie saw the Hunters out together in Wickham sometimes, or at Church on the rare occasions that she went. The fair girl, Belinda, was more like a fairy doll, Nessie considered, usually holding her father's hand as if they were par-ticularly close. She might almost envy them their happy family image, reminiscent of her upbringing but far removed from the life she led with Dick and their children.

Out of the corner of her eye Nessie saw the Taylor family walking in her direction so bade the Hunters good morning and hurried away from the Church. Jake Taylor wasn't above giving her the glad eye when he got the chance, whether accompanied by his wife Lily and son Adam or not, but mostly his affections were directed at any young girl who took his fancy. Nessie had further cause to feel aggrieved because sixteen-year-old Adam had been taken on as apprentice carpenter at the Manor House. How she wished there was a place somewhere for Charlie, but he wasn't the brightest lad and with his father's reputation well-known in the district no one was willing to give the boy a chance. At least her eldest, Benjie, now nineteen, had a regular job with the blacksmith, and both of the older girls, Kittie and Susan, seventeen and fifteen, were in reliable domestic service. Life was a good deal easier for Nessie with them living in, but she was always glad when they managed to get home together and the house was full again. She supposed even Charlie would be useful weeding and hoeing when the strawberry season started in earnest. June, her baby, was Nessie's closest companion. After losing the strawberry marked infant she had devoted her time and love to June, then a year and nine months old. Now she was growing into a young woman, at thirteen older than the Hunter twins but still shorter than Rachel. June took after Nessie in colouring with her chestnut-coloured hair and pale green eyes. She was timid, sensitive, always ready to rush to her mother's defence when Dick was in one of his difficult moods, eager to defend Charlie too when the world seemed against him. When the time came for her to go away in service Nessie knew she would be lost. But that was a whole year away.

The summer came and went, a summer during which the harvest of fruit was as plentiful as ever and Charlie Mead's physical strength was appreciated by several of the local smallholders. By the end of September Nessie's debt was paid and she could enjoy her sister Beth's wedding with a clear conscience.

Beth had surprised everyone by remaining single until she reached the age of twenty-three. From an early age she had shown herself to be flirtatious and showy, much too generous with powder and rouge. She liked to paint her full sensuous lips bright red in order to attract attention. Somehow she managed to dress in the latest fashions which showed off her well-developed figure to the best advantage. No one ever went as far as calling her a fallen woman but few doubted that she was well paid for her services which provided her with the necessary pounds, shillings and pence to spend on herself.

But she made a beautiful bride dressed in white satin with lace inserts. She was a clever needlewoman, following in her mother's footsteps, and together they had made the dress and those for the three bridesmaids, her nieces Kittie, Susan and June Mead, all dressed in pretty blue taffeta. Even Dick, who gave her away in the absence of her deceased father, managed to stay sober until after the ceremony and for once looked quite presentable in a dark suit borrowed for the occasion.

Relatives, friends and neighbours filled the Church of St Nicholas in Wickham as the bells peeled out across the Meon valley, though the main interest was whether or not Beth was already pregnant. In that she disappointed everyone. People gossiped and twittered. Had Beth Waterstone really turned over a new leaf? Was it possible that she hadn't seduced the handsome Harry Cropper, son of the lumberjack? Could this be a real love-match? By the expressions of adoration exchanged during the photographic session it would seem it was.

Nessie helped her elderly mother over the rough gravel pathway leading to the lych gate.

39

'That's the last of us to fly the coop, Ma,' she said.

'Never thought our Beth would be that,' Mrs Waterstone said. 'Even let our Esther get to the altar ahead of her by two years, and she the youngest.'

'Maybe Beth wanted to sow her wild oats first before settling down. She made a lovely bride – and fooled everyone into the bargain, but I guess it won't be long before we'll have to start knitting.'

'She's done well for herself, Nessie. Harry is hardworking and it's done young Charlie some good too if George is going to take him on for the winter months. Lumbering's no light work but I reckon your Charlie was built for the job. Let's hope he makes some'at of his self now.'

Things were looking up, Nessie thought, even if she did have to listen to Dick's coarse jokes about the newlyweds.

Autumn brought dark evenings and a spiky chill in the air but on Bonfire Night everyone for miles around joined in the celebrations on the green. For the past few weeks even the children had been collecting anything and everything to help build the mammoth-sized bonfire according to custom.

The Hunters walked in from Kingsmere, the girls dressed in warm coats, woolly hats, scarves and mitts.

'Now don't get too close,' Phoebe warned, 'and stay near us. Don't go wandering off by yourselves.'

But Rachel had a mind of her own. She saw a group of youngsters, among them some of her friends. Since the affair of the damaged picture she had become the most popular girl in the school. They danced round the bonfire enjoying the warmth from the crackling faggots, mostly stolen from people's back yards, running wildly when sparks flew in the air.

One of the older girls who had recently left school had a bottle of cider which she passed round to everyone who wanted to take a swig.

'Isn't this the Strawberry Girl?' she taunted, picking out Rachel. 'Ain't she the one who got a whack for sticking up for Charlie Mead?'

Rachel, in her innocence, didn't realise that the girl was under the influence of drink.

'What if I did?' she challenged with a toss of her head. 'Charlie Mead gets all the blame and it isn't fair.'

'Cm'on then, let's have a look at your mark? S'pose you think it makes you more important than the rest of us?'

'No!' Rachel decided it was time to return to the safety of her parents but the girls gathered round her excitedly, reminding her of a scene four years earlier. But she was older now and wiser. She wouldn't let them see that she was scared.

'Take 'er hat off. Hold back 'er hair,' Dottie Coombes said. Rachel backed away and there was a bit of a struggle. 'Reckon I'm as good a witch as you. I bet I could magic that away. Cm'on let's go to our secret hiding place.'

Rachel began to feel afraid. She was held fast by one girl on each side of her and the others brought up the rear. With some degree of panic she realised that most of these girls were the elder sisters of her own particular school friends.

'No need to be scared, Rachel,' Dottie assured her. 'You don't want to live for the rest of your life with that mark, do you?'

'It's getting fainter,' Rachel said in a small voice. 'The doctor said so. I'll have to get back to my parents or they'll be worried.'

'Not until we've put a charm on you. It'll work, you'll see.'

With the raucous noise at the bonfire no one noticed the small group of girls heading in the direction of the Manor House. When they reached a door in the high brick wall it opened easily and Dottie led the way across the grounds to a tall ominous-looking building known as the folly. They pushed open a rickety door. It was very dark inside and Rachel was frightened.

'I don't like it here,' she said. 'My mum will be looking for me.'

'Then she won't find you, will she, so shut up. And don't you dare tell anyone where you've been. This is our secret. This is where we come and talk. We make up stories and things, and cast spells on people.'

One of the girls had some matches and lit a candle. It was a cold, eerie place with no windows on the ground floor. A narrow spiral staircase stretched up in the centre – to where? Rachel wondered, but she didn't ask.

'Sit down, Rachel, and we'll all sit round you.'

'No!' she said indignantly. 'This place is dirty and I shall spoil my coat.'

'Then your dad will have to buy you a new one, won't he?' Dottie pushed Rachel to the ground and she found herself sitting in the middle of the group holding the candle.

'We need something to rub on your mark. What can we use?' Dottie began walking round. 'I know – we'll make a powder out of some leaves. There's plenty of 'em 'ere.'

Rachel was surprised at the amount of light the candle gave. She could see rubbish lying everywhere – leaves and paper, a few tufts of sheep's wool which had blown in from the meadows on the estate.

Dottie and her friend called Rose gathered handfuls of leaves and screwed them up between their hands. They held it over Rachel's forehead but it wouldn't stick so they threw it over her head. Then

41

they all held hands and danced round her, singing a lot of words she had never heard before. Dottie kept stopping to drink some more cider and soon could hardly stand up. They all fell about laughing hysterically. Rachel thought she'd get up and run but they made sure she didn't get away.

'That's the first bit,' Dottie said. 'Now we've got to blindfold you and then chant until the mark has vanished.'

Rachel found that it was no use remonstrating, she was quite powerless against so many of them fussing round her. They used her own scarf to tie round her eyes and then wheeled her round and round until she was giddy, all the while chanting gobbledygook.

'Oh, stop, do stop – *please* . . . ,' she implored, but no one took any heed of what she said.

'It'll take at least five minutes,' Rose whispered in her ear, and after that it went horribly quiet.

Rachel was so giddy she lost her bearings and when she came up against the wall slid down it on to the floor again. Dottie had tied the scarf so tightly round her head that it was several minutes before Rachel could free herself and then to her horror she found herself in total darkness. She rubbed her eyes but that only made things worse. Where were the others? Where was the door? She began to panic and rushed frantically this way and that but to no avail.

'Now take hold of yourself, Rachel Hunter,' she said to herself. 'You're not a baby and it stands to reason those girls were just making fun of you. You know they couldn't magic the strawberry mark away. Haven't you tried enough times yourself? Let your eyes get accustomed to the dark gradually.' She stood with her back against the wall and closed her eyes gently, then she opened them and waited. Out of the gloom she was able to see a pale strand of light – it must be the doorway, so she rushed at it and breathed a sigh of relief when it opened. There was no sign of anyone. She knew that she was trespassing on private land and would get into trouble if caught. She began to feel frightened again and very angry at Dottie, Rose and the others for leaving her stranded.

Far away on the night air came a shout, probably the men going home from the bonfire or pub. From another direction came the sound of cats fighting and a dog barked too. Rachel had only ever visited the big house with Belinda for the annual Christmas party and then accompanied by their father. Somehow she had to get out of the grounds without being seen but although she walked for what seemed like hours she couldn't find the high brick wall which surrounded the Squire's estate. In desperation she just kept walking not realising that she had left the park and was entering the woods.

42

The Manor House parkland was vast in itself and now Rachel found herself obliged to walk through a part of the woods she was unfamiliar with. But, somehow, she had to get to Kingsmere. She was tired and worried, aware of how anxious her parents must be. If only she could find a pathway which would indicate where she was but everywhere was deserted and there were only night sounds to scare her. Well, she thought with renewed hope, everywhere must lead to somewhere, she must keep going.

She walked for a further half an hour, then in the distance she could hear a baby crying. Life – there was life somewhere ahead, and she quickened her pace. A loud barking made her stop in her tracks. There in front of her baring its teeth was a vicious-looking animal. She stood frozen to the spot. Her father had taught the girls never to run from any animal but to brazen it out as if prepared for a full frontal attack.

'It . . . it's all right. I'm your . . . friend,' she managed to stammer in a frightened whisper.

The large alsatian dog responded with a low suspicious growl.

'Quiet, Jip!' a voice commanded, but the dog wouldn't be pacified that easily.

'Who's there? What you making that row for, Jipper?' A man stepped out of the trees and was astounded to see his dog holding Rachel at bay.

'God Almighty!' he exclaimed. 'And who are you, and what d'you think you're a doing of, frightening Jipper like that?'

'I . . . I'm ever so sorry, sir,' Rachel said. She hoped that politeness would be her passport from whatever peril she had walked into. 'I'm lost, you see.'

'Lost!' the man echoed. 'Should think you be, my dear. Out here in the forest all alone. Wherefore you goin' then, may I ask?'

'Who you talking to, Josh?' Now a woman appeared as if from nowhere. She peered ahead of her. 'A maid! A maid, all alone in the forest? You run away from 'ome, young miss?' she asked. Her voice was harsh and Rachel began to tremble with fear. Should she stay or take to her heels and run? But where could she go? Which way? Already she was lost and the prospect of being chased through the woods in the dark was worse than trying to talk herself out of difficulty.

'I've been to the bonfire on the green,' she explained in a meek voice. 'I went with some girls to the folly and then – well – I just got left behind.'

'Up to mischief, I dare say,' the woman snapped.

'Come now, Merle, don't be hard on the maid.'

43

There were more voices, and people emerged from the darkness until Rachel was confronted with quite a gathering. She could smell wood smoke and cooking – she had walked into a gypsy camp. All she knew about these people was that they made clothes pegs and faggots, and knocked on people's doors selling their wares. Sometimes they offered white heather or good luck charms as long as you crossed their palm with silver.

'I live at Kingsmere,' she said in a timid voice. 'I thought I was still in the Manor House grounds but, truth to tell, I don't really know where I am.' She ended the sentence on a high note as the situation became too much for her and she broke down and sobbed.

An arm went about her shoulders. 'Come now, Missie, don't you fret. We'll have you 'ome in no time. Your folks will be worried sick, I shouldn't wonder.' The woman called Merle urged her forward. Rachel was fearful that they might be going to kidnap her so she pulled back.

'Come along, my dear. Just you have a hot drink before we gets you 'ome. You'm cold and afeared, but never you mind, us travelling folk never turns a body away without refreshment.'

A clearing among the trees revealed several painted waggons, and by the light of one of the lanterns hanging on the front Rachel could see horses tethered to a tree in the distance. There was a comforting smell of food and warmth which helped dispel her fear.

She had never been inside a gypsy caravan before and was surprised at the cleanliness as well as the space it provided. The bed in the back looked mightily inviting but she knew she must get home.

'Please,' she begged, 'I ought to get home if you'll just tell me the way to go.'

Merle poured her a cup of tea from the iron pot on the stove. It was good to wrap her cold hands round the earthenware mug and sip. At first she wasn't sure she liked the tea, it wasn't the same as she had at home.

'Herbal, my dearie,' Merle said as if reading her thoughts. 'Do you good, though you look healthy enough to me.' The woman took one of Rachel's hands in hers and opened the palm. 'Mmm,' she murmured. 'A long life ahead of you, me dear,' she said. 'But a troubled one. You've had trouble already, I see. Let's see – a brand – is it a name?' Her voice drifted into a softer tone as she peered more closely at Rachel's hand. 'Poor child – a mark, a birthmark.'

'Yes, yes,' Rachel said eagerly. 'The girls were trying to magic it away in the folly.'

Merle shook her head. 'That's no good. They were trying to trick you and it's wicked to make fun of others.' She studied Rachel's hand in detail. 'Ever had owt to do with our kind?' she asked bluntly.

'No . . . no.'

'Mmm, must be my mistake, but take my word for it, Missie, your mark will go.'

'But everyone says that,' Rachel said indignantly. 'Even the doctor said it would fade by the time I was ten. I'm eleven now and I've still got it.'

'Have faith in what I tell you, Missie. It will go in its own good time if you stop fretting. Then you'll be prettier than your . . . er . . . sister, is it?'

'How could you tell I've got a sister?' Rachel asked in surprise. 'But I could never be prettier than Belinda.'

'Like a fairy doll, I do declare,' Merle said slowly, thoughtfully.

'Yes, she's smaller than me and very fair.'

Merle turned Rachel's palm this way and that, caressing gently until Rachel could feel a soothing element passing through her body. Instead of being frightened now she experienced a tremendous feeling of security.

'Yes, your mark will go but you'll have to be patient. You aren't fully grown yet, me dear, so I can't tell your destiny, but there'll be happy times and then . . . and then some unhappiness. But you'll find your own way . . .' Merle's voice became so soft that Rachel could hardly hear what she was saying, and then it petered out as if Merle was in some kind of trance.

Seconds later she dropped Rachel's hand abruptly. 'Drink your tea, child.' And to no one in particular outside the caravan: 'Fetch Kasan here at once.'

'What time is it?' Rachel dared to ask. She thought it must be midnight after such unimagined events.

'We don't have a need for clocks – but I'd say it's near to nine-thirty. Kingsmere's only a mile away through the woods, but Kas will take you there.'

'What's up, Merle?' a masculine voice called from the doorway.

'Come inside and meet – what's your name, child?'

'Rachel. Rachel Hunter.'

'Then see that Miss Rachel gets home to Kingsmere safely, Kas.' Merle took Rachel's hand in hers and clasped it closely against her chest. 'Godspeed, child – have a happy life.'

'You've been ever so kind,' Rachel began but Merle waved her away.

At the foot of the steps a young man waited. He smiled and took Rachel's hand as she descended the steps.

'We'll take the short cut through the woods. I think I know the cottage where you live,' he said with a warm smile.

Rachel thought she had never seen such a handsome young man before. He was very tall, with a mop of curly, jet black hair which reached down to his shoulders. In the gloom of the night if she hadn't known by his voice that he was a man she would have thought he was a girl. He was wearing a jerkin over dark trousers and had a knotted scarf at his throat.

'No need to be afraid, Rachel. There'll be no one but us in the woods at this time of night, not even the poachers.' His voice was strong yet strangely calm and Rachel had no qualms about walking along with him.

'I've never heard that name before – Kasan.' she said.

'Don't suppose you have. I was born in Ireland – suppose it comes from there. You can call me Kas, everyone does. How did you come to get lost then?'

Rachel poured out her story to him. It seemed to help to talk about her birthmark. She felt that here was someone who wouldn't make fun of her.

'Merle says it will fade if I'm patient but people have been telling me that ever since I can remember.'

'If Merle says so then you must believe it.'

'Is she your mother?' Rachel asked.

'Good gracious no! I haven't got any folks. Merle and Josh took me in when my parents died of a fever. I was only a baby, and they were travelling through Ireland at the time.'

'Do you like being a – gypsy?'

'It's a free life and a happy one. We don't poach and rob like some folks think we do. We try to live peaceably and take good care of each other and anyone else who crosses our path. Sometimes we're rich and sometimes – well, mostly, I s'pose – we're poor.'

'Does Merle tell fortunes?'

'She has the gift of seeing into the future and can tell a bit of the past too.'

'Is that a bit like magic?'

'No, nothing like magic. That's illusion – a kind of trickery.'

They walked in silence for a while and then through the veil of trees as the smokiness of the November night began to clear Rachel could see a lighter patch.

'There, see?' Kasan said. 'Kingsmere. And your cottage is down the road a bit on the right.'

'Oh, thank goodness,' Rachel said with relief. 'Would you like to come in and meet my parents? That's if they're home yet. I'll be in terrible trouble if they've been looking all over the place for me.'

Kasan laughed. 'I think I'll leave you to face the music. I reckon you can take care of yourself, but it was nice meeting you. And here – have this, Rachel.' He pressed something cold into her palm and when she looked she saw it was a round, smooth stone with a hole in the middle. 'For good luck – it's been my lucky charm for years. Perhaps it'll charm your birthmark away quicker.'

'Thank you but I couldn't take it,' Rachel said. But still she kept holding on to it tightly.

'I want you to keep it, to remember me by.'

'Will you be staying in the woods for long?' she asked hesitantly.

'No, I reckon we'll be moving on any day now, but one day maybe I shall knock on your door selling faggots or pegs or asking for work. By then you'll have forgotten you ever had a birthmark.'

'Oh, I do hope so, but I s'pose they'll still go on calling me Strawberry Girl.'

'That's a nice name. Strawberries are sweet. Everyone likes strawberries.'

A light spilled out on to the garden of Calder Cottage.

'Rachel, is that you? Where on earth did you get to,' Phoebe called with some degree of annoyance.

She turned to ask Kasan to go with her but he had vanished. Without so much as a rustle he had disappeared back into the woods. Rachel ran into the house and was about to explain about her visit to the folly when something prevented her.

'I got talking to some girls,' she said. 'They went off and left me and I got lost trying to find my way back to you. I . . . I met some . . . people and they brought me home through the woods. They were very kind.'

'Well, you're a very naughty girl for going off in the first place. Don't you ever do that again. You've had us worried out of our minds. Now get ready for bed and hurry up about it,' Phoebe said crossly. 'You never know who people are and there's gypsies in the forest. You should have stayed with Belinda.'

Rachel was quite glad to go to bed. She considered telling Belinda about her adventure but decided against it. This was her secret, her very own and the first ever from her sister. She stood at the window and looked out into the eerie night. Kasan would be about eighteen years old, she thought.

Long after she had blown out the candle and snuggled under the cosy sheets she lay awake thinking about her gypsy boy.

She supposed she had fallen in love with him at first sight. His soft friendly voice lingered in her head. She'd never ever lose her precious stone, his now her lucky charm. That made it *theirs*. She turned it over in her hand, held it close to her heart and wished with all her might that it would help to make her beautiful. And also that one day she would meet Kasan again, although she knew that was most unlikely.

Chapter Three

By the time the girls reached their thirteenth birthday Rachel could proudly push back her hair to show off her blemish-free forehead. All that remained was a pinkish stain, a pale thin outline which appeared more prominently when he was upset, angry or worried. Rachel was convinced that it was all due to Kas's lucky stone. She knew she must never lose it whatever happened and neither must she ever share her secret with anyone.

Her cross to bear as she entered her teens was that her nickname Strawberry Girl had stuck. Charlie Mead had started it and during the last couple of years others had picked it up, but hadn't Kas told her that it was a nice name? Strawberries were sweet, he had said, so it didn't bother her nearly as much as it once had.

Wickham's Spring Fair, held annually on May 20, was an exciting event. It was an important occasion when farmers met tradesmen at the huge market to pay their yearly accounts. Tents were erected where business could be transacted over a glass of beer or spirits and orders were placed for the forthcoming year. While the men completed deals their wives went shopping in Wickham Square, or the more adventurous crept surreptitiously into the travelling gypsy's tent to have their fortune told.

There was every sideshow imaginable to tempt young and old alike to part with their hard-saved pennies. Stalls of trinkets to attract keen buyers, and balloons and streamers giving an air of festivity to the market town. Loud music bellowed continuously and young men drank far more than was good for them as they gathered round the shooting galleries and boxing booths.

Wally and Phoebe Hunter allowed the girls to wander off and amuse themselves while they went to watch the sale of horses, sheep, cattle and pigs which totalled some several hundred in all and covered a large area. Business was brisk, sometimes carried out in a good-

48

humoured way but frequently a fight between competitors would break out and Wally and Phoebe temporarily forgot about their growing daughters.

The girls were fascinated by the enthusiasm of everyone as money flowed freely. Not that they had much to spend themselves as they were only allowed a shilling or two out of their birthday money to fritter away on what Phoebe declared was rubbish. Rachel's spirits lifted when they came to the fortune teller's tent. Was it possible that Merle was inside? she wondered. Dressed in colourful skirt and shawl, gazing knowingly into a crystal ball.

'Let's go in here,' she suggested eagerly, but Belinda was horrified.

'How can you think of such a thing. You know Mummy would be cross, Rachel.' She hurried on saying brightly: 'Let's have a go on the swings and roundabouts.'

After they had tired of being spun round and swung high into the air they went to find the toffee stall where they purchased large humbugs for a farthing. They were ambling along watching with amazement everything that was going on around them when a voice suddenly boomed out: 'Why, if it isn't the Strawberry Girl.'

Rachel turned quickly, readily on the defensive at the sound of Charlie Mead's voice.

'Don't call me that,' she said crossly. 'I haven't got a mark any more, so there.'

Belinda, white with apprehension, tried to pull Rachel away but she stood her ground, forgetting that Kas considered it a nice name. She was anxious to settle the matter once and for all. She pulled her hair back to show off her flawless white forehead as she stepped nearer to Charlie and his gang of yobs. Too late she realised that these young men had consumed more than their fill of beer. Charlie's breath reeked of it. He grabbed Rachel roughly, and although she tried to fight him off he was too strong and began to wrestle with her. To Rachel's surprise a young man came out of the crowd to her assistance.

'Leave her alone, you great bully. Don't you know that's not the way to treat girls?'

'Aw, who 'ave we got 'ere then? Cor, 'tis Adam Taylor! And what would you know, fancy boy?' Charlie sneered. 'Still clutching at your ma's apron, you are. If I want to tease the girls, I will.'

'Leave Rachel and Belinda alone,' Adam said.

'Want to make some'at of it then?' Charlie challenged, releasing Rachel and putting up his fists.

'No, I don't want to fight,' Adam said, 'but I will if it keeps you away from the girls.' He squared up to the bulky Charlie who by

49

comparison made Adam appear quite puny although he was only an inch short of six feet but very slim. Adam Taylor was a good-looking young man with dark curly hair and black eyes. He'd been above average with his school work so was not particularly popular with other young men in the village. At eighteen he kept himself to himself, keeping his mother company rather than going off gallivanting.

'Now, now, now, boys, that's not the way to go about things.' The boxing booth owner saw a golden opportunity to draw an audience. Already several people were showing interest in the situation which threatened to grow ugly. 'Come on inside, boys, and let the best man win.'

Charlie's friends roared their approval and before Adam knew it he was being hoisted to the back of the booth and urged to change into some large boxing shorts.

'Trade not going too well, me lads, so I'll give you a pound each for a good fair fight,' the man whispered. 'Got to get the people in though so I'll advertise two pounds for the winner.' He went to the front of the booth. 'Roll up, roll up!' he shouted, and had little difficulty in rallying a large number of people. 'Come and support these gallant young men in a most exciting three-round contest. Two pounds for the winner,' he yelled.

Belinda clutched at Rachel's arm. 'Oh, poor Adam,' she said. 'Rachel, we can't let him do it. Charlie will murder him.'

Rachel laughed. 'Nothing we can do about it – he didn't have to interfere, did he?'

'That's not very nice. He did it for you – and *I'm* very grateful even if you're not.'

'He got us out of an awkward spot,' Rachel giggled. 'He's all right – a bit of a Mummy's boy. He's quite nice-looking though.'

Belinda would have extricated herself from the situation, but by now onlookers were packed in closely behind them making escape impossible.

'I daren't look, Rachel,' Belinda said. 'I wish we could get away.'

'Somehow I don't think Adam will survive three rounds,' Rachel said, suddenly feeling remorseful, but they had to stick it out.

The fight began, the crowd urging it on, mostly yelling on Adam's behalf because he looked such an unlikely candidate. Blood was soon flowing from a cut on his lip. Both eyes were swollen up so that he could hardly see his opponent but still miraculously he kept on his feet. Rachel cheered with the rest of them but Belinda only peeped from between trembling fingers when the response from the crowd suggested that Adam might be down. Charlie was like a great lumbering bear after his prey but Adam managed to get in a few hard blows to his challenger's body which hurt. The final bell sounded. At last the three gruelling rounds were over and the boxing booth owner held up Charlie's hands as the winner, Adam's as a game loser. There were boos and jibes as Charlie received the two pounds, but the crowd quickly lost interest and dispersed. Rachel and Belinda remained, thinking that at least they owed Adam their sympathy. They stood at the side of the booth where they saw an argument in progress.

'You said a pound each,' Adam said snatching one of the pound notes the boxing booth owner had demanded back from Charlie.

'That was only to draw the crowd, lad. You surely didn't think I meant it? You two had a score to settle so I let you do it in my ring.'

'You're a liar and a cheat,' Adam said, blinking the blood from his eyes. 'Two pounds for the winner you said publicly, and that's Charlie fair and square.' The man grabbed the money from Adam's hand, he tried to take it back but it was securely held, and while Charlie beat a hasty retreat Adam threw a vicious punch which sent the owner of the boxing booth reeling on his own canvas.

Adam took to his heels. 'Get away from here,' he said to the girls before quickly merging with the throng of people milling around.

Few took any notice of the bloodied youth who fled from the fair meadow with two girls chasing after him.

'Rachel – we can't – we mustn't! Supposing Mum and Dad see us,' Belinda panted, finding it difficult to keep up with her long-legged sister. 'Let Adam go. He'll be all right when he goes home to his mother.'

'He won't want his mother seeing him like that. Wasn't he brave? I think we should make sure he's all right.'

Belinda had little option but to follow her sister who, being tall, managed to keep Adam in her sights as he ran towards the river.

Rachel guessed where he was making for and at the end of the fence by the mill she found him at the bottom of the steps at Dip Hole. He was frantically splashing water over his face, washing away the blood to make himself respectable.

'Can we help, Adam?' she asked.

'I'm all right. Don't worry about me. You get on back to your folks, and don't dare tell anyone what happened.'

'But it wasn't your fault. I mean – well – it was mine, I s'pose. I shouldn't have taken any notice of Charlie Mead. I didn't mean you to get into a fight on my account, Adam.'

He came slowly up the steps, drying his face on his neck tie.

'I hope I'd have done the same for any girl who was being molested by Charlie Mead. I may look feeble but he didn't get things all his own way '

'You knocked that horrible booth man flat!' Belinda said with undisguised admiration. 'That was very brave.'

Rachel saw Adam gaze at her sister with more than passing interest, but then – didn't everyone look at pretty Belinda with a sense of enchantment.

'Fair's fair,' he replied softly. 'I may not like Charlie Mead but he won the fight even if we weren't very well matched. That rotter didn't want to pay up at all – it was all a farce for *him* to make money. I hate cheats. He made me mad so I just lashed out. I reckon if I could have gone a few more rounds with Charlie I might have winded him and all.' Suddenly he laughed then said: 'Ouch!'

'Your poor mouth – you won't be able to eat, will you?' Rachel said.

'Right now I could do with a strong drink so I'd best get home to Ma and keep my head down. No doubt the boxing owner will tell the police he was assaulted and I won't be too hard to find, will I? You leave me and don't worry. Your father won't be very pleased at you getting involved in a brawl. I'll make my way home through all the side tracks.'

'Thank you for rescuing me from Charlie,' Rachel said shyly. 'I'm sorry you got hurt though. I think you should each have had your pound.'

'Charlie won the fight – I did try to get him his winnings. Maybe he'll buy me a drink one of these days.'

'Not if I know Charlie Mead,' Rachel said. 'We'll see you up at the big house perhaps when we visit our Dad one day.'

'I'll look out for you. I like working with your father, he's a good man.'

Adam glanced from Belinda to Rachel, and back at Belinda again. Then he hurried away. The two girls walked sedately back to the fair. No, thought Rachel, he fought for me. Belinda's not going to have him. Kasan was forgotten. Adam was her new hero. He was learning a trade, was attractive and well liked. She knew she must be the one to make advances though. Wasn't she still tarnished with the strawberry mark, even if it had completely vanished? She was convinced people still thought of her as the witch of Wickham so she had to make Adam notice her. Belinda would have the pick of young men, not just any eligible young man but probably a wealthy one. Their parents would see to that. Nothing but the best for Belinda.

On Saturdays when there was no school Rachel and Belinda usually went into Wickham to do some shopping for Phoebe, and as the days grew warmer they would stop by the river to feed the ducks. Occasionally they would have to go to the big house to find their father to take his lunch.

Phoebe noticed the sudden eagerness to run any errand which took the girls to the big house.

'They're growing up, Wally,' she said one balmy evening when they had strolled to the bottom of their large garden to feed the hens. 'I reckon there's a lad they fancy somewhere about.'

Wally looked fondly at his wife and smiled. 'And I can tell you who he is – young Adam Taylor.' He threw a handful of corn to the cackling chickens who came strutting after them. 'I've been wondering which of them 'tis he's after.'

'They're both nice-looking girls. I just hope they make good matches when the time comes. Somehow I don't think Belinda's that interested in boys though.'

'Rachel's the one with high spirits,' Wally said dryly. 'Have to watch her.' He did watch and with interest as Adam seemed friendly with both the girls.

As summer progressed the girls knew where to find Adam fishing and would spend long happy hours chatting to him. It was an enlightening time when they broadened their outlook and felt the first flush of young love. Belinda kept her feelings and thoughts close to her heart but Rachel had no such inhibitions.

One day when Belinda was in bed with summer 'flu Rachel had to take a basket of eggs to Beech Cottage. Everyone loved Minnie Fletcher and Rachel was pleased to sit awhile and chat to the old lady now in her eightieth year. She prepared tea and enjoyed a piece of fruit cake with Minnie before starting the long walk home through the woods. It was cool under the shade of the trees. Rachel hummed a tune as she went along swinging her empty basket. Her thoughts were all happy ones and she recalled meeting the travelling gypsies here almost two years ago. Where were they now? she wondered. What was Kasan doing? Did he ever think of her? She felt in her pocket and turned the lucky stone over in her palm. She didn't really need it any more, it had done the trick and taken away her birthmark, yet she knew she would never part with it, that would be courting disaster. Most of all she wanted Adam to like her more than he did Belinda so she held on tightly to the stone and wished with all her might.

The following day Rachel had to take her father's tea up to the big house. He was very busy and wanted to remain working for another couple of hours. Rachel sat with him in his workshop while he emptied the flask and ate the sandwiches Phoebe had prepared. Adam came in with some new wood from the store. He smiled politely at Rachel and nodded, not daring to say too much in front of Wally.

'You can get off home now, Adam,' Wally said. 'You've put in a good day's work so be on your way and get your tea.'

'I can stay, Mr Hunter, if there's anything I can do to help,' Adam offered. 'I know Squire wants to get that panel put in the drawing room.'

Wally surveyed the two youngsters and observed their covert glances.

'No, lad, your ma might worry if you aren't home by six.' He liked Adam well enough but maybe it was time to take precautions. He wasn't blind to what was going on so purposely kept Rachel talking until he'd finished eating so that she could take the empty flask home. Rachel knew she mustn't appear to be in a hurry but as soon as she was out of sight of the big house she took the tow path by the river and found to her delight that Adam was waiting for her by the old River Inn.

'I guessed you'd come this way,' he said. 'Where's Belinda today then?'

Rachel felt a flicker of jealousy. 'In bed with summer 'flu. She's a bit delicate and Mum's afraid she'll get pneumonia. I hadn't better be long as Mum will wonder where I am.'

'She'll think you're with your dad.'

'And I expect your mum will be expecting you for tea.'

'She'll only miss me when she wants me to do something.'

'Don't you wish you had brothers and sisters, Adam?'

''Course I do. You're lucky having Belinda.'

They walked along for a while then sat down on a grassy bank watching the water hurrying past. There was no embarrassment between them and as Rachel lay back looking up at the clear blue sky she said bluntly: 'You'll have to choose, Adam Taylor. I don't intend to play second fiddle while you wait your opportunity to get Belinda on her own.'

He pulled a blade of grass and chewed on it, then he turned to gaze down at Rachel. 'Who says I want to get Belinda on her own?'

Adam knew that what had first started out as youthful friendship with the Hunter twins was developing into something different. Now he knew his feelings were demanding more. He liked them both. Perhaps the dainty Belinda did have the edge but she was often sickly and more serious than her sister. He had always felt sorry for Rachel having that nasty birthmark which caused her to be the butt of

54

remarks by the likes of Charlie Mead. When her wayward curls blew away from her forehead he could see for himself that the mark was no longer there, and he had to admit he found her dark bewitching eyes hard to resist. She had the stronger character. She was forceful, carrying her twin along with a zest for life.

'Belinda's the prettiest,' Rachel breathed almost inaudibly as if afraid he might agree with her.

'She's pretty, yes,' Adam said. 'But you're – well – different.'

Rachel thought he was blushing slightly so gave him a playful shove. 'You're only saying that not to offend either of us,' she taunted wickedly.

'I like you both – but I'm older than you. Your parents . . .'

'What about our parents? They can't choose for you – if they could it would be Belinda.'

'No! You mustn't say things like that, Rachel. I'll choose for myself and if . . . if you let me kiss you, then it'll have to be you.'

'I don't want you to feel obliged,' she answered back pertly and got up and ran along the river bank.

Adam was soon on his feet chasing after her and when he caught her as she fully intended him to they fell together on the grass.

His hands spanned her waist and he slowly bent his head until his mouth touched hers.

'Now, does that convince you?' he asked. 'But we can't – well – be serious until you're older.'

'I'm nearly fourteen,' Rachel informed him proudly.

'When?' Adam asked.

'Next year – March.'

'That's months away yet.'

'Only seven months.' She sighed. 'S'pose you'll meet someone else and get married and forget all about me?'

'No question of me getting married yet awhile, Rachel. What have I got to offer a girl? I've only just finished by apprenticeship.'

'But I heard my dad tell Mum that Squire thinks very highly of you and would like to keep you on.'

'But how long for? Work's getting short. I love working with wood but there are other things I'd like to do more.'

'Nothing much you can do around here. There's the basket factory of course, but I can't see you working there, especially as Charlie Mead and his father have both got jobs there.'

Adam laughed. 'It's a good proposition. The factory has brought more work for local people and Dad reckons that at last Dick Mead might stay off the booze now that he's got a regular job as carter. Charlie's just right for storeman with his strength. What are you going to do when you leave school, Rachel?'

55

'They talk about me going into service.'

'And Belinda?'

'No, she's much too delicate to work – although she has thought about being a nanny but Mum said she'd better wait until she's sixteen or seventeen. They don't want her to go away from home but I expect I'll have to.'

'Perhaps you could go into the factory – I hope you don't have to go away, Rachel.'

It was the first sign of real interest and she was flattered. She smiled up at him seductively, smoothed his ruffled eyebrows and ran her finger over his cheek. Adam got up quickly, sensing that things could get out of hand if he wasn't careful. He respected Rachel and her family too much to let that happen.

During their clandestine meetings, though, they declared that they were sweethearts, that as soon as Rachel was old enough they would make known their intentions.

Belinda soon realised that things had progressed between her sister and Adam. When they met all together she began to feel in the way, an odd one out.

'Did you see Adam while I was ill, Rachel?' she challenged one night as they prepared to go to bed.

'Only once or twice,' Rachel said, hiding her guilt-stained cheeks behind the cascade of rich ebony-coloured hair which she brushed frantically. 'I saw him up at the big house when I took Dad's tea and we walked home together.'

'But he doesn't live this way.'

'No, but he wanted to ask after you.'

Belinda felt better but only temporarily as when they next went to church she saw Adam and Rachel eyeing each other with familiarity. Belinda felt cheated, not so much because of the new intimacy between her sister and Adam but because Rachel hadn't confided in her. She was well aware that Adam preferred the outgoing Rachel more than her so had to be content to stand aside and watch the boy she was attracted to fall in love with her twin sister.

October gales were followed by autumn mists and damp dark nights. Winter in the countryside meant that few folk ventured far after dark. Rachel didn't see Adam very often except when she went into the woods to gather firewood, or visited her father at the big house on some errand for her mother, but she thought about him all the time. Occasionally after morning service at the church of St Nicholas she and Belinda managed to have Adam to themselves for a chat, but it was all too brief. Rachel was convinced that she loved Adam and he

56

her even if he did show friendship to both of them. Her parents would think she was too young so she knew they must be discreet.

In the spring of 1914 the girls celebrated their fourteenth birthday and Rachel announced that she was going to support the suffragette movement which was constantly in the news. Wally and Phoebe listened to her pontificating on her views with a measure of amusement. After all, living in the country didn't allow their daughter much freedom to express those views. Rachel wrote letters in support of Mrs Pankhurst and her followers, talked of going to London, but then at the end of June the suffragettes were forgotten as world news dominated the headlines.

A wave of indignation swept over Europe when a nineteen-year-old student killed the heir to the Austro-Hungarian throne. The *Daily Chronicle* reported the incident as a 'clap of thunder', while *The Times* said that the atrocity in Sarajevo 'shakes the conscience of the world'. Events unfolded with extraordinary speed, completely overtaken when the Kaiser took offence at what he saw as British insolence by proposing mediation to avert the catastrophe of war.

But war was inevitable and by August of that year young men cheered as they made their way to recruiting offices to join Kitchener's Army, among them the local lads who had gone through school with Rachel and Belinda, Adam Taylor, Charlie Mead and Benjie Mead included. A special service was held in the church in Wickham with refreshments afterwards to bid the men Godspeed. Phoebe Hunter thanked God that at forty-nine Wally was too old, but several of the women wept as they said farewell to husband and sons.

Adam managed to persuade Rachel to go outside the school hall into a small copse nearby.

'I'll miss you, Rachel,' he said in a husky voice. 'I'm not going to pretend that I want to go and fight but neither am I a coward. Take care of yourself and when I came home we'll start walking out properly.'

'Oh, Adam, it's you who must take care. I shall look out of the window every night and pray for you wherever you are. Hold me tightly and promise you'll write.'

Adam hugged and kissed her. 'I don't know about writing, Rachel. The trenches don't sound the ideal place to use pencil and paper but I'll try.'

Rachel rummaged in her small bag. 'Here, this brought me luck and took away my birthmark. Keep it on you and it'll bring you luck as well.' She handed over the precious stone Kasan had given her. Adam needed it more than she did now.

At first there was something quite exciting about the local boys going off to do their bit in fighting spirit and the belief that hostilities would last a few months at most. It was an adventure offering escape from hard work on the land or jobs they didn't much care for. But Rachel soon realised that there were more sinister connotations to war than handsome young men in uniform. News came from across the Channel of fierce and bloody battles and everyone dreaded the arrival of military telegrams bringing notice of wounded relatives or worse still death at the front line.

At home everything had to carry on as near normally as possible. Hospitals were set up all along the south coast in readiness for ships bringing home wounded men. Women and girls left their regular jobs in service or on the land to train as nurses which left opportunities for young school leavers.

Belinda went daily with her father to the big house to help look after the family's children while Rachel went to work at the basket factory which was badly affected by the war as timber bought from Russia ceased to arrive. Much of the machinery was German-made so spare parts were unobtainable, but somehow the basket factory managed to survive.

Beth Cropper, still childless, was one of the many married women who stepped into the men's shoes though sadly she was one of the earliest war widows as Harry was fatally wounded during the early days at Mon. Beth quickly reverted to being flighty, and flirtatious with the men at the factory. most of all with her own brother-in-law, Dick Mead, so earning herself the nickname of Merry Widow while insisting on calling Rachel Strawberry Girl.

Rachel had to learn to stick up for herself which she did easily. She didn't enjoy the type of work much so was grateful that it didn't take the manager, Jimmy Cole, long to realise that she was capable of more exacting tasks. She was moved from the basket-packing benches to despatch where her arithmetical abilities and neat handwriting were an advantage, but unfortunately this didn't make her very popular with the other workers, many of whom had been employed at the factory ever since it started.

Nessie and Dick Mead continued to live together as man and wife but there was little love lost. Nessie worked hard keeping a clean and orderly home as well as working at the school. She wrote weekly letters to Benjie and Charlie, fearful that she might lose either or both of her sons. She had neither the will nor the desire to please Dick any longer so he responded to Beth's womanly wiles. Nessie felt that Beth had no shame and after Dick had gone off to the inn one evening rebuked her sister.

58

'Just widowed, Beth,' Nessie said as she folded the washing just brought in from the line. 'Whatever will people say?'

'Who cares what anyone says? With this war on we've got to make the best of things. It's not my fault that Harry got himself killed.'

'That's an outrageous thing to say. Haven't you got any consideration for what these men are going through? If you don't feel any grief for Harry just remember how his parents feel. It's made poor George an old man before his time.'

Beth took the ends of the sheet to fold. 'Poor old Harry, wasn't his fault that we didn't have a kid, I s'pose,' she said with momentary regret. 'His mum and dad blame me, naturally. Keep on about having an heir. It's obvious they don't want me around so I'm thinking of coming here to live. You won't mind, will you?'

'*Mind*!' Nessie said in high-pitched voice. 'Of course I mind. You should stay with the Croppers and help them through this sad time.'

'I just told you, they don't want me.'

'Well, is that surprising? You're an embarrassment to them I shouldn't wonder. And, no, you can't come here, there isn't enough room.'

Beth laughed lightly. 'No room, she says,' she mocked. 'With Benjie and Charlie away, Kittie and Susan living in, you've only got June here.'

'I intend to keep the boys' room just as it is ready for when they come back.'

'You mean you're using one of their beds for yourself rather than sleep with Dick? Don't think he hasn't told me how things are with you, Nessie, so you can't blame him if he looks elsewhere for his enjoyment.'

'And we all know where he gets it, young madam. Goodness knows where you get your sinful ways from, Beth Cropper. You didn't learn any of it from our family.'

'No, I learned all and more than I should have by coming here helping you when the kids were small. Dick always did have a roving eye, especially for me. You haven't got any passion in you – except, that is, for Jake Taylor.'

'How dare you! Don't mention that man's name in this house. You know nothing about him, nor me either for that matter, and if you had to sleep night after night with a man that reeks of drink and snores disgustingly you'd be glad of a bed to yourself, I can tell you.' Nessie knew her cheeks were aflame at the audacity of her younger sister. Memories came flooding back of a time she'd much rather forget.

'If you won't be a proper wife to Dick then you must expect him to find someone else. And if you don't shut up and let me come here to

59

live with you then I shall tell him about your affair with Jake Taylor.'
Beth stood over Nessie gloating. 'Dick might not realise that the
marked baby you had wasn't his, but you and I both knew that it was
Jake Taylor's bastard.'

Shock paralysed Nessie, albeit briefly, and then she smacked
Beth's face with the full force of her anger behind it.

'Jake was never more to me than a nuisance,' she yelled in self-
defence. 'There was never anything between us even if he and Dick
have always been rivals, and as to my baby being his . . .' She covered
her face with her hands.

Beth nursed her smarting cheek as she warned angrily, 'Now you'd
better watch out, Agnes Mead. I'll get my revenge for that, see if I
don't. In my own way and in my own time – but one thing is sure, I
shan't ever forget what I owe you.'

With a haughty toss of her head she rushed away from the silent
brick house leaving Nessie ashamed for having lashed out at her sister
but alarmed at what Beth might do. Everyone thought marriage had
changed Beth, but she had been clever to wheedle her way into the
Cropper household for her own ends. A good hard-working family
which provided plenty and to spare for their only son and his wife.
Since the death of Harry, Beth had reverted to her old ways. She was
free again to seduce any man she chose and for the moment that was
Dick. Nessie stood looking out of the window, remembering. Was it
possible that Beth knew too much? Enough to harm her? For if she
decided to tell Dick what she thought she knew of the situation all
those years ago, he was still capable of murder. Beth had shown signs
of being a devious schemer from her earliest years. Nessie recalled
her mother voicing her fears for the black sheep of her family. Yet
Nessie had cause to be grateful to her sister for the help she'd been to
her when the children were small. She'd been well paid though. Jake
Taylor had rewarded her for her services, and Nessie had been naive
enough to believe that her young sister was too innocent to suspect
anything. Now she realised that Beth was quite capable of causing
trouble.

Weren't there enough men around without her making a play for
Dick? No, Nessie thought, the eligible ones were fighting for their
country. Of the men left in the area, apart from the middle-aged and
elderly, there were a few who hadn't passed their medical and one or
two who had returned from Flanders with war wounds. Dick might be
rough and ready but he wasn't unattractive, and if a woman was of
easy virtue with loose morals as Beth was, the two of them might well
make satisfactory bed-fellows. Nessie couldn't help it if she felt
nothing for her husband now. Dick had been the recipient of Nessie's

youth. Degraded and abused, weighed down with sheer hard work and responsibility, she had at last reasserted herself to be independent of him. Since he had obtained regular work at the basket factory their daily lives had taken an upward turn. Was Beth, in her frivolous, capricious way, about to destroy everything that Nessie had worked for?

Chapter Four

'Love letter, Strawberry Girl?' Beth Cropper teased.

'What's it to you?' Rachel retorted with some embarrassment.

'Let's have a look. From – now who could it be from, I wonder? – oh, Adam Taylor, I bet.'

'It isn't anything to do with you. It's my private letter,' Rachel said heatedly.

Beth took a deceptive step backwards and then pounced, snatching the letter and dancing away with it across the yard. By the time Rachel caught up with her, Beth was reading it aloud.

'Oh, "love as always",' she taunted. 'Walking out together and you hardly out of school yet.' She tut-tutted as she re-read the letter before tossing it away on the breeze. Fortunately it fluttered straight into Rachel's hands. She quickly folded it and returned it to her pocket.

'Adam and I have been friends for a long time,' she said with a toss of her rich black hair. 'I'm sixteen anyway.'

Adam had been gone for nearly two years now and letters were few and far between so this last one was precious even though she was disappointed at the length of it. On one single side he explained that since completing his course in stretcher-bearer duties he spent all his time transporting casualties from the forward position back to the Regimental Aid Post, and from there on to the main dressing station.

Conditions were unpleasant, he wrote, but the job has to be done.

'I think often of the happy times we spent together, Rachel, and look forward to being back in Wickham again. My regards to your parents and Belinda. Please keep writing, it brings you closer to me even when I get several letters together. Your lucky stone is safe and proving its worth so far. Love you always, Adam.'

Rachel read and re-read the letter but guarded it jealously from inquisitive eyes, especially Beth Cropper's who from then gave her no peace. Every morning she greeted Rachel with 'Heard from lover-boy today?' and soon all the other girls and some of the men too tormented her about Adam. At first it hurt that her feelings weren't sacred any more, but she was used to being scoffed at so she was able to disregard much of Beth's taunting and concentrate on her work, boring though it was. Checking baskets going out, keeping neat accounting of all despatch work, was better than being on the packing benches, though she hadn't minded helping actually to make the baskets. The spring was a busy time when they were preparing for the strawberry season and one late afternoon Jimmy Cole asked Rachel to go along to the store shed to check on the stock there. She climbed up the tall ladder to get to the top stacking shelves and after counting carefully wrote down the number on a piece of paper. The shelves reached high into the sloping roof and Rachel was hidden while she was at the top. Beth Cropper evidently thought the store was empty when she came running in, chased by her brother-in-law, Dick Mead.

Beth was laughing in her usual coarse way. Everyone knew that grief for her late husband had been short-lived and an intimate friendship with Dick had developed speedily. Rumours were rife, most of them started by Beth herself who boasted her success in seducing any man who took her fancy.

'Come 'ere, wench,' Dick growled playfully as he caught her and threw her down on some sacks in a corner of the store shed. 'Can't get enough of you, my girl.'

Rachel descended a few rungs of the ladder as softly as she could, and then more swiftly as she became aware that what they were planning to do was not for her eyes. But when she reached the bottom she knew she had to creep past them and simply didn't have the courage. Dick pushed Beth's skirts up to squeals of her obvious delight. Rachel could only watch open-mouthed as in desperation she tried to squeeze in between some wooden crates. The horse-play went on for several minutes and then Dick, breathing heavily, sat back to undo his trousers. Rachel didn't think she had made any sound but he half-turned and in that instant saw her. As he shouted some obscenity she took to her heels and fled toward the door. He made a grab for her leg as she passed but she was fleet-footed and escaped out into the yard, Dick's voice echoing after her.

'You just wait until one dark night, Strawberry Girl. I'll have your drawers off you, see if I don't!'

Strong arms caught Rachel as she ran up against a brawny figure.

'You all right?' a deep voice asked.

Rachel didn't recognise the soldier who had stopped her in her tracks before she could emerge into the sunlight. She struggled to get away then realised that the voice was vaguely familiar.

'Charlie Mead!' Rachel managed to gasp. She wasn't sure whether or not she was pleased to see her old adversary. But then she laughed, her brain racing ahead in leaps and bounds. If Charlie was here then Adam might be as well. 'What are you doing here? When did you get home?'

'I got a blighty in me leg. T'weren't much, just enough to get me sent back to hospital. It went septic after they got the shrapnel out, but it's better now. At least I got the chance to come home for a couple of days.'

'No one told me that you'd been injured. I bet your mum's glad to see you, Charlie.'

'Yep. Reckon she is. Trouble is, I got to go back next week.'

'I don't suppose you've seen or heard anything of Adam Taylor?'

'Not lately. We did our training together then got separated.'

'He wrote saying that he's a stretcher bearer now. Is that dangerous, Charlie?'

''Tis all dangerous, Strawberry Girl. Shells flying about everywhere, and when you go over the top its either Fritz or you.'

'Oh, you poor thing. It must be dreadful.'

Charlie actually looked embarrassed at her sympathetic interest. Then he suddenly asked with genuine concern, 'Are you all right?'

The shock of seeing Charlie so unexpectedly had taken Rachel's fright clean away. He looked so handsome in his uniform; taller – could he possibly have grown? – he certainly didn't look as bulky as she remembered. Cleanshaven now where once much of his face had been hidden beneath coarse stubble, and the untidy matted hair of schooldays was cut very short and neatly combed. He looked every inch the proud soldier with a ramrod straight back.

'Yes, 'course I am,' she replied with a friendly smile.

'My Dad and Aunt Beth – did he molest you?'

'No, they were only teasing like they always do.'

'No need to lie for them, Rachel.' Charlie leaned forward a little to speak in confidence and she recognised a strange quiver in his voice at his use of her real name. This wasn't the big bullying Charlie Mead who had scared her when she was younger. 'I do know about them,' he went on in a low voice, 'and I bet they're up to no good in there right now. I heard what he shouted after you but he hadn't better touch you – or else.'

'Look, Charlie. I'll have to go. Mr Cole is waiting for these figures. I'm sorry you got wounded but I know how pleased your mum and the girls must be to see you.'

'T'won't be long before you knock off, will it? Can I wait for you and walk home with you?'

Rachel hesitated. Different though he seemed old memories weren't that easily erased. But he had been fighting in the front line – for her as much as for anyone else.

'Yes, 'course you can. There's the hooter now. Sometimes I work on a bit but there's no need tonight.'

Rachel hurried back to the despatch department and from the window saw everyone making a great fuss of Charlie in the yard. He only had a little 'blighty' according to him but it was enough to make him one of Wickham's heroes. Rachel finished up a few things on her desk and then went out into the evening sunshine.

'Are you sure you didn't ought to be getting home to your family, Charlie?' she said. 'You aren't here for long and I'm sure your mum wants to see as much of you as she can.'

To Rachel's surprise Charlie sighed, and his expression was one of despondency. 'I've had lots of time to talk to Ma,' he said. 'I don't particularly want to be at home when Dad's around, especially if Aunt Beth's there too. Been a bit of trouble at home, Rachel, since Benjie and me left for the war.'

Rachel walked along beside him in silence. There was gossip about the Meads – hadn't there always been? – which was why she supposed she couldn't help feeling pity for Charlie.

'I'm sorry,' she said softly. ''Specially for your mum. There's no love lost between Beth Cropper and me, though.'

'She's evil,' Charlie said vehemently, 'and so's me dad.' They had come to the bridlepath through the woods where the birds' evensong was the only accompaniment. 'Ma says Beth wanted to move into our house. Can you believe it? Carrying on right under Ma's nose? 'T'ain't decent. Ma ain't never had an easy life. Me dad ought to be the one out there in France fighting. Do 'im good, teach 'im a thing or two, I can tell you. No one would mind if he got done in.'

'Oh, Charlie, you mustn't say things like that.'

'You don't know what he's like, Rachel. Reckon you couldn't begin to understand what a rotter he's been to Ma.'

'I've heard rumours, Charlie, but it's drink, I expect.'

'Yeah, well, that's the excuse. But I've made me mind up. When this war's over and I come 'ome, he's got to behave 'imself or out he goes.'

Rachel admired Charlie's protectiveness towards his mother.

'Do you think the war is going to last much longer?' she asked.

Charlie grunted. 'Can't say – but we'll win in the end.'

'I wouldn't have thought you'd have to go back after being wounded.'

'I told you, t'weren't much. I'm glad it was bad enough to get 'ome to see me ma. I'm ready to go back to the trenches now, though I daresay I'll be put on light duties somewhere behind the lines for a while. Got to report back on Monday. No point in being back 'ome with all me mates out there. I hear even old Doc Grant's been called up.'

'Yes, but he hasn't gone abroad. We heard that he's on the Kent coast working in a hospital for the wounded. I wouldn't have minded being a nurse or joining the Red Cross, but I'm not quite old enough. By the time I am, I suppose the war will be over.'

'Won't be yet awhile, Rachel. You might get your chance.'

They had reached Kingsmere, but still Charlie continued to walk with her to the gate of Calder Cottage.

'I . . . I s'pose you wouldn't . . . look, Rachel, the person I most wanted to see at the factory was you.' She looked across at him in surprise. 'I won't ever forget that you saved me from a beating in front of the whole school.' He smiled. Rachel thought she had never seen him smile this way before, and was touched by his words.

'I'll never know why I did that,' she said. 'Most unladylike, my parents thought.'

'You shocked us all, even old Stanley, and I felt bad about you getting hurt . . .'

'Best forgotten, Charlie,' she interrupted. 'We're grown up now. Our schooldays are over and done with.'

'Well, I'm sorry for the way I teased you at school. Reckon I had my fair share of the same once, but things are different now. Being in the Army is hard, especially at first being away from home, but some of the chaps helped me through me training. I soon learnt that we all had to help each other, and I've met some good mates. But most of 'em have girlfriends. They carry pictures of them to look at when there's a lull in the fighting, but I've never had a girlfriend and I ain't likely to meet one in the trenches. I know you're keen on Adam Taylor, but, well, I was wondering if you'd write to me? I'd write back,' he hurried on. 'Not a very good scholar but me Sarge has been helping me.'

'Charlie . . . I'm very flattered that you should ask me but Adam and I do have an understanding.'

He shifted from one foot to the other. She couldn't help noticing how shiny his Army boots were, but then she'd never seen Charlie Mead so smartly dressed before.

'Yes, I understand that, Rachel. But – y'see – we don't know what's going to happen to us, do we? I don't know any other girls. Please, Rachel, say you'll write to me – just once?'

She didn't know why she agreed, to write to Charlie Mead of all people, but as they parted company she promised that she would.

The sun was sinking low behind the trees and Rachel's thoughts turned as they often did at the end of the day to Adam. Most evenings she wrote to him in the form of a journal, posting it off on Monday mornings, but tonight she just wanted to sit and think. Her mother had sounded quite disapproving of her agreeing to write to Charlie. What would Adam think? But he could never be jealous of Charlie Mead surely? She found it hard to imagine what it could be like for the men on the battlefields and the danger sailors faced at sea. Every Sunday at Church she sat with her family and listened, almost holding her breath, as names of those killed and wounded, some reported missing, were read out and special prayers offered for them and their families. Now she offered her own silent prayer for Adam – and Kas too. She hadn't thought about him for ages but somewhere he might also be fighting for his country. When she'd kept the lucky stone in her pocket she often wondered about him, but time was weakening the memory of the dark-haired gypsy boy. Her parents, being deeply religious, said there was no such thing as luck, good or bad, but Rachel had every faith in Kas's lucky stone. It had taken away her birthmark; she was sure it would help to keep Adam safe.

The summer days became shorter, light faded early and autumn gales wreaked savage destruction on the countryside, and still there was no let up in the war. The Germans suffered defeat at the Somme, several divisions having their numbers greatly reduced which weakened morale. Winter brought active operations to a temporary halt while the Germans retreated to a shorter front to prepare for the next battle.

Christmas 1916 was the bleakest for the troops. Two years earlier they had gone to war confident that they would soon be home but now there was no such optimism. The great breakthrough they had envisaged during 1916 had not materialised, and the cost in lives was huge, many thousands of British and Allied soldiers lost along with a comparable number of Germans.

Rachel spent the long winter months writing to Adam and Charlie, knitting gloves and socks for both of them. Adam's letters became more frequent and loving, while Charlie struggled to pen his thoughts in a childlike way. He was pleased to receive Rachel's regular letters and the snapshot she had sent him, but then the mail ceased to arrive. News came of the new Allied offensive on the Hindenberg Line, fighting had begun again in earnest and old fears were renewed.

During the summer of 1917 when the third battle of Ypres was unfolding, bombardments were timed with relentless accuracy and soldiers feared the mud of Flanders as much as the enemy. Ground was lost and retaken and stretcher bearer Corporal Adam Taylor, along with his comrades, found it almost impossible to struggle through the quagmire with the wounded. It was a relief to reach the Regimental Aid Post. As he wandered among the lines of men waiting to be treated he heard his name being called.

'Taylor – Adam Taylor? Adam picked his way carefully through the rows of makeshift beds in a large crowded hut behind enemy lines. At first he didn't recognise the lower half of a bloodied face which was all that was visible below the bandage and above the blanket. He bent lower to look more closely.

'Charlie Mead?' He reached down and grasped the hand which was held out to him. 'It's good to see you.' This was a rare treat – someone from home, someone from Wickham. 'How are you, Charlie? Not too badly hurt, I hope?'

Charlie's grin was instantly recognisable. 'Reckon being that this is me third blighty, I've had me share. Shrapnel in me leg first time. They sent me home then, that was last year. Only for a few days but I saw Rachel Hunter at the basket factory. I know she's your girl, Adam, but I didn't have anyone else except me ma to send me letters so I asked if she'd write to me.'

'I know, Charlie, Rachel told me.'

'And you didn't mind, did you? 'T'weren't nothing serious. I know'd she wouldn't want to walk out with me but I wanted to have a girl's picture to show off. 'Tis in me top pocket, Adam, if you want it.'

He patted Charlie's shoulder gently. 'You keep it, I expect it's the same as the one in my top pocket.' He patted the place next to his heart where he carried Rachels' last letter and photo. 'Lucky you, getting home, and if this is your third injury you'll probably go home again soon before me – p'raps for good.'

'Got it in me gut this time so reckon you may be right. Second time t'was in me backside so they soon got that splinter out. Anything's better 'an being taken by Fritz. I'd rather die than surrender to 'im.'

'That's the spirit, Charlie. If you do go back to blighty, give Rachel my love and tell them all we're doing our best to get it over and done with.'

Even as he spoke he could see Charlie's breathing becoming spasmodic, and he was desperately trying not to let Adam see the effects of the pain he was in.

'A doctor will soon be round to you and I expect they'll inject morphia before you go on to a field hospital. Want a cigarette, Charlie?'

His eyes had taken on a glazed look as he did his best to nod. Adam lit the cigarette for him and placed it between his dry lips. The medical officer was moving along the row getting closer to Charlie so

Adam stayed as long as he dared, offering what consolation he could, and then it was back to the trenches to remove more of the casualties. He wished he could have stayed longer to find out how Charlie got on. Things didn't look too good for him. Poor old Charlie Mead, a third blighty. Well, third time lucky, Adam thought hopefully. Maybe he'd get home for good when they'd patched him up enough to stand the journey across the Channel.

Another summer passed. Adam was weary beyond belief with the constant shelling and moving from place to place, camp to camp. Letters took some time to reach him but at last several arrived together at a time when he was back behind the lines in a small village sheltered by woods, his unit having been ordered a much deserved rest. He recognised his mother's small, even handwriting, the long loops penned a little shakily, he thought. He decided to read the two from her before opening Rachel's. Lily Taylor's letters contained many complaints about the effects the war was having on their food supply, and her fear of enemy bomb attacks was obvious. She should be out here, Adam thought before he opened the second letter. The news it contained shocked him. 'Charlie Mead was killed when the ship he was returning home on was torpedoed,' his mother wrote.

Adam searched for more detailed information but her letters were always short, never more than one single sheet, and the lone sentence telling of Charlie's death seemed to indicate just how cold and insensitive she was. She had no particular reason to feel any more sad than anyone else at the news, but war drew people together in shared compassion. Adam didn't know why his mother's attitude made him feel cross but he tossed her letters aside to rip open Rachel's hurriedly. In the first letter she said she had received a short letter from Charlie from a field hospital somewhere in Belgium where he was recovering well from his stomach wound. He had fallen in love with a beautiful Dutch nurse called Else.

'He is quite besotted with her,' Rachel wrote, 'and tells me that she is as fair as I am dark. I half expected to find my photo returned but at least he spared me that embarrassment.' It was obvious to Adam that she was much amused and probably relieved that Charlie had found a girl of his own. Mention of the dissimilarity between Rachel and the Dutch nurse reminded him of her twin sister, Belinda, who bore no resemblance at all. He tore open the second letter which confirmed what his mother had told him.

'Oh, dear Adam, such shocking news, made even worse because when you wrote you said that you had seen Charlie Mead. You sounded so concerned for him and hoped that by now he had reached

Wickham safe and well. Dearest Adam, how can I be the one to tell you – the ship bringing him home was torpedoed with all hands lost. His mother has taken the news so badly, they say she is inconsolable. Even Mr Mead seems a broken man.'

During the past two years Adam had been forced to come into close contact with dead and wounded soldiers. At first it had affected him emotionally just as it did his comrades, but eventually he had become hardened to the scars of the battlefield. Somehow, though, Charlie's death seemed more cruel than all the others. Now his thoughts searched out all the events of his past at home in Wickham. Memories went deep. He knew all the Mead family, Charlie especially – didn't he have cause to remember the notable puddinghead of Hundred Acres? But even Charlie hadn't been such a dunce that he couldn't fight for his country! Given his life for it. The stress of recent weeks and months suddenly took its toll. Bitterness, anger, hatred – all these emotions fought against the integrity of the real Adam Taylor. He couldn't stand the company of the other men a moment longer so went for a walk through the woods that reminded him of home and felt an uncontrollable desire to throw himself on the ground and weep.

In the Church of St Nicholas in Wickham, local people and villagers from miles around outnumbered the gentry who came to mourn the dead. Not for the first time a special family – on this occasion, the Meads – was singled out for prayer and sympathetic understanding.

The church was packed for Sunday morning worship and Rachel wasn't able to sit beside either her parents or Belinda. Instead she squeezed in at the end of a pew, then realised with some consternation that she was sitting beside Charlie Mead's mother, her face hardly visible through the black veil which covered head and shoulders over a black winter coat. Rachel felt embarrassed. Had she taken Mr Mead's place or that of another member of the Mead family? Nessie Mead lifted her head slightly so Rachel took the opportunity to whisper, 'Is this someone's seat? Shall I move?'

Nessie shook her head. Rachel thought she made a brave effort to smile but there was no mistaking the great burden of sorrow which engulfed the poor woman. The service commenced and during the singing of the first hymn, Rachel being taller than average, could see the rest of the Mead family occupying the pew at the front of the church. Even Mr Mead, who never ever crossed the threshold of any place of worship except for weddings, funerals and baptisms, was sitting beside his three daughters.

As the service continued with mention of the recent death of Charlie, Rachel could feel Nessie shaking with sobs beside her.

70

Charlie had vowed to take care of his mother. Why wasn't one of the girls here to comfort her? she wondered. The mother's grief transferred itself to those around her. On an impulse Rachel tucked her arm through Nessie's and held her hand. To her surprise, far from rejecting her Nessie leaned against Rachel as if gaining much needed support, and drew strength from the girl.

When the last hymn had been sung and after the final blessing Nessie turned to Rachel. 'Thank you for writing to my Charlie,' she said, her voice husky with emotion. 'He didn't have many friends and I know he wasn't very nice to you once, but he really appreciated your kindness.' Nessie squeezed Rachel's hand affectionately. 'Thank you too for helping me through his morning,' she said. 'I could see there wasn't going to be room for us all in that pew so I sat down where I could.'

She didn't know what to say, but very quickly local people began to gather round Nessie to offer their condolences so Rachel slipped away. Each little group of people, every family, was in sombre mood as they walked to their homes.

Dick was stunned by his son's death. After the shock, remorse set in for the way he'd treated the boy, and for a few weeks he tried to make it up to Nessie by staying at home in the evenings. But she remained uncommunicative and he realised that he had left it too late to make amends. Mrs Waterstone was ailing and Nessie was having to spend all her spare time at her mother's cottage. Beth should have been the one to care for their mother but having been refused a place at the Meads' home she remained with her in-laws. She was always one to watch out for herself and reckoned if she kept in with them she would come in for whatever there was going when the time came.

Dick was soon drawn back to The King's Head where a few drinks helped to take his mind off his troubles. Afterwards Beth would be waiting for him. She had the knack of twisting him round her little finger. Never lacking the ability to seduce her fifty-year-old brother-in-law, her unbridled passion was beginning to be too much for Dick. Yet he simply could not deny her. He tried to keep her at bay by saying that his place was at home with Nessie.

'She's still grievin' for our Charlie. I feel it too, I ought to be with her.'

In an old barn at the Croppers' homestead Beth knew she only had to lift her skirts to make him weaken, and later they lay huddled together among the dry hay as she did her best to console him.

'I shouldn't be here,' he said with remorse. 'Nessie's been a good wife to me, Beth. Many a woman would have upped and left me long ago after all I've put her through. I know she don't want me any more – reckon she didn't really want me ever, if the truth be told – but we've had twenty-five years together. Heading to be Darby and Joan now. Reckon it's time you found yourself a younger man. Someone needin' a wife.'

'There's no decent men around, and who says I want another husband? First time was bad enough. I like things the way they are, Dick. You and me are good together, only one thing on our minds. You can't say that with Nessie, now can you? Cold hard bitch if you ask me.'

'I ain't asking you – and I reckon I knows Nessie better'n you if you think that. We've had our good times. She's still pretty too, and not many women can say that after having six kids. I haven't done right by her and it's time I made it up. Not – well, not where this kind of thing's concerned, but if you want to chase around after someone younger I'll understand, Beth. I'm grateful for all you've given me.'

'And so you should be, Dick Mead,' Beth flung at him angrily. 'You take the best years of my life and then want to cast me off like an old coat.' She got to her feet and stood looking down at him with contempt. No, he wasn't much of a catch, she decided, but where was she going to find another man as easy to persuade as Dick? 'I've not had another man while we've been seeing each other.' She suddenly laughed, remembering the hold she had over Nessie. Now was the time to deliver her blow to this old fool. 'You were glad enough of me when Nessie didn't want anything to do with you – and you were always too drunk to know why she didn't want to sleep with you.'

Dick struggled to his feet to face Beth. 'What's that supposed to mean? Don't tar everyone with the same brush as yourself.'

She laughed in his face. 'That's just it, Dick, Nessie and me, we are out of the same mould. She's had her flings, same as me.'

Dick grabbed the giggling Beth and held her against him roughly. His bloodshot eyes bored right through hers as he gritted his teeth angrily.

'Tell me, you whore! Tell me what you mean – damn you!'

Suddenly his hands were round her throat, squeezing as his cheeks grew red with anger.

'Dick, stop! Let me go – you're hurting me.'

'Then you just tell me exactly what you meant about my Nessie.'

'*Your* Nessie, indeed. She was probably Jake Taylor's long before she was ever yours.'

'What stupid nonsense is this you're talking? I know well enough that Jake Taylor had his eye on her but I made sure of her by getting her in the family way – and I can tell you this, young miss, she were a virgin then all right. Not something I'm ever likely to forget – bloody hard work t'was. So what d'you think you know that I don't?' He forced her chin upwards until she thought her neck would snap.

'You aren't as clever as you think,' Beth said. 'How d'you think the rent ever got paid when you spent every penny on drink when the kids were small? I got paid a shilling to take the kids out when Jake came to collect his dues, and it wasn't paid in money!'

'You lying little cheat.' His grip tightened round Beth's throat until her eyes were bulging. 'Tell me you're lying – tell me.'

Beth gasped for breath. She hadn't expected him to take it out on her. Wasn't she the one who had given him what he wanted and needed? She hadn't thought he had this much strength left in him either.

'Let me – go – please, Dick. *Please*?' she begged.

He released her slowly yet never quite letting her free.

'Now, my girl, let's be having the truth,' he snarled viciously.

'You won't like it, Dick, and when I accused Nessie she smacked my face so I reckon it's true. But . . . but I don't want to spoil what we've got, Dick. She isn't worth it,' Beth pleaded.

'Let me be the judge of that. Tell me, I say, tell me.'

'It's just as I said. Jake Taylor always had a soft spot for Nessie. He used to visit her a lot until she had that last baby. He gave her the job of picking strawberries in the season. She used to go out after you'd gone to The King's Head.'

'You say he gave you money to take the kids off while he . . .?'

'Yes, and that's the truth, but it's all a long time ago now, Dick. What does it matter?'

'It matters because my wife deceived me – and no man will stand for that. So Jake Taylor got her after all – the *swine*!'

'The last baby she had – she wouldn't look at it – and I reckon it was because it was Jake's.'

'What makes you think that?'

'It was obvious. That hideous mark – the strawberry mark – the kid was tainted with sin. Even you said it couldn't be yours.'

Dick's eyes narrowed as he started to remember lots of little details – if only he hadn't been too drunk to notice at the time. He'd thought Nessie had rejected him because of the baby. She'd looked so ill – the infant so horribly disfigured – that for him there was only drink to take away the awful memory.

'You'd better be telling the truth, Beth Cropper, or I'll find you and kill you. Telling tales on your own sister, for your own ends. You're a wicked one and no mistake. If it's true I'll kill her, and you'll marry me and take her place just as you've always wanted to do. But it won't be the easy life you're a'hankering after. I'll make you pay for this as well as Nessie.' He pushed her up against the bales of hay, shaking with anger. 'You're a devious bitch, but I'll get to the bottom of this once and for all.'

Beth watched him shuffle away. She put her trembling fingers round her sore throat. He was capable of committing murder. She'd felt the strength of his rage in his hands. His victim was going to be her own sister Nessie, and after that . . .

'God Almighty!' she cried. 'What have I done?'

She seemed too paralysed to move, but move she must before a terrible crime was committed.

Chapter Five

Shortly after hearing of the death of Charlie Mead, Adam wrote to Rachel asking her to marry him.

'As soon as you can,' he said, 'visit my parents and mother will give you the ring. I do so want you to be friends. Mother doesn't go out much so you'll have to make the first move, Rachel, but I have written and told them about our plans.'

Our plans! Adam seemed to have changed so much lately, she could tell, from his letters in which he wrote of his need of her and she read all kinds of hidden meanings. She felt nervous yet excited as she prepared to go to meet his parents. She brushed her thick dark hair, black and silky as a raven's wing, and then stood still just looking at herself. The gilt-edged triple mirror had been her seventeenth birthday present from her parents. Rachel knew it had come from the big house via the auction rooms. Hadn't she changed too beyond all recognition? How many times had she stood on tip-toe to peer at the ugly raised mark on her forehead, mostly hidden by her hair, in that old speckled mirror she used to have. But now there was so sign at all of any blemish. Perhaps when she was officially engaged the unkind people like Beth Cropper would stop calling her Strawberry Girl. Her dark eyes twinkled mischievously as she recalled with a slight flutter the black-haired gypsy boy, Kas. 'Strawberries are sweet,' he'd said, meaning that he thought she was sweet too. Then he'd given her his lucky stone, and now Adam had it. It had worked magic for her, it could for Adam too. It must keep him safe – it *must*!

Rachel put on her best hat and coat and went downstairs. Belinda was standing at the window staring into space.

'Come with me, Belinda, please?' she urged. 'It's a nice day and I won't feel so nervous if you're with me.'

'I think you should go alone,' her sister said softly.

'I want you to come. I don't see you that often now, we can have a good gossip on the way.

'Yes, dear,' Phoebe said. 'You'll be company for Rachel.'

Belinda went upstairs to get her coat and hat. She was almost too obedient and whatever Phoebe or Wally suggested she agreed instantly.

Phoebe went to the gate to watch her two girls walk down the lane towards Hundred Acres about two miles away.

'The evenings are drawing in now so don't leave it too late starting back,' she called after them. She felt so proud of their appearance. Two smart young women and Rachel about to be engaged. She was secretly glad it was Rachel and not Belinda, and knew Wally felt the same. Not that they didn't want Belinda to marry, they did, but for her someone special, someone who would understand her delicacy.

Once Rachel was married their responsibility for her would be over. They loved her dearly and believed they had done their duty, but it had been no easy task bringing her up. They couldn't have chosen better for her than Adam Taylor, though, as they considered him a respectable lad. They hadn't been able to fault his letter to them. Phoebe and Wally were pleased to give their consent to the marriage but with one proviso: that they waited until Rachel reached the age of eighteen. Phoebe smiled as she watched the two girls link arms happily.

Lily Taylor looked pinched with cold when she opened the door to the two Hunter girls.

'Good afternoon,' she said politely but in a shaky voice. 'Come along in. After receiving Adam's letter I guessed you might visit me today.'

She showed them into the front parlour where a small round oak table was covered with a white lace cloth and set for afternoon tea with the daintiest of china.

'Now, let me look at you. The pretty one – you must be Belinda.' Lily Taylor was quite short and very thin underneath the woollen dress with its matching shawl. The girls thought she was rather old-fashioned with her small mobcap made of velvet. She had a grey pallor which seemed less prominent because of the blueness of her eyes, and in spite of her reputation of being unsociable, even a misery, she did have a warm smile. 'So you're my future daughter-in-law, Rachel?' she said turning to look up at the taller of the two girls.

Rachel gave a swift short curtsey more from fear than from politeness. 'Adam asked me to call to pay my respects,' she said in what was quite a small voice for her.

Heavy footsteps sounded through the hallway and a loud voice said: 'And we're delighted that you did, my dear.'

Jake Taylor was almost as formidable a character to the girls as Dick Mead but in quite a different way. Dick was usually too drunk to know whether he was insulting people or not so no one took any notice of him. But there was something about the toothy leer of Jake Taylor which made Rachel suspicious. He was handsome, there was no denying that, she thought, but something in those dark searching eyes suggested an unhealthy interest. Adam's parents were obviously younger than her own yet Lily Taylor appeared to be much older than Phoebe.

'Sit yourselves down and I'll fetch the tea,' Jake said, and when it was brought Lily uncovered a side table on which were plates of appetising sandwiches and cakes.

'So we're to have a wedding in the family?' Jake said with a wide grin. 'Let's hope the war doesn't go on for too much longer.' He gave Rachel a nudge. 'And I bet you do too.' His nearness made her shudder.

'My parents are happy about our engagement but have asked that we wait a while before setting the date to be married,' Rachel said as positively as she could.

'The war will obviously decide this ' Lily said. 'Let's pray that dear Adam comes home to us safely.' She glanced up at her husband. 'Give the child the ring,' she said, 'and then you can be off. I shall be glad of a little company.'

Jake took a small red box down from the high mantelshelf, opened it and displayed its contents to the girls.

'It's quite magnificent,' Rachel breathed with sparkling eyes.

'Then it's yours, my dear,' Lily said. 'As long as you promise to be good to my Adam and above all be faithful, like the good book says, unto death.'

'Oh, I will, I will,' Rachel said enthusiastically.

Rachel was so enamoured of the ring she didn't notice the fierce meaningful glance Lily gave Jake.

'Then let me do the honours,' Jake said, as he took the diamond cluster ring from its case and held Rachel's trembling hand.

'Oh dear,' he said as he tried to push the ring over her knuckle, 'I'm afraid you seem to have slightly larger fingers than Adam's grandmother.'

'My mother was petite, I take after her.' Lily took a closer look and then relieved Jake of the ring and put it on her own finger. 'Now, my dear, at least you can see how it looks. I'm afraid it would seem that you will have to be patient until Adam comes home. He'll have to have it made larger for you.'

Rachel felt the disappointment keenly but tried not to show it as Lily proceeded to pour out some tea.

'It's not a disaster,' Jake said. 'Nothing that can't be remedied. Now, if you delightful young ladies will excuse me, I prefer a beverage of the stronger kind.' He shook hands with each of the girls, kissed his wife lightly on the cheek and left the house.

Lily appeared to be more relaxed afterwards as she passed round the delicacies. 'If I could get out and about more I'd take it myself and have it altered,' she said. 'You could do it yourself, of course.'

'Thank you, but I'll write and explain to Adam first,' Rachel said. 'Our parents send their regards and asked if you would care to come to Calder Cottage one Sunday afternoon for tea?'

'Very kind, very kind, but I don't go out much these days. Perhaps we can all get better acquainted when Adam comes home.'

It became clear to Rachel that Lily Taylor did not enjoy entertaining very much. She feigned tiredness so Rachel and Belinda departed when it seemed polite to do so. There was a chill breeze blowing as the first colourful leaves fell from the trees. The girls had to hang on to their hats for fear of them blowing away.

'Are you very disappointed about the ring?' Belinda asked. 'It's a very beautiful one, Rachel.'

At that moment the wind whipped up into quite a frenzy and Rachel was unable to speak as she turned her head to one side holding her hat on to her wilful curls. At the same time a figure came rushing headlong into the girls from around the corner of the lane. It was Beth Cropper, clearly in a state of distress.

'Have you seen Jake Taylor?' she demanded breathlessly. I must find him . . . Dick's gone for Nessie . . .'

'Mr Taylor went out a short while ago,' Rachel said. 'Probably to The King's Head.'

'Can we do anything to help?' Belinda asked.

'Mmm . . . yes . . . no . . . perhaps . . . come with me.' It was unlike Beth Cropper to be so indecisive but she grabbed Rachel's arm and pulled her along with Belinda trying to keep up behind. 'Dick's going to kill my sister – I need help – Jake ought to . . .' her voice trailed away.

Rachel thought it all sounded melodramatic but Beth was an excitable girl so she allowed herself to be propelled along to the Meads' house. The back door was open. A flat iron lay on the floor along with other items strewn about as if the place had been ransacked. Then a moan led Beth into the living room where the girls found Nessie lying semi-conscious with blood pouring from a head wound.

'Nessie! *Nessie!*' Beth cried, bending down to her sister. I'm sorry, I didn't mean it to come to this.'

Nessie lifted a hand and pointed towards the door. 'He's gone after Jake,' she said in a weak voice. 'There'll be a fight. Find the constable to stop them. Go quickly, before someone gets killed.'

'I must tend to you . . . Oh, Nessie!'

'Go – quickly,' Nessie repeated in a stronger voice.

Beth looked apologetically at the two girls who were surveying the chaotic scene before them in wide-eyed astonishment.

'I'll go to find Jake Taylor,' Beth said. 'Could you help Nessie, please? Looks as if she needs a doctor – oh, dear God, I never meant this to happen.'

'I could go for the doctor,' Rachel offered.

'And I'll help Mrs Mead – at least find some towels to clean up the blood,' Belinda said helpfully as she started to take her coat off.

Beth tore off down the lane with Rachel in hot pursuit until they came to the Square in Wickham. Rachel made for the doctor's house while Beth ran on towards The King's Head.

Doctor Barber, a middle-aged, balding man who was Doctor Cyril Grant's substitute during his absence, was none too pleased at being disturbed on a Saturday evening.

'It's Mrs Mead, Doctor,' Rachel explained. 'She's been . . .'

'Well, spit it out, girl,' he said impatiently.

'She's been hurt – quite badly. There's a lot of blood and . . .'

'Where is she?'

'At her home. She lives at Hundred Acres.'

'I know where she lives,' Dr Barber grunted, turning inside to fetch his bag. 'I'll go in the trap.' He closed the door with a slam and Rachel turned to walk away. He could have offered to take her back with him, she thought, but he wasn't that kind of man. Not the friendly sort like Doctor Grant who had once rescued her from Charlie Mead and his gang in the woods. He'd lifted her up on to the saddle of his horse and taken her home. There'd never be another doctor as popular as he had been. Rachel heard voices, loud voices, shouting and hollering, and it was coming from the bridge over the river. She wanted to get back to help Belinda but curiosity got the better of her and she ran out of the Square towards the Mill.

Where on earth had all the people come from? she wondered. It seemed as if all of Wickham had turned out to witness the fight which was going on in earnest on the bridge. Rachel was thankful that Belinda was not here to see this, while she felt an urge to cheer Jake Taylor on. Dick Mead wasn't at all a likeable man and if he was responsible for leaving his wife in such a pitiful state Rachel could only hope he was going to come off the worse. Jake Taylor was several years younger than Dick Mead and although he enjoyed a drink he wasn't a renowned drunkard like Dick was. Both men were looking bloodied, Dick swearing as he punched, vowing to kill his old rival. Then Jake seemed to be getting the better of Dick who looked as if he were crumbling and losing his balance. Jake, realising he had the advantage, fought with renewed strength hitting Dick in the eyes until he could hardly see and in consequence Dick staggered backwards. One final push into the mill stream to cool him off hailed Jake Taylor the winner, and then to a gasp from the crowd he gave a loud groan and collapsed to the ground. Rachel pressed forward in time to see a last shudder as Jake Taylor breathed his very last breath.

The urgent ringing of a bicycle bell heralded the arrival of the village constable. Suddenly everyone felt compelled to return to their homes as quickly as possible and Rachel slowly made her way back to the Meads' house. Her lasting vision was of Dick Mead being hauled out of the stream by his mates, the constable waiting with handcuffs at the ready, while the landlord of the King's Head covered Jake's body with a blanket.

Rachel felt numb with shock. She didn't want to hurry and yet she needed to get back to her sister. Her boots felt heavy on her feet as if they were dragging her back. At the same time she was breathless by the time she reached the unhappy homestead still mourning Charlie's loss. She pushed open the back door, walked over the obstacles scattered in angry abandon and entered the small living room where Nessie was lying on the couch. Belinda, sleeves rolled up, was doing her best to restore the room to some semblance of order. Nessie opened her good eye, the one not blackened and covered by the same bandage which was protecting the wound on her head.

'Thank you for fetching the doctor, he's just left.' She tried to peer closer at Rachel, sensing the strain in the younger girl's expression. 'What . . . what's happened? Something terrible, I can see it in your face.' She eased herself up into a sitting position.' Belinda paused in her task and went to Rachel's side. 'What is it, Rachel?' she asked softly.

'Adam's father collapsed and died.'

'My Dick's killed Jake Taylor?' Nessie said in a frightened voice.

'They had a dreadful fight on the bridge. Mr Taylor pushed Mr Mead into the stream – and then Mr Taylor just groaned and fell to the ground.'

'Didn't anyone try to stop them? Surely Beth could have . . .'

'People seemed to be egging them on, Mrs Mead. The constable came too late to stop them – and I think Mr Mead's been arrested.'

'For murder?' Oh *no*!' She struggled to get up from the couch but pain forced her to lie back again. 'Doctor says my ribs are broken – what can I do? Dick needs me now. Where's Beth?'

'I'm afraid I didn't see her again. Is there anyone we can fetch? Where's June?' Rachel asked.

'She'll be here presently,' Nessie said. 'She went to visit my mother. You've both been so kind but I mustn't detain you any longer. Your mother will wonder where you are. It's quite dark now – you'd best get off home – but thank you for all you've done.'

'I don't think we should leave you, Mrs Mead,' Belinda said with kind concern. 'Rachel, you could go home and tell Mum and Dad where I am. I think someone ought to stay, don't you?'

Running footsteps could be heard then before the door burst open and Beth came in looking white with alarm.

'What's happening here?' she asked.

'What's happened to my Dick?' Nessie said shortly.

'They've arrested him and kept him in custody.'

'Thanks to you he really has committed murder now,' Nessie said.

'No, it wasn't murder – I waited to find out – and they think Jake had a heart attack. It may have been as a result of the fight but Dick didn't kill him.'

'As good as – the intent was there,' Nessie said with bitterness in her croaky voice.

'I think they're both guilty of those intentions, but the doctor has reported your condition to the constable and now Dick is being accused of assaulting you with intent to kill.'

Nessie's eyes filled with tears then she said, 'They'll never make that stick. I'll see to that.'

'But for goodness' sake, he tried to kill you – and me as well for that matter,' Beth said heatedly.

'Oh? Why? Rejected him, did you?'

Beth blinked and noticed the two younger girls still present.

'You can get off home,' she said in an accusing voice. 'Nothing for you to do here.'

Rachel glanced at Belinda and then enquiringly at Nessie. 'Yes, my dears,' she assured them, 'I'll be all right now and thank you again, Belinda, you were a wonderful help, you'd make a good nurse. Tell your parents I'm sorry you got involved in all this. Best not to say anything to anyone else though.'

Belinda hesitated, not wanting to leave the poor injured woman in Beth's hands, but Rachel took her arm and they left the house.

'I don't trust Beth Cropper,' Belinda said in a whisper. 'Should we have left, d'you think?'

'I don't know. I don't like her either, but they are sisters.'

'So different though, aren't they? Whatever makes Beth like she is? She quite frightens me,' Belinda said.

81

'She does seem to be an evil person. What an afternoon!' Rachel said. 'Poor Adam – who will tell him? Who's going to tell Mrs Taylor? To think we only left her a short while before her husband was killed.'

'Died, Rachel,' Belinda corrected. 'If what Beth says is true, Mr Taylor died of a heart attack, he wasn't killed.'

'But it was as good as. If he hadn't been fighting it would probably never have happened, and I doubt if he started it,' Rachel said.

'Wonder what it's all about?' Belinda said thoughtfully as she tucked her arm through Rachel's.

They hurried along the road to Kingsmere as Rachel told her sister some of the rumours she'd heard at the basket factory.

'They say Mr Mead and Mr Taylor are old rivals, going back as far as their school days. Beth is always saying that Mr Taylor waited until Mr Mead went to The King's Head and then he – you know?'

'P'raps that's only jealous gossip, Rachel,' Belinda said. 'Mrs Mead is such a sweet person. She was very loyal to her husband too, especially when the doctor asked her so many questions about their married life. It was rather embarrassing so I went into the kitchen and cleared up there as best I could. Mrs Mead would only say that she was as much to blame as Mr Mead – she said it was no one else's business and that Mr Taylor should be left out of it.'

'The trouble is when Mr Mead is drunk he'll probably beat her again,' Rachel said. 'Charlie told me how he intended to look after his mother when he got home after the war. He didn't have an easy life, Belinda. His father has been a very wicked man, I think.'

'We shouldn't judge,' Belinda said. 'We don't really know and we must honour what Mrs Mead requested, that we don't spread stories around.'

'Oh, you, Miss Goody-Two-Shoes,' Rachel laughed. You've lived too sheltered a life. If you worked at the factory you'd have to be more broad-minded or they'd make your life a misery. Still,' she added happily, 'I like you the way you are.' Rachel squeezed her sister's arm as they battered against the wind which cut across the river.

When they reached home Rachel ran up to her room on the pretext of putting her coat and hat away. She threw them down on the bed and then went to the window where she looked out into the cloudy night sky. Adam might soon be home. Then they could be officially engaged, she hoped. Would that be right? Or would it be what her mother referred to as 'unethical'? she wondered. Her heart was full to bursting with suppressed excitement. She felt sorry for Mrs Taylor, of course she did and especially for Adam, whose homecoming was all that mattered to her now. She prayed desperately that if they allowed

82

him to return to England his journey would be safe and not a repetition of Charlie Mead's fate. Thinking of Charlie brought back all too vivid memories of the afternoon. How could any man treat his wife with such violence as to break her ribs? She couldn't comprehend such vicious actions and realised how lucky she was that her parents were so loving to each other and to herself and Belinda. She knew her father loved Belinda best. In his own quiet way his fondness for her was evident to Rachel if no one else. When she was younger she had thought her horrid birthmark had disgusted him, but that had disappeared and she knew she was, if not daintily pretty like Belinda, not altogether unattractive. She tried to please him, endeavoured to show as much affection to him as to her mother, but she sensed there was a barrier between them. It was as if he were subconsciously trying to push her away. She wished with all her heart that she could be more like Belinda.

Still, Adam had chosen *her*, and she dreamed of the day when they could be married and start a family of their own.

The people of Meon Valley, especially residents of the village of Hundred Acres and nearby hamlets were shocked at the news of Jake Taylor's sudden death. Being rent collector for the manor he was well known though not altogether loved. There were rumours and counter rumours about the feud between the dead man and Dick Mead and when Beth Cropper gave in her notice at the basket factory everyone assumed she was the cause of the dispute. She was renowned for brazening things out, but now refused to enlighten anyone and unable to face the world deserted her in-laws and went home to care for her mother, Mrs Waterstone, grateful for the privacy of the isolated railway cottage.

Rachel and Belinda accompanied their parents to pay their respects to Mrs Taylor on Sunday afternoon.

'If there's anything we can do to help,' Wally said, 'you have only to ask. It's such a tragedy, and to happen when young Adam is away at the war makes it all the more difficult for you.'

'Squire is doing all he can to get him home,' Lily Taylor said. 'But it won't be until after the funeral.' She sniffed into a handkerchief but Rachel was quick to observe there were no real tears.

'You'll need help with preparing the tea, Mrs Taylor,' Phoebe ventured. 'I understand the funeral is in three days' time?'

Lily Taylor surveyed her visitors and decided that it was not unpleasant to be the centre of attention for once. The Hunters were a well respected family in the area even if they were not natives of the immediate locality.

83

She looked directly at Rachel. Such a tall girl compared with her sister. Amazing how the ugly birthmark had disappeared without trace, Lily thought. Sign of the devil all the same. Belinda was more like an angel. Strange for twins – one to be like the devil, the other an angel.

'Since you're going to be my daughter-in-law, Rachel,' she said pointedly, 'perhaps you'd like to help me?'

'Yes, of course, Mrs Taylor,' Rachel agreed readily.

'The girls usually do things together, Mrs Taylor,' Phoebe said. 'They're good girls. Well trained in the kitchen, I've made sure of that. It's a most distressing time for you so if you just tell them the way you want things done, they'll be happy to do the work.'

Lily sighed. 'You're very kind and I'm pleased that Adam has found himself a good wife, even if Rachel is a bit young. But they won't be getting married yet awhile, and when they do they'll make their home here, of course. I shall need my Adam now.' The handkerchief was delicately dabbed against her closed eyes briefly. Then she sat forward with defiance in her expression. 'I hope Dick Mead gets his punishment for what he did. How's a woman to manage without a man's wage coming in?'

'T'was a terrible business,' Wally said. 'But we mustn't forget that your husband died of natural causes.'

'More's the pity,' Lily said in a loud voice. 'Saved Dick Mead's neck – that's all! Grown men fighting – over what, I'd like to know? What was it to my Jacob that Dick Mead battered his wife? The woman's put up with it for years – everyone knows that. Filthy *swine*! *Drunkard*!' She was becoming quite heated, her normally white cheeks pink with anger, and then she glanced at Belinda's shocked look and sank back against her large feather cushion, exhausted.

'I'm afraid it's drink which has caused most of Dick's problems,' Phoebe said. 'Mrs Mead is a hardworking little woman and devoted her life to her children.'

'She should have left that mongrel years ago,' Lily retorted. 'If I'd known that Jacob was still hankering after Nessie Waterstone, I'd never have married him. Persuaded me on the rebound – well, now he hasn't got either of us. Good thing I come from a better class than he did and can keep myself, young Adam as well if it comes to that. But if my son weds your girl then he's got to work to keep her.'

'Adam is a fine, capable young man, Mrs Taylor,' Wally said. 'I've taught him a trade that he'll never forget and he isn't the kind of lad that would want his mother to keep him. I'm sure our Rachel will do her best to look after him the way you've done and keep up standards likewise.'

There was an awkward silence until Phoebe changed the subject by saying, 'I understand that Mr Mead is to be kept in custody for seven days, then he'll come up before the magistrate.'

'And I've already heard that Nessie Mead won't bring charges against him,' Lily said. 'I'm the one who should do that. He's responsible for picking the fight in the first place though heaven knows what it was all about. He's robbed my Adam of his father. He's a wicked no-good scoundrel and the police should prosecute – causing an affray, being drunk and disorderly – anything that would put him away for a bit.'

'Perhaps we should try to be charitable, Mrs Taylor,' Phoebe said. 'The Meads have had their troubles and I daresay Mr Mead drank more than usual to drown his grief over losing Charlie. Just when the boy was on his way home. Injured three times – you can't help but pity the Meads.'

Lily eyed the sanctimonious Phoebe Hunter suspiciously. What did she know about anything? She hadn't just lost her husband. 'S'pose you're thinking it might have been my Adam – he's still out there in danger. I've got enough to worry about without concerning myself over the Meads of this world. They've brought their damnation upon themselves.'

'We can but pray that Adam will be kept safe, Mrs Taylor, and that this wretched war will soon be over.'

Lily Taylor offered the Hunters afternoon tea before they went to the evening service in Wickham where there was much speculation and gossip among the parishioners. Phoebe and Wally kept their own counsel until they returned to Calder Cottage and the curtains were pulled against the darkened sky and howling winds which were persistent.

'They say there was never much love lost between Lily and Jacob Taylor,' Phoebe said, looking across the hearth at her husband.

Wally was deep in thought as he drew on his pipe.

'Who's to say what's between a man and his wife?' he said slowly. 'She's lucky that she's got means of her own and will be all right financially. It's Mrs Mead I feel sorry for. Bad enough to be ill-used by Dick but if he goes to prison how will she cope alone? Benjie's still in France and the girls are all away in service. She comes from a good family, except for that flighty sister, Beth. Mrs Mead didn't deserve what she's had to put up with.'

'If what Lily Taylor says is true and Nessie won't prosecute, what happens now?'

'We shall have to wait and see,' Wally replied wisely.

Rachel and Belinda were sitting at the table playing draughts, but Rachel's thoughts were not on the game. She had one ear tuned in to her parent's conversation and wondered how long it would be before Dick Mead was back at the basket factory. Or would he be dismissed? She felt a bit afraid of him but on the other hand she knew that whatever his destiny was it would have unpleasant repercussions for his wife. Seeing Mrs Mead lying on the floor in such a dreadful state was etched indelibly on Rachel's mind. She felt a desire to help her for Charlie's sake and for the girls'. The Meads were the kind of family that were avoided whenever possible, yet they had all made good, even dear Charlie, and Rachel for some inexplicable reason felt she had an affinity with them.

Chapter Six

Dick Mead pushed open the back door of the house and went in sheepishly. He wasn't sure what kind of reception he'd get. He knew he deserved to find the doors locked against him. Seven days in prison for causing a disturbance with a fine of five pounds to find as well wasn't going to afford him a welcome home. They'd let him out at eight o'clock on this wintry first day of November, still in the clothes he'd been wearing ten days earlier. Dirty and smelling of dried blood, he hardly knew how to face his family. They would be expecting him and probably the girls would all be here to protect Nessie.

It was bleak and gloomy outside but through the scullery door he could see the faint reflection of light from the oil lamp. He forced himself to move further in to the half open doorway. Nessie was sitting at the table, her elbows propped up as she sipped from a cup.

'Can I come in?' he asked hesitantly.

'Why shouldn't you? 'Tis your home as well as mine. The tea's just brewed. I'll pour you a cup. Get out of that stinking coat, for heaven's sake.'

Dick obeyed meekly and without question, probably for the first time in his life.

The two of them . . . there was no one else in the house and it felt ominous. Nessie placed the cup of tea in front of him and she thought she had never seen him look so humiliated before. A wave of pity swept over her but that was quickly replaced by contempt.

'The copper's on ready for you to have a bath,' she said. 'I daresay you're lousy so there's some Keating's powder for you to use. I'll burn those clothes. Mum found out some old stuff of Dad's you can wear. Goodness knows why she's kept it all these years. Just couldn't bring herself to part with his things, I s'pose, but Beth's been having a clear out.'

'Nessie . . .' Dick glanced up but found facing his wife was the hardest thing he had ever had to do.

'Yes? Get everything off your chest, Dick. We'll talk now while we're alone and you're sober.'

'I'll always be sober from now on, I swear to God I will.'

'Save your breath – I'll believe that when I see it. Now, what was it you wanted to say?'

'I . . . I'm sorry . . . really sorry. God, I never want to go to prison again – it's *hell*!' Dick buried his head in his hands and sobbed.

Nessie's heart swelled with a variety of emotions. How many tears had *she* shed over the past twenty-five years? But if Dick really felt remorse then maybe her bruises were worth it.

'Nothing to the hell I've got to suffer with these broken ribs, not to mention the bruises for all the world to see – and the humiliation. Not just humiliation now, Dick Mead, but twenty-five years' worth. Don't you dare sit there and feel sorry for yourself.'

''Tis the drink. Don't let me have another drop, Nessie.'

'How can I stop you? If you can lay you hands on a tanner you'll go to The King's Head. No, you can't go there any more, the landlord has banned you. Not that there's much point in you stopping drinking as you've probably poisoned yourself with the stuff already. Might as well go on and finish the job.'

Dick looked up ready to abuse his wife verbally but the sight of the large wound on her forehead where she'd bashed her head as she fell a week earlier subdued his quick temper.

'I s'pose I can't blame you for being hard on me,' he said. 'You'd be better off without me, but Jake Taylor's gone now. Nessie, I've got to know – how long were you carrying on with him?'

'Pity you didn't listen the other day before beating me to silence and you'd have heard the truth then. No point in going over the past but you're going to listen all the same. When the children were small I often couldn't find enough money to pay the rent. Mum helped me out a few times and she a widow. I could have died when Jake Taylor got the job of rent collector. I'd always managed to steer clear of him. He offered me the job of strawberry picking to pay our debts. It seemed a good idea but then when everyone else had left the fields one evening he turned up and – well, he forced himself on me.'

'You could have run, screamed or something.'

'How could I have known what was in his mind? It all happened so suddenly and I didn't have the strength to fight him off. After that what chance did I have? By always being out you played right into his hands. If I'd told you, you'd have killed him and me. But,' Nessie sighed, the memories painful, 'then at least I'd have been spared the agony of having that last baby with that awful disfigurement, I s'pose. All this has come to a head twenty years too late, Dick.'

'Was Beth right? Are you sure it was Jake's child?'

'Well, of course it was! What have I just been telling you? You never listen – you haven't got the sense our Charlie had. At least *he* loved me and wanted to protect me. He was coming home from the war to take care of me – and you'd have been *out*.' She pointed to the door fearlessly but tears began to trickle down her cheeks. Dick stretched out a hand and placed it over Nessie's.'

'I am sorry, Nessie love,' he said in a croaky whisper. 'I do love you, more'n anything else in the world.'

'And what about Beth? My own sister . . . God, how pathetic you are, Dick Mead. Have you no shame?' She pulled her hand away quickly.

'You shunned me. That's why – well, you know her, tart that she is.'

'And I know you for what you are – weak and selfish. It was lucky for us that that baby died. Its life would have been a living hell with that mark. I prayed that it would die and thank God my prayers were answered. But a lot you cared – even if the child had been yours, and you didn't know any different at the time.'

'But you still carried on with Jake, so Beth says.'

Nessie took out her handkerchief and wiped her eyes. She looked away from her husband now and remembered things she had spent years trying to forget.

'I didn't want to – I tried to make him leave me alone,' she said with desperation echoing from the past. 'He paid Beth to take the children out while you were at The King's Head. In the end,' she said slowly, 'when I got big, weary and ill, he tired of me.'

'So . . . so you don't wish you'd married him instead of me?'

Nessie didn't answer straight away. She had no love for Jake Taylor. There had been times in her youth when he'd seemed attractive, but never after that fateful June night. When her baby had died she'd been consumed with guilt, and after that all feelings for men faded.

'I might have had an easier life with Jake,' she said. 'At least he wasn't afraid of work and he'd have provided for his family.'

'That's easy to say knowing that he only had one son, and his wife having money of her own. It might have been a different story if he'd had to manage the same way we had to.'

'I married you and gave you five healthy children and a lot you cared about them or how we managed! If you'd been a good caring father you could be proud of them all. The fact that they've grown up respectable is no credit to you. They saw you for what you are – a lazy boozer and womaniser – and they were determined to make good themselves.'

'Oh, so now you're taking all the credit, I s'pose,' Dick sneered.

'I only did my best with what I had. I've had to work to keep the home together – and I did it for them. It's no use you having second thoughts now that you've nearly killed a man and lost one of your sons in the war. You're waking up too late, Dick Mead.'

'I'll change. Believe me I will. Give me another chance, Nessie? I've been without the booze while I've been inside so I'll prove to you that I can do without it for good.'

'How many times have I heard that before? I could cope with you getting drunk, Dick. I don't like it but at least I'm used to it. But not other women, and my own sister at that. I've had enough humiliation to last me a lifetime.'

Dick looked directly at his wife in an attempt to be honest.

'Have you any notion what it's like in prison?' he asked softly.

'No, and I don't want to know. You put yourself in there. Getting yourself in this kind of trouble not only lets you down but your family as well.'

Dick remained silent for several minutes while he drank tea which would have tasted good if he hadn't been compelled to have this conversation with his wife. They'd had some good times, he remembered. She hadn't seemed to mind that he was a bit of a lad in his youth. The children coming had changed everything, and that's when he'd turned to drink – no, that was no excuse, he'd always over indulge. Nessie was right. He was a rotter and she deserved better, but he'd made damned sure Jake Taylor wasn't going to get to her first. And to think he'd got her in the end, and Dick too sozzled to realise what was going on. He wished he could remember the baby. It all seemed a haze, something in the back of his mind that wouldn't quite go away. Yet in a strange way he was glad the faint memory was there. Of one thing he was sure, and that was that if he had known it was Jake Taylor's bastard he'd have killed it there and then. Yes, Nessie knew him so well, he'd have killed her too.

'It was just as well the infant died, Nessie. The world is a cruel place for disfigured children. I don't recall much about it – was it a boy or girl?'

'A little girl – and it was hideous. The mark of Jake Taylor was on her all right. I thought I'd never take to it.' Nessie suddenly gave way to anguished sobs. 'But I would – I *would*!' she cried, banging her fist down on the table. 'I was too weak and ill and angry to help it survive. Doctor Grant said the mark would fade in time. I didn't believe him but he was right. The Hunter girl's birthmark has gone completely and look at her now? She's a fine-looking girl. I was so wicked not to care for that baby, God forgive me.'

"Tis all in the past now, Nessie. We can start again.'

Nessie shook her head. 'Oh no, Dick Mead. Not after all you've put me through. We've got the girls to think about so the home stays the same. It's you who must change. Whether you stay or go is your decision. I'll cook and clean for you the same as I've always done, but you won't have a job. I don't want you round my feet all day and there'll be no money for drink. No doubt Beth will keep you satisfied, but not in my mother's house or here. If you want her then get out of Hundred Acres and don't come back.'

'You're turning me out?' Dick looked shocked.

Nessie shook her head again. 'I made my marriage vows, hard though it's been to keep them. The love's gone, Dick. I've had too much grief to bear. It's up to you.'

'I will make amends. I'll get a job even if it means walking miles to work every morning. While the war's still on they need men at the mill, the brewery, anywhere – I promise.'

'Don't make promises, Dick. I've heard them so many times before.' She stood up with the teapot in her hand. 'I must get on, the girls will be home presently.'

She cleared the breakfast things and then went upstairs while Dick filled the hip bath with hot water from the copper. She couldn't go down. She knew she'd end up scrubbing his back and before she knew it the old ways would be forced on her. This time it had to be different.

For a few weeks Dick gave a plausible impression of having turned over a new leaf, then while he was helping Beth's father-in-law, George Cropper the lumber-jack, clear fallen trees after the fierce autumn gales, his and Beth's paths crossed yet again. By late November both had disappeared.

Rachel watched eagerly for letters from Adam which never came. At weekends she and Belinda would go to the railway station and watch every train in the hope that Adam would return home.

'A watched pot never boils,' Phoebe said, trying to be light-hearted about it, but even she felt on edge lest something should happen to Adam before he could reach Hampshire.

Rachel was quite happy now at the basket factory. The two people she most feared, Dick Mead and Beth Cropper, had left and since the rumour had spread that they had gone off together she secretly felt greatly relieved. She felt awkward though whenever she met Mrs Mead or one of the girls.

'I don't know what to say to them,' she told her mother when they came out of Sunday morning service ten days before Christmas. 'Poor Mrs Mead has had such a terrible time, losing Charlie and all.'

91

'Just behave as if nothing has happened, dear, the way Nessie Mead does. She's a brave little woman and the girls are good to her. She works very hard and Squire's letting her stay on in the house. They have every reason to hold their heads up with pride. There's no need for folks round here to shun them. None of us is perfect.'

Phoebe tucked her arm through Wally's and urged him away from Wickham village. Usually people gathered around chatting. It was the one day of the week when folk had time and opportunity to exchange news and views with neighbours they might not see much of during the week.

'Why are we in such a hurry?' Belinda asked.

'It's too cold for your father to stand about,' Phoebe answered shortly.

Rachel raised her eyebrows in response to Belinda's glance. They were both aware that Phoebe didn't always practice what she preached. Not quite a snob yet not willing to be seen talking to any of the Meads they guessed. With their parents hurrying along the towpath by the river, the girls slowed their pace as they chatted. Rachel turned round suddenly when a bird made a curious whistle.

'That's a strange bird,' she said. 'I don't recognise the sound.'

'Could be a migratory bird, one that's lost its way,' Belinda said with concern. She was passionately fond of all birds and animals.

They walked on in silence until the sound came again, this time in close proximity.

Rachel stopped in her tracks. 'It's not a bird,' she said in a whisper, 'it's human. Someone playing tricks. Made me think of dear old Charlie Mead for a minute.'

She pulled Belinda on then stopped suddenly and turned – and there was Adam stealthily creeping up behind them.

'Adam!' Rachel exclaimed, lifting her skirts and running back to greet him.

He caught her in his arms and their lips met with fierce passion. When he released her Rachel found herself blushing. All their feelings so lovingly expressed in correspondence seemed exposed, but there was only Belinda to witness the scene.

'Come on,' Adam said with a laugh. 'You're going to be my sister-in-law so a kiss is permissible.' Belinda went shyly forward and lifted her face to his.

With a girl on each arm Adam walked proudly on to Calder Cottage, unaffected by the biting north-easterly wind which promised ice and snow.

'I'm only home for ten days,' he explained as they warmed themselves by the huge fire Wally stoked up. 'Mother isn't too pleased.

She had the notion that Squire could get me released from further duties.' He sighed. 'I know this is a dreadful time for her, but I was in at the beginning and I want to see it through to the end.'

'Is the end in sight, Adam?' Rachel asked.

'Who knows? The battle still rages on. It's all a game of advance and retreat then advance again.'

'How close to the front line are you?' Wally asked.

'We've been on the move a great deal this past few weeks which was why the news of my father's death took a while to reach me. The weather has been awful, up to our necks in mud and recently bitterly cold. There's devastation everywhere, villages and towns in ruins. Just when you think it's all gone quiet the shelling starts gain and then us stretcher bearers are called for.'

'I'm sure you're doing a very worthwhile job,' Phoebe said quietly. She didn't consider first-hand stories from the battlefield suitable for her two girls. 'We're very sorry indeed about your father's death. Will you stay for dinner, Adam?'

'No thanks, Mrs Hunter. I'd best get back to Mother, but she asked if Rachel might like to come to afternoon tea? I'll walk over to fetch you when mother has her rest if that's all right, Rachel.'

She went to the gate with Adam to see him off. He kissed her cheek lightly and whispered: 'We've got a lot of catching up to do, Rachel, and lots of preparations to make for the future.'

'If only this wretched war would end soon,' she said desperately.

'You'll have plenty to keep you busy – that way the time will pass much more quickly. Next year some time should see Fritz on the run. It seems strange to be back in Hampshire. Everything's so peaceful and quiet.'

'You must have been shocked by the news about your father, Adam? It was such a tragedy.'

He seemed reluctant to speak of the affair. 'We'll talk about that later,' he whispered as he squeezed Rachel's shoulder and strode away towards his own home. She watched him until he was out of sight despite the fact that her mother opened the front door and called to her.

'Don't stand about in the cold, Rachel. You'll catch your death with no coat on.'

But Rachel was warm with contented happiness. She knew it wouldn't last for long, how could it with Adam so soon to return to the front, but at least they could reaffirm their love for one another. A sudden stirring of branches from across the road in the woods made her glance towards the trees. She thought of her first love, a gypsy boy named Kasan, and then flushed with guilt as she ran into the house.

93

'Did Adam invite Belinda as well?' Phoebe asked.

'No, no, Mother,' Belinda said in agitation. 'Rachel and Adam are engaged. I wouldn't wish to intrude.'

Phoebe sniffed disapprovingly. 'Should have a chaperone,' she muttered at which Belinda ran to her mother and put her arms around her.

'Don't be so old-fashioned. Of course Adam wouldn't want me hanging on, neither would Rachel if it comes to that.'

'I wouldn't mind,' Rachel said, but in her heart she knew she would. She loved her sister dearly but hadn't they spent all their early years doing everything together? Being thought of and treated as one for much of the time, except when Belinda was ill or too delicate to participate in whatever was involved. They were two such different people. Belinda's perfection made her feel quite inadequate.

As Rachel stood at the high window upstairs looking out as she brushed her hair, she drifted into a world of her own, wondering just what the future held for herself and Adam. The scene was a wintry one, yet she indulged in fantasies of being a free spirit. There were times when for some inexplicable reason she felt the urge to take off like a bird. To soar into the unknown leaving behind all rational thought and etiquette. The woods opposite looked drearily brown and lifeless but in her mind Rachel could visualise the colourful caravans of the Romany travellers dotted among the trees. How she envied them their freedom, and not only because she had happy memories of Kasan who had been kind to her. So far his lucky stone had proved to be just that. Her birthmark had disappeared and Adam was safe. She wished she had been able to give Charlie Mead a lucky stone as well. Perhaps, though, he was bet off out of the war. She tried to imagine how he would have reacted had he seen his mother in such a battered state. Poor dear Charlie who had caused Rachel such misery in her childhood and yet had become her friend. She was glad about that. She felt she had contributed to making his life a little more bearable.

When she thought about the Meads' home she experienced twinges of fear. How could she be sure that Adam or any man come to that wouldn't take to drink and become violent? But not Adam, he was too mild and courteous. The gypsies seemed to all outward appearances to be rough but having been helped by them Rachel believed them to be protective of one another, always ready to offer a helping hand with the utmost respect. She thought that they probably didn't wash very often or brush their hair. Most of them could neither read nor write, so she'd been told. They lived and loved freely with few cares. There was something wild and exciting about their lifestyle or so it seemed to her.

Rachel saw Adam approaching Calder Cottage so waited until he had knocked and Belinda had let him in. Then she went downstairs wearing her dark red woollen coat with the black velvet collar which she protected by wearing a fashionable silk scarf her parents had given her a year ago.

Belinda smiled up at Rachel as she stood beside Adam in the hallway. But was there just the tiniest hint of envy behind the sweetness of that smile? Rachel felt a pang of guilt at her own good fortune. Guilt that was rapidly forgotten as they set off down the lane, Adam's hand beneath her arm.

'Let's walk through the woods, Rachel,' Adam suggested. 'Where we can be alone to talk for a while.'

She looked expectantly at him. She was almost the same height as he in her high-heeled buttoned boots.

'How's your mother, Adam?' she asked. 'I don't want to keep you away from her – after all, that's why you're home.'

He sighed. 'Mother never stops complaining. She should be out there in France, then she'd have something to grumble about.' He stopped and turned Rachel to face him. She felt herself growing warm with anticipation. The sparkle behind Adam's dark eyes drew a loving response from hers. He held her arms gently and allowed his lips to meet hers. It was sweet and lovely but lasted only a brief moment. 'I want you to tell me, dear, exactly what happened that afternoon when you were visiting Mother,' he said. 'I know my father was not all he appeared to be. I expect you think our home was a happy one, Rachel, but I doubt that it was very different from the Meads'.'

'Oh, Adam, you mustn't say that. Everyone knows how Mr Mead drank too much. So many stories have been going round, who can possibly know the truth? Belinda and I were just leaving your house when we met Beth Cropper in a great hurry. It all seems so long ago now. I do think they should have got you home much sooner.'

'But that wouldn't have saved Father. Mother insists that Dick Mead killed him, but according to the death certificate he had a heart attack and died instantly. Did you see the fight they're supposed to have had?'

'I wasn't very close but your father pushed Mr Mead into the mill stream and then collapsed himself, I understand.'

'If only I could find Dick Mead or Beth Cropper they'd tell me exactly what it was all about, but they've vanished.' Adam held Rachel's shoulders with urgency. 'Rachel, I need to know – that's why I didn't call on you the moment I arrived home. I wanted to, believe me I did, but mother was being difficult, saying she wishes she was dead too, that she'd kill herself if I had to go back. I had to get the doctor to her. He sedated her and then I visited Mrs Mead. She wasn't much help though.'

'Poor woman, I don't suppose she was. She seems to be the victim in all this. Beth had been carrying on with Mr Mead for ages, but what happened that day to bring about such violent reaction I don't know. Beth seemed to blame herself and for a while went to live with her mother. She left the basket factory and no one saw much of her. Mr Mead did seem to have turned over a new leaf. He was working hard, doing odd jobs wherever he could find them. Unfortunately, so June told me, he worked for the Croppers and I suppose Beth called to see her in-laws. Suddenly no one knew where they'd gone. It's been quite a scandal as you can imagine.'

'But what's behind it all? Dick Mead has been a drunkard for years and Beth Cropper – well – we all knew what kind of woman she was. So why did it all blow up out of all proportion, and what did it have to do with my father?'

'Rumour has it that there was rivalry between your father and Dick Mead, but from a long time ago. What could it matter now after all these years? Surely your mother must know, Adam?'

'If she does she isn't telling, and I hate having this awful antago- nism against dad. He's dead, nothing can bring him back now. I know there was some kind of feud between Dad and Dick Mead but I never thought it was serious any more than the fight Charlie and I had.'

'That was my fault, Adam. For having that horrible birthmark. You couldn't blame Charlie for taunting me about it. He'd been taunted enough himself for being a half-wit.'

'And he was nothing of the sort. Not very bright but he never had a chance, and what could you expect having a father like Dick Mead? Away from him Charlie changed as you saw for yourself when he came home.' Adam pulled Rachel towards a huge fallen tree trunk and they sat down together in the most secluded part of the wood. 'I fought Charlie because I couldn't stand by and listen to him making unkind remarks about you and calling you Strawberry Girl.' He kissed her firmly on her mouth. So hard in fact that she was forced to open her lips. In response Adam opened his mouth and the lesson in teaching Rachel how to express her love began.

The next few days passed by swiftly, Adam eagerly seeing Rachel at every opportunity, always there to meet her when the day's work was done at the basket factory. When she had a half day off they visited a jeweller in Fareham who made Adam's grandmother's ring a size larger to fit Rachel's finger. Christmas Day their engagement was made public and Rachel thought she must be the happiest girl in all of Hampshire, except that they had barely another forty-eight hours to spend together before Adam had to say his goodbyes.

Mrs Taylor refused all invitations to spend any part of Christmas with the Hunters.

'It isn't seemly to celebrate when I'm still in mourning,' she told Adam.

'Aren't you being just the tiniest bit of a hypocrite, Mother?' he said. He was realising that he was now the man of the house and needed to adjust accordingly. Being a corporal in the Army meant that he had learnt to assert himself and give commands on occasion. Although he felt profoundly sorry for his mother he was determined to show her that she was not going to dominate his life as she had in the past. 'You and Dad weren't exactly close, were you? He went out because you made his life a misery – what was it? – some kind of penance for his womanising?'

Lily Taylor looked at her son sharply. 'Who've you been talking to? What have the Hunters been saying? Filling your head with all kind of wicked rumours, I s'pose?'

'Mr and Mrs Hunter have been most considerate and sympathetic. They aren't the gossiping kind, but goodness knows, Mother, everyone knows what Dad was like. You haven't been a proper wife to him for years.'

'And what would you know about such things, my boy? A couple of years in the Army doesn't give you the right to speak to your mother as you like without respect. I've not enjoyed good health since the day you were born.'

'That's hardly my fault. Dad's gone now so you can stop putting on an act. You're not old. I expect Rachel's parents are getting on for ten years older than you. It's time you got out and about more. Mix with people, make them welcome here and when you get an invitation to go somewhere for afternoon tea then go and enjoy yourself.'

'Don't be so tiresome, Adam. You don't understand about a woman's problems in middle life.'

'Then you must have been in middle life for the past twenty years! I'm twenty-two, Mother, and you've always made your poor health an excuse for living like a recluse. Dad waited on you hand and foot. The truth is you've got into a rut. Has the doctor ever said there was anything physically wrong with you? Well, has he?'

'I don't hold with doctors. They don't care about old women like me, much less understand.'

Adam was losing patience. 'Mother! You are not old. I've got to go back tomorrow or I shall be classed as a deserter. As soon as this

97

wretched war is over I'm coming home to marry Rachel and I want her to have a pleasant mother-in-law.'

'If she's coming to live here she'll have to tow the line and abide by my rules.'

'Then I'll ask Squire for a tied cottage.'

'No, Adam please – don't do that.' She began to weep and this time her tears were real enough. 'You're being deliberately cruel, Adam.'

'I . . . I'm sorry, Mother, but you don't help yourself. I shall worry about you while I'm away. I'd like to think that you had friends to keep you company sometimes. You aren't the only person who's in mourning, you know. Think of all the other women who have lost husbands and sons in the war. Give some sympathy to them and people might be more friendly.'

'Friendly!' she scoffed. 'No one has ever wanted to be *my* friend.' Lily Taylor considered herself a cut above the rest of the community having private means, so she didn't need friends.

'Why should they? Father had an unpleasant job to do collecting rents – he wasn't exactly the most popular or friendly person in the area. You have your small private legacy but what do you do to help those less fortunate? You can afford to have a woman help with the housework or washing but so far everyone who's ever worked for you has been subjected to some of your tasty tongue-pie – and people, however poor, will only take so much. I'm sorry, Mother, but you've done yourself a great disservice. But you're still young enough to make a fresh start, if only you had the inclination.'

'I never heard such rot, Adam Taylor. It's a good job your father isn't here to hear you talking to me like this.'

Adam only grunted. 'I'm going to see Rachel. It's our last evening to be together so I don't know when I'll be home. Don't wait up.'

He flung on his greatcoat and went off still buttoning it up. His loyalties were divided which didn't help his frustration. He loved his mother but she was a hard difficult woman whom few could get on with. Now local people had given up and if the truth were told avoided her as much as possible. The Hunters had offered her the hand of friendship, inviting her to Calder Cottage for Christmas Day and Boxing Day too, but she'd enjoyed playing the martyr which embarrassed Adam. He had spent as much time as decency allowed with Rachel and his future in-laws but now he was going to have to leave Wickham with some measure of guilt.

Rachel tried to soothe his troubled mind by saying, 'It may not be for long, Adam. Think of the future when you come home for good. That will please your mother – and we'll be together for always.'

They went for a walk along the crispy frosty bridlepaths, their last chance to be alone – for how long? Adam's brief sexual experience in

France had developed his virility and he found it difficult to keep his feelings in check. He knew he must. Rachel and the Hunters were respectable people – but Rachel had shown that she was capable of showing her affection with some degree of passion.

'Rachel,' he began hesitantly, thinking selfishly of what he needed from her to seal their betrothal. 'You wouldn't consider? No, I mustn't ask . . .'

'Of course I don't mind, Adam,' Rachel responded eagerly. 'I know your mother won't be easy to live with but I'll be as patient as I can and try to fit in with her ways. I'll visit her often while you're away and try to make her like me, even though I know she likes Belinda best.'

Adam felt as if someone had poured cold water over him. How could dear innocent Rachel have any idea what was in his mind? Girls thought only of pretty weddings, the frills and fripperies. Consummating the marriage would be merely a duty, he supposed, and that very definitely after the church ceremony. During his leave and many visits to Calder Cottage he had grown used to the talk of collecting items for a bottom drawer, flowers, bridesmaids, and every other thing which was to make their wedding day memorable, but now on the eve of his departure he thought how negative it had all been. He would carry back to the front a lasting picture of his fine fiancee, of the happy moments shared, the kisses, cuddles, even a little horse-play. If only Rachel realised how desperate he was for a more physical bond to remember her by.

'Goodbye-ee, goodbye-ee . . .' The paper boy whistled the tune of the hit song of 1917 as he delivered the morning news, reminding Rachel of her emotional farewell to Adam who was by now back across the Channel.

As 1918 was heralded in there was renewed hope that the war would be brought to an end as quickly as possible but when February snowdrops carpeted the woods hopes were dashed. By the end of March came an uneasy peace between Russia and Germany. The one thing the Allied Commanders had hoped to avoid was happening as troop trains began to travel west and new tactics were employed to devastate the Allied lines in France. Germany's Erich von Ludendorff looked as if he was to be successful in beating the British back to the Channel. The Allies lost 400,000 men in three weeks and the Kaiser was confident of winning the war.

Rachel waited and watched anxiously for news. Since Adam's leave the war seemed that much more real. He had given graphic descriptions of some of the events at the Front but counterbalanced the horrors by telling her of the way the men made their own amusements when they went back to quieter towns and villages for a brief respite. Here they could relax and there was always someone who was capable of organising a Follies Show to entertain the war weary soldier. But as the Meon Valley bore the first signs of spring with crocuses and daffodils in bloom the news was too gloomy even to think of men singing and dancing and generally enjoying themselves.

By the summer a crippling epidemic of influenza brought a month long lull in the fighting on the Western Front but when battle resumed with renewed ferocity the opposing army was at last halted and when the Allies mounted an offensive with some twenty divisions near Amiens the enemy collapsed. A black day indeed for Germany which changed the character of the war.

Towards the end of September the Allies were sweeping all before them regaining ground in Flanders where the war first began.

But a different war was raging around the world and millions of people were dying. The worldwide epidemic of Spanish Influenza was taking its toll everywhere, Great Britain included. Through the hardships of war people were undernourished and had little resistance to this virulent strain. No successful vaccine could be found to combat the disease which resulted in more US servicemen dying from it than from war wounds.

Those who survived though were jubilant when the Armistice was signed at Compiegne in November 1918 and the sound of gunfire ceased after four long years of war.

Wickham mourned not only for the war dead but the many local people who had been flu victims.

Mrs Waterstone, Nessie Mead's widowed mother, was among them. Wally Hunter became seriously ill and for a while his condition caused great concern, but with loving nursing by Phoebe and Belinda he made a good recovery.

Rachel took it upon herself to nurse her future mother-in-law. She was a difficult patient though not as seriously ill as many others.

'*Please* drink this juice, Mrs Taylor,' Rachel urged. 'The doctor says it's important to have plenty of fluids. Eating doesn't matter but I've brought you some broth Mother made for my father.'

'Leave me alone to die,' Lily Taylor moaned. 'My husband's gone and now Adam. There's nothing else to live for.'

'There's everything to live for, Mrs Taylor. I'm sure no news is good news and Adam will soon be home.'

She looked out of the window at the bleak mid-winter. A year ago Adam had been able to spend Christmas at home even though it was a sad homecoming after his father's death. The celebrations which followed the end of the Great War gave way now to counting the cost in human life. Many wives and mothers didn't know whether or not their loved ones were alive or dead. Those who did return told stories of horrific injuries – shell-shock, hundreds suffering from the effects of being gassed – what was Adam's fate?

Chapter Seven

Rachel and Adam hesitated outside the railway cottage which had been Mrs Waterstone's home for many years.

'Are we doing the right thing, Adam?' Rachel asked. 'We more or less promised your mother that we'd live with her after we got married. I don't like going back on my word, and it isn't characteristic of you either.'

He pulled Rachel closer to him and kissed her cheek. 'War changes people,' he said. 'I know Mother dominated me before I went away. She'd made Dad's life a misery, always grumbling – and I don't want to have my marriage ruined by her interference.'

'But she expects us to live with her. While we were waiting for you to come home she kept reminding me of your promises, and she'll surely blame me if we get this cottage.'

Adam hugged Rachel to him in desperation. 'I can hardly believe I'm home, darling,' he said. 'Thank goodness Squire was willing to write to my unit and confirm that my job was safe, otherwise goodness knows when I'd have been demobbed.' He glanced up at the ivy-covered cottage. 'I've always loved this little place. I came here with your dad to put up a new fence and gate for Mrs Waterstone just before the war. It's small but pretty and I know the old lady was happy here. I believe houses reflect the people who live in them.'

'Don't forget Beth Cropper was born here and lived with her mother until she went off with Mr Mead.'

'But she's the black sheep of the family, Rachel. The rest of them are all nice hardworking folk.' He held her at arm's length. 'But you're sure, aren't you?'

'About what?'

'About marrying me for one thing, and this cottage for another?'

'Oh, dearest Adam, you know I want to marry you more than anything in the world. It seems as if we've had to wait for ever.'

'But you're still only eighteen, Rachel. It's quite young . . .'

'But I shall be nineteen by the time we get married at Easter,' she interrupted him. 'And of course I love the cottage. A tent would have done as long as we're together, but this will be our very own. Well, yours to be exact.'

'Once we're married what's mine belongs to you too. I know I'm very fortunate having this money left to me by Dad, and we're so lucky that the rail company wanted to sell the cottage cheaply just at the right time.'

'Mm . . . all the same, Adam, I'm not sure that my parents will approve and it might make your mother ill.'

He laughed. 'It would if Mother thought it would make me change my mind, but it won't. When I was a child we had a grandmother living with us and there was always friction. I believe that's why Dad went out drinking so often.'

'But he wasn't a drunkard – not like Mr Mead.'

'No, he knew when to stop – and that was when he was under the influence enough to go and find some woman who was willing to oblige him.'

At that moment voices grew louder at the back of the house and a figure emerged from between bushy shrubs.

'You the new tenants then?' the gypsy woman asked in a gruff voice.

'Not yet,' Adam said stiffly.

'Newlyweds unless I'm mistaken.'

'Yes, you are mistaken. We aren't married yet. Not that it's any concern of yours.'

The middle-aged woman eyed first Adam then Rachel suspiciously, and Rachel was reminded of Merle, the woman who had told her fortune so many years ago.

'Take some white heather to wear on your wedding day, m'dearie – for good luck.' She thrust a sprig towards Rachel but Adam pushed her hand away.

'If she wears white heather then I'll buy it for her,' he said firmly.

The woman's face darkened. Rachel felt some foreboding at her expression and was suddenly afraid. When she'd walked into that gypsy encampment as a child she had felt no fear and they had been kind to her. Kasan had given her the lucky stone which had taken her birthmark away and she had dreamed romantic dreams about him. She must remember to ask Adam about her stone. An eerie feeling crept over her as if it was important to have her stone back to ward off the evil that was emanating from this woman.

'Take care, young man. All is not as it seems, believe me.'

'Of course I don't believe you. You can't frighten me just because I won't give you any money.'

'This house ain't yours nor never will be.' She stepped around Rachel cautiously. 'Be . . . be kind to the woman . . . yes . . . be very kind.' She hitched her basket of wares on her hip and hurried away.

'Whatever did she mean, Adam?' Rachel asked in a frightened voice.

'Goodness knows, but nothing for us to worry about.'

'Adam . . . she meant your mother. "Be kind to the woman" she said. She must have seen your mother's distress.'

'Rachel!' Adam sounded annoyed. 'Surely you don't believe all this good luck nonsense, and seeing into the future?'

'Well, yes, I do. My stone helped to take away my birthmark, didn't it? And it brought you back home safely.'

'No, Rachel, dearest. Your birthmark faded quite naturally, and I was one of thousands of others destined to return home.'

'You kept my stone, didn't you, Adam?'

'Yes, Rachel, I did. For almost all the war, and then at the last offensive when we had to go out into the trenches to try to save the poor devils who were cruelly wounded and many more gassed, it must have fallen out of my pocket. But losing it hasn't brought me any bad luck, has it?'

Rachel fell silent. She shivered with a sudden chill as the wind whistled round the side of the house, and when she looked up she saw Mrs Mead standing against the wall watching them. Adam followed Rachel's glance.

'Hullo, Mrs Mead,' he said with eagerness in his voice as he propelled Rachel forward. 'The gypsy woman wanted me to buy white heather for luck. Don't hold with such silliness myself.'

'Hullo, Adam, Rachel,' Nessie Mead said with a hesitant smile. 'I'm never quite sure whether it's safe to upset the gypsies. I suppose I've had enough bad luck in my time to make me cautious. I crossed her palm with silver in return for a sprig of white heather which I've put in Ma's living room – just in case.' Her smile broadened and she motioned them to follow her into the cottage. A few bags were propped by the doorway and one or two sacks in the yard awaiting disposal.

'I've cleared everything now except a few pieces of furniture which I thought you might be able to make use of. It's hard when you first set up home as everything costs so much, but you'll be able to make nice things, Adam, and I daresay Rachel's father will help.'

'We'll have a lifetime to get our home together, Mrs Mead,' Adam said. 'It's very kind of you to think of us though.'

104

'Not many folk round here can afford to buy a house or cottage, but it's the right way to start out and I hope you'll be very happy here. My parents were and we all had a happy childhood even though times were tough, especially for Ma after my father was killed on the railway.'

'How old were you then, Mrs Mead?' Rachel asked.

'Seventeen, and I was married three months later. I was the eldest you see. My Benjie was born a couple of months after my mother had our Esther. She didn't even know she was going to have another baby when Dad had his accident. Wonder she didn't lose it with the shock. Reckon that's why our Esther has always been special to her – *was* special to her. Can't get used to Ma not being around and it'll seem mighty strange not having to visit her here. Nearly forty-six years she lived in this cottage. Don't expect you'll stay here that long, though. Things are changing and young folk want to move into the towns.'

'I'm sure we shall love living in your parents' home, Mrs Mead,' Adam said. 'It'll be nice to remember her.'

'No, my dears, you must forget the past and start afresh. She'd give you her blessing, though, just as I do. Now I'll be on my way. I'll get our Benjie to come by and get rid of the rubbish and take these bags on to a jumble sale. Just be happy together.' She looked directly into the faces of the young people. Strange, she thought, how absurdly alike they were. Made for each other, Ma would have said, because their noses were exactly the same type. Noses could make or break a face. Some people had slightly crooked noses, while others were short, or long and thin. Both Adam and Rachel had good straight noses, almost perfect in shape. Reminded Nessie of someone, now who was it? Someone she knew well, someone she'd had intimate dealings with – why, of course Adam's father, Jake Taylor. She looked away guiltily, fumbling in her coat pocket for the key which she handed over to Adam.

'I'll leave you to it then.' She couldn't bring herself to look at them again but Adam and Rachel walked her to the gate, and with a slight inclination of her head Nessie Mead raised her hand half-heartedly as she hurried away down the path alongside the railway line.

'Did we say anything to upset her?' Rachel asked perceptive to the sudden change of mood.

'No, I don't think so. Mrs Mead was good to her mother and she's still grieving, I expect. She's sad that her mother has gone, and doesn't like to think of someone else living in the old family home.' Adam squeezed Rachel affectionately. 'And that someone will be us after Easter.' They almost danced back to the open doorway of the cottage and once inside they closed the door firmly against the outside world.

Nessie had a long walk back to her house at Hundred Acres. A long slow walk with things churning over in her head. Rachel Hunter and Adam Taylor looked so . . . so *together*. She couldn't get the uncanny likeness between them out of her mind. The Hunter twins were so unalike – supposing they weren't twins at all! But Nessie couldn't imagine Phoebe Hunter carrying on with the likes of Jake Taylor, and anyway the Hunters weren't locals so she wouldn't even have known him in her younger days. Fool, she told herself, if the twins shared the same birth date they could hardly both be Phoebe's *and* have a different father. As she walked other things came into her mind. Rachel was such a fine young woman now that the birthmark had faded. If her own daughter had lived, hers and Jake's, would she look as attractive as Rachel Hunter? Nessie's footsteps quickened in time with her thoughts. Stupid impossible thoughts, she told herself. But Rachel Hunter did have that birthmark and she was about eighteen now, just as her daughter would be had she lived . . . had she lived . . . had she lived? Oh, dear god, supposing she hadn't died? Nessie's feet fairly flew up to her front door where she let herself in and sank down in the nearest armchair in the front parlour. Her baby hadn't been baptised so had no name. She'd never seen a death certificate. There'd been no funeral. She'd hated the child until it had gone and then she loved it passionately and wished it back again, birthmark and all.

What had Dick done all those years ago? Given it away? It was possible. He was capable of anything, but no, that didn't make sense. If he knew that their daughter was alive somewhere would he have been so angry when Beth told him that the child wasn't his? He ought to have been pleased. No, the child wasn't important to Dick, one way or another. What had angered him was that his old rival, Jake Taylor, had been his wife's lover. What a mess she'd made of her life, Nessie thought now. Jake Taylor was dead, and her mother. Charlie too. Dear Charlie, her protector as he'd grown older. And that was another strange coincidence, she reflected with renewed interest. First Charlie had taunted Rachel Hunter when they had come to the area to live. Then in some ridiculous way they had ended up friends. Was it because . . . dare she begin to believe that it was because there was a blood tie? Both *her* children? Charlie, Dick's offspring, and Rachel, Jake Taylor's? Nessie got up suddenly and took off her coat, then she went through to the kitchen and made herself a pot of tea. She drank tea until every drop was drained from the big Brown Betty teapot. Silly fool, she reprimanded herself. What wishful notions she was conjuring up. Incredible, fanciful, unreasonable fantasies which could in no way be true or Adam and Rachel would not be permitted to marry. She tried to cast her mind back to the dreadful day when her last baby had been born. It was so long ago and a great deal had happened since, but hadn't Doctor Grant and Minnie Fletcher confirmed that her baby died soon after birth?

Still, it was not an unpleasant thought that Rachel Hunter might be a replica of the child she had borne. Rachel was a nice girl who'd been upset when Charlie was killed in the war and shown genuine compassion.

The Meon Valley seldom experienced the sounds and smells of motor vehicles but on this early March day heads turned and people ran out of their cottages to see the unusual sight of a 1912 Morris Oxford chugging its way through the narrow lanes. When villagers saw that the driver was none other than their beloved Doctor Grant home after service in the Army, he was besieged and forced to halt his journey several times.

I should have crept stealthily in by night, he thought with a wry smile as he admired new babies and listened to tales of goings on during his absence. It was early evening before he sounded his horn as he came into the Square at Wickham. It wasn't much like spring with the damp drizzle falling softly and no one appeared to be interested in his arrival here. He parked the car and switched the engine off. Nothing much had changed, he supposed. But he had. The bout of influenza he'd suffered had left him feeling persistently weary and depressed. He'd lost weight and at times felt as if he had no future. But it lifted his spirits to be back where he'd learnt to live again after being jilted. He loved the countryside and the people of Wickham especially.

He got out of the car and closed the door as quietly as he could. He needed time now to come to terms with his mother's death. His fate might so easily have been the same as hers since it had been a cruel strain of influenza. He wondered how the locals here has fared and how many of his old patients had survived. He needed a meal and he guessed his old housekeeper at the surgery would have one prepared as he had notified Doctor Barber of his visit. But first he wandered around, gazing with interest and many memories at the old buildings. The large Mill was just as he remembered. Built in 1820 it contained beams from the United States Frigate *Chesapeake* which was captured off the coast of Boston in 1813 by *H.M.S. Shannon*. Cyril Grant smiled to himself as he came to Dip Hole where steps led down to the river which enabled people who didn't have pumps to draw water. Living in Kent where the large town of Maidstone afforded better amenities had made him forget how these local folk lived. He passed the brewery and malt house which stood on the banks of the Meon and made his way to the Church of St Nicholas from where he could hear strains of organ music. The heavy iron-studded doors was unlocked so he went inside and sat quietly in the back pew to listen. He was lost in tranquility so didn't notice the Vicar coming through the aisle. A light touch on his arm made him jump to his feet.

'Vicar! How good to see a familiar face,' he said huskily.

'And I might say the same to you, my good man.' The Vicar hardly recognised the doctor who now sported a beard and was several stones lighter than four years earlier. 'How are you, Doctor Grant? Welcome home,' he said, offering a hearty handshake.

'Not as fit as I was a few months ago. This wretched 'flu hit me badly just when I should have been able to help my mother, but sadly she died.'

'I'm sorry indeed, and to hear that you're not feeling as well as you'd like to be, but a few weeks back amongst us will soon put you right, I'm sure.'

Cyril Grant sighed. 'Not back for good, I'm afraid. I suppose if I'm honest it's time to move on and there's still a lot of my mother's estate to attend to so I'm going to settle back in my old home town of Maidstone. I'm here just to finalise the selling of my practice to Doctor Barber who seems to have fallen in love with the area and people just as I did. I'm a bit old at fifty-one to be starting again but the town is growing and there's room for a new practice near the family home.'

'You do surprise me. You've been greatly missed and we've all been asking when you would return but Doctor Barber hasn't divulged anything of your plans.'

'Good! I'm pleased because I specifically asked him not to as I needed to come back and say goodbye to all my old friends personally. I daresay some of the young men didn't come back after the war and this 'flu has probably taken several of the old people off.' He patted the pew beside him. 'Do you have time to sit and tell me what's been happening hereabouts, Vicar?'

'I'll surely make time, Doctor Grant, but at least let's be civil and talk over a meal.'

'I think I'd better pay my respects to Alice who has no doubt prepared a banquet for my home-coming. I'm sure there'll be sufficient to include you.'

The two men returned to the centre of the Square where the doctor's house stood. After they'd admired his new acquisition standing proudly at the kerbside, Cyril rang the bell and both Doctor Barber and Alice greeted him enthusiastically.

108

An awkward silence followed through as both housekeeper and Doctor Barber were stunned by the change in him. When he removed his hat Alice noticed that what was left of a once fine head of hair was iron grey and his cheeks were quite sunken, giving him a gaunt appearance. But, as they sat round the table enjoying the appetising meal Alice had lovingly prepared, they quickly realised that Cyril Grant was still the kind, caring doctor everyone loved. Afterwards the men retired to the sitting room where Alice served port wine and the Vicar disclosed the names of the young men lost in the war.

'Poor Charlie Mead,' Cyril said. 'I can hardly believe he was suited to the Army '

'He changed quite dramatically,' the Vicar said. 'He was wounded twice and came home to recuperate after the first injury. It was difficult to believe he was the same boy. Getting away from his father and going into the Army made a man of him, and he vowed to look after his mother.'

Doctor Barber stood before the hearth to light his pipe, afterwards holding the edge of the high mantelpiece with one hand as he brooded over past events in Wickham.

'Which is more than that scoundrel of a husband of hers ever did.' The doctor gave a detailed account of Nessie's condition after Dick's beating and of the fight between Dick and Jake which ended in Jake's death.

'What were the two men fighting about?' Cyril Grant asked. 'I know they were once rivals but that was when they were youngsters, so Mrs Waterstone told me.'

'Something to do with Nessie Mead's sister Beth,' Doctor Barber said.

'But she married Harry Cropper and settled down, I thought?' Cyril said.

'Harry was one of the first victims of the war,' the Vicar explained. 'Beth's in-laws were a good influence over her and she seemed to have changed for the better, but when she went to work at the basket factory she began to flirt outrageously and I'm afraid her own brother-in-law was easy prey, though what their relationship had to do with Jake Taylor no one seems to know. Eventually they went off together and no one knows where they are,' Vicar said. 'Mrs Waterstone was shocked and angry. Fortunately she had Nessie to look after her until this 'flu saw her off.'

'Mrs Taylor didn't seem too upset by the death of her husband,' Doctor Barber said thoughtfully. 'She put on a show of crocodile tears to impress. I understand she has means of her own. To my surprise she doesn't appear to mind that young Adam is to marry

Rachel Hunter, though I believe there's some conflict as to where they'll live. She expects them to live with her but Adam intends to buy the railway cottage.'

Cyril Grant answered vaguely at first as he wondered how the delicate Lily Taylor would manage without Jake's strength to manipulate. Then the penny dropped as two names linked together filled him with utter shock and despair. Adam and Rachel. Half-brother and sister. They *couldn't* marry – but they weren't to know that! He couldn't admit to what he and Minnie Fletcher had connived to do nineteen years ago!

Voices floated over his head and thankfully the other two men thought he was overtired after his long car journey so suggested that he should retire He did so gratefully but sleep eluded him. Had he come back in the nick of time? Should he keep quiet and pray that they would have no children? It seemed an impossible situation but by dawn he knew that he had to see Adam and tell him that marriage to Rachel Hunter was out of the question. His head ached in anticipation of the questions he would be asked. Adam was no fool. He was going to demand to be told the truth, but that too was impossible. Whatever would Nessie Mead's reaction be to discover that the baby she thought had died was alive and had grown up right under her nose? Cyril searched his memory for the way things were before the war. Yes he remembered that Charlie Mead had enjoyed taunting young Rachel. He recalled seeing Adam and the two Hunter girls together but it had never crossed his mind that anything would come of it. Heavens, he thought, Adam Taylor, why couldn't you have chosen Belinda instead of Rachel!

He knew he needed time before he acted and whatever decision he took must be carried out with discretion. For the next couple of days he travelled round the villages meeting up with old friends and familiar faces to get the feel of the place again.

When he visited Phoebe and Wally Hunter he learned that Rachel and Adam were to be married at Easter and there was great excitement as preparations were made. It was to be a grand occasion when all the villagers would join in the celebrations. He didn't have much time to think out a plan so rode over to Beech Cottage only to find that Minnie Fletcher had moved away to live near the sea with her sister.

Cyril felt desperate. He visited Nessie Mead who was delighted to see him but she avoided any gossip about Dick and her sister. She was still mourning her mother as well as Charlie. The shock of what we did with her child would kill her, Cyril thought. She'd had a hard life and fate had dealt some cruel blows, how could he deal her another one? She might be glad that Rachel was her daughter but that would hurt Phoebe and Wally, not to mention the two youngsters themselves.

Cyril tossed all manner of ideas around in his head, and during the service on Sunday morning prayed for guidance to do the right thing. He greeted Rachel and Adam afterwards with courtesy, offering his warm congratulations. How could he do this to them? Better to stay out of it and hope for the best, but he was a doctor and knew the dangers. He had a week before the banns would be called. The longest week of his life.

Still no nearer to making up his mind how to do what he knew he must, he took a drive out to Romsey and then on to Winchester to see some old friends. The countryside was at its best on a rare bright sunny day and the small wild daffodils in the woods hinted at a hidden spring. His friends were overjoyed to see him though concerned about his health and it was late when he left the town to return to Wickham. He decided against taking the better road via Southampton and Fareham. When the moon got up there would be enough light to see his way back to Wickham through Bishop's Waltham and the Chase. The drive was pleasantly uneventful. He had passed the Hunters' cottage at Kingsmere when he saw a lone figure ahead of him jauntily walking back towards Hundred Acres. At least he could offer the young man a lift, he decided, then cowardice tempted him to pass by when he realised who it was. But wasn't this the opportunity he had prayed for so earnestly?

Adam turned when he heard the car coming up behind him. He knew who it must be and guessed the doctor would offer him a lift. Such opportunities rarely came his way in such an area as Wickham so he accepted gratefully.

'Just said goodnight to your fiancée, Adam?' Cyril Grant said.

'Yes. It'll be nice when we can be together in our own home, Doctor Grant.' Adam was more interested in the car and how to drive it than his forthcoming marriage, though. He smoothed his hands over the leather upholstery and admired the polished grain of the wooden dashboard.

'This is real luxury,' he said in admiration. 'Something I shall never be able to afford.'

'You don't know, Adam. I'd never anticipated progressing beyond doing my rounds on my bicycle. My mother, you see, owned a rather large family home which I inherited after her death. If I'd married and raised a family I'd have needed the house. Instead I've settled for a modest town practice and a new vehicle to go with it.'

'Yes, I heard that you were only back to visit us all. I'm sorry that you aren't going to return here to live, Doctor Grant, and I know Mother is disappointed.'

There was a moment's awkward silence then the doctor pulled in to a clearing in Bere Wood and they talked briefly about the war and its consequences.

'Lots of things have changed here, Adam,' Cyril Grant said gently. 'I know war plays havoc with people's lives both on and off the battlefield. I was sorry indeed to come home and hear about your father.' He turned in his seat to face the young man. He couldn't have it on his conscience that he'd let this opportunity to execute his duty pass by – a duty he must tackle sympathetically but honestly, yet without revealing more than he need.

'It didn't take long for someone to tell you all the local gossip then,' Adam said dispassionately.

'I knew that there had always been a difference of opinion between your father and Dick Mead.'

Adam was glad that it was dark. He knew people still gossiped about the fight and the reason for it but there had never been anyone who could tell him how the feud between the two men originally started.

'I only know what people say and Mother tells me it's all nonsense. Folk round here didn't think too highly of Dad because of his job, but rumours have it that it might have had something to do with Mrs Mead or maybe Beth?'

'Whatever the cause, Adam, it all happened a long time ago, before my time. I think perhaps your father was keen on Mrs Mead and Dick won the day. Better I daresay for Nessie Mead if she had married your father. Dick didn't do her any favours, did he? And now gone off with Beth Cropper.' Cyril Grant shook his head sadly.

'I expect both men were to blame for the fight, Doctor Grant, but it was the heart attack which killed Dad and no one can say different.'

'Very sad for you and your mother. She's lucky to have you and I hope you'll be good to her.'

'She wants Rachel and me to live with her after we're married, but I've put my foot down. She'd make Rachel's life a misery – any woman's come to that – and being that Dad left me some money, I can afford to buy Mrs Waterstone's cottage.'

'I admire you, Adam, I just which you'd chosen any girl but Rachel.'

There, it was out, now he had to justify his remark. Adam was clearly shocked. Cyril Grant could feel the boy's defensive reaction.

'But I thought you of all people would be pleased. I thought you liked Rachel?' he said.

112

Cyril placed a hand on his shoulder. 'No one is fonder of Rachel Hunter than me, Adam. I've watched her grow into a fine young woman, and life was pretty cruel to her in the beginning.'

'I know, I felt sorry for her with that awful birthmark.' Adam leaned forward. 'Is it because you think if we have children they'll have birthmarks too? Belinda didn't have one. They're not a bit alike and they're twins.'

'My dear Adam, I'm afraid this is a painful duty I have to perform but what I'm about to tell you must be in the strictest confidence. It seems fate brought me back to Wickham in the nick of time. You can't marry Rachel Hunter – you simply can't – and I'm so very sorry.'

'That's a dreadful thing to say, Doctor Grant! Why ever not?' Adam's tone was highly indignant.

'You know I wouldn't make such a statement without very good reason, Adam. The plain truth is that you're related and any affection you feel for each other is probably because you . . .'

'Related? Me and the Hunters?'

'Only Rachel. This is very difficult for me, Adam. I'm not at liberty to disclose certain events concerning Rachel's birth. Suffice it to say that I believe you share the same father.'

'But how can that be? Rachel is Belinda's twin sister and they –'

'No, Adam. They aren't twins at all. When Phoebe gave birth to Belinda she had only the one infant, much loved and wanted after many years of waiting. Rachel was born in questionable circumstances, unloved and unwanted. It was touch and go whether or not she would live. The Hunters lived miles away. No one ever thought they would choose to move to the very area where Rachel was born. Phoebe Hunter took the poor mite in and mothered her as if she were her own. They've been good to her and no one has ever suspected anything.'

'You're just telling me this – this fairy story. It's all a pack of lies! Is it because you don't want me to know what a rotter my father was? I suppose Mrs Hunter was another of Dad's fancy women? It seems he was well known for cheating my mother. I thought you were a friend. I'll walk home, thank you very much.'

'Calm down, Adam. It wasn't like that at all. I can confirm that you and Rachel share the same father. Beyond that I can reveal nothing. Even Phoebe and Wally Hunter don't know Rachel's real parentage so I must ask you to keep this knowledge to yourself. But you must see, Adam, that you cannot go through with a marriage to Rachel. Now, if it had been Belinda, everything would have been fine.'

'I never thought my father was capable of such blatant adultery, let alone with Mrs Hunter.'

113

'Adam, please try to think things through. If Rachel's real mother were Phoebe Hunter would she have allowed you and Rachel to marry? She has no idea that you're related which is why only you and I can share this knowledge. Please believe me, Adam. If there was any other way – if I had any doubts – but I know it to be true. You must have wondered why Rachel and Belinda are so different in looks and character?'

Adam sat with his head in his hands. 'I don't want to believe you, but I've never known you to be anything but upright and honest. Is it that you want Rachel for yourself?'

Cyril Grant placed his arm on Adam's shoulder. 'Now you're being ridiculous,' he said softly. 'She's a fine person – but she's not for you, Adam. She's your half-sister.'

'What can I do?' he cried in despair. 'What can I say? How can I tell her it's off?'

'You'll need to sleep on it for a few nights, I suspect. We can talk again if you like? I'm due to leave Wickham in a couple of days' time but I'd like to see this thing settled before I go.'

'You sound as if you feel responsible?'

'Only in as much as I saved the life of a child once, Rachel's, and found her a good home. Your father and her real mother believed she died soon after birth. To all intents and purposes she's the daughter of the Hunters. I can hardly believe that you and she – it's just incredible, Adam, a quirk of fate, if you like, but you must try to understand that I had no option but to prevent your marriage from taking place once I realised what was about to happen.'

'What if you hadn't returned here?'

'Then no one would be any the wiser – in a way I wish I hadn't, but I have a conscience. There would be risks, Adam.'

'Will you visit them with me?' he asked after a few minutes had elapsed.

'No. It might be better if I don't. Too much would have to come out into the open, and too many people would be hurt. The only way I can suggest is for you to say that you've changed your mind, Adam.'

'But I love Rachel, Doctor Grant, and she loves me.'

'Then if you really love her you know you're doing wrong in going through with this. I . . . I can't stop you, of course, though I know I should stand in church and forbid the banns. I don't want it to come to that, Adam. Think of your own reputation, your mother's, Rachel's and her family's. I know how much this hurts, believe me, and how much it's going to hurt Rachel. I was jilted myself many years ago, but there's no other way. Either you must engineer a quarrel to finish it or you must tell her that you've changed you mind. She's still young, only just nineteen, and you'll soon find someone else.'

114

Somewhere in the distance midnight chimed but Cyril Grant knew he must see the night through with Adam.

'Come back to the house,' he begged. 'We'll have tea and get warm while we talk – if it helps.'

'I don't want to go anywhere. Yes, I do, I want to go away as far as I possibly can, but there's my mother. I've got to confront her and see what she can tell me.'

'I doubt that she knows anything about the matter, Adam. She seldom took an interest in the doings of others. She was always too busy complaining about her health. I could never find much physically wrong with her. I fancy she feigned ill health to keep your father at bay. So, you can't altogether blame him for seeking satisfaction elsewhere.'

'In any vacant bed it would seem! Maybe we don't have to look too far to know which one.' Adam spat the words out angrily. It was all slotting into place now, but Cyril Grant lifted his hand in protest.

'No more speculation, Adam, please. It's all in the past and we don't want to hurt people unnecessarily, do we? I've always had reason to believe that you're a young man of integrity and I want you to think this over very carefully before you go to see Rachel. Who her real parents are isn't important any more. As far as she's concerned, Phoebe and Wally Hunter are her mother and father, and you must let her go on thinking that.'

'Doesn't she have a right to know the truth?'

'I doubt that any of us know the real truth, and how would it help her? The shock of hearing that she's not Phoebe's daughter, Belinda's sister, might be too much for her. It could turn her brain, Adam. Nothing can change the circumstances but you're not in a position to offer Rachel marriage now that you know that you're half-brother and sister. I'm sorry. I wish it didn't have to be me coming between you and Rachel, but professionally I must advise against marriage.'

'I'm beginning to wish I'd never come home,' Adam said suddenly. 'Then I'd never have known.'

'It might have come to light, sooner or later, and then think of the terrible heartache it would have caused.'

'T'would be easier if I went away but that would kill my mother just as the truth would. But I don't know how I can do this to Rachel! What a mess! Poor Rachel.' He thought of how she believed in good luck, that it had removed her birthmark and brought him back from the war. She would think so ill of him, her love changing to hatred, and she'd believe it was all down to his losing the lucky stone.

The two men sat and talked the matter over until the first light of dawn began to appear.

115

'You'll never be ready for your work, Adam. Can you go home to bed and for once tell a white lie and say you're ill?'

'No, Doctor Grant. I'll go home, have a wash and shave then get off to The King's Head where I'm working on some new outside tables. Thank goodness I'm not working with Mr Hunter at present. He's still suffering from the effects of 'flu so he has to work inside. I'll be glad to go to work to think out what I can say to Rachel and her parents. They aren't going to think too much of me, are they?'

'Better the upset now than in a few years' time when who knows what might happen. You've got a lifetime to prove to yourself that you've done what's right, Adam. It's hard. I know what you're going through and we'll hate ourselves for what we're doing to Rachel – but you must see, Adam, it's the only way.'

'I wish I didn't believe you but it ties up with things I know about my father. I'm sure you respect the Hunters and like Rachel too much to do anything to hurt them unjustly.'

'You won't do anything silly, will you?'

Adam shook his head, and as early morning farmhands and carters set about their morning's work, heads turned in surprise to watch the motor vehicle going through the lanes at this early hour.

Adam took his mother a cup of tea after he had washed and shaved with an unsteady hand as he couldn't pare away the shock of the night's revelation.

'You're up early, Adam.' Lily Taylor sat up in bed wide awake having been disturbed by the sound of the car engine. 'Where have you been all night?' One look at her son confirmed that he hadn't slept in his own bed. 'You haven't taken advantage of Rachel before the wedding, I hope? I thought I heard the doctor's car outside?'

Adam had decided against confiding in his mother just yet but she was a wily old bird and knew something was wrong.

'The doctor brought me home, Mum. I've been talking to him – you know, about the war and everything. The time just drifted by.'

'Time doesn't drift by unless you're up to no good. I suppose even the good doctor isn't above drinking to forget the horrors of war. You look awful, Adam, fit for nothing – I hope you're not taking after your father and soaking yourself in beer and whisky and the like?'

'I haven't touched a drop and neither has the doctor as far as I know,' he replied patiently.

Lily Taylor had never been an affectionate woman though in her own way she had coddled Adam and been possessive. He needed someone to confide in now. Going away to war had toughened him but the bitter blow he had received was just beginning to affect him

116

and his chin quivered as the wound in his heart could only be soothed by tears. He suddenly knelt by his mother's high bed and buried his face in the quilt, sobbing.

'Adam! Dear boy! Whatever's the matter?'

He hated himself for his weakness but it all had to come out.

'Doctor Grant tells me that I can't marry Rachel, Mother. Dad fathered us both. Tell me it isn't true, please? Tell me he's wrong?'

The cup rattled in its saucer as Lily took in what her son had blurted out. Adam glanced up in time to see cup and saucer falling from his mother's hands as she sank back against her pillows. He managed to retrieve the china but the tea was spilt everywhere. His mother's cheeks were ashen as she cried. 'No! *No*! It can't be true. Your father was no saint, heaven knows, but not a bastard child – not here in Hundred Acres. You mustn't believe it, Adam. It's just vicious gossip.'

'But it must be true, Mother. You know Doctor Grant would never come between Rachel and me for the sake of vicious gossip.'

'It can't be true, I tell you. It isn't true!' She began to gasp and her cheeks turned from grey to bright red and then to purple. Adam ran for the brandy and held his mother close until she revived. 'Never speak to me of this again, Adam, nor anyone else,' she panted, clutching at the front of her nightdress.

'But if you know anything, Mother, anything at all, please tell me, for God's sake?' he pleaded.

'I know of no child, Adam. There have always been rumours about your father and his affairs but a lot of them to spite me because I had money of my own. Stupid jealousy, of course. People are so wicked and full of treachery.'

'But Doctor Grant wouldn't say such a thing if there wasn't some truth in it, would he?'

Lily lay back her eyes closed, her breathing spasmodic. To anyone else she could have been at death's door but Adam had witnessed such attacks all his life and no longer feared them.

'The Hunters came from several miles away in the New Forest so how could they have known your father?' she said after recovering. 'It's true the two girls are very different – I always suspected something fishy. Now Belinda is the one you should marry, Adam. She wouldn't object to living here with me. Gentle, quiet and sweet-natured, and I know she adores you.' She sipped more brandy. 'Rachel could be quite fiery, I should think, and you can't deny she chased you. She thought no one would look at her because of that strawberry mark.'

'Now you're saying unkind things, Mother, and I don't want to hear. I'd better get off to work. I need time to think.'

117

Lily pleaded with Adam to stay at home even if there was nothing she could say to console him. She was as shocked as he and the thoughts which raced around in Adam's head brought him nothing but confusion. He knew his mother would be delighted if the marriage were called off. He felt defiant yet the more he thought it over the more he realised that he had to do what Doctor Grant had insisted upon. He kept arguing with himself. Supposing there was no truth in the rumour? Then all this trauma was for nothing. But if it were true – and so much pointed to his father's disloyalty to his mother – he daren't risk the health of any offspring he and Rachel might have.

When Adam could stand the strain no longer he visited Calder Cottage straight after work before going home for his tea.

'Why, Adam!' Phoebe Hunter exclaimed. 'Rachel wasn't expecting you this early. I believe you're going to see the Vicar this evening?'

She looked at his work clothes with disapproval.

'I . . . I . . . need to see Rachel urgently, Mrs Hunter. We . . . we . . . won't be going to see the Vicar after all.'

'Oh dear, what's happened? Not your mother is it?'

'In a way. She's had one of her attacks. It's made me realise that I can't go through with buying the cottage. It wouldn't be right to leave her on her own.' Adam followed Phoebe into the living room where the meal had just been placed on the table. 'Oh, I'm sorry,' he apologised, 'I didn't stop to think. Your tea . . .'

'Sit down, lad and have some with us,' Wally invited.

Hurrying footsteps sounded on the stairs and Rachel came bounding into the room.

'Adam!' she said excitedly. 'I wasn't expecting you just . . .' She stopped and the pleasure faded from her bright eyes as she saw the solemn expression on his face. 'Is something wrong?'

Adam looked down at the cap he was twisting between hot sweaty hands. How could he say what he'd come to say? What right did he have to upset this harmonious family who'd never harmed anyone? Curse Doctor Grant, he thought venomously. But he had no choice.

'Something's wrong in a manner of speaking.' He dared to glance up at the faces waiting for an explanation. He realised that Belinda was home. He hadn't expected that and nodded by way of acknowledgement.

'I'm not going to buy the cottage, Rachel,' he blurted.

'But I don't mind, Adam,' she said with a nervous laugh. 'I told you I'd do my best to be nice to your mother. It'll be all right in time.'

'I . . . I'm sorry,' he stammered. He wasn't making a good job of this but there wasn't a nice way to do it, he knew. 'I'm sorry – this is

118

going to come as a shock – but – I can't marry you, Rachel. It wouldn't be right.'

'Whatever d'you mean? Wouldn't be right?' Rachel's voice was high-pitched and demanding. His mother was right, she *did* have a fiery streak. He hadn't meant to say it wouldn't be right, he'd meant simply to state that he'd changed his mind.

'I shouldn't have let things go this far before telling you,' he said. 'But coming back from the war, there was an urgency in everything. Truth is, Rachel, I never meant . . .'

'Well, go on,' Phoebe urged with an edge to her tongue.

'It . . . it's Belinda that I love and want to marry. I'm sorry, Rachel, I never meant to hurt you, honestly. I felt sorry for you and you did chase me . . .'

'I think we'd all better sit down and have a cup of tea,' Wally said with a firmness unusual for him.

'Just as well to come to this conclusion before the wedding than afterwards, I s'pose,' Phoebe said haughtily.

'T'will be wedding nerves, Adam,' Wally said, trying to calm the tense situation. He went out to the scullery where the kettle was just on the boil over the stove. 'You've been through a trying time being away from home for so long and losing your dad. Postpone the wedding, why don't you? For three months to give you time to settle down?'

Adam shook his head. 'No, I'm sorry. Rachel – I hate myself and I won't blame you for hating me, but I just got carried away with it all. You made it seem so easy but I just can't marry someone I don't love.'

Adam despised himself. He lied too readily for he did love Rachel and knew that marriage to her would have been lively and full of fun.

She burst into tears and fled to the safety of her bedroom, throwing over her shoulder as she went: 'I hate all of you – *all* of you – and especially you, Belinda. You always get the best of everything.'

Phoebe went chasing after her which left Adam and Belinda facing each other.

'I've always been fond of you both,' Adam said. 'I know I shouldn't have let Rachel become so attached.'

'You seemed equally attached, Adam,' Belinda said quietly. 'Perhaps if you do what Father suggests and postpone the wedding it will be all right?'

'No, Belinda. I know my own mind. I didn't want to hurt Rachel but you and she are so different. You will marry me, won't you?'

'Oh, Adam, no. I couldn't – I just couldn't – it would be so painful for Rachel. And I love her too much to be so cruel.'

Adam left Calder Cottage feeling an utter failure. He crossed the road and disappeared into the woods where he walked until he was

119

too weary to place one foot before the other. A new thought came into his head which brought a mite of comfort to his troubled mind. He had every right to love Rachel because she was, after all, his sister. Maybe that was why they had become friends in the first place.

Chapter Eight

The news soon spread round the villages, quickly followed by a rumour that Adam was secretly courting Belinda up at the big house.

Rachel looked pale, but her large dark brown eyes smouldered with humiliation and she refused point blank to go to work. Phoebe knew that she was ready to erupt and dreaded to think what might happen if she crossed paths with Adam Taylor or his mother. Not that it was very likely. Lily Taylor seldom left the house, and Adam had no cause to come to Kingsmere while he could see Belinda at the big house at Hundred Acres. Phoebe wanted what was best for both her girls, especially Belinda. It grieved her to think that Adam might have been playing one sister off against the other. He was a nice enough young man but his recent behaviour had shocked them and caused alarm, suggesting instability. Supposing he married Belinda and then changed his mind again!

'You've got to face people eventually, dear,' Phoebe said kindly to Rachel who was helping her with some baking one morning.

'And have them laugh in my face?' Rachel retorted. 'I don't need to go into Wickham or any of the other villages.'

'But your father can't keep you, and you can't do nothing for the rest of your life. You were very rude to Vicar when he came to see you. He might have been able to help you. No one blames *you*.'

'No, they just feel sorry for me and I don't want their pity. I've had that all my life. I never thought Adam Taylor felt so sorry for me that he'd actually get engaged and then break it off. I could understand it if I still had my birthmark, but I'm not that ugly now, am I?'

'I'm sure it's got nothing to do with whether you're ugly or pretty, Rachel, but you know you're very nice-looking, and I still believe that Adam is very fond of you and always will be. His mother's behind it, you mark my words.'

Rachel was kneading the bread dough vigorously. She paused, staring unseeingly at the copper pans hanging on the brick wall. Yes,

Mrs Taylor had shown a fondness for her sister. She preferred Belinda, that was it, probably considered it was a risk for her beloved son to marry a girl who'd had such a horrible disfigurement. She was thinking ahead to her grandchildren. Rachel had thought Adam was standing up to his mother but now she realised that he was very much under her influence still. With a painful cry she wiped her hands on her apron and ran up to her bedroom where she flung herself down on her bed and wept huge tears of despair.

Phoebe sighed but left her to drain her unhappiness with weeping. What else could she do? The situation was unpleasant, the atmosphere tight whenever Belinda came home now. It was Phoebe's turn to pound the dough. She could hardly believe it of Belinda when she'd asked that she might invite Adam home to tea on Easter Saturday. How was she going to break the news to Rachel?

'It's too soon,' Phoebe said to Wally when they were alone preparing for bed that night.

He found it difficult to deny his own true daughter anything.

'We've a lot to be thankful for that the two have been so close up to now,' he said thoughtfully. 'They've grown into fine young women, each developing her own character, and now must fashion their own destiny.'

'I don't know much about Shakespeare but didn't he say something like: "There's a divinity that shapes our ends, Rough-hew them how we will"?' Phoebe asked.

Wally grunted. 'Probably. What difference does that make? I'm sorry it's turned out like this, Phoebe. Given you a lot of worry. In a way I was glad it was our Rachel that was getting wed first. After all, we know nothing of her background and it would have been a relief to see her married and settled down. All I want is to see Belinda happy. If only Adam had had the decency to wait before switching from Rachel to Belinda. Can't think what came over the boy. He ought to have let Rachel down gently.'

'He was very unkind, I thought. She's taken it badly and I'm sure she'll not want to be here when Adam comes to tea.' Phoebe slipped the wide, high-necked winceyette nightdress over her head and buttoned the front opening. 'We could refuse, I suppose. And if they're thinking of rushing into marriage we can forbid it until Belinda is twenty-one.'

'Now who's being unkind?' Wally asked. 'Maybe we should have insisted on making Rachel and Adam wait until he'd been home from the war longer? I mean – we don't know what effects the war will have had on him. People change. They're exposed to all kinds of disease abroad. But, for the moment, we can't do anything much. If Adam

122

can change his mind once, he'll as like as not change it again. We must try to persuade Belinda to be discreet and wait until this scandal has died down, though I suppose there's no harm in Adam coming to tea. Perhaps it'll break down some awkward barriers. If we try to stop it, Phoebe, they'll start courting in secret and we all know where that can lead.'

'But not our Belinda. You surely can't think . . .?'

'No, 'course not, she's much too sensible. She's shy and Adam wouldn't do anything to hurt her. Yes, I reckon t'will bring things out into the open if Belinda brings him home to tea on Easter Saturday, but you'd better warn Rachel in good time.'

Rachel accepted the news quietly. After copious weeping came days of morose solitude. During the quiet of an afternoon she took to walking alone through the woods. Subconsciously she was running away from things which had hurt her and looking for things long past which had brought her pleasure.

She followed sounds of children playing or dogs barking, anything which reminded her of the gypsy travellers, but the woods remained empty of such people. What a fool she'd been to give Adam her precious stone. Now she knew she'd never find Kasan again, let alone enjoy good luck. That myth was quashed – a merciless answer to happy expectation. She longed to be free of the noose around her neck. It was getting ever tighter as bitterness towards Adam and Belinda grew. How insensitive they were, she thought. She'd always thought that Adam was attracted to her sister, but to drop her and take up with Belinda immediately was the last straw. Well, Belinda was welcome to him. She could invite who she liked to tea but Rachel wasn't going to be made to feel small. She didn't know where she'd go but somehow she would escape any confrontation with Adam Taylor or her sister.

She told no one of her plan to go out on that Saturday afternoon. It was a crisp cold day with high winds and she wrapped up warm and took a small bag of sandwiches with her, planning not to return until well after dark. Her parents were in their bedroom getting ready so Rachel stealthily crept down the stairs, praying that they wouldn't creak. Once she had reached the back door it was easy. Her boots hardly touched the ground as she raced through the long garden, past the almost barren vegetable patch, skirting the fruit trees, brown and lifeless now. She ignored the indignant clucking of hens in their coops as she picked her way over the rubbish plot. When she reached the hurdle fence she had to hitch up her skirts, but long legs made it possible to get over without too much difficulty. Walking through the

123

paddock wasn't quite as trouble-free though as the two horses put out to grass there were inquisitive and expected Rachel to have apples in her pocket. She stopped just long enough to talk to them and pat their noses and then took to her heels and ran the last few yards to the gate. She made certain that she secured it behind her and then made for the bridlepath near the river.

Rachel had no definite plans to go in any particular direction. It occurred to her that she could start walking towards her grand-parents' home in the New Forest. Something urged her to get back to her roots, to the place of her early childhood where she'd been happy with much loved grandparents to run to when in trouble. But when she reached the Waltham Chase Road it looked long and cheerless. Not one carter was in sight so there was no hope of getting a lift. It was Easter and after the solemnity of Good Friday when everyone excepting her had attended the Church Service in Wickham people were spending the time closeted by their own firesides. The north-east wind lashed at her cheeks so she turned back in the direction of Wickham through copses, over streams and ditches, always careful to avoid any rider or walker by keeping to the thickest part of Bere Forest.

She had no idea what led her to the Church of St Nicholas in Wickham but she turned the iron handle and went inside. She sat in a pew at the back admiring the mass of beautiful flowers which had been especially arranged for the Easter Day services. All the arrange-ments for her wedding crowded into her mind, disturbing the peace of this ancient building. Her mother had intended to supply the floral displays to decorate the altar and church for her wedding on Easter Monday. Hers and Adam's. Rachel stood up and walked slowly down the aisle imagining her father by her side, Belinda in her sky blue dress standing solemnly behind them carrying a basket of spring flowers. Everything had been arranged, even to the carriages and reception in the old school hall. Who had cancelled everything? she wondered. Her parents, or Adam. God, how she hated and despised *him*! What right did he have to treat her so callously? She felt her finger-nails digging into her palms as outrage filled her senses. Her whole body stiffened and then relief flooded through her as a gentle arm was placed on her arm.

'Rachel, dear?' Nessie Mead was shocked to feel the hostility in the girl's manner. 'Are you all right?'

'Yes, of course, why shouldn't I be?' She pulled free with irritation then lowered her head in shame. What had this woman done to offend her? A woman who had known pain and misery for as long as Rachel could remember. 'I . . . I'm so sorry. I didn't mean to be rude.'

'Shall we sit down and have a chat? I've been placing some flowers on my parents' grave and the bitter cold wind has chafed my hands.' Nessie laughed softly. 'Stupid, isn't it, to come into this cold church to get warm?'

They sat side by side and each silently remembered another time when they had sat together, to mourn the loss of Charlie. Rachel was filled momentarily with remorse. She had sat in this very place and prayed many times for Adam, Charlie, and other local men away at the war. Not that was all over, but life was far from peaceful.

'I was sorry to hear that your engagement to Adam Taylor was broken, dear,' Nessie said. 'I expect it feels like the end of the world, but remember there might be better times ahead.'

'I doubt it, Mrs Mead. Setting up home with Adam meant so much to me,' Rachel's voice cracked.

'I know it did, Rachel.' Nessie wasn't sure what to say to this grieving girl who obviously felt that she had lost everything. 'Perhaps it wasn't meant to be. We don't always understand why things happen and we rebel against life, but invariably things turn out better than we deserve.'

'How could he do it, Mrs Mead?' Rachel quelled the tears which threatened. She must be a woman and stand tall and proud for she had done nothing to be ashamed of. 'To break it off so suddenly and turn his attention to Belinda – how could he be so unfeeling?'

'I'm afraid that's the way of men, Rachel. If you find a good one – like your mother did – then you're a very lucky person. I must admit I thought Adam was a decent lad, but how can we tell what people are really like? I'm sure he didn't mean to hurt you and cause you such misery. You must remember that he's all his mother's got and I fancy she might have swayed him.' She shrugged. 'For some reason best known to herself.'

'I know she didn't like me very much, although I tried to please her. But I can't understand Belinda either. We've always been close and vowed never to quarrel or part from one another – how could she do this and not expect me to despise them both?'

'You're both grown woman now. How old are you, Rachel?'

'We were nineteen on March the seventh.'

'You're still young, my dear. You and your sister have to make your own choices and decisions in life now, and you've got a lifetime to find real happiness. I know you don't understand it at present, but one day you'll laugh at it all and be glad you didn't make a big mistake.' Nessie stood up to leave. She felt Rachel's dark brooding deeply. She felt compelled to share in her torment and wanted to do something to restore the girl's faith in human nature. As she stood looking down at the dark head she felt a ridiculous urge to invite her home where her own daughters might help to cheer her up. She could love this girl who might have been her own baby. She felt Rachel's need too keenly for comfort and was letting her imagination run amok. She must go and persuade Rachel to go home too. 'I must get back home. June will be in for her tea,' she said. 'It's lovely to have my family around me – and I'm sure your parents want you to be with them.'

Rachel allowed herself to be guided to the lych gate and in the lane beyond they said their goodbyes and parted. But Rachel only walked a few yards to the bridge, then turned back. The church was as good a place as any to hide away until her former fiancé had taken his leave of Calder Cottage. She idled her time away looking at the slabs of grey marble which marked the burial place of descendants of the Uvedale family. She knew the history of the church and most of the old families of Wickham off by heart from schooldays. The long walk in the cold had made her hungry so she huddled in a quiet corner to eat her sandwiches. Bored, her thoughts turned again to the reason for her solitude. Bitterness built up inside her with no outlet. She had been wronged and someone had to pay. Why was it she who had to leave the comfort of her home to avoid her sister's pleasure? Adam had used her to get to Belinda. Rachel could see it all clearly now and burned with a sense of injustice. It wasn't fair – it simply wasn't right! She hurled the wrapping paper across the grey stone floor which had been thoroughly swept ready for the services tomorrow. She'd have happily scrubbed them to make them look nice for her wedding day on Monday. But it wasn't going to happen, and all because Adam Taylor was too much of a coward to leave his mother. Hadn't she said that she was willing to live with her? Things wouldn't have been easy but she would have made the best of it.

Dusk was descending, the light coming through the high windows making the interior of the church eerie. She wanted to go home but knew she mustn't. They would all look at her with regret. Adam might try to make amends with soothing words but nothing he could do or say would pardon him for the misery he had caused her. Cold and unrelenting she paced the floor, hatred for the world at large mounting inside her. She kicked out at the nearest pew. That too was unrelenting. Made of good solid oak which had taken a few other knocks in its time, it now refused to yield to Rachel's sacrilege. Neat rows of hassocks lay beneath each pew waiting for worshipper's to kneel. No more would she ever kneel to pray, she vowed, picking up one after another and hurling them across the church. Soon the place was littered with hymn and prayer books, and such was Rachel's frenzy that she removed the large Bible from the lectern and hurled it towards the altar. A huge vase of flowers toppled and lay in an untidy mess on the carpet. Then, as if possessed by the devil himself, she dashed the rest of the flowers to the floor and trampled on them, giving vent at last to all the resentment which had been building up over the past three weeks.

At the door she turned and surveyed her handiwork. Her dark eyes glistened with glee and she let out a harsh laugh. Her dark hair, escaping from her hat, blew across her eyes and mouth. Her fury stimulated her and she tore around the church once more, kicking at everything in sight. Then, picking up her bag, she let herself out of the door and began to run.

Clouds scudding across the night sky quickly blotted out the moon and stars. Like a demented animal Rachel ran until her body weakened and she was forced to drop to her knees at the roadside. A grassy bank took her weight. It was wet and she realised that a slight drizzle had given way to torrential rain. She didn't care. She was free at last: free from pitying glances, free from obstacles which had shackled her from the day she was born. There was no one to answer to out here in the wild. She had run, walked, hurried along an unfamiliar road, but what did it matter? She began to laugh again, a high-pitched unnatural hysterical sound that came from someone else not her. Her head felt light, her sides ached, yet she revelled in the feeling of the rain as it cascaded down to mingle with her tears. The world was totally unreal. She was no longer Rachel Hunter but someone with no name, no identity. Her heart gradually slowed its frenzied pounding and she drifted into a state of exhausted sleep.

Chapter Nine

Rachel believed that her mother was standing over her trying to waken her, but it was a wet nose which nuzzled her cheeks and ears. An excited whimper, not the voice of a human, made her sit up sharply. The dog's urgent barks were music to her ears. He needed someone to love and she stretched out her arms to hug him.

'Wonder where you've come from and what your name is,' she said. He wagged his tail frantically, still talking in his own way, and then crouched down, scraping his paws backwards. When she didn't move he rushed at her, whining louder. 'You're as wet as I am,' she said. 'And if it's food you want, I haven't got any.' He ran round Rachel playfully and then, obviously annoyed because she wouldn't get up, began to bark his short urgent demands. Rachel was stiff, cold, and definitely not herself.

'I don't know where you want me to go,' she said, 'but I'm not going to get very far at this rate.' It was a painful struggle to pull herself up and she found it difficult to make her legs and feet work. They were quite numb, but with some perseverance she took a few steps, then one or two more, the dog chasing his own tail, going round and round her excitedly. 'Do stop,' she said, 'you're making me giddy. Come on, let's try to find out where we are.'

Her hat was too wet to put on her head and the water squelched in her boots. Rain and sleet had saturated her coat so that it was twice as heavy as normal. She walked a few yards. What was she doing out of doors before it was really light? Had she really stayed out all night? Where on earth did she imagine she was going?

Suddenly there was a noise behind her and she felt a heavy hand on her shoulder.

'And where might you be off to, young lady?'

Rachel turned to face a rough-looking man of about thirty. He was wearing an old army cape and a cloth cap.

'I . . . I'm just walking,' she said nervously.

'At this time of the morning? You mean you're stealing my dog.'

'No! No, I don't want your dog. He found me.' The icy cold rain enveloped her and she felt as if she were being swept away on the crest of a wave to somewhere where nothing mattered any more. She swayed . . . made a grab for the nearest support . . . felt herself being sucked down into a dark, ice-cold cavern.

Unfamiliar voices grew louder, stirring her from unconsciousness.

'She were stealing my dog, I tell you!'

'Stand back and let me have room to look at the girl.' Rachel felt warm breath against her cheek as if someone had bent over her. 'Her heart's beating all right, but she looks mighty pale. What's a nicely dressed girl like her doing out in this weather, and before six o'clock? Fetch me some weak tea with plenty of sugar.'

Rachel was too afraid to open her eyes. She wasn't sure that she could. Pain was attacking her everywhere. Each muscle felt like a tightened cord binding her.

'Come on now, dearie, open your eyes. Keep awake – don't faint off again. You'm quite safe. No one 'ere's going to harm you.' Rachel thought the woman's voice, although gruff, sounded kind. She opened her eyes slowly and it was as if she had come home. No, it wasn't home, not Phoebe's warm cosy place, but somewhere she'd sought refuge before, a long time ago. The colourful interior of the caravan shocked her back to life. Brightly coloured flowers painted on the walls and bow ceiling made her feel as if she were lying in a beautiful garden.

'Where am I?' she asked in a small voice. 'One minute I was talking to a dog, I think . . .'

''Tis my dog,' the young man retorted sharply.

'I think he found me,' Rachel said. 'I must have fallen asleep and when I woke he was nuzzling my face.'

'I think you'd better get out of those wet clothes, Missie,' the woman said. 'You'm soaked to the skin. Out, everyone, while I find som'at for the girl to put on.'

'You're very kind,' Rachel managed weakly. 'I don't want to put you to any trouble. Perhaps I'd better be on my way.'

The woman laughed. 'And where might that be? You ain't got no luggage. Even us 'as moves about 'as belongings.'

Rachel frowned. Where had she intended to go? Why was she on an unfamiliar road and in the middle of the night? From a long way away came the sound of church bells. She gasped and sat up, crashing her head on the roof of the van. The church, God's house, what

129

terrible, wicked thing had she done? Blood rushed to her cheeks and she began to sweat as all the painful memories returned. She sank back on the bed.

'Oh dear Lord, what a dreadful sin I've committed,' she cried.

The woman insisted that she sipped her tea. It didn't taste very nice and Rachel made a face.

''Tis herbal tea and t'will do you good. We must get the chill out of your bones. You'm delirious, I reckons. A nice sponge down with warm water will make you feel better. What's your name?'

The woman bathed Rachel's face with a cold flannel first and then insisted on helping her to discard her sodden clothes.

'My name's . . .' she began vaguely. She was in disgrace. The police might be looking for her. What she had done must be a criminal act. 'I can't remember, and I don't know where I am or what I'm doing,' she said lamely and without conviction.

'I'm sure a nice young woman like you 'asn't committed no offence. S'pose there's a young man at the bottom of this?' The woman washed Rachel's body all over and she didn't have the energy to protest. Strange but sweet-smelling clothes were put on her and at some time she had the feeling that lots of pairs of inquisitive eyes were peering at her. Left alone she fell asleep, blissfully at first but then tormented by fierce and violent dreams. Someone was trying to catch her but she fought like a wild cat to escape. Occasionally a pretty little woman came to her and tried to calm her but then the woman was dragged away and beaten.

Rachel cried out with fear, flailing her arms around. Was it rain pouring down her face? The cool sponge tempered the fever. Someone insisted she should keep drinking from a china cup. Where was she? Who were these people? The agony seemed to go on for ever, and then a man's calm gentle voice lulled her to sleep, but it wasn't Adam or her father. Her grandfather's perhaps? Hadn't she set out to visit them in the New Forest? But her head felt as if it were in the clouds and she floated away, safe at last.

The sun poured in on Rachel's face. She knew by the smell of the fresh drying earth that it was a clear, crisp spring morning. She was herself again, all fever vanished, her body cool and free from pain. For a long while she lay taking in her surroundings. There was no sound of anyone about and it crossed her mind to get up and make a run for it. But she realised as she turned over on to her side that she simply didn't have the strength.

Something below her moved and she looked down from the berth where she had lain for what she thought must be several days and noticed that two cupboard doors stood open. She peered inquisitively over the side and saw bed covers spilling out on to the floor of the gypsy waggon.

Once she had been afraid of gypsies but now, with memories of Kasan returning to remind her of their kindness, she felt happy and contented, believing that she was safe among friends.

The waggon shook gently as the woman below her levered herself out of the lower berth and stood up, stretching with grunts and groans.

'Good morning,' Rachel said. 'I believe I must be in your bed. I'm sorry if I've put you to any trouble.'

The woman, short and somewhat overweight, turned to look at her uninvited guest. Her black hair was twisted into a thick rope tied with a piece of coloured material which she now tossed over her shoulder. A voluminous nightdress covered her completely and Rachel was amazed at the brilliant whiteness of it.

'Not trouble, Missie, exactly, but we had to delay our moving on 'cos of you. Me name's Sybil, what's your'n?'

'Rachel. I don't know how to thank you, but I'm afraid I can't pay you any money for taking me in.'

'Have I asked for any such?' Sybil retorted sharply.

'I didn't mean to offend you,' Rachel apologised. 'I mean, you've cared for me, given me drinks and dry clothes.'

Sybil grunted. 'No more'n we'd do for any other traveller. Now I'd best get washed and dressed. Then we'll see if you fancy any breakfast.'

At the far end of the van on the stove stood a pan of steaming water, and on the cupboard at the side a wide-topped bowl. Sybil moved towards it pausing to draw brightly coloured curtains across which divided the van into two sections.

Rachel sank back against soft pillows, eager to study in detail the interior of the caravan. Everything was bright and cheerful and spotlessly clean. She was surprised at its roominess with locker seats and cupboards, side windows as well as the one at the back above her bed. She sat up and drew back the chintzy curtains. Being tall she had to keep her head lowered where the bow top curved. When she moved too quickly she experienced a dizzy feeling, probably because she was weak. She wasn't sure how long she'd been here but felt sick when she realised the anxiety her absence must have caused her family. She hoped they hadn't made themselves ill with worry or that her father might have got a soaking if he'd gone out looking for her – but that was unlikely. They were only concerned for Belinda and Adam, and their future. Once word got out of what she'd done in the

131

church it was unlikely anyone in Kingsmere or Wickham would want to set eyes on Rachel Hunter ever again. They'd know it was her because the last person she had spoken to in the church was Nessie Mead. Somehow Rachel knew that Nessie wouldn't deliberately tell on her, but being the kind person she was would want to help trace Rachel. The last place in the world anyone would look would be among a group of gypsies and Rachel smiled with satisfaction. She felt so much better and at home, and fervently hoped these good people would allow her to remain with them.

'But you'm a gorgio, Missie,' Sybil said when Rachel voiced her thoughts to the older woman later.

'Whatever's that?' Rachel asked with indignation. 'I'm sure whatever it is I'm not.'

Sybil threw back her round head and laughed. ''Course you'm a gorgio – you b'aint a Romany, that's certain.'

Rachel felt ridiculous and hung her head while Sybil continued to chuckle as she scrambled eggs in an iron pan over the stove.

'I wish I was a gypsy,' she said softly.

Sybil spun round. 'A young woman like you?' she said in disbelief. 'What would you know about the way we live compared with your easy life? Not that I'd change, mind you, oh no! Freedom's what us folks like.'

'And that's what I want to be, Sybil. Free. Free to smell the fresh air and do what I want to do.'

'And what might that be, may I be bold enough to ask, Missie?'

'Live near the sea with the wind and spray on my cheeks.' Then Rachel fell silent. Was that really what she wanted? Wasn't it a cosy cottage to share with Adam Taylor? But he'd deceived her, she recalled. Now she didn't feel she could trust any man. During the time she'd lain ill in this waggon, in moments of waking she'd had time to think, to relive the events of the past – was it days, weeks, months?'

'How long have I been with you, Sybil?' she asked.

'No more'n about five days, but who's counting?' Sybil put two warmed plates on the table and dished up the eggs. 'Now you get this down you and you'll feel stronger, Missie.' She broke chunks of bread from a large homemade loaf. 'Here, eat this, the dear God's grain which he provides, and may He set you up well and strong again to return to your folks.'

At first the bread tasted strange and was rough to Rachel's throat but she found the eggs appetising and was soon enjoying the bread too. She felt confused in her mind. Sybil talked of God which brought a guilty flush to Rachel's cheeks. She would be punished for what she'd done to God's house. There could be no escape and she shivered with fear.

'You cold?' Sybil asked bluntly.

Rachel shook her head. 'No. Someone walked over my grave, I expect.'

'Not for a long time yet, me dearie. What's ailing you, Rachel?' Sybil leaned across the small table and peered into her eyes.

'I . . . I've committed a terrible sin. You mentioned God and his goodness but He'll have me punished for what I did.' Rachel's voice cracked. She seldom cried but suddenly couldn't help herself and wept uncontrollably.

''Tis 'cos you'm weak. There, there, child – don't distress yourself. Whatever's ailing you can't be that bad. You didn't kill anyone, I'm sure of that. We'll talk about it when you'm stronger.'

'No, I must tell you now. D'you believe in God? I thought gypsies didn't. I thought you were a law unto yourselves.'

'We'm believers, same as other folks, Rachel,' Sybil said solemnly. 'Not all of us, you understand, but this family does and we've got a good spiritual leader who teaches our children and keeps us on the straight and narrer. He came to see you when you was in a terrible fever. He said a prayer and that seemed to quieten you down. Whatever's wrong, Missie, I'm sure Lemuel can help you overcome it.'

'I . . . I went wild, Sybil. My mother always said I had a wild streak, not a bit like my twin sister.'

'Now don't you go upsetting yourself again. There's plenty of time to tell us if you wants to.' Sybil wiped her mouth on the corner of her apron. 'We'm moving on today or tomorrow.'

Rachel felt the blood drain from her face.

'You're planning to leave me behind then?' she asked anxiously.

'In your state? Never! But if you was wanting to go home we could find a carter or someone to take you. Where d'you live, Missie?'

'Um . . . I'd rather not say, Sybil. And I meant what I said about wanting to stay with you. I'll work to earn my keep – do whatever you say, honestly. Just please don't leave me behind.'

'Best tell me honestly, young woman, what trouble you're in? Is it that you'm in the family way?'

'Good gracious, no!' A warm flush crept into Rachel's cheeks. She finished her breakfast and then faced Sybil dry-eyed as she calmly gave a brief outline of her story. Sybil was intrigued and leant her fat arms on the table as she listened without interrupting.

'So you see, I simply can't return home. I . . . I don't know whether they'd send me to prison for what I did, but my parents and Belinda must feel so ashamed of me.'

133

'There's such a thing as forgiveness, Rachel. Don't you think that by now your folks are beside themselves with worry? They'd be that pleased to see you safe and sound that I reckon they'd forgive you anything.'

'I'd like to believe they'd understand, Sybil, but I'd only hurt them all over again if I went home. And I don't think I could bear to see Adam and Belinda together. I hope they'll be happy, but people might pity me and I've had that all my life. I must go somewhere to find work. I'm quite good at figures so perhaps I could go to the town – by the way, where exactly is this? I've no idea how far I walked that night.'

'A deal too far, Missie, by the state of you when Davy found you. This is Portsdown Hill and we'm on our way to the Isle of Wight.'

'Portsdown Hill,' Rachel echoed. 'Did I really walk that far?' She remained thoughtful for several minutes, pleased that she managed to put so much distance between herself and Kingsmere. 'Please can I come with you?' she begged. She knew it was impolite to invite herself but this was too good an opportunity to miss.

'Oh, don't know about that. We'll have to see what Lemuel says.' Sybil seemed troubled by Rachel's request. She got up from the table and put a large shawl round her shoulders. 'I'm going to feed me horses to I'll leave you to clear and was up the breakfast things. If you feels faint, though, you sit down and rest.'

She put a large-brimmed hat on top of her hair which was now pinned up into a plump bun at the back of her head. The hat wobbled about and Rachel wanted to laugh, then she remembered her sister and wished she was here with her. How could she have felt so angry towards Belinda? They'd always had such a happy childhood to-gether, and their growing up years had been amicable too – until now. They had shared everything, tears and laughter, until Rachel had fallen in love with Adam Taylor. And all the time he had really loved Belinda. It was so cruel.

'This is the washing up bowl, Missie. There's one for your clothes and a different one to wash yourself in. There's a kettle of hot water on the stove. Later on you can come with me to fetch some wood. Always plenty 'o work to be done, living' free like we does.'

Rachel worked with a willingness she had seldom shown at home. The sun was warm as it shone through the open doorway, breathing new life into her as she watched the gypsies going about their daily tasks. One or two of them eyed her suspiciously, some of the men nodded but it was with the children Rachel made friends first. They soon lost their shyness and before long about a dozen were vying for a front line view, so when the washing up was done Rachel sat down on the top step and chatted to them until they were called away.

'They 'as their books to read,' Sybil explained. 'Lemuel makes sure as 'ow each and every one of 'em can read.'

'Don't they go to school?' Rachel asked.

'How can they, dearie, when we'm on the move? If we stay long in one place then the school man comes and makes sure they go. But he can't fault the learning Lemuel's given 'em.'

'They're lucky to have someone like him then.'

'Yes, and you'll like Lemuel – he'll see you at noon.'

Rachel wasn't quite so confident after that. Sybil spoke of him with respect as if he were some kind of elder. Rachel envisaged a tall, severe man who would demand that she return to her own family. It wasn't likely that they would want her tagging along. She wasn't one of them and they didn't mix with gorgios.

But when Sybil took her across the field to a solidly made plain caravan the man she met was nothing like she had imagined. He was dressed similarly to a priest in a small-brimmed black hat. He was of medium height, his back rather bent, but when he lifted his face to look at Rachel his smile was friendly, his grey-blue eyes intelligent and sympathetic. He held out his hand and helped her up the steps, inviting her inside the van.

'Peace be with you, child,' he greeted her and Rachel felt calmed. He invited her to sit down. 'There's no need to look so worried, my dear. I hope you don't find me or my travelling friends frightening?'

'No, I'm very grateful for the kindness which has been shown to me. I don't know what Sybil has told you, but –'

'Sybil has repeated your story as best she could but perhaps it would be better if I were to hear it from your own lips?'

Rachel began hesitantly. Lemuel listened with such patient interest that she soon forgot any fear of being judged harshly, and her outrageous actions seemed less shocking as she sensed his understanding.

When she finished speaking she waited for some comment but he had his yes closed while he pondered her predicament.

He pulled on his goatee beard which was a soft shade of grey with white patches. When he opened his eyes he looked at her kindly.

'I believe you may have more affinity with us Romanies than you realise, Rachel. You have the – the –' He waved his hand in small circular movements until he found the right word. 'The spirit,' he said. 'Few people ever bother to discover who were are – the race we're descended from, the work we strive to do, and they know nothing of the way we live. A young girl like yourself, obviously from a happy home and well provided for, would normally have been scared of being rescued by gypsies. I know you were quite sick as a

135

result of being exposed to the elements overnight but you showed no alarm at finding yourself in strange surroundings when you came out of the fever.'

'I met a group of gypsies once before when I was lost in Bere Forest. They were kind to me then and a young man took me home. I have cause to be grateful to you all. There's no reason to be frightened of you, and I'm really serious about wanting to remain with you – though I'll understand if you don't want me.'

Lemuel surveyed this strange young woman with misgivings.

'If we agree to your accompanying us to the Isle of Wight what then, my dear? Supposing you become homesick? This may seem like some kind of adventure, but you will probably soon tire of our way of life.'

It was Rachel's turn to remain silent. She couldn't deny that she had doubts, but she'd had plenty of time to consider her crime and the penalty she might have to pay. She missed her family, and a reminder of the vexation she had caused her mother made her chin tremble and tears fill her eyes.

'I do love my family,' she told Lemuel solemnly. 'I know what I did was wrong. I felt so betrayed which made me angry and vicious. Now I'm sorry, but I can't expect them to forgive me that easily. I can't go home, Lemuel,' she pleaded. 'I simply can't. If you won't let me stay with you then I must move on by myself.'

'I understand, Rachel. We all have to make up for our own wrongdoing and in time I pray that you'll find a way to redeem yourself.' His voice was soothing yet firm. He stroked his bearded chin thoughtfully as he surveyed her appraisingly. 'Travelling with us cannot appease your guilt. Only when you have said you're sorry to those you have wronged can you expect to feel pardoned, but here in the great outdoors you can begin to make your peace with God. A time of self-examination may be easier among strangers though I fancy you won't feel a stranger for long.' His smile gave her comfort and a measure of hope. 'One thing, however, I must insist upon.'

'I'll do anything – *anything*.' Rachel sat forward eagerly, but Lemuel raised his hand to restrain her.

'Not so fast. Thus committing yourself, my child, without knowing my condition could be dangerous. After all, you know nothing of me and the people here. Trust must be earned, Rachel. Oh, I know you're young and anxious to please and I have few doubts that allowing you to become one of our family will be anything but beneficial to us all, but hasty words and actions may be your downfall – a lesson already forgotten?'

136

Rachel flushed penitently. 'Impetuous,' she said humbly. 'That's what my parents say. How can I show you that I am really sorry? And what is your condition, please?'

'You may not like it,' he warned. 'Put yourself in your parents' shoes, Rachel. You cannot have the remotest notion of the desperation they've been feeling over the past week. Only a mother can know such anguish, so you must send word to them that you're all right.'

'But I can't do *that*!' she shrieked. 'They'll be able to trace me and I shall be forced to go home.'

Lemuel said nothing. Rachel was forced to submit to his impervious stare even though the devil inside her rebelled angrily. He wasn't offering her forgiveness, no one ever would, least of all her parents. How could she return home? This strange man seemed to be mesmerising her with a power even she was unable to break, and after the heat of revolt came tranquility. She sat with her head lowered.

'A picture postcard would suffice, my dear.' Lemuel broke the silence in a gentle but firm voice. 'Posted from the mainland with no suggestion of where we're heading. The first step towards reconciliation will have been made. Try to imagine their relief that you're safe.' He leaned forward and took both her hands in his with a force which gave her renewed strength. 'It will spark off many questions, I suspect, but at least they'll know you're alive and well. The first step across a precarious bridge for you too, Rachel, as you pen those precious words "I'm sorry".'

'Can I think about it?' she asked in a small voice. 'I . . . don't want to say I'll do it and then let you down. I'd like to travel with you as far as the ferry –'

'Perhaps you're thinking that you'd like to go home, after all?'

'Oh no!' She shook her head vehemently. 'I know I can't do that. I loved Adam dearly and found it hard to believe that he could treat me so badly. I never want to see him again – least of all married to my twin sister.'

'The passage of time will make the burden easier to bear, my dear Rachel. By all means travel with us to the ferry, but I meant what I said. My conscience wouldn't be clear if I allowed you to continue with us without word to your parents. If you decide to go on alone then I shall have to examine my conscience even further and may be obliged to inform the authorities.' Lemuel stood up, towering above her, a veritable gentle giant. 'Go back to Sybil and make yourself useful. She's not finding life too easy these days as her rheumatism gets worse. She had a daughter once.' Rachel looked up quickly, her expression curious. 'No – Sybil will tell you herself in her own good time.' Lemuel took Rachel's arm and guided her through the doorway to the steps. 'Think very carefully about what you should do.'

137

Rachel had plenty of time to think while she washed pots and scrubbed cupboards. She was kept busy all the time as they prepared their vans to move on, and all the rubbish collected was built up to make a huge bonfire which was lit on their last evening on Portsdown Hill. It made a spectacular sight, and Rachel felt she had been accepted as one of them as she joined the group singing songs while the men played violins and squeeze boxes, before Lemuel conducted evening prayers asking for safe passage to the Isle of Wight.

They were up at dawn next morning to complete packing crockery and utensils in storage boxes for safety. Food was placed in the built-in cupboards underneath the rear of each van. Rachel learned these were called pan-boxes and served as larder and kitchen cupboards. She was amazed at the orderliness with which the gypsies both lived and organised the travelling procession. The younger couples with children headed the convoy, each van closely followed by grand-parents and older relatives' waggons. Lemuel travelled fifth in line, followed by Sybil and Rachel, with one or two hawkers' waggons bringing up the rear.

Rachel quickly forgot the misgivings she'd had about leaving this part of the world behind. It was like embarking on a brand new adventure. Even the horses seemed to sense the excitement as they trotted along, manes flowing and shiny horse brasses jingling. By mid-day they had travelled the five miles to Portsea. Here they rested on a piece of wasteland and had a meal of bread with cold ham before the first few vans moved towards the ferry crossing at the south-western tip of Portsea Island. Sybil went with Rachel to a nearby shop and Post Office where provisions were bought and Rachel purchased a postcard and stamp.

'Take your time now, child, and think what you'd like to say,' Sybil said. 'I ought to persuade you to leave us and go home but I knows you won't do that. Maybe 'tis your destiny to come awhile with us.'

'Can you look into the future, Sybil?' Rachel asked. 'Can't you read my palm or something and tell me truly what's going to become of me?'

'We all makes our own destiny, Missie. You've a lot to learn yet. For instance, never knowingly harm other folks or cause distress – now you just make amends with your folks and give 'em some peace o'mind.'

Rachel went to sit on a low wall and rested the postcard on the pillar at the end. She wrote her parents' name and address in the space provided then in her neat handwriting she began: 'Dear Mum and Dad'. She sighed and changed that to 'Dearest Mum, Dad and Belinda'. After several minutes of composing and recomposing

138

sentences in her head she was still sucking the end of her pencil. What could she say? How could she put into words both love and hate? How could she expect them to understand? Her message must be simple. She dared not say where they were heading or that she was living with gypsies. That in itself would probably cause one or both her parents to be ill. In an almost childlike expression of her thoughts she told them what she was feeling.

'I love you all so much and I am full of remorse for the things I have done and the pain I have caused you. It is better that I stay away for a while, but do not worry about me as I am staying with some very dear people.'

She wanted to tell them how kind the gypsies had been to her in looking after her when she was ill, but that might add to her parents' concern so she simply signed her name and quickly dropped the card into the post box.

Sybil gave her a hug as they walked down the road.

'You'll feel better now, dearie. You've done your duty and they'll known you'm safe. Even if they set about trying to trace you, 'tain't likely they'll look among us travelling folk.'

Rachel smiled to herself. If she happened to meet anyone she knew from Wickham they wouldn't recognise her wearing a brightly coloured woollen scarf round her shoulders and another silk one over her hair. It hadn't taken her long to realise that she would be more easily accepted by her newfound friends if she made the effort to dress the same as the other women, and Sybil had taken her under her wing in this respect. There hadn't been open hostility but one or two of the younger women had eyed her with great suspicion especially when the young men talked pleasantly to her.

Rachel had given little thought to the methods of transport available to the gypsies or any other travellers come to that in order to reach Ryde on the Isle of Wight. As they waited patiently on the jetty they watched Lemuel's van being pulled on to one of the barges by his faithful piebald mare, called Goldie on account of the golden streaks down her nose. Then Sybil's van was taken aboard, though her horse, Astra, shied at the shouting and noise as cars revved up to take their place alongside. When every space on the two barges was occupied the steamer gave the signal for the ropes to be cast off and they gently moved out into deeper water.

'Have you been to the Isle of Wight before?' Rachel asked Sybil.

'Gracious me, yes,' she answered with a gruff laugh. 'Fair held every spring and most travelling folk gets there if they can. 'Sides, Lemuel's chest ain't usually too good after winter so the sea air does 'im good. Meets up with all our old friends, we does – won't be much chance of anyone spotting you now, Missie.'

139

Rachel tried not to show her apprehension as the water slapped against the sides of the barges and she was grateful that the crossing was relatively calm and took little more than half an hour. The horses could smell land and needed no encouragement to get up the ramp and on to the country road away from the sea. They travelled south and soon caught up with those who had already reached a large field lying in a hollow between rolling downland hills, and by early evening the last of the brush waggons joined them. They made camp here where Lemuel suggested they remain for several days.

Rachel's first task was to go in search of sticks and suitable firewood with some of the older children. At least she felt free of the past, knowing that no one could come after her with the sea separating her from her family. After the evening meal the horses were put out to grass and most of the older members of the group retired early but Rachel wanted to explore.

'You won't mind if I have a look from the top of the hill, will you, Sybil?' she asked.

'As long as you wrap up warmly against the evening chill. You can hardly get lost on this island but don't stay out too long.'

Rachel put on her warm woollen coat and wrapped her brightly coloured shawl round her shoulders. She was hurrying across the grassy hill when a young woman called after her.

'Wait for me, Rachel. I'll come with you.'

Rachel turned to wait for Ena, a slim girl of about seventeen who was slightly shorter than herself. Her sallow skin and high cheekbones were complemented by a cascade of rich raven black hair, but there was something about the twist to her full red lips which made Rachel suspicious of her. Rachel had watched the girl from the window by her bed on several occasions darting to and fro between the waggons and even sitting cross-legged beneath the one she lived in with her parents and several children. They had never exchanged any conversation before but Rachel was often aware of being watched by Ena.

'Where are you going?' the girl asked.

'Just to look at the view. I wondered if we might be able to see the sea from here.'

'Haven't you seen enough of the sea for one day?'

'Don't you just love it? The salty smell, the sound of the waves, the vast expanse of it? It fascinates me.'

Ena grunted, unmoved by Rachel's enthusiasm. 'Sea's just something that stops folk from going places, as I see it,' she said. 'Where d' you come from, anyhow? Ain't you never seen the sea before?'

'Yes, once or twice, but I lived in the countryside and didn't visit the seaside very often.'

'Why did you run away from home then? Reckon you had it nice and comfortable. Did you do something real bad?'

Now Rachel understood why she was viewed with curiosity. Sybil had kept her secret which made the others sceptical about her motives.

'In a way,' she replied hesitantly. 'I didn't hurt anyone. I . . . I just wanted to get away by myself for a while. I got soaked to the skin and caught a chill so I'm grateful to Sybil for taking me in.'

'T'was Davey what found you.'

'Yes, I know – well, it was his dog actually.'

'You sure you wasn't trying to steal his dog?'

'No, of course not! Do I look like someone who'd steal a dog?' Rachel raised her voice indignantly.

'Thieves don't look any different from other folks, Rachel. But I reckons you must be all right or you'd have taken whatever you wanted and been gone by now.'

'Time, Ena. What's what I need, time.'

'Time!' the younger girl repeated. 'Time don't cost nowt.'

'The best things in life are free. There,' Rachel said reaching the top of the hill and turning round and round to view the landscape. 'This is free – the air, the wind, the sky, the sea. It belongs to us all and we can take what we need of it. Love is free too, but sometimes there's a price to pay for that.'

'You lost someone maybe. Your ma or pa?'

'In a way, yes. I thought I would have been married by now. We loved one another so much. I still can't believe my fiancé could change his mind at the last minute like he did. I'll never understand it.'

'You going to have a baby then? Is that why you can't go home?'

'Good heavens, no! While Adam was away at the war his father died. We got engaged and planned to get married when he came home for good. He was buying a cottage for us to live in . . .' Rachel's voice trailed away. She sat down on the grass and plucked at a daisy. She had wept all the tears she could; now it was comforting to talk with a girl of similar age. 'Then he suddenly announced that it was never me he loved but my twin sister.'

'You poor thing.' Ena's voice was full of genuine sympathy. 'Gosh, you must hate 'im and your sister.'

'Sometimes I feel that I do and at others I know I can never hate them. I just hope he's good to Belinda. Now you can see why I can't return home.'

'We-ell, I reckons that gives you good enough reason for staying with Sybil.'

141

Rachel got to her feet and gazed seaward. 'She's been very kind. I don't know what I'd have done if Davey and his dog hadn't found me.'

'Jes s'long as you ain't got designs on 'im, that's all. 'Cos I'm warning you, no gorgio's goin' to take one of our men!'

Rachel began to understand why she was viewed with such suspicion.

'Is Davey a special friend of yours then?'

Even in the growing twilight Rachel could see Ena's dark eyes glinting. 'Very special,' she said. 'We've got a secret as well.' She suddenly darted up to Rachel's side and, standing on tiptoe, reached up to whisper: 'I'm in the family way. No one but us knows yet.'

'Shouldn't you tell your mother, Ena?'

'Nah. She'll find out soon enough.'

'Are you planning to get married?'

'Gypsies don't always. Davey's saving up to get us our own waggon though. Trouble is, our families don't get on. When me ma finds out about me there'll be trouble. Reckons I'll tell her when we get to the Fair. Plenty of drinking then and the men'll be ready for a showdown.'

'But that's awful! Can't Lemuel stop them?'

'They'll fight it out away from the waggons. Lemuel's been teaching us about God and stuff, but our families don't go along with all that. They jest pretends they do to please 'im. Mind you, if we could get married I'd like it to be in a church with lots of flowers.'

'If that's what you want then you must work to get it. I'm quite good at sewing. I'll help you make a pretty dress. But first I think you should confide in Sybil or Lemuel. They could talk to your parents and Davey's. Get it sorted out sensibly by talking it over.'

'Gypsies only knows one way of sorting out disputes and that's with their fists.'

'Then perhaps we could help to change their minds. I could go with you when you talk to your mother.'

Ena laughed this to scorn. 'They ain't got a very high opinion of you as 'tis. Thinks you're after something. You must learn not to poke your nose in where it ain't wanted.'

'I'm only trying to help, and you must prepare for the baby, Ena.'

'Plenty of time for that. Now you go on back to Sybil and I'm going to wait until Davey comes with our supper.'

'Supper?'

'He's gone after rabbits. We'll have a canoodle in the woods first then take the rabbits back, skin 'em and cook 'em. Don't you tell on me, mind. You 'aven't seed me at all.'

Ena picked up her skirt and ran down the other side of the hill where she disappeared into a thicket of trees.

Rachel took a long last look at the fading view before she walked slowly back to camp. Now she knew that the gypsies thought she was on the scrounge and must be careful not to take anything for granted. She felt some pity for Lemuel, knowing that he was doing his best to educate these folk yet all the time they were only pretending to believe what he said. He couldn't be a real Romany, Rachel thought. He might have been accepted by them for helping them with their finances and teaching the children to read but she didn't believe he really belonged among them any more than she did. Maybe he had a skeleton in the cupboard too! Perhaps he had not always been so saintly. Was there something in his past which made him particularly understanding when others did wrong? She'd probably never know, and it didn't really matter as she felt she could trust him implicitly. He was kind and wise, a fatherly figure to them all but one Rachel valued as a friend.

Chapter Ten

During the next few weeks they travelled round the island selling clothes pegs, but as soon as the wild daffodils burst into bloom Rachel and the other girls spent each morning gathering them from the woods. Then with baskets laden with neatly tied bunches, they went from village to village knocking on doors. Rachel was amazed at how quickly the pennies earned turned into pounds, and any embarrassment she felt at hawking soon disappeared. She greeted householders with a nice smile and some looked surprised at how well-spoken she was.

'Tain't fair,' Ena complained. 'They buys from you much quicker 'an from me.'

'Well, you could try being pleasant,' Rachel said. 'I know you get a lot of back-ache, Ena, but people aren't likely to look upon you favourably when you've nearly always got a scowl on your face. You don't bother to wash your face let alone your hair. Tidy yourself up and be nice to people if you want them to buy your wares.'

'Hmph! S'pose you thinks yourself a cut above the rest of us? Jest 'cos you'm tall and slim and pretty – and I've got a big belly?'

'There's no need to be crude. Have you told your mother yet?'

Ena said nothing for several seconds and Rachel guessed that her mother was none too pleased with the situation which was why Ena was so bad-tempered.

'She guessed,' Ena said dismally. 'Right telling off I got an' all, but she ain't told me dad yet.'

'What about Davey's parents?'

'He's a man. Don't make no difference to 'is people. He can deny 'tis his if he wants.'

'But he wouldn't do that, surely? I thought you really cared for each other.'

'I fancy he's gone off the idea of marriage or setting up 'ome together!'

'Perhaps he thinks you're a bit too young. He is quite a bit older than you, Ena.'

'Yep. But he said that didn't matter. He liked me 'cos I was a young bit 'o stuff and I loved 'im all the more 'cos he was growed up, not soppy like the other boys. He treated me growed up as well.'

'I'm sure everything will be all right. Once your back doesn't ache so much and you don't feel so rotten first thing in the morning, he'll begin to look forward to the baby coming.'

'He still takes all he can get,' Ena stated crossly. 'Never mind how sick I feel or how much me back's breaking he's making the most of a good thing.'

'How old is Davey?'

'Jest turned thirty.'

'How long have you been going together?'

Ena sighed. 'Reckon I've always chased after 'im, since I were a nipper. 'Cos our families were always feudin' it seemed to make 'im more attractive. When he went away to war I wrote to 'im and when he came back – cor, there was no waiting for 'im. Never mind about the risks, never mind about not being married. "I'll make you mine right now," says he.' Ena laughed cynically. 'Great it were. Davey had money in 'is pocket and we had a good time without thinking about the consequences. Ma says I must confess all to Lemuel, but what good'll that do? Damage is done. Too late to have second thoughts, but I reckon Davey is.'

'Why don't you talk to him, Ena?' Rachel suggested. 'Tell him you want your baby to be born in wedlock.'

'He don't seem to want to talk about it.'

'Maybe he's worried about finding a van.'

'Don't think he's bothering about that either. No . . .' She looked directly at Rachel with anger flashing in her dark eyes. 'If you want the truth, Rachel, he's got his sights set on you. I wish to God you'd never joined us. Why don't you go back to your own kind.'

Ena began to weep, quite noisily at first, until her cheeks were streaked with grubby finger marks as she hastily dried the tears away. Rachel felt sorry for her.

'Davey means nothing to me, Ena,' she said softly. 'I was so grateful to him for finding me and taking pity on me. Please don't cry.' She placed her arms round the younger girl and took her basket from her. 'You shouldn't be doing this kind of work now. The baskets are too heavy in your condition.'

'And what would you know about my condition?' Ena snapped. 'Unless you've been in the same boat – and I wouldn't put that past you. How do we know you 'aven't had a baby and been turned out?'

145

'I swear to you I haven't,' Rachel said. 'And I swear to you I don't want Davey. He doesn't even like me – he thought I wanted his dog, remember?'

'He's changed his mind about that. Thinks you're posh. Likes the way you talks and dresses. Wants me to have nice clothes but how can I in this state?'

'I'll help you, Ena. We'll sew a pretty summer dress which will help to cover up – well, you know.'

'Say it, go on, my bulge. I never thought Davey would change jest 'cos I got big. He likes doin' it but he don't like the result. Reckons *I* should have been more careful, if you please. Goddammit, he never gave me time to get prepared! But he ain't goin' to get away with it. My brothers'll sort 'im out.'

'Now, don't be hasty, Ena. Let's get you prettied up and then see who he prefers.'

Rachel did all she could to help. As the weather grew warm with bright spring sunshine she insisted that Ena sat on the verge in the shade while she herself went from cottage to cottage. They spent their evenings sewing until Ena had a light floral dress to wear but although it hung loose from the shoulders nothing could hide her expanding figure.

The group travelled on to meet up with other gypsies where the Spring Fair was to be held. They set up camp and in the cool of the evening Rachel went to a nearby house to ask if she might fill her carrier with water. At the gate Davey caught up with her.

'Here, let me. I need some too so I'll ask if they'll fill both containers.'

'We-ell, thanks, Davey, but I don't mind asking.'

He was tall. He smiled down at her with the kind of smile which instantly put her on her guard.

'You've got the hang of the way we live pretty good, haven't you?'

'I expect when the winter comes I shall wish I was back home,' she replied. 'But I am grateful to Sybil for letting me stay awhile with her. I've enjoyed helping Ena too. She looks nice in her new dress, don't you think?'

Davey didn't answer immediately so Rachel looked up at him expectantly. She noticed that his sandy hair was recently washed and combed and his checkered shirt was freshly laundered.

'I don't think about anything else but you, Rachel. When we've got the water will you come down to the woods with me?'

She felt her cheeks burning, not from embarrassment but from anger. She snatched at her water carrier but Davey held on tightly.

'Let go! Let – it – go!' Rachel shouted. 'How dare you suggest such a thing, Davey?' They tussled for several minutes but he was the stronger so Rachel turned on her heels and ran back to the caravan.

'Didn't you get the water then?' Sybil asked.

'Davey's getting it. I . . . I'm going to have to move on or something,' she said despondently.

'Why? What's up?'

'It's Davey. He's got Ena in trouble and now he's after me.'

'I heard she was expecting. She's too young for Davey really but she asked for it. He's always been a bit of a lad and since he went in the Army he's worse. Thought there was trouble brewing between the families but Lemuel won't have none of it, you mark my words. Don't you take no notice of Davey.'

Rachel wished it was that simple but every time she left the caravan he was hovering in the vicinity. That night he knocked on the van door well after dark. Rachel saw him through the window.

'Go away, it's late and we're in bed,' she called.

'I've brought a rabbit for Sybil.'

She was standing before the mirror brushing her hair. She opened the top half of the door and leaned out.

'Now look here, young Davey, don't let me see you hanging round here again. Rachel don't want anything to do with you. You've got responsibilities to Ena. You put her in the family way – now go and look after her. If I'm not much mistaken she's going to have twins.'

'Twins?' he echoed.

'Your twins – not surprising really since your grandparents had two sets and your own parents got twin girls. You'll have a lot of mouths to feed so you'll do well to work a bit harder instead of chasing pretty faces. And I'm telling you, Davey Smith, we ain't going to stand any nonsense this year at the Fair. Lemuel's going to send your family and the Wellses back to the mainland if either one of you gets making trouble.'

'T'aint no business of your'n or Lemuel's what feuding we gets up to. I only wanted to thank Rachel for helping Ena with her work and making the dress.'

Sybil half turned. 'She's heard – and since when has us folks needed thanks for what we do to help one another? 'Tis my guess your family don't know about Ena's condition so I reckons you best get home and tell 'em smartish – before I do.' With that she slammed the door shut and Davey was left alone with his rabbits tied to a pole balanced on his shoulder. They heard his feet shuffling away and when Sybil had gone to bed Rachel peeped out of the window by her bunk.

There was a high, bright moon which showed clearly the outline of the different types of caravan. The horses were all tethered either to a

147

tree or pegged to the ground near to the owners vans. An owl swooped low close by, evidently picking up a mouse or vole before flying off to its nest in the woods. Everything seemed eerily quiet and then Rachel spied figures moving about stealthily across the grass. As her sight became accustomed to the night gloom she could see Davey being marched along by his father, a short stocky man.

The caravan belonging to Ena's family was across the field and when Davey and his father reached it they stood outside, shouting and banging on the windows. Rachel was too far away to hear what was going on but suddenly the door of the van opened and Ena was pushed out and down the steps. Rachel forget about her head and banged it noisily on the roof as she tried to sit up to see what was happening.

'What you doing?' Sybil called from the lower berth.

'Sorry, Sybil, but I was looking out of the window. It looks like trouble between the Smiths and the Wellses.'

'There's always trouble between them two lots. Get off to sleep now and don't worry your head about them.'

'But I think Ena might be hurt. It looked as if they threw her out and down the steps. Davey's bending over her, best I can see. Maybe she's hurt. Should I go and see?'

'We-ell, maybe – but Lemuel usually sorts them out. Don't think he ought to be woken up though. 'Tis late enough.'

'I'm not afraid,' Rachel said. 'I should at least help Ena.'

'You might get a beating yourself – and you'm a gorgio, I daresay you aren't used to such goings on.'

'Poor Ena, she was so unhappy about Davey not wanting her as well as about the baby. Do you really think she's having twins?'

'Sure of it. And we don't want anything to happen to the babies, do we?'

Although Sybil didn't actually say so, Rachel felt certain she wanted her to go investigate so she got up and wrapped her shawl round her before unlocking the door and creeping out. She thought an element of surprise was the best approach so skirted the field, keeping close to the vans, but just as she reached the Wells' van another figure emerged from between two latecomers' vans. Rachel had watched them hitching their waggons earlier just as the sun was going down but didn't know who they were.

'What's all this noise?' the young man asked in the voice of authority. He was tall and of medium build, and all Rachel would distinguish in the darkness was that he had a mop of dark hair on his head and round his chin.

'What's it to do with you?' Davey's father snapped.

'Everything. We've had a long, tiring journey and we need to get some rest. Might have known it would be you two families, you're always arguing about something. We aren't going to put up with fighting any more so what's your problem?'

'Oh, hark at you, Kas Dolan, and who d'you think you are?' Davey scoffed.

Rachel clutched at the front of her nightgown and drew back into the shadow of the nearest van. Kas? Had she heard aright? Kas Dolan – was it possible that it was her gypsy boy from all those years ago? If it was it was a miracle seeing that Adam had lost the lucky stone he'd given her.

'We want some peace and we mean to get it,' Kas said shortly. 'What are you quarrelling about this time?'

A head appeared through the top half of the Wells' van door. 'Kas? Is that your voice I heard?' The door opened fully and a figure stood silhouetted in the half light. 'S'pose you might have guessed. Davey's got our Ena in the family way,' said Mr Wells.

'Is that all? Then the sooner they marry the better,' Kas said. 'But can't it wait 'till morning and we'll hold proper court with Lemuel?'

'Best settle it now with our fists,' Ena's father said gruffly. 'Davey Smith's no good and he's too old for our Ena?'

'Shouldn't Ena and Davey decide that?' Rachel's voice sounded cool and cultured in the evening air. All heads turned in her direction.

'And who the hell are you?' Kas said impatiently.

'Rachel – Rachel Hunter. Ena is expecting twins. I came to see if she's hurt. You had no right to throw her down the steps like that,' she added to Mr Wells.

Ena slowly uncurled herself and sat looking up at everyone. 'I'm all right,' she said in a small voice.

'Twins?' Kas echoed, then he laughed. 'As if there aren't enough of you lot already. You'd best get up and get back to bed. That goes for the rest of you. When I see Lemuel tomorrow morning I'll tell him there'll be a wedding to prepare for.'

Rachel was amazed to see them move quietly away to their own vans. Kas turned to face her.

'Why do I seem to think I know the name Rachel Hunter? Let me look at you. Come closer.'

'I doubt that you'd remember me,' she said softly. 'I was only a schoolgirl when we met several years ago. I was lost in Bere Forest. You walked me home and gave me a lucky stone.

With a firm hand on her shoulder Kas turned her into the moonlight. 'Mm . . . yes, now I recall. Yes, Rachel Hunter,' he said slowly and thoughtfully, 'the Strawberry Girl.'

Rachel felt herself blushing furiously and was grateful that it was semi-dark. She buried her face in her shawl.

'Fancy you remembering, though I never forgot you,' she said.

'But you're not a Romany or even a traveller. Come from that pretty little cottage somewhere – I know, in Kingsmere wasn't it? What brings you here to the island?'

Rachel sighed. 'It's a long story,' she said. 'Too long at this time of night, and you said you wanted peace and quiet.'

'You mean you're saying with the group? You've joined the Romanies?' His voice was filled with incredulity.

'I'm staying with Sybil – for the present anyway. I . . . I had to get away for a while, but like I said, that's a long story.'

Kas turned Rachel round and propelled her through the caravans away from the camp to the edge of a field beneath some trees.

'Suddenly I'm not tired any more. I want to hear this intriguing story. A gorgio living with the travellers. It isn't the first time, but not one of your sort. This story's got to be good.'

Rachel felt that he was mocking her. 'No, there's nothing good about it, Kas, and if you think it's amusing then I won't bother telling you.'

'A woman with spirit, I like that. You should fit in well with our sort. I'm sorry if you thought I was laughing at you, but you must admit a young woman from your type of background coming to rough it with travellers does sound highly unlikely.' They walked to the far end of the field where several horses were tethered. Kas patted each one in turn and then led the way up the wooden steps to his van. 'Come in for a few minutes. Night time is a good time for talking.'

Rachel shrugged and gabbled a few meaningless words, hesitant lest someone else might be in the van.

'No, Strawberry Girl, I live and travel alone, mostly. Since the war that is. Merle died in the 'flu epidemic while I was still away at the war and Josh died long before that.' He jerked his head towards the door. 'Come on, I won't bite. I can hardly believe it's you. The strawberry mark will prove it though.'

'No, it won't,' she replied. 'Merle was right about that, it faded – though sometimes a slight red patch shows. Your lucky stone helped I daresay.'

At that Kasan laughed. 'Come on, the kettle's boiling its head off. I make a nice cup of cocoa. Sybil won't even miss you.'

'But it's getting late.'

'I'm not that tired really. Had a long wait to get across on the ferry which I find irksome. Didn't feel I could handle a fight at this time of night. Any idea what it's really all about?'

150

Rachel followed him up the steps and into the van. It wasn't as colourful as some of the others but was tastefully decorated and tidy. He seemed less of a gypsy now than she remembered. Maybe going away to war had changed his lifestyle. She watched him mixing cocoa and milk in some dainty china cups before he added boiling water. She told him what she knew of Davey and Ena.

'They were all suspicious of me to begin with,' she said, gradually finding it easier to talk to Kas. 'I've tried to earn their trust and my keep, but now Ena says Davey prefers me to her.'

'And how do you feel – about Davey, I mean?'

Rachel looked at Kas fearlessly. If she'd had even the slightest inclination toward Davey, which she hadn't, she knew that Kas's arrival would have changed her mind. By the light of the lamp she realised how many years had passed since their meeting in the woods. It must be all of eight and they had both matured. Rachel was no longer a child but a young woman and Kas must be well into his twenties, she thought. His hair was cut much shorter than she remembered and his thick growth of beard made him look older, but his dark brown eyes still reflected the gentle warmth which had made her trust him when he walked her home.

'I don't have any feelings towards Davey,' she said. 'That's what my story is all about, Kas. Heartbreak, disillusionment . . .' She passed a hand across her brow as painful memories returned. 'Maybe the war had something to do with it, maybe it was misguided pity because of my birthmark – it was all so ugly.'

'I'm sorry, Rachel. I didn't realise. I shouldn't have asked – some other time. Drink your cocoa. We'll talk another time.'

She put her hands round the small cup. The pretty design on the china reminded her of home. Phoebe, Wally and Belinda . . . Now that they had received her card they probably seldom gave a thought to her or what she was doing. An ache crept up from the pit of her stomach, an ache of homesickness, and for a brief moment she felt the urge to escape, back to the safety of Calder Cottage and the people she knew and loved in Kingsmere.

'I was going to be married,' she began eventually.

Kas didn't press her to continue or try to stop her. He listened with the utmost patience until she finished. Then he remained silent as if there was nothing to say, no condemnation, no words of sympathy either.

'Thank you for telling me, Rachel,' he said softly. 'That is some story – and I feel it isn't over yet. This is just waiting time. Sooner or later you'll want to go back where you belong.'

'I don't think so, Kas. I'm happy here with Sybil and the others. Lemuel has been understanding in allowing me to accompany them but on the condition that I sent a card to my parents, which I did. They have no idea where I am, though, and it's best that way. It sounds silly but there's something of the gypsy in me, I believe, because I feel part of the group.'

Kas smiled warmly. 'I know exactly what you mean. I'm not a true Romany, neither is Lemuel, but we've been cared for by these good people and accepted. That makes them very special. They don't ask questions or make demands, neither do they condemn, but offer help and kindness – which is a good deal more than so-called Christian folk.'

'I'm afraid I was brought up to believe that gypsies were evil rogues but I soon found out that wasn't true.'

Kas laughed heartily. 'A little harmless poaching perhaps when we're hungry but most of us want to earn an honest living.'

'How was it for you in the Army?' Rachel asked. 'You shouldn't have given me your lucky stone.'

'It wasn't so lucky, was it. It brought you unhappiness.'

'Only after Adam had lost it.'

'We'll find another one. There's plenty on the beaches here. That's where I found the first one.' He sighed. 'War opened my eyes to lots of things. Living in the trenches wasn't as hard for me as many of the other chaps. Perhaps I was better equipped to look after myself than them. I felt as afraid as any soldier but I knew better than to show it. Yes, Rachel, I have to admit that on the whole, stone, or no stone, I was luckier than the poor blokes who got 'blighties'. At least I came back.'

'Was it awful?'

'War is needless, terrifying and cruel. I wish I could say it makes better people out of us, but I doubt it. When it comes down to it we all have to look after ourselves. No one owes us anything, Rachel. But we owe it to our own self-respect to be trustworthy and care for our fellow men.' He placed his cup on the side and took Rachel's from her. 'I hope we'll get to know one another much better while we're here. Now I'd better see you back to your van.'

The moon was up, lighting their way across the open field. 'I nearly didn't come,' Kas said. 'I mostly travel around on my own these days, never sure whether or not I'd like to get a decent job and live in a house. This is a waiting time for me too, Strawberry Girl, while I try to forget the war and decide what I want to do with my future. They put me in the cookhouse in the Army so I've even toyed with the idea of going abroad, to Australia or New Zealand, and getting hotel work.'

'My parents often said how difficult it was for men to adapt to civilian life again – maybe that's what changed Adam, I don't know. It was all so sudden, so unbelievable.'

'Would you still have him if he came after you?'

'He won't ever want me now that he's got Belinda. I can't honestly say that I don't still have some feelings for him, but I could never trust him after what he did. I don't know why I'm so different from Belinda either. She would never have behaved the way I did, and after being brought up in such a loving, respectable home why do I have this urge to be free of it all?'

'Perhaps you're just the outdoor type. At this time of year that's what I like about this life – and the horses, of course. In France, and I'm told Australia, there are thousands of wild horses.'

'I like horses, too, but I don't suppose I shall ever have one of my own.'

'I'll loan you one of mine – to ride, that is. I may buy another at the Fair. There's usually a bit of dealing goes on.' He looked up at the night sky. 'It looks as if we're in for some really good weather.' He put out his hand and touched Rachel's arm lightly. 'Goodnight, Strawberry Girl.'

'Please,' she said shyly, 'would you mind not calling me that? If people hear you call me that they'll copy and want to know why – and my mark has quite gone so it isn't really true any more.'

'I'm glad for your sake that the mark faded. It wasn't that bad – made you special, didn't it?'

''Specially bad, I expect,' she said with a light-hearted laugh. 'That's all in the past and I'm into a new life now. I never ever expected to see you again so I think I was meant to run away.'

'But you would go home if you felt you wanted to?'

'Maybe, one day, a long time from now.'

A lengthy silence ensued while Kas studied her thoughtfully, then he said: 'I'll be taking my horses to the nearest beach every morning for a dip. They love it and it gets them used to the sound of rough water. If you'd like to come, watch out for me about seven o'clock.'

'Thanks, I will,' Rachel said, and with a slight wave of her hand she tiptoed up the steps and was soon lying on her bunk. But sleep wouldn't come, she was too excited. She drew back the curtain and watched the moon hanging like a pale yellow balloon in the heavens. Shadows were everywhere and somewhere in close proximity was Kas, the boy she had dreamed of, now a man whom she regarded as a friend. She couldn't believe her good fortune that he still remembered her. She lay still, knowing that too much movement would disturb Sybil. Had she seen this meeting in Rachel's future? Everyone knew that Sybil had the 'gift', but according to Lemuel's teaching it was not for everyday use. But Rachel often caught Sybil watching her with a faraway look. What did she know of Kas? Rachel wondered.

At 6.30 a.m. Rachel was wide awake, still feeling excitement running through her veins. As softly as she could she slid from the top bunk and went through to the kitchen end of the van where she poured cold water into the bowl to wash herself.

There was a nip in the morning air as she unlocked the door and stood outside on the platform at the top of the steps. Most waggons had detachable steps but Sybil's had been specially made only to fold up over the staging during transit. Rachel stood listening and watching for movement across the field. There was little sound except the neighing of horses but then a man's voice heralded a fine black horse with Kas astride it, leading two more on a rope. As soon as he saw Rachel he waved and pointed to the gate at the far end of the field. She ran down the steps and reached the gate ahead of him to open it.

''Morning,' he called cheerily. 'Come on, you can take the mare.'

'I don't think I should, I haven't ridden for ages.'

'She's yours and you'll never guess what her name is?'

Rachel laughed up at him. 'Daisy? Blossom?' she asked.

Kas shook his head. 'Strawberry Girl, of course.'

'Oh, Kas, you've only just thought of that, haven't you?'

He leaned down from his great height and grinned. 'If I can't call you Strawberry Girl then it's a good name for No-Name. She's a bit high-spirited and not always obedient – like most women – but she deserves a name and I only got her recently so I hadn't christened her yet. We'll do it this morning. Come on, they're raring to go.'

'But there's no saddle.'

'So you ride bare-back like the rest of us. You'll soon get hardened to it. At least they've all got bridles.'

Rachel tried unsuccessfully to jump up on the horse's back.

'Come round this side and I'll help you,' Kas said.

After a great deal of laughing Rachel finally managed it, and with the rope attached to the bridle firmly in her hands they set off down the twisting lane.

It took several minutes to reach the path which led to the beach but soon they were galloping along the sea-shore with the feel of a cold spray on their faces. Although it was a fine spring morning the sea was rough, but that didn't deter the horses who were eager to feel the water splashing round their hooves. Kas made sure that Rachel kept alongside him, with the smaller pony cantering along behind. It was a

154

small secluded bay and after exercising the horses and enjoying a paddle Kas cupped some seawater in his hand and splashed the chestnut mare with it.

'I name thee Strawberry Girl,' he said. He patted the horse and in return she lovingly nuzzled his neck and face. 'Now you be good to your namesake. I'm letting her adopt you while she's with us.'

Rachel sat down on the sand and put her shoes back on. 'Do you think I ought to be living with your people?' she asked hesitantly.

'Gypsies, Rachel. Gypsies. Never be afraid to call us what we are. I'm concerned for you,' he said. 'I know you've let your parents know that you're all right, but you came from a good home and while this may seem an adventure, how long is it going to last?'

In her heart she knew that it would last at least as long as he was here. Aloud she said with as much indifference as she could muster: 'Indefinitely. I don't want to make plans or decisions, Kas. I'm happy to be living free for the present.'

'But you will go back when you feel you should?' Why was he pursuing this question? He was the same Kas she remembered, yet he was different. So grown up, showing such thoughtfulness for her welfare. Was he still thinking of her as a schoolgirl?

'As I told you before, maybe one day,' she said impatiently.

An uneasy silence prevailed as they made the return journey.

The van door was open as they reined in outside Sybil's door and a delicious smell of frying bacon wafted to greet them.

'Come on in for breakfast, Kas,' Sybil called.

'How did you know it was Kas?' Rachel asked as she ran up the steps.

'Ah! Knew some'at was up, didn't I? You stayed out half the night and spent the other half day-dreaming, then up at the crack of dawn again? Saw Davey fetching water and he told me Kas had come. I guessed where you'd gone and I knows the sea air make a body hungry.' Sybil turned from the stove to hold out her arms to Kas. 'My, 'tis good to see you again, lad.'

He embraced her warmly and then sat down at the table which was already set for three. Rachel listened attentively as Kas and Sybil discussed recent events.

'Merle didn't suffer too long, Sybil,' Kas told her. 'Once the 'flu took hold t'wasn't long before she got pneumonia. It wasn't easy to gather the clan together so soon after the war but I honoured her wish that all her earthly belongings should be burnt along with her waggon. The Army gave me compassionate leave 'cos I'd put her down as my next-of-kin. Then the Armistice was signed so I never went back to France.'

155

'What've you been doing since? I sees you got a nice new waggon.'

'Merle and Josh left me all their money. It wasn't that much because they'd bought a couple of houses near Christchurch. Two joined together, not very large but smart. Reckoned they'd settle down as town dwellers eventually,' Kas laughed, 'but I knew better. Romanies don't settle and as long as they lived they wanted to be on the move. I bought me van with me own money I saved through the war. I used some of theirs to buy the horses. Thought that would please Josh. The chestnut mare's the latest and I want Rachel to ride her.'

'Friendship's going by leaps and bounds,' Sybil said with a note of disapproval.

'We met years ago,' Rachel put in quickly, and between them the incident was related to the older woman whose expression changed to one of understanding as if she now had a clue to some unsolved puzzle.

'Now,' she said to Kas, 'you were going to tell me what you've been doing since the war. Hawking on your own can't have been easy?'

'I'd learnt a bit about making cart wheels before I went in the Army and they showed me the rest. Gun carriages have to have strong wheels and there's a lot of maintenance needed on vehicles of all kinds. I did a bit of smithying, helped with the horses, learnt a bit about car engines too, so I reckon I can turn my hand to a few things nowadays.'

'Think you've come up in the world then, young Kas?'

'I'm still the same, Sybil, but there's no harm in trying to better myself, is there? Reckon I'm not so young either at twenty-six.'

'Who owns the houses at Christchurch now then?' Sybil asked. Rachel had discovered since living with the travellers that they were astute businesspeople, kept no secrets from one another, and few seemed poor.

'I do. They're rented out by an agent so I can't live in either of them unless the tenant dies or gives notice.'

'Still, it's nice to know you've got an income and property to sell one day if the need arises.'

'The income has to be used to keep them in good repair. Merle left it all tied up as Josh wanted. I won't misuse it, Sybil. They were good to me, probably better than my own parents would have been. I know I'm not a true Romany, no better than an Irish tinker if what they told me about my family is true, but I'll always think of myself as belonging to Merle and Josh. Who I was and what happened before they found me doesn't matter.'

156

Rachel listened with interest until she heard Kas say: 'Got to get this young woman back to where she belongs, don't you reckon, Sybil?'

Rachel stopped chewing. 'What do you mean?' she demanded.

'Living like this isn't right for you, Rachel.'

'Now hold on a minute, Kas,' Sybil said. 'Rachel was took poorly when Davey found her. We looked after her and helped her through a bad time, but I reckon she's old enough to make up her own mind. She can return home any time she wishes – ain't that right, Rachel?'

'Yes, of course, and no one's going to tell me when. I'm enjoying the life. I feel free –'

'All right, Strawberry Girl,' Kas laughed. 'I was just testing you, that's all. But I feel certain when winter comes you'll be back home like the shot out of a gun.'

'We'll see,' was all Rachel would say, determined to prove him wrong. Everything she ever wanted was here. The sea, freedom to come and go as she pleased, to live without too many rules, and now the company of her first love. That he had given her little thought over the past eight years didn't matter. She suspected he might be the one to move on first but meanwhile she meant to make the most of having him near.

Ena and Davey were married a few weeks later in a small church at Godshill, the prettiest village Rachel had ever seen.

'The old Romany custom was for the couple to join hands in front of witnesses,' Sybil explained. 'But Lemuel don't hold with it so he persuades the young'uns to go to a church if the parish priest will perform the ceremony. Nothing will ever stop the Smiths and Wellses from fightin' and feudin' but 'tis only proper that Davey should do right by Ena.'

They were sitting side by side in the beautifully decorated church. Davey, dressed in a smart blue suit, was standing beside Kas, his best man, down in the front right-handed pew. Rachel had helped with and supervised the sewing of a beautiful cream silk wedding dress for Ena, and pretty pale blue ones for two of her sisters who were bridesmaids. Rachel was surprised at how well-dressed everyone was but she had been warned that the wedding breakfast afterwards might end in some kind of affray.

As the service proceeded she looked round the church and the memory of the night she ran away came back to haunt her. How could she have done such a wicked thing? Rachel felt crushed with shame until Sybil patted her knee as if she knew and understood how she felt.

"'Tis Ena's day,' she whispered. 'Be happy for her.'

Rachel did her best to forget the past and entered into th spirit of the celebrations, glad to help any way she could. She realised though, that despite its being his wedding day, Davey watched her every move.

Each morning Rachel went to the nearest beach with Kas to exercise the horses and afterwards worked all the harder to help Sybil keep the waggon clean and to make the pegs and hurdles which were their livelihood.

By the time the Spring Fair was in progress more travellers had congregated on the island and the authorities asked that the gypsies use a larger piece of spare ground between Newport and Brading.

After they had moved, each morning at dawn while the dew was still wet on the carpet of bluebells in the nearby woods, Rachel and some of the gypsy girls picked vast quantities of flowers which they sold along with other wares as they mingled with the crowds at the Fair. Shouts and screams echoed across the downs and through the valleys, and the organ-grinder kept up a continuous stream of tunes from his barrel-organ. It was a good time for business with everyone in high spirits, and in the evenings although they were tired Rachel and Kas returned to the fun fair to enjoy the bright lights and amusements.

Kas insisted that they have a go on the merry-go-round. The large wooden horses were painted and decorated in vivid colours and Rachel sat on one on the inside while Kas sat next to her on the outside. They were laughing happily, their voices drowned by the loud music as the horses went up and down on their poles and the merry-go-round circled round and round. Suddenly Rachel felt herself go cold. The colour drained from her cheeks. She caught a glimpse of a couple standing close by whom she recognised instantly as Beth Cropper and Dick Mead. Before they circled round again Rachel leant over the side of her horse away from Kas, keeping her face hidden. He caught her and pulled her up, thinking that she was feeling giddy and falling.

'You all right, Rachel?' he shouted above the music, and then a woman's voice reached her among the hub-bub of noise.

'Rachel! Rachel Hunter! Fancy seeing you here!'

Anyone but Beth Cropper, she thought. Anyone! But she was trapped and as the merry-go-round slowed and stopped, Beth came running up to her.

Kas looked first at Beth Cropper and then at Rachel, curiously. He helped her down.

'I hardly recognised you,' Beth said. 'Never expected to see anyone from Hundred Acres or Kingsmere here.' She searched Rachel's face then Kas's before letting her astonished gaze dwell on their clothes. 'You here for the day or on holiday or something? Never expected to see you dressed like a bloomin' gypsy!'

Rachel fancied Dick might have nudged Beth's arm to prevent her from saying any more. For this occasion, and to please Sybil, Rachel was wearing a brightly coloured floral skirt with a low-necked white cotton blouse, and round the scarf over her hair she wore a band of jangling coins.

'All part of our fancy dress for the evening,' Kas put in quickly. 'Now, if you'll excuse us, I have to see a man about a horse.' He propelled Rachel away among the sightseers while Beth and Dick looked after them in complete astonishment.

Chapter Eleven

Rachel hurried to escape from the fair, jostling people out of her way. Kas had difficulty in keeping up with her but when he did he held her back and drew her behind the fortune-teller's tent.

'For goodness' sake, Rachel, slow down!' he said angrily. 'Who were those people and why are you trying to run away?'

'Oh, you don't understand! You can't understand. They're from Hundred Acres and it was that man who beat his wife and nearly killed her. He's Charlie's father, and Beth is Dick's sister-in-law. I'd have rather have met anyone but them. Anyone!'

'What do you suppose they're doing on the island?'

'Goodness knows. Dick stayed with his wife for a while after the scandal but then he and Beth went missing. As far as I remember no one knew where they went.'

'Then perhaps they're hiding as well as you?' Kas suggested.

Rachel leaned against the tent pole and sighed miserably. 'You could be right, Kas,' she said thoughtfully. 'I don't think they'd want anyone to know where they are, so why did Beth want to talk to me? Once she'd recognised me you'd have thought she'd be the one to rush away.'

'It was a natural reaction at seeing a familiar face from home, I expect. You'd probably have done the same thing.'

'But I didn't. I was trying not to let her see me 'til you pulled me up.'

Kas began to laugh. 'I thought you felt giddy. I didn't want you falling off and hurting yourself.'

Rachel looked up into his dark eyes. He put his face closer to hers. 'I want to look after you, Rachel,' he said in a low voice. 'My gypsy girl – at least you really look like one of us now. Your friend thought so.'

'Not my friend,' Rachel said heatedly as she turned her head away. She wanted Kas to kiss her and felt certain he almost had but she was

160

afraid. Afraid of feelings which were growing deeper every day. Afraid that Kas was only teasing, playing a game until he chose to move on alone. Afraid of the new situation she was in knowing that Beth and Dick were here on the Isle of Wight. 'Suppose they return to the Wickham area and tell my parents where I am?'

'Just suppose?' Kas echoed.

'You're only making fun,' she challenged him with flashing eyes and burning cheeks. 'They could come to find me.'

'I reckon you could make a stand for yourself. I know you're not twenty-one yet but you should be able to make up your own mind. We could solve the problem, of course,' he added mysteriously.

'How?' Rachel asked.

'You could go home voluntarily or . . .' he held his head to one side indecisively as he placed his hands on Rachel's arms '. . . you could marry me?'

The blood drained from her cheeks.

'Now you really are making fun,' she said, experiencing a cold sickly feeling in the pit of her stomach. 'I don't want to go home. I'm loving it here.'

'And the second alternative?'

She lowered her gaze thoughtfully. 'If I thought you were being serious it might be worth considering.'

'Then let's work on it together.'

'But you intend to move on by yourself,' she said.

'Who says? After the war and losing Merle and Josh, I needed some time to think out what I wanted to do. Like you, I love being a free traveller, Rachel. The climate here is kind. It's good for Lemuel and he's getting old and frail so I reckoned he might need someone to look after him. Sybil's not so young either. The war changed everything but there's time enough to make decisions. Little did I ever expect to find you here with our people, and I'm sure your friends will take a little time to get over the shock of seeing you here, especially dressed like that.'

Suddenly Rachel saw the funny side of it. 'Fancy dress indeed,' she laughed. 'That was good.'

'It wasn't bad at short notice. It was obvious you were upset at seeing them so I had to think quickly.'

'Thanks anyway. Maybe they're just here for the day, but I shall be on my guard from now on. Beth Cropper can never be a friend, she's a horrible person. I worked with her and she's hateful – you can't imagine.'

'Then we won't think about her any more. Have you had enough of the fun fair?'

161

She nodded. 'I daren't stay here any longer.'

'Let's go and fetch the horses and take a ride along the shore.'

Rachel didn't need a second invitation. She and the chestnut mare were now firm friends and she loved every minute she could be riding, or grooming her horse, as well as the opportunity to be with Kas.

They returned to the field and told Sybil where they were going.

'Just be careful,' she said, waving a warning finger at Kas.

'We shan't go far into the water and there's no sign of fog.'

'I wasn't thinking of those kinds of dangers. 'Tis the custom that if you'm walking a girl out, then you 'as a chaperone.'

Kas went up to Sybil and placed his arms round her shoulders.

'I'm over twenty-one. I know Rachel is younger. You should know me better than to think I would do anything to harm her in any way. I promise I'll look after her and bring her back safely to you before midnight.'

Sybil grunted, then gave Kas a shove. 'Be off with you before I gets me shawl and comes too.'

'You're welcome if you can bear to ride up behind me.'

'And I would if I were a few years younger. Midnight, mind, and not a minute later.'

Kas winked saucily at the older woman as he led Rachel to where the horses were tethered, and to the distant sound of music and laughter from the fair they trotted along deserted country lanes towards their favourite bay, leaving the merrymakers to their fun.

As they neared the cliff the horses began to show excitement at the smell of the sea. They quickened their pace, tossing their long manes with impatience. It was a steep run down to the beach and then the horses were all full rein. Kas galloped away on the great black stallion he called Kitchener, and although Rachel did her best to catch up, Strawberry Girl was not so fast. Before she could reach the other side of the bay Kas was racing back towards her. She turned her mare towards the cliff away from the water with Kas in pursuit. When he caught up with her he made a grab for her, pulling her off. With his large hand and an arm spanning her small waist he kept her dangling alongside his horse. For jew a few seconds he allowed Kitchener to ride on before he brought him to a halt and to the sound of Rachel's screams let her down on the sand. He jumped down himself and rolled her to the ground, teasing her before his lips met hers with almost brutal force.

'Quite a lot we can do before midnight, gypsy girl,' he whispered as he clasped her tight in his powerful arms.

'No, no, we mustn't,' Rachel said breathlessly. 'Sybil . . .'

'Sybil isn't a prude. She didn't think we were coming to the beach to say our prayers.'

162

'We could,' Rachel suggested provocatively.

'And what would you pray for, gypsy girl?'

She turned her head away from him, but she could still feel his warm breath on her cheek. 'I don't know.'

'For everything to be back to how it was three months ago?'

Rachel shook her head. 'No,' she said solemnly. 'Three months ago Adam told me he'd changed his mind. I wouldn't want to have to go through that humiliation again. There have been times when I've desperately wished I could turn the clock back to six months ago, but there's no going back. And now . . .' She looked into his face with a measure of uncertainty in her expression. His rugged handsome features made her breathless with apprehension.

'And now?' he prompted.

'Now I don't want any of this to change – ever.' She sat up and hugged him to her. 'Oh, Kas, I never thought I'd be so happy again.'

'Because of me?'

She nodded. 'I thought of you often in the past, and when I met up with the travellers on Portsdown Hill I felt comfortable with them. It's almost as if I am really one of them. I know I'm not, of course. My parents and grandparents are all thoroughly respectable . . . Oh, I'm sorry, I didn't mean –'

'Yes, you did. Gypsies and travellers have acquired a bad reputation, not always deserved. If it's true that I came from Irish tinkers then their reputation is even worse. But none of that matters. It's what we are inside ourselves that counts. When you suddenly find yourself away from people you've always known and in a frightening situation you have to develop a close bond with others in the same situation. While I was doing my Army training some of the chaps weren't very friendly to me, especially when they'd had a drink or two, but once we went across the Channel we were all on the same level, officers and men alike.

'Kas, it must have been awful for you and all the others, especially dear Charlie Mead who was wounded about three times. He was the village dimwit when he was young, and I dread to think of what he went through before he got drowned on his way home. Life can be cruel, can't it?'

'It can. But why are we being so morbid when all I asked was what you'd like to pray for?' Kas pushed her back on the sand and bent to kiss her again. 'This maybe? And this – and this . . .'

'Oh, yes please,' she whispered.

Each kiss was more fierce than the previous one. Rachel wasn't sure what was happening to her. She had thought Adam's advances had brought a glow to her body but now she felt as if she were on fire.

She clung to Kas, silently begging him not to stop, yet she wasn't sure what else there was to follow. His breathing deepened until with a groan he lifted himself away.

'That's enough. The horses . . .' He stood up, took a deep breath and went after Kitchener.

Rachel sat up, hugged her knees, watching Kas and realised just how much she loved him.

Next morning over breakfast Rachel hardly said a word until Sybil spoke.

'So, you've a great deal to ponder over this morning, Missie?' she said harshly.

'I . . . I'm sorry, Sybil. I was miles away.'

'Not so many, I fancy, young Rachel. I hope you and Kas behaved properly.'

'We were back well before midnight.'

'That's not what I asked.' Sybil leaned across the table. 'How well informed are you about the ways of men and women?'

Rachel flushed deeply. 'I only know what I feel, Sybil, and it's like a bubble inside which won't burst.'

'Then it's time we had a cosy chat, me girl. That bubble's not for bursting! You don't want to end up like Ena, now do you? She chased Davey, making up to him like some street woman, and look where it's landed her. You have to restrain yourself, Rachel. A man gets to the point where he can't no longer – that's the danger. Then it's mighty pleasant but there are consequences. Your reputation will be damaged for good an' all.'

'I wouldn't lead a man on, Sybil,' Rachel said, remembering the little her mother had taught her about such things.

'I should hope not. I sees you and Kas –'

'You mean you can see in the stars that we're right for each other?' Rachel asked eagerly.

'I don't hold with such things,' Sybil said with a haughty sniff.

'But you can't deny you have the gift?' Rachel went round to Sybil's side of the small table and hugged her warmly. 'You've been so good to me, Sybil. Please, *please*, I beg you, tell me if it's right for me to love Kas. Does he love me?'

'Ah, now that's some'at you'll have to ask 'im.'

'I think he does. Well, I'm sure he does or he wouldn't have asked me to marry him, would he?'

'Got that far, 'as it? Seems like I ought to have come with you last night.'

'We didn't do anything wrong, Sybil, honestly. After all, we don't know one another that well.'

164

'And talking of marriage already?'

Rachel kissed Sybil on her cheek. 'You know from the stars that it's right, don't you?'

'I have a premonition that it might be in your destiny – but marriage ain't always the answer to everything. Most marriages have 'appy times and sad'uns as well. Slow down, dearie, and get to know one another properly first. Work together, find out what it is you wants from life – it may not be the same thing.'

'Happiness is all I want, Sybil.'

'And your folks, your real flesh and blood? Where do they come into it?'

'Oh, why did you have to spoil it?' Rachel ran her fingers through her long dark hair. 'I'd forgotten – no, not about my family. I pray for them every night and think about them all the time. But at the Fair last night we met a couple from home.' She sat down at the table again and told Sybil about Beth and Dick.

After she had finished Sybil said,' If they're living together illegally 'tisn't likely they'll want to go back, let alone tell folk they saw you dressed like a gypsy. I daresay they have enough problems of their own without giving you much thought.'

'You're probably right, but it did give me an awful fright.'

'And did they seem happy?'

'I s'pose so. I didn't wait to find out. They've both caused their families so much distress. I know I did my parents, but now they know I'm all right I don't think they'll worry too much. I always got the feeling that they would have been relieved to get me married off but it was Belinda's future which caused them most concern. I suppose by now she and Adam will be married and living in the railway cottage. I'm sure Dad will have helped them to do it up nicely.'

'And was the cottage more important to you than the man?'

'No, Sybil. I honestly loved Adam very deeply – still do in a way – but now I know he can never be mine, I try not to dwell on all that happened. I just hope he's good to Belinda. I was even prepared to go and live with his awful mother. She always preferred Belinda. I suppose it was all her doing that he changed his mind.'

Sybil took Rachel's hand and after a few minutes she realised the old gypsy was smoothing it gently the same as Merle had done years ago. Sybil's face was solemn, her eyes glazed as if she had gone away somewhere a long way off. Rachel kept silent, and then Sybil began to mutter.

'Not so . . . not so . . . reasons, deep dark reasons.' She turned Rachel's palm over, studying it carefully before placing her hand down on the table.

'What do you see?' Rachel asked in a whisper.

Sybil opened her eyes wider and smiled. 'That happiness isn't so far away from you, child, and you could do a lot worse than love Kas.'

'Oh, I do love you, Sybil!'

'Ah, but wait on – I didn't say it would all be smooth sailing. I believe you're a very privileged young lady. The past is often clearer than the future but yours is shrouded in some kind of mystery. The future isn't clear either which means that troubled times may come, but in the main I believe with Kas you may find truth.' Sybil stood up and banged hard on the table. 'And now I've broke me promise to Lemuel. I must away to speak with him.'

'But there's no need to tell him what you saw.'

'I never saw nothing – 'tis jest a feeling, a sense I gets, and he must be told or I'll never sleep easy again. Get on with the chores, Miss, if you please.'

Sybil pulled her coloured shawl about her shoulders and hurried from the waggon. She was away so long that Rachel began to feel troubled but she worked hard, washing dishes, sweeping and scrubbing the floor. She was polishing the windows when Sybil returned.

'Get over to talk with Lemuel, child,' she said gruffly.

'Oh dear, is he very angry? It's all my fault and I'll tell him that,' Rachel assured Sybil.

'Bless you child, Lemuel angry? Never in a million years. 'Tis the wise one he is, and more amused than angry. All the same he feels a little talk might help you just now. Brush your hair first.'

Rachel did as she was told and then walked calmly across the field to Lemuel's caravan.

'Ah, Rachel, my dear. Come inside. It's going to be a grand day, a heat wave has begun. Not that I like the heat, mind you, it knocks the stuffing out of me, but it sets us all up for the winter.'

Rachel sat down a little nervously but Lemuel handed her a cup of tea and then chatted about everyday occurrences until the door opened and Kas joined them.

'I'm in no position to preach at you,' Lemuel said, smiling at both of them as they sat side by side on the window seat. 'But the relationship between you must be taken slowly and with caution. Your upbringing was so different. Rachel, you escaped what you thought of as an impossible situation. You've made new friends and been guided by Sybil while Kas had the unhappy experiences of war to contend with. I understand that you met several years ago and no doubt, Rachel, you were at an impressionable age. Kas became a sort of hero. Now, it may well be that destiny has brought you together again – you certainly make a fine couple, indeed, a handsome one –

166

but it would be wise to live from day to day, learning about each other before making a commitment. Legal marriage is not for you until you reach the age of twenty-one, Rachel, and although the Romanies observe their own rules, I believe you should wait until you come of age.'

'We both know this, Lemuel, and although I have asked Rachel to marry me I know we must wait until after March 1921,' Kas said. 'And even then I'd prefer that we have Rachel's parents' blessing.'

'If you truly love each other this will be a great strain on you both,' Lemuel warned with a kindly inclination of his head. 'Easier, though, if you honour and respect each other. I can't stop you if you want to go off by yourselves but it would please me if you remained with our group. Rachel has become like a daughter to Sybil and you Kas, having lived away from us for a while, have much to offer the warring factions among us.'

'I can't promise always to be able to keep the peace, Lemuel, and I've had the notion as you know to build up a reputation as a good honest horse dealer and smithy, but for the present I'm content to stay among you.'

'You have a worthy ambition, Kas, and I hope you'll realise it. You've shown wisdom in your thinking and you're clear-headed in making your plans so I can only wish you well. But for Rachel our way of living is an adventure and the day will come when she feels a desire to return to her family.'

'One day I may want to see them again,' she put in quickly, 'but I really do enjoy the life here and want to stay.'

Kas put his hand over Rachel's and squeezed. 'No one is doubting how you feel at present, but none of us can know what the future holds. Our way of life isn't always easy, you know. When the going gets tough I think you'll want to go home as Lemuel says.'

'I don't know that – and neither do you,' Rachel said firmly. 'It doesn't do to try to anticipate the future.'

'So for what reason did you want Sybil to look into yours?' Lemuel asked. Then with a smile he added, 'I understand, child. When we're young we all wish to know our fate, but if were meant to know we'd be born with this knowledge. The world might be a happier place but that's not how it is. Choosing the right path, making sensible decisions, knowing right from wrong, trying not to hurt others – isn't that what we should be concentrating on?'

'I didn't really want to know my future,' Rachel said, somewhat shamefaced. 'I only wanted to know whether Kas loved me as much as I love him.'

Lemuel looked from Rachel to Kas questioningly.

167

'Rachel, at this moment I love you very much,' Kas said, putting his arm round her shoulders. 'But how can we be certain that it isn't the joy of meeting up again, the situation we find ourselves in? I wouldn't have suggested marriage if I'd had any doubt, but we must learn more about each other first. A chance meeting in the woods, a lucky stone which turned out to be not so lucky, is not a basis for marriage. I'm sure what Sybil sees in our destiny is correct. She's wise, she uses her talent wisely. But let's enjoy our friendship first.'

Lemuel covered their hands with his own and blessed them before they left his van, arms entwined, heads together as they talked and discussed plans which might or might not be realised. Rachel was happier than she had ever been and throughout the summer indulged in daydreams as she worked to help pay her way among her gypsy friends.

As the weeks and months passed she forgot about seeing Beth and Dick Mead, presuming that they had been day trippers on the island. The people of the Isle of Wight seemed happy enough to accept Lemuel's group who chose to remain after many others had left following the Fair. Kas purchased two more horses and became a frequent visitor to the local blacksmith who admired Kas's expertise and allowed him to share the use of his anvil in return for assisting him when he was overworked.

Just before Christmas Rachel and Kas decided to go to the main-land by ferry. They visited the shops in Portsmouth where Rachel bought small gifts for her parents and Belinda, and enclosing greeting cards had them wrapped ready for posting.

'We can't post them here,' she told Kas. 'It's too risky as it'll be the same postmark as my last card. Could we take a bus ride to the next town to post them?'

'I've got a better idea,' Kas said. 'There's sure to be a ship in port bound for London and we can pay one of the seamen to post it for you.'

'Is that safe? He might go off with it?'

'That's a risk we have to take – or maybe we shall see a carter heading for a different county. Let's go to a cafe and have something to eat and drink to warm us up and we'll see who's about.'

They walked along the main road until they came to a suitable cafe. It was a miserable damp kind of day and they enjoyed platefuls of stew which was both satisfying and warming.

'We'll take a walk along the docks presently,' Kas said as he stirred his cup of tea thoughtfully, then he suddenly grabbed Rachel's parcel and dashed to the door with it. The driver of a Lyon's tea van was just about to close the door as Kas rushed up to him and began talking. To Rachel's surprise the driver got out again and the two men shook hands. They seemed to be enjoying a chat and then the driver touched his cloth cap and got into his van, driving away bearing Rachel's precious parcel.

Kas returned smiling. 'An old mate from the Army,' he said. 'He's on a delivery round which will take him all over the southern districts so he's going to post your parcel as far away from here as possible.'

'Do you think he'll do it? He might forget until he gets home and then it'll be too late to reach Kingsmere before Christmas Day. Where does he live?'

'Near Reading. It's his last delivery round until after Christmas so he's travelling all through Sussex and Surrey before going home. He learnt to drive in the Army and it's earned him a decent job now. A nice chap is Percy. He won't let us down. I offered him a tip but he wouldn't hear of it.' Kas lifted Rachel's chin. 'Happy now?'

She nodded, and although she smiled her eyes were moist.

'Missing your folks?' Kas asked gently. 'There's still time to get home, you know.'

'It'll be my first Christmas away from the family, but I don't mind. I've got you and Sybil, and the others. Ena should soon have her babies. She's scared so I'd like to be near to help if I can.'

'We don't need to rush back now. Is there anything else you'd like to do before we catch the ferry? Let's go back to the shops again. I want to buy you a present.'

They paid the bill and returned to where bright lights sparkled in the gloom and a band played carols for the benefit of shoppers. Kas bought a silver bracelet for Rachel, and small gifts were purchased for Sybil and Lemuel. When they passed a wool shop Rachel went in to buy white wool to knit matinee jackets for Ena and Davey's babies. As they walked down a side street which led to the ferry she bought a fine set of horse brasses for Kas from a small shop overflowing with all manner of treasures which kept them occupied until they realised that they would have to hurry to catch the Portsmouth to Ryde passenger ferry.

'It's getting dark already but I hope you've enjoyed the day?' Kas asked.

The journey back was uneventful and they were pleased to reach the cosiness of Sybil's waggon.

Christmas celebrations were like nothing Rachel had ever dreamed of. Everyone joined in to help cook the traditional fare, and the smell of chickens cooking over open fires whetted the appetite. Huge cauldrons hung above wood fires to steam Christmas puddings, and later others were used to boil fresh vegetables.

'Just as well it's not raining or snowing or worse,' Rachel said to Sybil as they warmed plates on the smaller stove in the van.

'Then we'd have had to each cook our own in the waggons. 'Tis part of Christmas to celebrate all together and I daresay you ain't never been to such a gathering as this before.'

Rachel agreed that she hadn't. Now she was so much a part of the Romanies' way of life she hardly gave a thought to how her family were spending Christmas. But after the day's exciting events Lemuel conducted special prayers in a nearby spinney which sheltered them from the winds and then Rachel was overwhelmed with homesickness. It was as if a heavy cloud descended on her and her alone as they sang softly, 'Holy Night, Silent Night'. The voices echoed through the cold crisp air tunefully reminding Rachel of the sing-songs round the piano at Calder Cottage, her father's fine voice complementing the women's. Were Adam and Belinda celebrating at Calder Cottage? she wondered. Had he managed to persuade his mother to join them? Were they missing her? Even after all the food she'd consumed she suddenly felt empty. Why was she here? What was she doing leaving all the comforts of home to live with a group of gypsies? Tears trickled down her cheeks and she hung her head, unable to sing another note. Kas held her close to him as he felt her trembling. He didn't need to ask what was wrong. He knew that however much she tried, Rachel Hunter would never be a true gypsy. For a while all this was appeasing her conscience but one day, maybe far off in the future, she would need to return to her people. He wanted to marry Rachel more than anything else in the world but were their worlds too far apart for a relationship to last? They had another fifteen months to wait before they could be married and a great deal could happen in that time.

Before the service had ended a loud wail echoed across the field. It came from Davey Smith's waggon and although they honoured Lemuel's attempts to continue his reading and prayers they were all uneasy for Ena. She had become so large that it had been difficult for her to get about much during the past few days. Her whole body seemed to have swelled to unsightly proportions. A special delivery tent had been erected with a makeshift strawbed prepared which afterwards would be destroyed as was the custom. Most of the old customs had been lost but Rachel loved to sit and listen to Sybil who related how women had once been considered *mochardi*, the Romany word for unclean. If in the presence of men, women should sit with their legs pressed tightly together, and always pass behind a man who was sitting down. Sybil still retained some of the old ways and insisted that Rachel must never let her hair down or brush and comb it in front of any man.

When the service was over the women moved towards the birthing tent where Ena screamed. They stood round, huddled together in small family groups, waiting anxiously.

'It must be awfully cold in there,' Rachel whispered to Sybil. 'Shouldn't she be in the waggon?'

'T'would be awkward because everything would have to be taken out of the vardo, the living waggon, or destroyed afterwards. A separate tent is best and let's hope those babes won't take too long a'coming.'

The night passed and Ena was given some herbal medicine to calm her and stave off the labour pains for a while in order to give her some rest until the babes dropped lower. But by early morning her terrified screams had resumed and could be heard all round the field. Davey came banging at the door at five o'clock.

'Sybil, Rachel, come quickly. Ma says some'at's wrong. She's bleeding bad.'

'All right, Davey,' Sybil called. 'Give me time to get me clothes on.'

Rachel dressed quickly and then tried to help Sybil who suffered a great deal of stiffness first thing in the mornings.

'Shouldn't a doctor be called?' Rachel asked. She wanted to rush to Ena's side but realised that she knew a little of such happenings. When they entered the delivery tent the sight of so much blood filled her with horror.

'I'm going for a doctor,' she whispered to Sybil.

'We don't hold with such things,' the old woman said but Rachel was quick to observe that no one attempted to prevent her from rushing across the field and saddling Strawberry Girl. It was Kasan who tugged at the mare's reins.

'And where d'you think you're off to?' he demanded.

'Ena needs a doctor, Kas. She's bleeding badly. She should be in hospital.'

'We don't use doctors and hospitals. Our women are well experienced in such matters.'

'I don't care – I'm not going to stand by and watch her suffering any more, Kas. Please, let go of the reins.'

'Rachel, listen to me. They won't thank you for interfering . . .'

She pulled on th reins and gave a click of her tongue. Strawberry Girl set off at a trot. It was as if she sensed the urgency and when Rachel asked her to jump a gate instead of their stopping to open it the mare cleared it with several inches to spare. Once or twice her hoofs slipped on the icy damp surface of the lane but as soon as they reached Newport Rachel made for the Police Station she'd noticed in

171

the town. The sargeant on duty heard her coming and came outside to see who it was in such a hurry at this early hour, especially during the festive season.

'I need a doctor, Sargeant, urgently,' Rachel said. 'One of the gypsy girls is in labour and bleeding badly.'

'Humph! Not likely he'll want to turn out for them on a Boxing morning.'

'It may be a matter of life and death. Will he want that on his conscience?'

'You don't sound like one of them? What's it to you, Miss?'

'Oh, what does it matter, for goodness' sake. Please, help me, it's really urgent.'

'Doctor Grinstead lives down the other end of the High Street but I doubt that he'll be awake or sober enough to go anywhere.'

Another horse came galloping up to the door. 'Have you found anyone, Rachel?' Kas asked. 'I think you're right. Ena's in a bad way.'

'I'll telephone him while you bang on his door,' the sargeant said. 'Between us we might rouse him.'

Rachel spotted the brass plate on the gate of a large double-fronted house. She ran to the front door and began knocking with the heavy wrought iron knocker. Kas banged on the window where light could be seen through a chink in the curtains.

After a few seconds they heard a man's voice muttering as bolts were being withdrawn and when he opened the door he growled. 'All right! Damn you gypsies, all right. 'Tis Christmas, for God's sake, can't a man even have a bit of peace on one day of the year? What's up?'

'One of our women's in a bad way, Doctor,' Kas said. 'She's having twins and she's haemorrhaging. Come on, I'll take you on my horse and bring you back when it's all over.'

'I hope it won't be all over – not for the woman anyway,' the doctor grumbled. 'Twins are always trouble,' he said as he put on his overcoat and wrapped a thick woollen scarf round his neck.

'Your bag, Doctor,' Kas said impatiently.

The little man seemed bemused as he went off into another room to fetch his medicine bag, pulling his cap down firmly on his head. He was unsteady on his feet but not completely inebriated and the cold night air soon sobered him up as they galloped back to the field.

There were no screams now and Kas and Rachel exchanged worried glances as they helped the doctor down from Kitchener and ushered him towards the tent.

172

'Get some strong coffee, Rachel,' Kas whispered. 'God knows what will be required of him. At least we can keep him warm and hopefully in command of himself.'

But Rachel hesitated as Sybil appeared at the tent flap. 'She's all right,' she said, 'and one of the little'uns – but the boy's dead. I'll see to some'at for the doctor, Rachel. You best go in and comfort Ena.'

Ena was only semi-conscious. She had lost a great deal of blood and required stitches which Doctor Grinstead inserted with unsteady fingers.

'Lucky to be alive, this young woman,' he said. 'Should have had pre-natal attention.'

'But she carried well, Doctor, and we folks know a thing or two about having babies,' Ena's mother said. 'I've had seven of me own. T'weren't no need for you to be called out – Christmas an' all.'

'I'm going to give her an injection to prevent further bleeding.' The doctor proceeded cautiously and afterwards looked up quizzically at Rachel. 'I suspect you're responsible for sending for me, young woman. Whatever these good people think or say, it's a good thing you did. I couldn't have saved the one infant any more than they could, but if the mother had continued to bleed they wouldn't have been able to save her either. See that she gets rest and plenty of warmth. Get her into a waggon at once. I'll be back later on to see how she is.'

Kas took the doctor back to Newport while some of the men from the Wells and Smith families carried Ena gently into Davey's waggon. He was missing, so Sybil and Rachel remained with her while Ena's mother bathed the baby girl and dressed it in fine white clothes.

Much later, when Rachel was returning from the woods with kindling wood, she came across Davey hiding behind a tree.

'For Goodness' sake, what are you doing here?' she admonished. 'Ena and your baby daughter need you.'

'Daughter?' In spite of Davey's weight and size he held a fair resemblance to a troubled schoolboy. 'Is it all over then?'

'Yes, and you might well have lost Ena as well as your son. I'm so sorry Davey, every man wants a son, I know, but this time it wasn't to be. They couldn't save the baby boy.'

He emerged from his hiding place and fell on Rachel, sobbing like a child. 'T'were all my fault. I should never – she's too young to be saddled with infants, she's no more'n a nipper herself. I couldn't bear to hear her, Rachel. I never heard no one cry like that before.'

Rachel patted his broad back and then pushed him away. 'Come on now, Davey. Pull yourself together. You should be proud, you have a lovely little girl. She's small and sweet. You're going to love her, and

173

work hard to provide for Ena and the babe. It's true she had a bad time but then lots of women do, especially when there's twins, but she's all right now and the doctor has treated her. She needs rest, plenty of it, but I'm sure she wants you to tell her how pleased you are that you have a daughter.'

'Oh, Rachel, dearest Rachel, you're so clever and wise. I wish it was you I'd married.'

'Nonsense,' she retorted angrily. 'Don't let me hear you whining such rubbish again. I'm certainly not clever or wise or I wouldn't be here.'

'You thinking of going home to your folks?' Davey asked, wide-eyed.

'No, not while I can be with Kas. I like being here with you all but if you say such silly things to me, I shall have to move on. You're Ena's husband. You were married in church and made vows which you must honour.'

They walked back to the camp in silence and when Rachel urged Davey to go inside his waggon Ena stirred. Rachel thought she looked quite lovely as she lay between fresh clean sheets but her big dark eyes were full of fear when she realised Davey was there. Rachel pushed him forward and then left them alone together.

Rachel shared nursing the new mother and baby with Sybil who was always ready with herbal tea and plenty of other remedies. The baby girl, weighing only four and half pounds, had a healthy enough cry and nothing would pacify her. Rachel cradled her in her arms at every opportunity, pitying her the loss of a twin which she knew all about.

'You're like me now,' she crooned softly. 'My twin and I are parted, but we'll make it up to you just as these good people have helped me.'

She sat for a long while nursing the baby until eventually she slept. During the next few days it was Rachel who bathed, dressed and fed her with plain boiled water until Ena could be persuaded to feed the child herself.

Ena gradually recovered from the ordeal, but in spite of Davey's attempts to show compassion and affection, she was quick to blame him for what she had suffered so it wasn't surprising that he appeared to become increasingly indifferent towards his little daughter.

'Why should I want to hold it?' he snapped when Rachel suggested he take a turn at nursing the baby.

'She's your child, she's adorable, and she needs to know you're her father.'

''Tis Ena's, not mine. Let her do the nursing and feeding.'

174

'A baby needs two parents, Davey. You're nothing but a selfish coward, running away just when Ena needed you.'

'That weren't no time for a man to interfere. Ena's got what she wanted – tricked me into marriage, she did – so she must take the consequences. Lucky one of 'em did die. At least we've only got one extra mouth to feed.'

'You hadn't better let Lemuel hear you speaking so indifferently about God's precious gift, or Kas either. The baby may be the consequence of your selfishness, Davey, but now she's born you must devote your lives to looking after her. I can't wait to be married and have a baby.'

'If you'd come to us a bit sooner it might have been you lying there,' he said in a low voice, nodding towards the bed.

Rachel felt indignant colour flooding her cheeks which brought an amused grin to Davey's mouth. She felt angry at his inference and hoped Ena hadn't heard.

'You sound like some love-sick young boy,' she spat at him. 'What makes you think I'd give you a second look, Davey Smith? Get off about your work before I tell your mother.'

He leered at her for a second and then slunk away. Among the Romanies a man was very much head of his household but it was the woman who did the lion's hare of the work to support the family as Rachel had discovered. There wasn't so much work to do now that the holly wreaths had been made and sold, and for a week or two life drifted by uneventfully while Ena's baby was cosseted and admired. Rachel and Ena became very close, but once Ena was on her feet again, even though she was pale and listless, Rachel made sure she left the young parents alone. Ena seemed relieved though when Rachel occasionally visited her and took over looking after the baby.

'She's going to give you so much pleasure,' Rachel said one day after she'd managed to lull the baby to sleep following what Ena described as days and nights of fretting.

'Brought me nothing but misery has that one,' the girl said dismally. 'Davey don't want nothing to do with her nor me.'

'He'll come round when she begins to grow and you feel more like your old self. It's early days yet, Ena. You must take all the nourishment you can and all the herbal medicines Sybil and your mother give you.'

'Davey don't want more babies so he won't even sleep with me. Might as well not be married.'

Rachel tried changing the subject. 'What are you going to call her?'

'Oh, they're all quarrelling over the name. The in-laws insist on Elizabeth after Davey's gran, Ma wants Mary 'cos she was born at Christmas, but I fancy Carol. That's Christmassy too, ain't it?'

175

'Carol is very nice. Why not all three – Carol Elizabeth Mary? But you and Davey must decide. Make him something special for his supper tonight,' Rachel suggested. 'Wash your hair, put on a clean dress or skirt and make yourself nice so that he can't help but notice you.'

'Mmm,' Ena mused, 'maybe I will. I want my Davey and so does Carol.' Then she turned on Rachel aggressively. 'You sure you ain't carrying on with my Davey? 'Cos if you are I'll scratch your bloody eyes out.'

'*Ena*!' Rachel exclaimed. 'I've got Kas, why would I want Davey? He's *your* husband, and I told him you were married in church and he must honour his vows.'

'So you've been seeing him behind my back?' Ena accused.

'No! I told him off for running away and leaving you when you were having your baby. I wish I hadn't bothered,' Rachel shouted impatiently. 'You're welcome to Davey, I don't even like him.'

She flounced out of the waggon and went in search of Kas.

Chapter Twelve

A few days later Ena came knocking at Sybil's door.

'Is that gorgio bitch here?' she called. 'My Davey's gone and I bet she's gone with him.'

Sybil opened the upper half of the door.

'If you mean Rachel, she's here, see for yourself, but you're not welcome to come inside if you can't keep a civil tongue in your head.'

Rachel glanced up from peeling potatoes. 'I haven't even seen Davey,' she said calmly.

'You ain't been over to see Carol so when Davey didn't come home last night I thought you'd gone off together.'

'The trouble with you Ena, is you've got a vivid imagination. I told you, I don't want Davey. He's probably gone to the other side of the island for some reason. Kas has gone to look at another horse. Maybe Davey went with him.'

'Got tired already of helping with the baby?'

'No, you know I love taking care of Carol, but if it causes trouble between you and Davey then I'd best steer clear.'

'She stops crying for you. She takes one look at me and bawls her bloomin' head off.'

'That's because she can feel your hostility. It's no use blaming her, she didn't ask to be born,' Sybil said. 'You played with fire, young Ena, and you got burned. You can't make a man love you. Just the fact he was a Smith made him attractive,' she went on. 'Well, now you got his child so be thankful for that.' She waved a warning finger at Ena. 'Look at yourself for reasons why Davey might have gone off, though I doubt very much that he has, and don't come 'ere accusing and blaming other folk.'

'I'm sure he'll be back,' Rachel said.

But Davey didn't and no one knew where he was. They assumed he'd taken the ferry back to the mainland but enquiries of people they knew revealed nothing.

'You wouldn't think anyone could lose themselves on a small island like this, would you?' Kas said as he and Rachel rode together across the downs one morning. Rachel remembered the shock of seeing Beth and Dick at the fun fair just when she was feeling safe. For weeks she was convinced that every door she knocked at would be opened by one of them but Kas had assured her that they were probably only day trippers.

In a secret hollow they let the horses roam freely while they lay on a blanket on the grass.

'It's possible Davey's found work on one of the farms,' Rachel said. 'Maybe he'd be happier living in a cottage with Ena and the baby.'

'Davey's a wanderer. He wants to get away from their families but he should have taken Ena and the child. He made a commitment so he should stick by it.'

Rachel turned to look at Kas. 'Do we have a commitment – a real, honest commitment?'

He pulled her into his arms. Rachel loved the raw earthiness of him. His sometimes unruly hair, the thick growth of beard round his chin and the smell of horses on his jacket and breeches. His mouth was moist and enticing on hers.

'I love you, Rachel Hunter,' he said huskily. 'Isn't that commitment enough: sometimes you tempt me beyond endurance, Strawberry Girl. I have a mind to jump the budget instead of waiting to do things the gorgio way.'

'What's jumping the budget? I know Romany marriages are recognised in English courts and it seems so easy, just joining hands in the presence of witnesses. Sybil told me all about that.'

'Jumping the budget is an Irish custom. You know the box I keep my tools in? That was the only thing Josh found belonging to my parents and that's what tinkers call their budget. We could hold hands and jump over my box and we'd be man and wife as long as there were witnesses from both families – but you don't have any family here, and neither do I.'

'Wouldn't Sybil and Lemuel do?' Rachel asked.

Kas laughed. 'You know damn' well Lemuel would never agree to such a ceremony, and neither would you.'

'I might be persuaded,' she taunted him. 'I rather like the idea of jumping the budget. Even if we get married in church we could still do that, couldn't we?'

'I shall insist upon it,' he said. He caressed the firmness of her young breasts, wishing that it was warm enough to remove some of her clothing. He could feel her bosom beneath her blouse harden to his touch and by the way she put her legs together he knew that she was as impatient as he.

178

'Unfortunately my darling, gypsy girls must guard their modesty. We shouldn't even be here without a chaperone – but oh, dear God, Rachel, I want you so badly.'

She wound her fingers through his coarse hair as they indulged in passionate kisses and when his moans became uncontrollable Rachel would willingly have given him her all but Kas rolled away in desperation.

He helped Rachel to her feet and they called the horses.

'A canter along the shore,' Kas said with a wicked grin. 'If only it were summer we could cool down in the sea.'

Their happiness knew no bounds as Strawberry Girl and Kitchener splashed through the white-foamed waves while Kas and Rachel laughed and chatted happily until it was time to return home.

There was still no news of Davey and a few days later Kas told Rachel he had to go away for a few days.

'Can't I come too?' she asked.

Kas shook his head. 'No. I'm not sure how long this business will take but I'll be back as soon as possible.'

He was gone for less than two days and when he returned he brought Davey with him. The men bore the marks of some kind of scuffle.

'Whatever happened?' Rachel asked.

'Davey was reluctant so I had to persuade him.'

'Kas, why should you put yourself at risk for him?' Rachel demanded angrily. 'He's got a father and brothers and I'm sure Ena's family would willingly have dealt with it.'

'That's exactly why I went, my darling.'

'How did you know where to find him?'

Kas tapped the side of his nose. 'That's enough questions for now. He's back, though whether Ena is capable of keeping him is another matter.'

Rachel could get nothing further out of Kas and for a while things seemed improved between Ena and her husband.

After wintry weather the grass showed greener and the freshness of spring blew in on the wind from the sea. Primroses and crocuses followed delicate snowdrops, and the goods the gypsies had industriously made all winter could now be hawked through hamlet and village.

At Easter the entire group went to church at Godshill where Ena and Davey's baby girl was christened, Rachel and Kas being godparents.

The gown Rachel made for Carol was much admired but the infant's crying was still a source of concern. But she always stopped for Rachel.

'I might almost think t'were you'n,' Ena's father said during the festivities which followed the service. 'If I didn't know what our kid went through to have her.'

'Don't you see, Mr Wells, it's because she's missing her brother?' Rachel looked at Sybil who was sitting nearby. 'Isn't that right?'

Sybil pursed her lips doubtfully. 'S'pose you could be right but I don't know about such things.'

'I'm one of twins and I know how close Belinda and I always were until . . .'

'Until she took your man from you, child. Now that wasn't a kind thing to do, twin or no. But I reckon it might be some'at like that with this 'un. Maybe she needs extra loving and 'tis Ena what ought to show her that.'

Rachel helped Ena with her dress and hat for the occasion and Davey did show some interest in both his wife and daughter but only for that Sunday. Then he disappeared again without a word.

Over supper that evening in Sybil's van Rachel begged Kas not to go looking for him again.

'No,' he said. 'I told him I wouldn't. He'll get more than a beating if Ena's family go in search of him so it's up to him now.'

'I can't understand him not wanting to be with Carol at every opportunity,' Rachel said.

'You don't know Davey,' said Sybil. 'He likes the women but he didn't want to get tied down. Ena's only got herself to blame. She threw herself at him and when you came on the scene she meant to have him before you did.'

'I was never interested in any of the men here,' Rachel said sadly. 'I was just looking for a safe haven – and I found it with you, Sybil. I can't ever repay you.'

'But you have, child. You do all my work now, or most of it. You might have been the daughter I lost.'

'A daughter – you never said?' Rachel questioned.

Tears came into Sybil's eyes, dimmed with age now yet still far seeing.

'I haven't talked about her for years. Pretty golden-haired child she were, and I was young too. We'd done well that year, me and my man, just bought a new van, so off I goes to market to buy new fripperies. No one will ever really know what happened but when I got back the van were burnt to the ground and –' Sybil sniffed and blew as tears streamed down her wrinkled cheeks. It was several minutes before she recovered and then she said, 'My little Kitty were burnt to death and me man died trying to save her.'

Rachel and Kas did their best to comfort her but she got up and indicated that she needed to be alone. From the doorway they watched as she walked slowly towards Lemuel's waggon.

'They seem very close,' Rachel observed as he opened the door to welcome Sybil.

'He's a great comforter, is Lemuel,' Kas said. 'A wise counsellor if any of us needs to talk things through.'

'Sybil's pretty wise herself. If she's got the gift why didn't she know what was going to happen?' Rachel asked.

'That's why she won't use her "gift" as you call it. She had an inkling of danger that day but was so enthusiastic about the new van she ignored the warning signs. She blames herself and needs to go to Lemuel for comfort.'

'It's all so sad,' Rachel said as she cuddled up to him. 'I feel so sorry for Ena too. I thought my troubles at home were bad enough and I always thought gypsies had a happy trouble free life.'

'But now you know 'tis a hard living.' Kas kissed the top of her head. 'Still want to stay or are you getting nostalgic for Kingsmere?'

She lifted her face to meet his loving gaze. 'I think about them all, of course, and then I'm consumed with guilt for the way I behaved. I want them but I want you more, and I have to prove I can live my life responsibly.'

'I think you already did that, by fetching the doctor for Ena and acting so swiftly while we all stood by wondering what the hell to do. I want us to be married and have children. I long for a son of my own, but I couldn't bear to see you going through what Ena did.'

'I interfered, and for what?' Rachel said thoughtfully. 'Ena's aunt delivered the babies with Sybil's help. The doctor may have prevented any more bleeding and he gave Ena iron pills afterwards, but he admitted that he wouldn't have been able to save the little boy. I acted on impulse, and now Davey's gone off and left her.'

'You just keep on acting on impulse, that's the way I like you.'

A whole year had passed since Rachel had joined the gypsies and as spring sunshine warmed to the longer days of summer she enjoyed the early morning rides whether across dewy downs or along the seashore with Kas and his horses. One of his new mares was with foal and as the time drew near he refused to be parted from her so Rachel peddled the besoms they had made through the winter, along with bootlaces and clothes pegs, with Ena. At last Carol was less fractious and the two girls took turns to push the rickety pram along dusty lanes

181

leaving the other free to knock on cottage doors. Shabby the pram might have been but the baby was kept clean and fresh-smelling so that many a householder admired Carol and brought goods they didn't really want to help the gypsy girls.

At an isolated farmhouse they received no reply except for a fierce growling from a large Alsation dog attached to a long length of strong chain who guarded the premises.

'All in the fields, I expect,' Rachel said as she turned away.

'Look, there's a cottage right up there through the lane,' Ena said. 'Wonder if anyone lives there.'

'Bit of a long way to walk if it's empty,' Rachel said. 'Still, we might as well. Probably no one else thinks of going up there. Let's try – that's if we can get the pram along the rough track.'

They secured the besoms across the bottom of the pram and set off, hardly realising what a long steep incline it was up to the cottage door. The weather was pleasantly dry and sunny, and once past the farm buildings to the right they enjoyed a vista of ploughed fields and meadows with a fine display of wild flowers among which were a host of large red poppies. Rachel was reminded of the painting in Wickham's school hall and related the story to Ena of how Charlie Mead defaced it to depict herself and the ugly strawberry birthmark she'd once had.

'Can't imagine you being ugly,' Ena said.

'It wasn't very nice. When I was really little I didn't realise why everyone pitied me and paid much more attention to Belinda. I had a rude awakening when I went to school and had to defend myself against teasing boys like Charlie Mead. Poor old Charlie,' she added wistfully.

'Why d'you say poor old Charlie? He didn't have any sympathy for you.'

'Not at the beginning but he had this rotten father who drank too much. Charlie changed so much went he went into the Army. He was wounded three times and then the boat he was coming home on was torpedoed. I felt so sorry for his mother. She was heartbroken. It was her I talked to in the church before I . . .'

'Now don't start on about that again,' Ena said. 'I don't suppose you damaged anything that couldn't be mended or replaced.'

'But a church! I can't believe I was capable of doing such a thing.'

They struggled along in silence for several minutes. Rachel tried hard to forget her crime but every now and then it washed over her to make her feel utterly miserable and guilty again.

As they neared the cottage they could see that the windows were open and curtains were fluttering in the sea breeze. They hadn't realised how near to the coast they were.

182

'Just look at that view,' Rachel said. 'The sea looks so inviting.'

'Lucky sods who live 'ere. They've probably got a track down to the beach. Maybe we'll get a drink of lemonade if we're lucky.'

But there was no reply to their persistent banging.

''Tis no good, Rachel. All this way for nothing,' Ena moaned.

'We could sit in their garden and eat our bread and cheese though,' Rachel suggested with a giggle.

They were cautious as they went round the side of the cottage which appeared to be well kept. Beyond a small flower garden was a vegetable patch and a woman's happy laughter came from somewhere in the orchard farther on. As Rachel moved towards the sound she saw a woman bending over a brick well lowering a bucket. A man leaned against her, holding her still while his groping hands explored beneath her skirt. The girls watched with a mixture of embarrassment and curiosity the horse-play in progress as the man turned the woman over to bend her backwards over the edge of the well, but she struggled free and as they broke apart Ena gasped.

'Davey Smith!' she exclaimed. 'The swine! I'll . . . I'll kill 'im!'

Rachel held her back, alarmed and equally angry when she recognised the woman as Beth Cropper. They stood mesmerised as Davey hauled up the bucket full of water and the two lovers went into a clinch before realising that they were being watched.

Rachel heard a hidden oath from Davey, and Beth ran towards the two girls.

'Why, if it isn't the Strawberry Girl again,' she sang out. 'Now I know my eyes didn't deceive me before. You've become a gypsy girl.'

'And you've pinched someone else's husband,' Rachel retorted.

'Yes, *mine*!' Ena made to lunge at Beth but Davey got between them.

'You tricked me into marriage, Ena Wells,' he said.

'Not Ena Wells – Ena Smith if you don't mind! This is your child that I sweated and nearly died for. What sort of villain are you? Nothing but a cheating rat!' She beat against his chest while Rachel turned on Beth.

'And you've caused nothing but trouble all your life, Beth Cropper. You cheated on your own sister, not that her husband was much good but you never gave him a chance to get back with Nessie Mead.'

'Oh, hark at you, Miss Goody-two-shoes. For your information Dick has gone back to Nessie, so there!' She took a step nearer Rachel, menacingly. 'Why have you left Kingsmere anyway? What are you doing here on the Isle of Wight? If you go back and tell where I am you'll be sorry.'

'But you just said Dick has gone back to Hundred Acres so he'll tell that he saw me at the fair, and who cares where you are?'

183

As they squared up to each other Rachel could see that Beth's face was now deeply tanned from the sun and her skin was wrinkled. She looked well used and much older than her thirty-two years. A cry from Ena made Rachel turn in time to see Davey throw off his wife. She ended up on the grass.

'I don't want you,' he shouted. 'I never did. You're too young and nothing but a little slut. You chased me, remember – always begging me to get between your legs – and finally you got what you wanted. But you don't own me. Beth and I are happy together so it's going to stay that way.' He looked across at Rachel. 'Might have been different if you'd been willing,' he said with snigger. 'Toffey-nosed bitch, sending the mighty Kas after me. He didn't get off so lightly at the pub though. I only agreed to go back because you was threatening to kill your bloody self,' he added to Ena. 'Well, go on and do it for Christ's sake. This 'un'll take care of the babe. You never wanted 'er any more'n I did. You just want any man – whore!'

Suddenly Beth realised that Rachel might be a threat so smacked her face and without thinking Rachel reciprocated. For a few seconds the two women pulled each other's hair, bit and scratched, giving vent to the hatred which they'd always felt for one another. A shout from Davey brought a halt to the fracas as they realised that the pram was running away, but Ena was going the other way to a path that led down to the sea, her agonised cries echoing behind her.

'Go after her,' Rachel shouted to Davey as she tore downhill to catch the pram but not before it had hit a piece of rock and toppled on to its side. She slid the last few feet to reach Carol who protested loudly as she lay on the ground, thankfully protected by her clothes and the blanket she'd been wrapped in. Rachel caught her up in her arms to console her as Beth and Davey ran to her aid.

'I told you to go after Ena,' Rachel said.

'No, 'tis no good, Rachel. I don't want Ena and 'tis wrong to pretend. She'll have to wake up to the fact. I've tried to tell her often enough. I should never have wed her, but I let you, Kas and Lemuel talk me into it. If you won't have me then I shall stay here with Beth.'

'I wouldn't be too sure of that, Davey Smith,' she retorted. 'I've had enough of being used by useless men. If you want Rachel then that's it. You never told me you had a baby. You sure it's Ena's not Rachel's?'

''Tis Ena's all right,' Davey said calmly. 'I've always fancied Rachel, I don't deny it, but she loves Kas.'

'For goodness' sake stop going on about who wants who,' Rachel shouted. 'Go after Ena, I tell you.'

'No, she'll get over it – you go after her if you like.'

Rachel put Carol back in the righted pram. 'Ena's desperate,' she said. 'You watch the baby while I go after her then.'

Beth turned the pram round to return to the cottage while Rachel ran across the garden to find the path down which Ena had disappeared. All kinds of terrible consequences ran through her mind as she went. Ena was capable of doing something awful in her quest for Davey, she might even throw herself off the cliff, but when Rachel came to a clearing she could look down to the beach below and saw Ena making for the sea. Could she reach her in time? Would Ena really do anything so final?

Rachel realised that she really was determined and by the time she reached the sea shore Ena was in the water up to her neck.

'Ena! Ena!' Rachel called. 'Don't be silly, turn back – turn *back*!'

Rachel wasn't a strong swimmer, she didn't get to the seaside often, but as a child her father had made sure that his daughter was capable of taking care of herself. She knew she must rid herself of some of her clothing which would otherwise hamper her progress so she kicked off her shoes and the ankle socks she was wearing, also her skirt and petticoat and then ran into the water. In spite of the warm day the water struck cold and took Rachel's breath away momentarily but she managed to keep Ena's head in view for a while before she lost sight of her. Rachel went on until she was out of her depth so she knew wherever Ena was she was certainly out of hers. She turned to doggy paddle as she called Ena's name then to her dismay saw a head bob up for a few seconds. It was some distance away. Rachel swam to where she thought Ena had surfaced and thankfully was nearby when she came up again. The sea was fairly calm, but the expanse of it shocked Rachel as she grabbed the struggling Ena round the neck and began to pull her towards the shore which seemed deserted until a couple of fishing boats drew in behind her. Within seconds of reaching the beach the men were out of their boats and helping Rachel to drag Ena to safety.

'Turn her on her side, Miss,' one shouted.

'Pump the water out of her lungs, Jack,' another said.

'Ena! Ena! Come on,' Rachel urged. At last she spewed the sea water out. Rachel sat back on her heels exhausted.

'Well done, Miss,' the man called Jack said as he went to Rachel's side. 'Not many a young woman could a'done that. You all right, me dear?'

'Yes,' she breathed in a hoarse whisper. 'Will she be all right?'

'I daresay. Ought to call the authorities really. Can't have young women walking into the sea, t'aint right.'

'Please, don't do that,' Rachel begged. 'She's had a nasty shock. She's got a baby too. I'll look after her, I promise.'

185

Ena began to moan and cough so Rachel massaged her back until she had recovered. The fishermen went back to their boats after Rachel had thanked them for their help. The last thing she wanted was a fuss. She did her best to pacify the distraught Ena, uncertain how she was going to get her back home. Both girls were soaked and dripping but they weren't aware of how they looked until Beth arrived with blankets to put round them.

'Come back to the house. Can she walk?' Beth asked.

'We'll have to help her. Why didn't Davey come? He could have carried her.'

'He's up at the top with the baby.'

'Is she all right?'

'Yes, she seems fine,' Beth said. 'A hot drink and you'll both be fine too, I reckon.'

They didn't talk any more as they helped Ena up the cliff. It was a slow process and Rachel was aware of Davey standing at the top of the path without making any attempt to help.

'Now see what you've done,' Rachel accused when she faced him.

'Silly bitch,' he muttered. 'Out of her bloody mind, she is.'

Rachel pushed him out of the way and took the wailing Carol out of the pram.

'Here, hold her,' she said to Davey. 'Good job the pram is large. Ena can sit in it to get her back to the cottage. Mind her legs don't drag on the ground, though.'

Ena looked ashen and hollow-eyed, and they had almost reached the cottage before she recovered consciousness.

'Where am I?' she asked, then looking round her and seeing Davey carrying Carol, she closed her eyes again with a cry. 'No, no, why didn't you let me drown?'

'Don't talk silly, Ena,' Rachel said. 'Whatever would your family have said if I'd stood by and let you do that – besides Carol needs you.'

'No, she doesn't. You're better with her than me. I'm no good as a mother.'

'You should have thought about that before you took your knickers off,' Davey said.

'Oh, shut up the pair of you,' Rachel said crossly. 'Bad enough to be soaking wet without all this bickering.'

Davey put one hand on the pram handle and helped to push the last few yards to the cottage.

'Have you got any spare clothes, Beth?' Rachel asked. 'Anything so long as it's dry, just to get home.'

'Where is home?' she asked.

186

'Just off Pedlar's Lane, near Yarrow's Wood.'

'I might be able to borrow a cart from the farmer,' Davey said.

'There's no need. We'll get home all right. Ena will be fine when we've had a cup of tea.'

While Beth heated the kettle Rachel and Ena changed into the clothes Beth had found for them. Ena needed help. She seemed to have lost all her energy.

'You must move about to keep your circulation going,' Rachel explained.

'Come on, Ena, for God's sake stir yourself. 'Tisn't the end of the world. Rachel saved your life. At least you could show your gratitude.'

'Why didn't you save me?' Ena asked in whisper.

''Cos I can't swim. 'T'was lucky Rachel could.'

'Here we are, have some hot tea,' Beth said as she poured it from a pretty teapot and added two spoonfuls of sugar to each of the cups.

Ena cupped her hands round the cup and sipped slowly as she avoided looking at Davey. Rachel watched the two of them. It seemed such a shame that with a lovely baby like Carol a rift divided them. She glanced across at Beth who eyed her suspiciously in turn. After that they avoided eye contact. Of all the places to come, Beth and Dick had chosen to hide away on the island just as she had done. It was an incredible coincidence too that Davey had met up with them. As yet she didn't know how, but was he with them when Kas found him and made him return home? Would Kas have remembered them from the day at the fair? Davey was young-looking for a thirty-year-old and handsome. Beth would be about thirty-two now, Rachel guessed. If it wasn't ruled out by his marriage to Ena they might have been made for each other while poor Dick Mead, at least fifty she thought, had obviously outlived his usefulness. Rachel thought of Nessie, his ill-used wife. Would she take Dick back? No one would blame her if she refused after all she had been through, but knowing Nessie Mead, Rachel felt in her heart that she would soften just as she had when he was let out of prison.

Davey kicked the chair leg as he moved and everyone jumped. Rachel's gaze met his and she saw that he was about to say something to Ena. A shiver went through Rachel and she shook her head at him. Some presentiment warned her that whatever was on his mind, now was not the right time to make it public. Davey went outside, mumbling to himself.

'He don't want me nor Carol,' Ena said in an embittered voice.

An awkward silence filled the room then Beth said, 'Well, you are a bit young for Davey, dear. Not much more than a school girl and he's a grown man.'

'Not too much of a schoolgirl to lie a'bed with, nor suffer hours of bloody labour to bring his twins into the world.'

'*Twin*!' Beth was shocked.

'S'pose he never told you nothing about me, nor the babe, nor his responsibilities? Where d'you meet 'im? Didn't take you long to make 'im comfortable, did it?'

Ena was recovering fast and couldn't hide her aggression, but running footsteps made them look expectantly towards the door as Davey rushed in.

'Horse coming up the lane,' he said anxiously. 'And 'tis Kas. How the hell did he know where to find you?'

Rachel stood up and went to the window where to her relief she saw Kas on Kitchener riding up to the cottage door. Now she need not be afraid any more. He would sort them all out. He knocked before entering immediately. With his hand still on the door latch he looked from one to the other.

'What in God's name's been going on here? I came out looking for you, Rachel. One or two people saw you in this area and then when I went down on the beach a fisherman said that a young girl nearly drowned.' Again his searching eyes roamed the room, alighting on Carol sleeping peacefully now in the pram. 'Thank God you're all safe.' Then he glared at Beth. 'You again,' he said. 'You and Davey deserve each other. Wherever there's trouble you're in the middle of it, just as you were when I found Davey at the pub. Where's your other man?'

Beth stood up smoothing down her dress, the bodice of which fitted just that bit too tightly but showed off her figure to advantage.

'Gone back to his wife. Too old for me. I need a younger man like Davey. Or if you've come to take him back and you're available . . .'

'Shut up, woman,' Davey snapped. 'Don't cheapen yourself, same as Ena did. Kas has got designs on Rachel 'ere.'

'Mm, maybe I can change that,' Beth smirked. 'Come on, Rachel dear, you don't want to see this nice little family split up, do you? How about it? Why don't you go back to Kingsmere and I'll have Kas while the gypsy girl gets her man back to help her with the children?' She sidled round the table towards Kas, tantalising him with her full lips as she wiggled her hips.

'It's a good job for you I'm not in the habit of ill-treating women, Ma'am. Just one look at your face and I know what kind you are. Rachel and I will be wed next year and neither you nor the devil himself can come between us.' Beth's eyes glinted with anger but she turned her attention to Davey. 'Yes,' Kas went on, following her gaze, 'if it weren't for Ena and the child you'd be welcome to him. As 'tis I can't make you stick by Ena, Davey, it's got to be your own decision. But if you stay with this woman then don't think you can ever come crawling back.'

'Oh yes he can,' Ena shouted. 'I love Davey and he'll always be welcome in my bed. Davey, please come home with us – *please*.'

Kas appeared to have reached the end of his tether. He drew his hand through his thick mop of hair with impatience.

'You can have a ride back on Kitchener with me, Ena. But it's got to be now,' he said sternly.

'No, let her stay here,' Beth suggested, at which Davey paled visibly. 'I never wanted kids of my own, always had to look after Nessie's brood instead of having a good time. But I might quite like looking after Carol. She's yours, Davey, and she's sweet.'

Ena grabbed Carol in her arms. 'No, you bitch! You ain't going to touch my baby. I'd sooner Rachel had her than you.' Ena went to stand by Kas who led her outside. Rachel followed.

Kas helped Ena up on the horse and then handed her the baby.

'D'you mind walking, Rachel? Someone has to push the pram and I'd better lead Kitchener. I wish you could ride as well. One day we'll have a pony and trap.' He smiled at Rachel, despising Ena and Davey for involving her. It never ceased to amaze him how well she fitted in with their way of life when he would have expected her to be far too genteel for such a rough existence. The more he witnessed her strength of character the more he loved and admired her, yet he couldn't shrug off that fear that one day she would want something better. He was building up good contacts as a blacksmith as well as horse dealer, planning that in a year or two he could offer Rachel a decent home in a picturesque cottage here on the island or a town house if she preferred. But for now he was content to be with her at every opportunity.

Rachel fetched the pram. 'Thanks for the clothes,' she said to Beth. 'Well see that they're washed and returned.' She looked at Davey. 'You're making the biggest mistake of your life if you don't come home with us.'

'What's it worth, Strawberry Girl, to take Davey and leave Kas?' Beth said. 'You haven't told me how you came to be a gypsy. Fancy one of the Hunter twins falling in love with a gypsy boy! Do your folks know where you are and how you live? I'll keep quiet, though, if you persuade Kas to stay with me.'

'No contest, Ma'am,' Kas said firmly. 'Well, Davey, what's it to be? Your family won't be pleased.'

'And you'll take great pleasure in telling them where we are. Maybe we'll move on, back to the mainland, and head for London

189

where no one'll find us,' Davey said. 'Just keep that wife of mine off my back. I've made my choice and I'll see to it that Beth here soon forgets you.'

'Good luck then – until she meets someone she fancies better,' Kas said.

Ena cried into the baby's shawl all the way back. There was no doubt that she loved Davey passionately and to have to leave him behind with Beth Cropper was more than she could bear. Kas and Rachel hardly spoke as they slowly walked the narrow lanes. Rachel could understand from her own experience exactly how distressed Ena felt and vowed to help the younger girl get over her heartbreak.

Over supper with Sybil and Kas that evening she expressed her concern.

'I know she's got her family, and her mother will help to provide for Carol, but she's so young to have to bear such a burden. Davey has been very cruel.'

'Now the Wellses and the Smiths will start feuding all over again,' Sybil said. 'A bad business, but that Davey Smith never was much good, only after one thing. I'm mighty pleased you put him in his place, Rachel.'

'I s'pose Davey will tell Beth how he came to find me when I ran away,' Rachel said. 'She'd take great delight in telling my parents where I am and what I'm doing.'

'But I doubt that she wants her people to know where she is,' Kas said.

'Dick's probably already told them. Still, after all this time I don't think anyone will come looking for me. I've sent cards and messages telling them that I'm well and happy, also how sorry I am for what I did. They probably can't understand how devastated I felt at being rejected so coldly, but I know just how much Ena is suffering, after the way Adam hurt me.'

'Maybe he hasn't married your sister?' Kas suggested. 'Perhaps if you were to go back . . .'

'Oh, Kas, dearest Kas,' Rachel said, clutching at his arm. 'I'm so happy now. Don't let's ever talk again about my going back to Kingsmere. I can't think of a single reason that I'd want to or be persuaded to.'

He kissed her lightly on her cheek and Rachel glowed with contentment. Sybil stood up abruptly.

'You'm looking tired, young Rachel. I reckon 'tis time we turned in.'

'Will Ena be all right on her own with Carol or should I offer to stay with her?'

'She's got family – and they'm none too pleased with you 'cos they think you've been a bad influence on Davey. I knows that ain't true, Davey don't need any encouragement, but best to keep things quiet for a while. Ena'll get over all this in time.'

Kas kissed both Rachel and Sybil goodnight and left. But Rachel couldn't sleep. The horror of trying to reach Ena in the sea kept returning to haunt her and she knew by the creaks and groans coming from the lower berth that Sybil was restless too. Eventually sleep came just before dawn but almost immediately they were aroused by a fierce banging on the door.

'I'll go,' Rachel said, instantly awake even after so little sleep. She pulled a wrap around her shoulders and opened the upper half of the door to find a distraught Mrs Wells outside.

'Is our Ena here with you? I only left her half an hour ago to get the family's breakfast and now she's disappeared. Don't tell me she's gone off after that scoundrel Davey Smith again?'

'We haven't seen Ena, Mrs Wells,' Rachel said. 'Not since we left her van last evening.' She recalled how Ena had hugged her fiercely before they'd left, and her own promise that they'd always be like sisters. Ena had wept and then pushed Rachel away, her eyes like steel. She had experienced a momentary pang of guilt that Ena still blamed her for Davey's cooling towards her.

Sybil came shuffling up behind Rachel. 'Best get out and look for her,' she said. 'Probably couldn't sleep no more'n the rest of us. There's trouble somewhere, I'm sure.'

'Oh, Sybil, I know you don't like "seeing" but for God's sake, 'tis my Ena and I'm afeared that some'at 'as happened, if not to her then to Davey or that wench he's living with. I stayed the night with her 'cos I was worried. She felt murderous towards that hussy. Please help me.'

Sybil frowned and turned away, not wanting to say what she sensed. Rachel knew the signs now and she too had an uneasy feeling about Ena.

'Please, Sybil,' she urged, 'can you tell us where to look for her?'

Sybil sat down heavily in the chair and rocked back and forth with her eyes closed. Rachel thought she looked many years younger. Was it possible there was something to this gift after all? Sybil couldn't help having it, Rachel thought with some sympathy. With a moan she sat upright. 'Try the spinney,' she said, and all the weary lines were back in her ageing features. 'Hurry.'

Rachel gave no thought to the fact that she was only dressed in her nightdress and shawl as in bare feet she raced across the field, with Mrs Wells following behind at some distance. Rachel's long legs carried her swiftly to the woods where even the birds were silent.

191

'Ena! *Ena!*' she called, but there was no response. Dry twigs crackled beneath her feet as she ran on. Which way to go? 'Where, Sybil, where?' she pleaded. Pausing for breath she wondered why the spinney. It was just such a place where Ena and Davey canoodled on many an occasion, she knew. Had Ena lost her reason? Did she think she'd find Davey here in the spinney waiting for her?

A cold shiver went through Rachel and she moved forward slowly, breaking the low branches of small young trees as she pushed deeper into a thicket, and then she caught at the front of her nightdress. Farther on between the leafy branches of a tree she could see two bare feet gently swinging with the weight of a young girl's lifeless body.

Chapter Thirteen

Rachel pushed her way through until she was standing, mesmerised, beneath Ena's limp body. Then she turned and ran back to halt Mrs Wells.

'No, no,' she cried. 'Don't look, don't come any closer. We must fetch Kas and some men to cut her down. I think –'

'It's too late,' Mrs Wells said. 'I know she's dead. I should never have left her on her own after what happened yesterday. If only I'd woken her and taken her to our van. She was sleeping so sound, and when the baby woke I took her with me to let Ena rest. God! Dear God! My Ena!'

In spite of her own shock Rachel did her best to console the older woman and they retraced their steps out of the spinney, but by now word had gone round and some of the men were already on their way. Rachel spoke briefly to Mr Wells before she led Ena's distraught mother to Sybil's waggon. Sybil gave them both some herbal tea and then Mrs Wells began to weep.

Rachel felt too numb to cry at first. Her body felt cold with shock and horror and she just buried her head in her hands and thought this must be the blackest day of her life. When the tears began there was no stopping them, especially when the men brought Ena's body out of the spinney. The next thing Rachel saw were policemen and a police surgeon, and later on she was questioned as to how she came to find the body. It was all so terrible – the travellers went into deep mourning, even though it was considered a crime to kill oneself.

'Poor Ena,' Rachel said to Kas as she leaned on him for support. 'I never thought she'd try it again. Perhaps it would have been better if I'd let her drown. She didn't struggle much so I didn't really think she was too intent on finishing herself off. How could she do such a thing?'

'She must have loved Davey more than any of us realised, dear,' he said. 'You did so much for her, and you did save her life yesterday –

today there was nothing anyone could have done. She'd made up her mind and sooner or later she'd have succeeded. Thank goodness Carol is too young to understand.'

'What will happen to her now? Will her family look after her?'

'I'm sure they will. But she'll want for nothing. We're her god-parents remember.'

Lemuel was a great comforter and Kas took Rachel along to his waggon during late afternoon where he consoled her and prayed for Ena's soul.

'It was all my fault,' Rachel sobbed. 'If I'd gone home when you wanted me to, Davey and Ena would have settled down nicely with Carol. I did my best to help Ena. I wanted us to be friends, and most of the time we were, but I know she still blamed me for intruding into the family group here.'

'You've done a great deal of good by being amongst us, Rachel, my dear,' Lemuel said in his quiet, soothing voice. 'Ena's mind was always a troubled one. Every other young woman she met was a threat. If only Davey had moved on before things went too far. He used her and she became too possessive.'

'I thought once they were married and had the baby things would be all right,' Rachel sobbed.

'Marriage is a partnership. It's not the means to get one's own way, Rachel. Davey may be thirty but in many ways he's very immature. I wasn't wholly convinced that it was right when they got married but for the sake of the twins Ena was expecting marriage seemed the sensible way. None of us was blind to his roving eye, especially where you were concerned. Let's hope he's going to settle down now with this other woman.'

Rachel falteringly explained who Beth Cropper was and the troubles she'd caused in Wickham, and Lemuel listened sympathetically.

'Kas, someone must go to Davey and tell him what's happened,' he said. 'Her family will arrange the funeral but he should attend. It's his duty and you can tell him I said so.'

After the inquest they were allowed to proceed with making the funeral arrangements. Davey reluctantly returned with Kas but he was morose, spoke to no one and hardly showed any sadness at what Ena had done, let alone remorse.

Because it was suicide many of the usual funeral rites observed by the Romanies were waived, but her body lay in state in a separate tent where relatives and friends could pay their respects. Three of Ena's elder brothers kept vigil as was the custom and a candle was kept burning at the head of the coffin day and night. Her bereaved family fasted on bread and water for the three days before Ena could be buried, then items of jewellery and a few trinkets which had been her favourites were placed in the coffin. At last Ena lay at peace and looked quite beautiful in her best clothes. A hearse drawn by four of the gypsies' best horses was followed by family and friends, either walking or on carts, all sombrely dressed in black. There was much weeping and wailing as the simple coffin was lowered into a corner of the local churchyard and then they returned to the field where a special meal had been prepared.

During this Lemuel announced that he had something to say. He said a special prayer for Ena before too much drinking took place and then he said, 'Ena left a letter to me. As you know she was no great scholar but her wishes are clear enough. She wants Rachel and Kas to take Carol and bring her up as their own.'

A gasp went up. Already the Wells and Smith families had begun arguing as to who had the legal rights to the child. Davey made it quite clear that he intended to return to Beth Cropper and wanted neither his waggon nor any of their belongings, much less take charge of the baby.

Loud murmurings went round the group while Lemuel stated that the remainder of Ena's belongings were to be burnt the following day, though anything which might be of use to Carol was to be preserved.

'I can't believe it,' Rachel whispered to Kas. 'Surely Ena must have known the trouble this would cause between the two families.'

'Not nearly as much trouble as if they had to decide between themselves who took charge of Carol if Davey wasn't prepared to, and Ena obviously knew he wasn't interested,' Kas said. 'That was what hurt her the most, to have borne him a child he cared nothing about.'

'Shouldn't we forgo it and let Ena's mother have her?'

'No, that would start a riot. It's in black and white and we must carry out her wishes. Don't tell me you don't want her?'

'No, Kas, I love her already as if she were my own, but I do have some sympathy for the families. It doesn't seem right.'

'Maybe not in the kind of lifestyle you were brought up in, but among these people things are different.'

After the drinking began so did the quarrels and although Lemuel did everything he could to maintain some order, begging them to respect the dead, the men took themselves off to the nearest pub and soon rumours came back of violent fighting spilling out into the streets.

Sybil and Rachel were jointly to take care of Carol until Rachel and Kas got married. The child settled down contentedly with them, unaware of the dreadful happenings of the past few days which had taken their toll on Sybil in particular. She looked drawn and was glad to get to bed. Rachel tidied round and was relieved to climb into the upper berth, though troubled thoughts kept her awake until nearly midnight.

In the early hours of the morning she woke up coughing and choking. The wagon was full of smoke. She almost fell off the top bunk, and holding the skirt of her nightdress over her nose and mouth, shook Sybil frantically, pulling at her bedding until the older woman scrambled out of her bed.

'We're on fire,' Rachel screamed as she gathered up the baby, bedclothes and all, and heaved at the door to get out. She ran down the steps and carried Carol to safety, laying her gently on the ground before shouting for help to anyone who might hear. Then she returned to the van to help Sybil.

Within minutes the place was alive with men carrying buckets of water, old blankets, and anything which would douse the smoke. As yet no one could detect the source of the fire and there appeared to be no flames. The horses were disturbed by the acrid smell and their whinnying and stomping had already roused Kas.

'God,' he breathed taking Rachel into his arms, 'thank goodness you're safe. And the baby too.'

'Sybil's safe though she's very shocked. Lemuel came and took her back to his van with Carol. Have we lost everything, Kas, I daren't look?'

The early morning mist helped to dispel the smoke and with the dawn light Rachel could see that the van, though blackened, was still intact.

'Why were there no flames?' she asked.

'Because this is arson. Whoever did this cowardly mean thing didn't mean to kill you, Sybil or the baby – just get their revenge.'

'Revenge for Ena's death you mean?'

'I'm afraid so. Her family were angry that Sybil couldn't foresee what was going to happen, they're a suspicious lot, and Davey's people felt slighted because Ena wanted us to have Carol. They blame you for everything. Stupid creatures should have realised that Sybil and Carol could have died from smoke inhalation, and then they'd be wanted for murder! You're young and strong, my darling. The person they most wanted to harm was the least likely to be affected. Thank God you're all unharmed. You acted bravely and promptly, Rachel. I'd been awake some minutes – I woke with an

196

uneasy feeling. Have you noticed anything?' Kas pointed to two empty places in the group of waggons. 'They've up and gone.'

'Together?' Rachel asked in surprise.

'Probably not actually together. I daresay Davey's family will try to see him and persuade him to move on with them. They've taken his and Ena's van and when they find a suitable spot they'll burn it. By now the Wells family will have reached the ferry anxious to be first across.'

'All so needless and sad,' she said. 'Will we be able to live in Sybil's van again?'

'That's up to Sybil. She may want it destroyed or she may decide to have it repainted. Thankfully there'll only be smoke and water damage. Now I want you to get some sleep. I've got some investigating to do with Caleb Sanders.' The Sanders were a good family whom Lemuel had met and converted to the Christian faith several years earlier. They had six daughters and four sons and kept themselves to themselves.

Kas sighed. 'At least with those two families out of the way, we shall be a more harmonious group.'

'I feel so guilty. It really was all my fault for staying on.'

'You've become one of us now and you're here to stay – if you want to.'

'Oh, Kas, I want to more than anything and now I've got to, to care for Carol. That's what Ena wanted so we're committed to each other – for ever.'

He guided Rachel to Lemuel's van where Lemuel and Sybil waited with the baby.

'I suspect we shall find the evidence we need underneath Sybil's van,' Kas told Lemuel.

'It's a bad business,' he said. 'No amount of teaching could change their ways, always drinking and fighting, so it's best they go their separate ways.'

During the late morning Kas returned to Lemuel's van carrying a large galvanised bucket.

'As I thought, Lemuel,' he said. 'A bundle of damp rags, probably the remainder of Ena's clothes, mixed up with some very wet bracken. They must have set fire to it before they left – and they must have been preparing to go since before the funeral. What are you going to do, Sybil?' he asked. 'The van is wet now and will need complete redecoration.'

'Yes, I think I shall stay put for the time being. You and Rachel will be wed this time next year so you'll be wanting a new van, I daresay. T'will break the spell if I stay on – if I let it be destroyed it means that I've been burnt out twice. Third time maybe t'will be me as well.'

197

'When your time comes, Sybil, you'll have no say in how or when or where,' Lemuel said in his calm, wise way. 'If you take my advice you'll have your van all done up nicely ready for next year's wedding festivities.'

'I've got a suggestion,' Kas said. 'I'll do up your van, Sybil, and while I'm doing it, you, Rachel and Carol can stay in mine.'

'But where will you stay?' Sybil asked.

'Caleb's offered to help, and his two brothers, so it'll all be done in time for Christmas. I expect I can make up a bed of some sort for myself in your van.'

'You're welcome to stay here with me, Kas, until Sybil's is habitable,' Lemuel said.

There was no lack of offers of help. Most of the travellers were relieved to be rid of the Wellses and Smiths though no one voiced their opinion. While the women peddled their goods, the men spent a few hours each day repairing damaged wood, and Lemuel, who was an accomplished artist, painted beautiful pictures on the walls and the wood panelling for the new ceiling. Rachel helped Sybil make new curtains and bed coverings and by late autumn the van had been completely refurbished. Carol, who would be a year old at Christmas, was growing at a good pace and was too big for the small wooden crib passed down to Ena from her mother. Kas spent every spare minute making an iron cot where she could be safe when she reached toddler stage.

Gradually the traumatic events of that summer receded though were never quite forgotten by any of the group, especially Rachel. As Christmas drew near and she began to think about sending greetings to her family in Kingsmere she regretted that she was not able to see Belinda and share the experience with her. She doubted that her sister would have much sympathy with the gypsy way of life, but there were times when she missed her dreadfully and more often than not it was the happiness they had shared together which Rachel remembered rather than those final days.

Carol was looking more like Ena all the time and when Rachel recalled that she too was a twin she felt all the more pain of being parted from her own sister. But then her thoughts would move on to the way Beth Cropper had stolen Davey from Ena, a situation akin to her own when Adam had so insensitively announced that he had made a mistake and it was Belinda he loved. Rachel was happy beyond belief with Kas but recognised her love for him was different in a way she couldn't define from the young love she'd had for Adam.

Christmas was a happy occasion. Rachel was becoming very adept at cooking over outdoor wood fires in large pots hanging on a crane

198

above, and the seasonal fare was eaten and enjoyed with relish. During the Yuletide evenings, while chestnuts were roasting in the embers, the families grouped around the camp fire singing carols and songs. Afterwards, Lemuel added a blessing which set a seal of friendship between everyone present.

The year 1921 promised to be special for Rachel. On March 7 she would celebrate her twenty-first birthday, and her marriage to Kas was arranged to take place on June 1 at noon. She and Sybil spent the long dark cold evenings sewing by the light of an oil lamp, making Rachel's wedding dress of cream lace with an underskirt of taffeta. Some of the women in the group were talented needlewomen and helped with the fitting and tacking. Caleb's wife Precious had a special aptitude for floral work and made some sample head-dresses with the first early spring flowers. Rachel was able to choose the design which suited her best, and this was to be made up on the day with pink roses to complement her dark hair which still fell forward in a beautiful wave on the left side of her forehead, the way Phoebe had trained it from birth. Attached to the head-dress would be a finely woven net veil, exquisitely embroidered, loaned to her by Sybil who had kept and treasured it since her own wedding day.

'I daresay your mother would have had something similar to lend you. "Some'at borrowed, some'at blue", says the old rhyme. My, oh my, young Rachel, I feels vexed for your folks that they won't be seeing you dressed up in your finery. We must get someone to take a picture, just in case you ever gets to meeting up with them one day.'

'I'm sure I will,' Rachel said. 'When I'm thirty maybe.' She sighed. 'Mum and Dad will be getting on, ten years from now. I think Dad must be turned sixty this year. I'd love to see them all, especially to wish Belinda a happy twenty-first birthday on March 7.'

'No reason you can't make your way there in time for that,' Sybil said, but Rachel smiled wistfully at the old woman who had been like a second mother to her and whom she loved almost as much as Phoebe.

'No, Sybil dear,' she said. 'My mind is made up. At first, I confess, I was very homesick but as the weeks and months have passed I've grown away from them and close to you, and here I stay.'

'Never thought so much could happen in so short a time. Our lives ain't usually so dramatic, believe me,' Sybil said.

'But always colourful,' Rachel answered with a bright laugh.

Sybil laughed heartily too. 'Yes, you could say that, dearie, and put like that it don't sound so bad.'

Kas took Rachel into Portsmouth just before her birthday and when she bought a gold pin brooch with filigree flowers at each end and the name 'Sister' across the centre for Belinda, he bought a lovely engagement ring with opals and rubies set in a cluster for Rachel. The shop gift-wrapped Belinda's brooch and afterwards they went to the Post Office and bought a registered envelope for safe posting. Enclosed with a card was a short letter from Rachel sending her special wishes and adding that she herself was to be married to Kas on June 1. She didn't include any address or whereabouts but used the Post Office as surety.

'Looking for you in Portsmouth would be like looking for a needle in a haystack,' Kas joked which put Rachel's mind at ease. 'I expect you feel sad that you can't celebrate your birthday with your twin sister?'

'I try not to think about it too much,' she said honestly. 'My feelings are pretty mixed up. Being twenty-one is rather special and I expect my parents thought they would be arranging a really slap-up party for both of us in the village hall at Wickham.' They were enjoying a mid-day meal in a pub, sitting close to a roaring fire. She set aside her knife and fork and stretched out her hand to cover Kas's. 'But what's in a party when I've got you and Sybil? I just know everything is going to work out well at last. I'm really happy and very excited.'

They toured the shops, buying any necessary items for the home they would share together in the summer, and on a street corner Kas stopped to buy matches from a beggar.

'We sell matches ourselves,' Rachel said, amused.

'And we're reasonably well off compared with him. He's blind, Rachel. Probably lost his sight on the Somme, poor devil. So many of them didn't have a chance. We're lucky. We can walk unaided, we can see and talk, we're not disfigured by burns. Two years on what have we to show for the appalling loss of life? Like Lemuel teaches we must never forget to count our blessings.'

Rachel squeezed his hand. 'You're such a good man,' she said. 'I must be the luckiest girl in the world.'

Kas put his arm around Rachel's waist, teasing her. 'Just you wait, my girl, until my Irish temper flares. You may not think you're so lucky then.'

But Rachel could never imagine Kas doing anything to hurt anyone.

There was a great celebration to mark Rachel's coming of age on March 7 and her official engagement to Kas, and then there was much to do in readiness for their wedding. Carol was toddling now. She was a pretty child with light golden hair, so unlike her parents who had the rich dark gypsy colouring. There were times when Rachel even wondered whether Davey was Carol's father after all or if Ena really had tricked him? Could he have had his own suspicions perhaps and that was the reason he'd been so indifferent to her and the baby?

Rachel wanted Carol to be a little flower girl so made her a dainty pale pink organdy dress which she smocked in pretty colours across the front. She looked a picture on the day with small white shoes, socks decorated with pink bows, and pink flowers in her hair and in the little basket she carried. One of Caleb's six daughters, Charity, aged sixteen, was Rachel's adult bridesmaid and also wore pink.

Rachel, looking radiant, travelled to the small village church on a decorated cart with Lemuel who was acting on her father's behalf. He had become friendly with the Vicar who had invited him to take part in the service by reading the lesson.

Kas, with his best man Caleb Saunders at his side, turned to look proudly at his bride as she walked down the aisle. He had feared that at the last moment she would remember her family back at Kingsmere and the occasion would become to emotional for her. But her large dark brown eyes smiled confidently at him and he admired her courage, knowing that somewhere inside a corner of her heart was stored a wealth of love for her family and a deep sorrow for the way she had vexed them. Her skin looked like porcelain beneath the transparent veil which covered her head and face. Kas remembered the strawberry mark and thought she would still have been very beautiful even if it had not faded, and he would have loved her just the same.

The ceremony over, the happy couple emerged into the sunshine where many well-wishers greeted them and showered them with confetti so that Rachel was hardly aware of the transport awaiting them. As their friends waved them off, back to the camp for the wedding breakfast, Rachel noticed that they were sitting on a brand new trap.

'Oh, Kas,' she breathed excitedly. 'Is this what you've been making when you've been going off secretly at night?'

'Well, I had to occupy my time while you women were busy with your needles and pins,' he said, kissing her cheek. 'I hope you like Bella?'

Rachel looked in front of the trap. It wasn't a pony. It wasn't a donkey pulling the trap, though both types of animals were owned by members of the group.

'She's a darling, Kas,' Rachel said. 'But what exactly is she? Pony, horse or in between?'

'A miniature horse, darling. My wedding present to you together with the trap. I know you like riding but it isn't easy with Carol to care for and with this you'll be able to take Sybil out and about as well, until we fill it up with our own children.'

'You're so thoughtful, Kas. What a wonderful day this is and a marvellous wedding present.' Their lips met in a passionate kiss heedless of onlookers as they travelled through the country lane.

'But I don't have anything so wonderful to give you,' she said.

'Just yourself – and that's all I want, until you present me with our first son.'

People waved and called their good wishes as the little horse, its fancy plumes fluttering in the breeze, trotted handsomely along pulling the trap with its happy occupants, attracting many an envious onlooker.

After the eating, drinking and merry-making Rachel had to be pulled away from Bella to join in the dancing, the music provided by Caleb's old squeeze-box.

'I think she's the prettiest little animal I've ever seen,' Rachel told Kas as they twirled in time to the music. Bella's coat was the colour of a young fawn, her sandy mane interspersed with white. 'We shall have to work very hard now to save some money. You must be broke, Kas, but I really appreciate how hard you've had to work already to make this day so extra special for me. I'm totally yours now, you don't have to be concerned any more. Suddenly I feel free of all that's gone before.'

'Together we'll reach the stars,' he whispered with a twinkle in his eye. 'And now, before we leave, we must observe a special custom to bring us good luck.'

Everyone made a huge circle and before the chief witnesses, Lemuel for Kas, Sybil on behalf of Rachel's family, the newlyweds held hands and jumped over Kas's special box to the sound of affectionate applause and cheers which echoed behind them as they set off in Kas's waggon to go farther south on the island to spend a week alone together.

When they reached a secluded corner of the field owned by a farmer Kas knew they tethered the two horses, Kitchener who had pulled the waggon and Strawberry Girl who had trotted alongside, to a nearby tree, and very soon the two lovers were lying together pledging their love anew.

The next few days seemed timeless as each morning they rode along the shore with the sun on their backs and the soft sea breeze wafting through their hair. Rachel's happiness knew no bounds.

On the quiet Sunday afternoon which she thought was the last day of their honeymoon, as she gazed out of the window watching for Kas to return from the farmhouse, she saw Precious and Charity coming into the field driving Bella and the trap. For a moment she thought something must be wrong with either Sybil or Lemuel but anxiety

202

changed to delight when to her utter astonishment she saw all the other waggons following behind.

Rachel ran out to greet them all, at the same time calling to Kas who was coming from the other direction. 'Kas, Kas, the others are here!' She hardly knew which way to run first and greeted Kas with such enthusiasm that he nearly lost all the water from the canister. 'Oh, Kas,' she accused in response to his wicked grin, 'you knew all the time. You arranged for us all to move south – oh, I *do* love you,' she said earnestly.

Kas put the water down and hugged his wife to him. 'And I love you more and more each day,' he said as he kissed her hair. 'It was time for a change and I knew you weren't quite ready for the mainland yet so I scouted round the island and found this spot. The farmer grows strawberries so we shall all have work for the next few weeks at least.'

'The farmer doesn't mind so many of us?' she asked, waving to the gypsy families as they drew nearer.

'He needs extra help. It seems Beth and Davey have been working here recently but they've gone back to the mainland. He thought they were going to try their luck in London. Thank goodness they've gone. Lemuel called a meeting before we got married and there was a unanimous decision that it was best to put the past behind us and start afresh here after all that had happened. I hoped it would be what you wanted?'

'It's a lovely way to start our married life,' she said with tears streaming down her cheeks as she greeted Lemuel, Sybil with little Carol, and her other friends.

There was great jubilation at setting up camp in the field the farmer had leased them on an annual basis, provided those who could would work on the farm and in the fields when he required help. The spirit among the community was harmonious and Rachel could relax, knowing that Beth Cropper and Davey were not around to taunt her any more.

The weather throughout the strawberry season remained glorious, and when Rachel's back began to ache as she filled her basket she would look up at the blue sky and offer a prayer of thanks for a happier life than she could ever have imagined.

Later in the year haymaking and harvest kept the men busy while the women picked apples and plums, preserving what they were given by the farmer for the winter. By early autumn Rachel knew she was pregnant but no sooner had she got used to the idea of motherhood than she miscarried.

'Kas, I'm such a failure at everything I do,' she bemoaned.

'Darling, you haven't failed me and that's what matters. Yes, I hope we shall have a family of our own, every man's ideal is to have a son, but your health is more important so get strong before we try again.'

Carol was an active toddler who used up Rachel's energy and time, but she loved her desperately and often mourned the loss of Ena in such tragic circumstances. She felt guilty at her own happiness, especially when she found herself pregnant again, but for the second time, in spite of Sybil's herbal remedies and every precaution, she miscarried again and a year later lost a third baby.

Kas insisted that she visit a doctor for a thorough examination but no cause could be found for the miscarriages and the local doctor referred her to the hospital in Newport. The doctors there considered she was a healthy young woman who for some unknown reason simply was not ready to carry a pregnancy full term. Kas decided that for the next year or so they would forget about starting a family which depressed Rachel.

'I feel miserable now,' she confessed to Sybil one morning when the men were all out at work. 'Kas won't let me do any work at all.'

'You've got your work cut out with young Carol,' Sybil said. 'Forget your troubles, dearie, then it'll happen when you ain't thinking on it.'

'Look at me, Sybil,' Rachel said. 'Tell me what you see – please? Dare I hope?'

'You must always hope, Rachel. I ain't capable of seeing no more.'

'Years ago when I got lost in the wood and by chance met up with Merle, Josh and Kas, Merle read my palm,' Rachel recalled thoughtfully. 'I didn't ask her to, she just did, and said I'd find happiness then be unhappy. I wonder what she meant – what she saw?'

'We all 'as unhappy times and then happy ones again,' Sybil said. 'Don't you fret, child, t'will all come right in God's good time. You jest be a good wife to Kas, 'cos he's a good man to you and everyone else.'

'But how can I be good to him when I know he wants a son and I can't give him one?'

'Jest stop worrying yourself, and 'im as well. I knows you misses teaching the children but that can't be helped since we've stayed on the island longer than intended. The authorities were bound to put their foot down eventually and insist they went to school. Lemuel misses teaching the little'uns, and I fancy he ain't so well nowadays. You can always help him. Cleaning his waggon, cooking his meals.'

'Oh, Sybil you know he doesn't have to do anything for himself. There's always someone doing for him.'

204

'Then see if he needs help with writing and suchlike. He always has his head in books when I goes to see him. Goodness knows what he's up to.'

At first Rachel had no inclination to visit Lemuel but when she saw him taking an early morning walk she thought how much older he looked. He wasn't a man who accepted help readily so she had to be discreet. The summer of 1923 had been tiring and now, as autumn leaves fell, dropping their blanket of yellow, gold and red, the bitter north-east winds whipped them up again to fly like miniature kites across the island. Rachel could hardly believe she had been with the group of gypsies for over four years, and come Christmas Carol would celebrate her fourth birthday.

'You've matured in this time,' Lemuel said as Rachel reminded him how long she'd known him. 'And I've grown much older.' He looked sad but smiled in his usual way.

'Only four years older, Lemuel,' she said to cheer him.

'But four years is a long time when we're past our prime. I've had my threescore years and ten, and a few extra.'

'Maybe you're just a bit weary,' she said. 'The summer is tiring. Funny, isn't it, how all through the winter we look forward to spring and summer, and by the time autumn comes we're looking forward to sitting round the fire again?'

'That's why the good Lord gave us four seasons. "To everything there is a season", and mine are running out, my dear.'

'Are you ill, Lemuel? Shouldn't you see a doctor if you are?' Rachel asked kindly as she set the table in his waggon for his evening meal.

'My chest gives me some pain, and my sight is not as good as it was.'

'You've done too much writing, Lemuel. What is it that's kept you so busy?'

'I – well, I've had a fortunate life, Rachel. I wasn't born into this type of lifestyle but that of the privileged classes. My father had a government post in India and it was there that I first learnt of the Romany ways. I had a special interest in languages and so I studied the Romany language in particular.' He sighed, remembering his youth. 'I didn't always practise the Christian faith, Rachel. I enjoyed the good life, money and a good education, then the woman I thought I was going to marry helped me to lose my father's inheritance.'

'How?' Rachel asked.

'We went into business together. She and her accomplice embezzled quite a fortune, leaving me with nothing but the clothes I stood up in. My family disowned me.'

'Weren't they caught? Wasn't there anything you could do to get it back?'

'The love of money, my dear, is the root of all evil. It would take too long to tell you of my follies as well as hers. Suffice it to say that finding myself alone and penniless, like you, I found some gypsies who happened to be retracing the Romany journey from India across Europe to England. They took me in and in return I taught their children and wrote down much of what they could tell me about their ancestors and the true Romany way of life. I still haven't completed my manuscript, but when I have I hope to find a publisher – that's if I'm spared. Not many gypsies are Christians but their way of life taught me a great deal, and I feel I owe it to the world to tell future generations about these people.'

'Perhaps I could help you?' Rachel offered.

'That's kind of you, but you have Carol to take care of and she's at a demanding age. Perhaps when she goes to school you'll be able to spare an hour or two each day.'

'I'm sure Sybil or Precious Sanders would look after Carol, Lemuel. I'd like to help and I know Kas would like me to.'

Through the long winter days Rachel sat with Lemuel and wrote as he dictated. She became so absorbed in the story that all her own past disappointments were forgotten. Time became the important factor as she realised with regret that Lemuel's eyesight was failing and on top of that as the winter progressed he developed a bad cough.

When Rachel arrived at his van one morning and found him still in bed she became really concerned.

'It's al right, my dear,' he croaked. 'Nothing that a rest for a couple of days won't cure. The book can wait. In fact if I'm unable to finish it I shall pass it on to you to do as you think fit. You're young and you'll have a family soon, then when they're growing up you can bring the book up to date.'

Rachel sponged his hands and face and realised that he was running a temperature. She made him a warm drink and then went to tell Sybil.

The group rallied round to nurse him as they always did in times of crisis, for they knew that Lemuel was a very sick man.

'We should have returned to Bere Forest to shelter for the winter like we always used to,' Sybil said.

'But the climate seemed good here,' Kas said. 'And there's been work for most of us. The farmer has been exceptionally kind. Should we call in a doctor?'

'He'll mend,' Sybil said knowingly, 'but I think he's pining for the mainland. Maybe it's time to leave the island.'

Rachel went cold. She didn't want to leave this idyllic place where she had found happiness, except for having a baby.

The matter was discussed at length when Carol had been put to bed behind the dividing curtain and Kas and Rachel were quiet and alone.

'I think we ought to get a doctor to visit Lemuel,' Rachel said.

'I agree, but we have to honour the elders' wishes, and Sybil seems to think Lemuel wants to return to Portsmouth. I know the island suits us, but there is a bleakness about it in winter with those biting winds from off the sea. His cough is worsening and we don't want him to develop pneumonia.'

'Goodness, no,' Rachel said in alarm. 'But we don't have to go too, do we?'

Kas inclined his head with a wry smile at his young wife. 'I'm afraid we do,' he said. '"Whither thou goest I will go. Thy people shall be my people",' he recited. 'We stick together. I know you dread returning where you might be recognised, but everything has changed now. You're over twenty-one and you're my wife. Your family would be overjoyed to see you again, I'm sure.'

'But they won't acknowledge my having become a gypsy.'

'As long as you don't want to return to them, there's no harm in a visit just to test the waters.'

'If we go to Portsmouth it's for Lemuel's sake,' she said. 'I don't think I'll ever have the courage to return home even for a visit, though I'd love to know how they all are.'

'Once we're settled again you can write to them and give a box number for them to reply. And who knows?' Kas added 'You might have better luck with a baby somewhere else?'

The idea was attractive for that reason alone but Rachel voiced her misgivings to Sybil when it was confirmed that they were all planning to move back to the mainland.

'The worst of the winter is almost over,' she said. 'And Lemuel seems to be improving, doesn't he?'

'He's much weaker, Rachel, and wants to leave the island. There'll be no arguments, we do what's best for him. The bronchitis has gained a hold and our remedies ain't working.'

'I thought perhaps Kas and I could stay here?'

Sybil screwed up her ageing eyes and stared intently at her.

'I can understand why you don't want to go,' she said in a low voice, 'but in the end 't'will be best.' Rachel watched as her appearance changed. She looked younger, more aggressive, as she added, 'The past needs to be remembered – there may be changes . . .'

Rachel realised that for that brief moment Sybil was 'seeing' – but was it into the future or the past? Fear clutched at Rachel's doubting heart but in a moment Sybil reverted to her normal self.

207

The sea was choppy and rain fell heavily as the ferries carried the group two by two back to the mainland. Rachel was convinced that the journey was doing Lemuel no good at all. He was well wrapped up in his waggon but his racking cough could be heard distinctly. When she took her turn at tending him she realised that he was getting weaker each day and by the time they reached the outskirts of Portsmouth his condition appeared to be serious.

'I think it's pneumonia,' Kas said. 'Rachel, you and I will take him in his waggon to the nearest hospital and the others can hold up on some waste ground until we can carry on to Bere Forest.'

It was evident that they were not particularly welcome as they entered the grounds of the hospital but when Kas spoke to a doctor stretcher bearers were summoned and Lemuel was rushed inside where he was given immediate attention. Kas and Rachel sat on a bench in the corridor waiting for the doctor's verdict.

'Poor Lemuel,' she said gloomily. 'He's been so good to everyone and always known what to do in a crisis. It'll be awful without him.'

'Who says we're going to be without him? He's tough, and with the right treatment may make a good recovery.'

It seemed like hours before the young doctor returned to them.

'What a wonderful gentleman,' he said with a smile. 'I'd say you got him here in time. He's weak and exhausted but tells me that he's been very well looked after and that it's his own fault. He's been working to hard on his history of the Romanies.'

'But how his he, Doctor?' Kas asked.

'A touch of pneumonia but with plenty of bed rest and the best medication we have there's every chance Mr Davidson will make a good recovery,.' He glanced at Rachel. 'Perhaps you could fetch a change of clothes and his toilet things as we'd like to keep him in for at least two weeks, I should think.' The doctor smiled and Rachel felt annoyed that he seemed to find the whole thing amusing. 'A most convenient way of travelling round,' he went on. 'You have all his possessions on the spot. Your caravan is the subject of much enthusiasm. So charming and brightly painted – but I'm afraid you can't leave it here.' He actually looked apologetic but Kas assured him that they would remove it once Lemuel was settled.

Rachel felt quite relieved as she ran back to the van and collected some of Lemuel's possessions. When she joined Kas again he said, 'They're taking him to the men's medical ward and we can go along too so that we know where he'll be.'

Swing doors opened and a trolley bearing the much loved Lemuel appeared. Rachel held his hand. 'It's going to be all right,' she said affectionately. 'You'll be in the best place and we'll be able to visit you.'

Lemuel squeezed her hand, then she felt that she was being scrutinised. Looking up into the porter's face, the never-to-be forgotten Adam Taylor, the shock was too much. She closed her eyes, wanting to believe it was he yet willing him away as she slid to the floor.

Chapter Fourteen

When Rachel recovered she found herself in a small waiting room where a nurse was undoing the top button of her coat and calling her name. Kas was there too looking as shocked as Rachel felt.

'Are you all right?' he asked.

Rachel nodded and was grateful for the cup of hot sweet tea a young probationer nurse brought her. The doctor came in and felt her pulse.

'A bit fast, and you're very pale,' he said. 'Are you sure you're all right?'

'I'll be fine,' she said in a small weak voice. 'I thought I saw someone I knew.'

'You did, Rachel.' Adam poked his head in at the doorway. Adam, the man she'd loved and wanted to marry, the man she had run away from. She took a sip of tea but the cup rattled in the saucer as she trembled with emotion. 'I'm sorry if seeing me here was too much for you – but seeing you again has given me a shock too.'

He came further into the small room – the same old Adam, his features kindly and sympathetic, his smile warm as he studied Rachel as if unable to believe his eyes.

'Well, if there's nothing else we can do for you,' the doctor said, 'we'll get back to work.' As he turned to go he added, 'And when you've rested awhile you can visit Mr Davidson.'

The nurse followed him out and Rachel was glad to be left alone with just Kas and Adam.

'Rachel,' Adam said as he closed the door and walked towards her eagerly, 'I can hardly believe it really is you.'

'Dressed up like a bloomin' gypsy?' Rachel mocked defiantly. 'That was how Beth Cropper described me.'

Adam looked puzzled. 'Beth Cropper? You've been with her?'

She shook her head. 'No, but we did meet up on the Isle of Wight.'

210

'You've been on the island all this time?' Adam frowned as if he found this too much to comprehend.

'Yes. I joined some lovely people, Romanies most of them, and as they were going to the Isle of Wight they agreed to take me with them. I was ill, you see, Adam – after all that had happened, I just couldn't face going home. I felt so ashamed.'

'No one blamed you for anything, Rachel. It was all a mess, a horrible misunderstanding.'

The colour began to return to her cheeks. Misunderstanding indeed, she thought. Then she looked at her beloved Kas. His eyes flashed warning signals, his expression was troubled, and Rachel realised she should have introduced them.

'This is my husband, Kas Dolan,' she said. 'But you knew I was getting married. I wrote to Mum and Dad to tell them. I hope Belinda got my present and card for her twenty-first birthday?'

'Yes, she did. It was such a relief to them when you sent the first postcard. They – we were all worried sick about you, Rachel, and as Belinda said it wasn't you who should have run away. She would have moved out until we got married.'

'And when was that?'

Adam looked down at his feet nervously. 'We waited to see if you could be found. Your mother put a notice in the paper asking you to return but when you didn't and they received your card – well, at least they knew you had come to no harm, and so we got married the following July. We've got a little boy, Billy, he's over three now.'

'Rachel,' Kas interrupted, 'don't you think we ought to go to the ward to see Lemuel?' It was clear that he felt ill at ease and was anxious to break up the conversation with Adam. Meeting this man from Rachel's past was as much of a shock to him as it was to her.

'Yes, of course. That's why we're here.'

There was so much Rachel wanted to talk to Adam about, so much she wanted to know about the family. Adam and Belinda had a little boy, it wasn't fair – it just wasn't fair.

'I'll take you to the men's ward, but before I do there's something you should know, Rachel. Your father is in that ward. He's been very ill indeed this winter.'

'Dad? Here? What a strange coincidence,' she said, but the way Adam averted his eyes warned her that her father must be in a very bad way.

'He . . . he's going to get better, isn't he?'

'That's not for me to say, but I'm sure he'll be overjoyed to see you again, and I know your mother and Belinda will.'

Rachel passed her hand across her brow. 'I don't think I've ever fainted before,' she said. 'It was silly.'

211

'Are you sure you're all right now?' Kas asked, taking her arm to help her up.

'Yes, perfectly,' she said, with eyes shining happily. 'Poor Lemuel will wonder what's happened to us.'

Adam hesitated, meeting Kas's gaze uncertainly, then led the way through long corridors.

'I think we'll see Lemuel settled in first then we'll visit your father, Rachel,' Kas said. 'Perhaps you should be prepared for a change in him.'

When they reached the swing doors to the ward Adam pushed them open and went at once to the desk to speak to the sister in charge, then he turned back to Rachel and Kas.

'Your friend is here, on the left behind these screens. Sister says you can only stay a minute or two as rest is important for him. I've explained that you're Mr Hunter's daughter and haven't seen him for a while so she said you could see him for just a few minutes as regular visiting time isn't until this afternoon at three.' Adam lowered his voice. 'She's a bit of a stickler for the rules but she's an excellent nursing sister. When you're ready your father is halfway down the ward on the right hand side. He's better than he was when he came in but hasn't improved as much as they'd hoped. I'm sure seeing you safe and well again will work wonders.'

Adam touched her arm lightly, nodded politely at Kas and left the ward.

Lemuel was already dozing. 'You can relax now and concentrate on getting well again,' Rachel said softly. 'I think we should leave you in their capable hands, but you only have to ask if there's anything you need, anything at all, and we'll bring it in for you.'

Lemuel opened his eyes. 'I know, child, but I want for nothing. I have a warm bed, perhaps just a bit warmer than in my van, but I shall miss your company. Yours, Sybil's, and of course you, dear boy. You've all been so very kind. A little rest is all I need and I'll be up and about again in no time.'

'Of all the people to bump into here it had to be Adam, the man I was going to marry,' Rachel said with a hint of excitement in her voice. 'He's a hospital porter and I'm afraid you'll think me very weak, Lemuel, but at the sight of him I fainted. He was just as surprised to see me and he's told me that my father is in this ward. Now, maybe, after all this time, I can make peace with my family.'

'God works in mysterious ways, his wonders to perform,' Lemuel said. 'Perhaps it was the right time to come back to the mainland and my sickness is a means of reuniting you with your family. I'm happy for you, child. Everything is going to be all right.'

212

'And you're going to get well very soon,' Rachel said with a bright smile. 'And I'm sure you'll be most comfortable here.'

He closed his weary eyes and Kas led Rachel away. She hesitated. How ill was her father? Would he recognise her? Would he be pleased to see her? She clutched at Kas's arm.

'I'm not sure I can go through with his,' she whispered suddenly. 'Perhaps it would be better to come back another time after I've seen Mum and Belinda?'

A rustle of starch and the ward sister was at her side.

'Taylor says you're Mr Hunter's daughter? I didn't know he had another one. You live away?' She didn't wait for any replies but strode swiftly down the ward, indicating that Rachel and Kas were to follow to where an elderly man sat propped up on pillows. His eyes were closed but at a glance Rachel could see that her father had changed little except that his colour was poor and his hair maybe a little greyer. 'Mr Hunter.' Sister shook his arm. 'A surprise for you. Your daughter's come to see you.'

Wally Hunter opened his eyes expectantly and the sister began to walk away. 'Just five minutes,' she said brusquely, 'it isn't official visiting time until three o'clock this afternoon.'

'Thank you, Sister,' Kas said, 'we'll only stay a minute.'

Rachel bent over her father and gently kissed his cheek. 'Dad,' she whispered, her voice cracking with emotion. Oh, how she loved him, and how vexed she was with herself for hurting him, but she couldn't put into words all that was in her heart. He neither spoke nor moved and when Rachel peered into his eyes they looked back at her, uncomprehending. 'It's me – Rachel,' she said. 'I've missed you terribly and I'm so sorry you're ill. You must get well quickly now that I'm home.' In her eagerness to show him how pleased she was she sat on the side of the bed and took both his hands between her own. For a moment she fancied she felt him squeeze in response and then Sister was back.

'Please don't sit on the bed,' she said stiffly, 'and I think that'll be enough for now.'

Rachel stood up, reluctantly letting her father's hands go, and as she kissed him again she noticed that a solitary tear trickled down his cheek.

'This is Kas, my husband,' she said. 'I do so want you to be friends.'

Kas took Wally's hand in his just for a second. 'It's nice to meet you, Sir,' he said. 'I hope we can visit you again soon.'

Kas led Rachel away. Neither spoke, nor were they aware of curious onlookers as they drove away in Lemuel's waggon to join up with the rest of the group.

Inside Sybil's van Rachel wept unashamedly. 'I don't think he knew who I was,' she wailed. 'I thought he squeezed my hand but he said nothing and showed no sign of pleasure at seeing me.'

'Don't fret, Rachel,' Sybil said. 'I daresay t'were a shock and now he'll lie there and wait for you to visit again. I've got a bit 'o stew on the stove so as soon as you'm ready we'll sit and eat.'

'We'll take Bella and the trap when we go back to the hospital,' Kas said. 'It'll be nice to meet your mother and sister, Rachel, but I'll make myself scarce after the introductions.'

'But I want you to stay with me,' she said.

'We can't leave the pony and trap unattended in the hospital grounds for long. It's better that we have our own transport then we can get back to Carol.'

'She's no trouble,' Sybil said. 'Precious and Charity will take her for a while when I needs a nap.'

'I'd like Mum and Belinda to see her,' Rachel said. 'But she isn't mine – and it's no good pretending she is.'

'But you will have your own child one day. Our baby will come in its own good time.'

Sybil clattered about with pots and pans and they sat down to eat. Rachel watched the clock on the wall, apprehensive yet eager to return to the hospital.

'I don't think we should get there too soon,' Kas said. 'Let your mother and sister get used to the idea of you turning up first.'

'I'm sure Adam will have got word to them somehow by now. I wonder where they live. Kingsmere would be too far for him to travel daily to work.'

'Are you sure you feel all right?' Kas said. 'You could go back another day. How d'you feel about meeting Adam after so long?'

'It was a surprise, but he hasn't changed.'

'And you don't hate him any more?'

Rachel looked up at the unusually acrimonious tone in Kas's voice.

'Nothing will change what happened,' she said softly. 'But what good does it do to harbour grudges?'

''Tis time to bury the past,' Sybil put in. 'You're all older and wiser now – and families need each other. I jest knows you ma is going to be overjoyed to see you, Rachel.' She sniffed as she often did when something bothered her. 'Hopes your pa recovers soon.'

Rachel was too bothered by events herself to notice Sybil's uneasiness but as they drove off in the trap she felt a vague queasiness come over her. She prayed she wouldn't faint again. She'd never done so in her life before, why should she have done today? Concern over Lemuel, she supposed, added to which was the surprise of coming face to face with Adam Taylor as well as the unexpected blow of finding her father in hospital too.

By the time they reached the hospital Rachel knew that she was about to be ill and she had to make a dash for the nearest lavatory. She looked red-eyed and putty-coloured when she rejoined Kas.

'Rachel, you shouldn't have come, you look awful,' he said.

'It's all right. It's just the emotional shock. Let's get to the ward and get it over with. I . . . I can't help wondering . . . will they be pleased to see me?'

'Of course they will,' he reassured her as he put his arm round her, and they walked the long corridors in silence.

As they turned off the main corridor and went into the passageway leading to the men's medical ward Rachel saw her mother and Belinda outside Sister's office. Rachel disengaged herself from Kas's arm and ran forward. But a few yards short of them she stopped. Her mother was crying and Belinda was comforting her. Rachel's feet moved slowly forward in spite of her subconscious telling her to turn back. Then Belinda saw her.

'*You*!' she accused in a tight aggressive whisper. 'Why couldn't you stay away? On top of everything else, how could you do this to Dad?'

'Do what? Oh, Belinda, I've wanted to see you all so often – tell me what's the matter?'

'Dad's had a stroke – a really bad one. He can't talk or move – and it's all your fault! You should never have visited him without giving us a chance to warn him,' Belinda said.

Phoebe turned then and after staring at Rachel through tear-filled eyes held out her arms. Rachel, the unwanted child with the hideous birthmark whom she had accepted as a gift from God, and whom she still loved in spite of everything, fell into them with pitiful sobs. Neither was capable of speaking. There was so much mutual love and understanding in their hearts.

Belinda's gaze moved towards Kas. So this was Rachel's husband. Tall, dark and extremely manly, she noticed. But for the fact that he was a gypsy Belinda had to admit that her twin sister had done very well for herself. Or was he just a stop gap until such time as she could return to take Adam away from her?

'Mum, oh, Mum – maybe Dad'll get better,' Rachel said croakily. 'I'm sorry – really sorry if it's my fault.'

'I doubt if it's anyone's fault, Rachel. He was a sick man. Years of chest trouble had weakened him, and he had hardening of the arteries so the doctor said.' Phoebe dried her eyes as she held Rachel at arm's length. 'Just to see you again, my dear, *dear* Rachel – I can hardly believe it.' She wept again and Rachel wept tears of relief.

215

Then she took her mother's arm. 'I want you to meet Kas, Mum,' she said. 'He and Sybil have been so kind to me and we're very happy. Lemuel, the leader of the Romany group who found me, is quite ill. We brought him in yesterday. He's a lovely man. Little did I think that Dad would be here too, let alone Adam working in this hospital.'

Kas shook hands with Phoebe Hunter, a strong, warm clasp which gave her a measure of reassurance, but Belinda seemed reluctant to shake her brother-in-law's hand. All kinds of suspicions were racing round in her brain. Were they really man and wife according to the church or had Rachel lied to them when she said they were legally married? It wasn't Romany custom, she knew. If they weren't legally married . . . Belinda hadn't yet recovered from the shock of Adam coming home for his dinner with the exciting news of seeing Rachel again. He would never discuss why he had changed his mind about marrying her, and Belinda could never quite convince herself that his affections for her were genuine. But they'd been happy, especially when Billy came along – until now when she felt that their future was threatened.

'Rachel has talked about you always,' Kas was saying. 'I'm delighted to meet you both but I wish it was in happier circumstances.' He turned to his wife. 'I'll go to visit Lemuel in case he thinks we're not coming. You can join me when you're ready.'

'Why are you standing out here?' Rachel asked her mother when Kas had left them. 'Can't we see Dad? Visiting time will soon be over.'

'He doesn't know any of us,' Belinda said abruptly. There was a degree of guilt in her short-temper. Since she and Adam had moved to live near the hospital in Portsmouth their visits to Kingsmere had become much less frequent and she knew there was no valid excuse, while at least Rachel had a legitimate reason for running away from Kingsmere. 'The doctor is still with him,' Belinda explained. 'Dad had the stroke shortly after Adam returned after dinner. We were only allowed in for a couple of minutes.'

'Oh dear, this is terrible,' Rachel said. 'You're right, Belinda, I shouldn't have rushed to see him, though they only allowed me a couple of minutes this morning as it wasn't visiting time.'

'It would have been a shock to see you again whenever you turned up,' her sister said sarcastically.

'But I'm sure it pleased him to know that you came, dear,' Phoebe intervened.

'He wept,' Rachel said. 'I actually made him cry . . .' She sobbed again into her handkerchief.

'Crying won't help now,' Belinda said. 'I doubt that he was pleased to see you after all the heartache you caused Mum. Dad would never

216

allow us even to speak your name after you desecrated the church and ran off.' She had no intention of letting her sister forget her shame.

Phoebe put a restraining hand on Belinda's arm. 'That's enough,' she said, softly but sharply. 'That's all in the past now. Naturally we were both grieved at what happened and we still don't know what caused such an upset. I doubt if any of us are entirely free from blame, Belinda. Your father loves you both and we must be happy that we're back as a family again.'

'As long as she doesn't expect us all to change into gypsies,' Belinda said scornfully.

Rachel could hardly believe there was so much hatred in her sister's voice when it was she who had fared best out of the two of them. Adam was evidently working hard to provide for his wife and child.

The swing doors opened and closed behind two doctors, the young one Rachel had seen earlier accompanied by an older dark-suited consultant. There was a serious expression on their faces which brought the three woman instant consternation.

'My husband,' Phoebe said falteringly, 'is he going to be all right?' The older man placed his hand on her shoulder.

'I'm very sorry, my dear. There isn't anything we can do now. So sad, just when he seemed to be making a recovery. Strokes take people in different ways. Another one may follow quickly or he may linger, though he'll never be able to walk or do things for himself. For the moment we must just wait and see. By all means visit him, though, and talk to him. We can't be sure how much people can hear in this semi-conscious condition.'

Phoebe was too distressed to ask further questions and the doctors went with the ward sister into her office.

'Can we all go in?' Rachel asked.

'Of course, dear. It might help him to know we're beside him altogether.'

'She's the cause of all this,' Belinda hissed. 'I reckon it would be better if she stayed away.'

Phoebe put a hand on each girl's arm. 'We're here to help your father,' she said solemnly. 'Quarrelling won't do that. We must try to support one another.'

Rachel looked at Belinda apologetically but her sister glowered back. Phoebe went first and kissed the man she had married nearly forty years ago. He was a good man, honest and upright, a devoted husband and father, though he had never seemed quite the same after Rachel had disgraced the name of Hunter. Phoebe had pleaded desperately hard with him on the runaway's behalf for forgiveness, but Wally had accused her of spoiling Rachel at Belinda's expense.

217

Phoebe was sure she hadn't. Both girls had been treated the same but who else was there to try to make up to Rachel for that awful birthmark? They didn't know anything of her background or where she'd come from so couldn't be prepared for such an outburst as she'd displayed in Wickham Church. Phoebe blamed herself. Somehow she'd failed Rachel over the affair with Adam Taylor. It had all been a nightmare which had caused tongues to wag and Wally just hadn't been able to bear that. Now, just when things had quietened down and the past was forgotten, here was Rachel, looking more mature but very happy with her handsome husband. If seeing her again had brought on Wally's stroke it was a high price to pay to have this rebel child back, Phoebe thought as she gazed at her beloved husband. She felt so helpless, there was nothing even she could do for him now. He was there but not there, alive yet dead to all that was going on around him. He looked pale and drawn and Phoebe seemed quite unable to speak the words she had rehearsed.

Rachel stood aside to let Belinda kiss her father.

'It's all right, Dad,' she whispered close to his ear. 'We won't let anything else upset you. Just nod or lift a finger if you'd like her to go away.'

Rachel went cold and a sick feeling caught in her stomach. She watched for some sign of response from the father she loved so dearly but there was none. Belinda went on whispering and then with a sigh stepped back.

'Suppose it's your turn,' she said to Rachel, 'but if he doesn't acknowledge us, it isn't likely he will you.'

Rachel hesitated. How she wished it was just her and Kas here. Earlier today her father had acknowledged her and squeezed her hand, now she was afraid of causing any further agitation. The screens were round each side of the bed and as Belinda stood back to allow Rachel access to the bedside she was acutely aware of the heat of her sister's anger. But she bent over her father and kissed him on each cheek.

'It's me again, Dad – Rachel,' she said softly. 'I'm sorry to find you so poorly. We all want you to get well quickly. I know I have so much to thank you and Mum for, and I'm sorry I had to go away in disgrace. I hope you've forgiven me? You must know I wouldn't have hurt either of you for the world but I was devastated when Adam jilted me. I could have borne it if it had been for any other girl, but my own twin sister . . .' Rachel could no longer cry. She felt stronger now and able humbly to voice her case, as she knew Lemuel would wish.

Rachel lifted her father's frail hand and held it between her own. Yes, sure enough, his fingers moved. There *was* life there. She freed

218

his hand so that she could cup his face lovingly and as she gazed down into his face his eyelids fluttered for the briefest of moments.

'I felt his fingers move,' she said, turning to her mother. 'And he's just fluttered his eyelids. He can hear us all right. Now he'll get stronger, I'm sure.' She pressed her cheek against his, willing him to fight, willing him to forgive her. 'Dearest Dad,' she murmured, 'get well again. Please, for me.'

It was Kas who gently persuaded her to leave. 'Let your mother and sister have the rest of the visiting time, Rachel,' he said quietly, sensing Belinda's hostility. 'We can come again. Lemuel is anxious to see you before the others get here.'

The others! Yes, Rachel had been and still was part of a much larger family than just the Hunters. She hugged her mother as she left her father's beside and after a few minutes with Lemuel who was much brighter and rested, Sybil and Precious arrived.

The nurses soon insisted that only two visitors were allowed for each patient, so Rachel and Kas went outside to find Carol and some of the other children who they looked after while the adults took turns to visit Lemuel. The time passed quickly and a loud bell echoed through the corridors when four o'clock came. Lemuel's flock gathered with much chatter over the welfare of their beloved leader, but when Rachel saw her mother and Belinda emerge from the main doors she ran to them.

'Did he respond to you, Mum?' she asked. 'Do you think he'll be all right?'

'You're deluding yourself, my dear,' Phoebe said solemnly. There's not much life left in his body.'

'But, Mum, it's his brain,' Rachel said. 'It's what's in his brain that matters.'

'Well, don't kid yourself that there are any kind thoughts for you,' Belinda said.

'I just want to get home and have a cup of tea.'

'How are you going to get back to Kingsmere?' Rachel asked. 'We've got a pony and trap. We could take you.'

Belinda scoffed. 'Pony and trap! You think Mum would be seen dead with a group of filthy gypsies!'

'Excuse me,' Kas put in as he joined them. 'True Romanies are never filthy. Because we choose to live a nomadic life doesn't mean we are any less clean and honest than you. I suggest you come and stay with Rachel and me to see for yourself. Mrs Hunter, you'd be most welcome to remain with us while your husband is in hospital.'

'Mum's staying with us,' Belinda snapped aggressively.

'And where is that?' Rachel dared to ask.

'Just a few roads away, within walking distance.'

'Who's looking after your little boy then?' Rachel enquired. 'I'd love to see him, Belinda.'

'Of course you would, dear,' Phoebe said in an attempt to pour oil on troubled waters. 'But perhaps another day. He's with a neighbour for now.'

'We'll see you tomorrow then,' Rachel said, kissing her mother's cheek. 'Lemuel will have to stay in hospital for at least another ten days.' She hesitated, not wanting to leave without some kind of reconciliation with her sister, but Kas tugged at her sleeve.

'If there's anything we can do, please let us know,' he said to Phoebe. 'We shall be making camp on Portsdown Hill while Lemuel's in hospital.'

Belinda guided her mother in the opposite direction. It was some while before Rachel felt calm.

The next morning while Kas was outside feeding the horses Rachel washed and dressed Carol. She was still experiencing a feeling of nausea and found Carol's exuberance difficult to handle.

'You'd better go and find Daddy,' she said as she lifted the child down from the table. 'A run before breakfast might burn off some of your energy and give you an appetite. Tell Daddy it'll be ready in ten minutes.'

Rachel helped Carol on with her coat and hat but when she opened the van door a surprise awaited her. Kas and Adam were a few yards away in earnest conversation.

'Daddy! Daddy! Breakfast in ten minutes,' Carol shouted eagerly as she ran down the steps and flung herself at Kas.

Rachel had to support herself on the framework of the van. Now Adam would believe that Carol was really their child – but what was he doing here in the camp at this time of the morning?

The two men exchanged glances when they saw Rachel at the door of the van.

'Come in, Adam,' Kas said as he hoisted Carol up in his arms.

'What brings you here?' Rachel said in a husky voice. She felt sick to her stomach and everything began to swim. 'How did you manage to find us?' She forced herself to go back inside the waggon and sit down. She closed her eyes, knowing there was bad news to come yet not wanting to believe it.

Adam went up the steps two at a time and stood inside, looking round, noting everything about the interior of their home.

'This is very pleasant,' he said. 'I'd no idea there would be so much room.'

'I'm afraid I haven't tidied round yet,' Rachel said. 'I was just getting breakfast.'

'Rachel,' Adam said, and came to stand directly in front of her, 'I'm here because the news is grave.'

'It's about Dad?'

He nodded. 'He had another stroke in the early hours and I'm afraid he died about five o'clock. I'm so sorry Rachel, but I'm glad fate intervened and brought you to the hospital. At least you saw him.'

'But . . . I . . . killed him.'

'No, of course you didn't,' Adam said quickly. 'He was a sick man. Your mother told me to tell you that you mustn't blame yourself. The doctors have said that it could have happened at any time.'

'But Belinda will always say it was my fault. If only Lemuel hadn't needed to go into hospital. Why didn't we go to Southampton, Kas? This might never have happened.'

'And we might not have met up again. It had to be, Rachel,' Adam said. 'And for your mother's sake too – perhaps most of all for her sake. She'll need you now.'

'She's got Belinda.'

'She'll need you both, Rachel.'

'Did Dad manage to talk – did he say anything?'

'No. There was no response while we were there. I'm afraid you must have imagined what you thought you felt and saw because it was what you wanted so badly. If you hadn't seen him when you did it might have been too late.'

Rachel buried her face in her hands and wept.

'Can I offer you a cup of tea, Adam?' Kas asked. 'I'm sure Rachel needs one. Darling, I'm sorry that this happened but your father was well over sixty.'

'That doesn't seem old though, does it?'

'His chest had bothered him for a number of years,' Adam said.

'Could the shock of what I did and then me turning up unexpectedly really have caused a stroke.'

'Most unlikely,' Adam said, trying to be as prudent as he could. 'I've got time off to help your mother and Belinda arrange the funeral,' he hurried on. 'You'll both come, of course? Mrs Hunter's expecting you to. What about the little one? I didn't know you had a daughter.'

Rachel looked at Kas.

'She's not really ours,' he said. 'We wish she was. Unfortunately Rachel has had three miscarriages, but her turn will come.' He smiled warmly. 'Carol's mother was a friend of ours. It's a sad story. When

221

she died she left a note asking us to bring her up as our own which we've been pleased to do. One day our children will be her brothers and sisters.' The blackened kettle began to sing and Kas warmed the pot. 'Yes, we shall be at Mr Hunter's funeral if you're sure that's what Rachel's mother wants? No need to worry about Carol, there's plenty of our folk who will mind her.'

'Look,' Adam began, 'I'm sorry Belinda has been difficult. I hope you can find it in your heart to excuse her bad manners. She doesn't mean to be rude but she's been worried about her father and it was a shock seeing you again, Rachel – for all of us. It's your right to be at your father's funeral. I'll let you know as soon as we know the time.'

'Will it be at Kingsmere?' she asked.

'Yes. Mr Hunter's wish was to be buried in the churchyard at Wickham. Apparently a will has been left to be read by his solicitor after the burial.'

Rachel felt numb. It was all so final. Why couldn't it have been Lemuel who had died? He was older, there were no blood relatives who would mourn his passing, and no one would have blamed her. She blinked away more tears hating herself for such selfish, ungracious thoughts, but no matter how anyone tried to comfort her and exonerate her from blame she knew she must accept that she was partly responsible for her father's death, and the guilt would weigh heavily on her. Kas passed her a cup of tea and she took it without realising what was taking place around her. Kas and Adam talked amicably but after one or two sips of the hot sweet liquid Rachel had to rush outside to vomit.

'I'd better leave you,' Adam said as Kas led Rachel back inside the van. 'It's a rotten business, and I'm sorry to be the bearer of bad news. Belinda and Mrs Hunter need me, there's so much to arrange. I'll let you know about the day and time as soon as I can.'

'We shall be calling to see Lemuel every day,' Kas said. 'To save you coming out here again you can leave a message with him or we might see you there. It's hard work cycling up the hill.'

'Yes, I'll see you at the hospital, later today or maybe tomorrow.'

Rachel watched him walk away pushing his bicycle, with Kas in earnest conversation and Carol jumping alongside. The years rolled back. If only she could roll them back still further to when she and Adam had been happily engaged. But there was no going back. He was married to Belinda and she was married to Kas. Her mind spun like a top with confusing emotions. If only . . . if only . . .

It was a grey February morning, frost crackling beneath their feet and the sky overhead thickening with snow clouds as Kas secured black plumes on Bella's head. She stood quiet as if she knew that this was no joy ride but a solemn occasion. Rachel looked drawn and pale in her black coat and woollen shawl which she had draped over her black hat to protect her ears from the icy north-east wind. As she got up in the trap she turned to raise a gloved hand to Sybil and Carol who were watching from the window of Sybil's van. Kas got up beside her looking every inch the country gentleman in a thick dark coat and sombre grey trilby hat with a black band which he'd borrowed from Lemuel. He put a thick rug over Rachel's knees before they set off at a trot. Sybil had insisted that she have a bowl of thick nourishing broth, made with her usual concoction of herbs, to stave off the nausea which Rachel had experienced ever since their arrival in Portsmouth.

Sybil's mouth was tight-lipped as she let the curtain fall. She had sensed trouble for Rachel but happiness too. What was taking place was out of her jurisdiction but she feared that there was more trouble to come before the girl who had become like a daughter to her would be truly happy. She couldn't rightly say what emotion it was she saw in Rachel's dark eyes. A mixture of sadness, torture and longing – but for whom?

The tops of the hedgerows glistened with frozen dew as Rachel recognised familiar surroundings. Her emotions were mixed, not of sadness, torture and longing but a strange kind of relief at coming home. She saw barren fields, powdery white waiting for spring planting, trees with branches like horny brown fingers pointing skywards, and evergreen bushes and shrubs brightly coloured with red berries. As they neared Wickham the local flock of rooks was making the most of the wind to swerve and dive, chasing each other, cawing endlessly with their mournful chatter as if in sympathy with Rachel's grief.

It seemed ironic to Kas that he and Rachel's former fiancé could have become instant pals in these unexpected circumstances. Kas wished he had taken an instant dislike to Adam Taylor but the truth was he had felt an affinity with him at their first meeting. He searched in vain for some logical explanation for Adam treating Rachel the way he had but he seemed the most unlikely person to behave in such a manner. Kas was doing his best to comfort her in her sorrow. He was anxious for today's sad events to be over and done with, for Lemuel to get well enough so that they could travel on, but a sense of foreboding plagued him. Of course, he feared Rachel becoming too nostalgic about the past. He watched her and Adam together, so kindly disposed to each other, with no apparent rancour over what

223

had happened four years earlier. It didn't seem quite natural to him. Surely Rachel should have experienced some embarrassment and bitterness at Adam's change of heart? But the only bitterness evident was between the two sisters. Kas could hardly credit how totally unalike they were in looks. Belinda was of slighter build and fairer complexion, decidedly pretty, but her round blue eyes could cut as sharply as the blade of a knife. He couldn't help wondering whether she hadn't played some devious role in past events. It was clear that she saw her sister's return to the mainland as an intrusion. Did she, like Kas, have reason to be apprehensive about the future? He vowed that he would do all in his power to get Rachel away from this area as fast as he could after today and spare her any more agony.

They had arranged with Adam that they would only travel to the outskirts of Wickham and await the funeral cortège down a small farm track which Rachel knew of, and it wasn't long before they heard the horses and carriages coming through the lane. Kas removed his hat as the procession passed and then urged Bella forward to join at the rear. He felt that Rachel at least should have been invited to travel with her mother and sister in their carriage, but she had chosen to be an outcast, a gypsy, and so must bear the consequences, he supposed.

The village church was full as the much respected and loved resident of neighbouring Kingsmere was brought inside by estate workers acting as bearers and the service commenced. Rachel felt quite faint as she once more relived her rebellious actions in this sacred place. She sat down quickly, pulling a veil over her face, but all eyes turned on her and Kas with curiosity. As she was tall there was no way of hiding. Perhaps word hadn't got out that she was going to be there? Her reappearance caused hushed whispers and a constant turning of heads.

The service over, family, local villagers and friends filed out to the open graveside. Phoebe kept turning round, trying to urge Rachel and Kas to move closer to the family, but Rachel kept her distance, her head bowed against inquisitive glances. A handful of earth was thrown on to the coffin. Rachel saw Adam place an arm round her mother's and Belinda's shoulders to support them, and then the family stood back as people paid their last respects. Rachel waited until last. She wanted to refrain from giving Belinda any cause for complaint. As they moved forward Kas took a small posy of snowdrops from his large pocket which Rachel held for a moment and then let slip from her fingers on to the coffin of carved oak. Her father would have been proud of it.

'I'm sorry,' she whispered as she bade him goodbye.

At Calder Cottage the tiny rooms were filled to overflowing not so much with relatives as friends. During Rachel's absence over the past four years her grandparents had passed away at a great age. Strange, she thought, that her father had died while still a comparatively young man, which only confirmed her belief that it must be her fault. A glass of home-made wine was offered but Rachel was forced to decline and could merely pick at the sandwiches and other delicacies which followed. A cup of tea went down gratefully and as time passed people began to forget the reason for Rachel's hurried departure. They were curious about Kas and word had soon circulated that there was a child. No one dared ask outright but Rachel suspected that there was speculation as to Carol's parentage. If it pleased them to think that she had been compelled to marry Kas because she was pregnant then she doubted that anything she said would make them think otherwise.

It was almost three o'clock when Phoebe diplomatically explained that the solicitor was anxious to deal with legal matters which involved just the family, and get back to his head office in Winchester. Belinda and her mother stood at the front door and thanked the visitors for coming. Rachel was buttoning her coat too.

'Can I come to see you, Mum?' she asked as she hugged her mother.

'This is still your home, Rachel dear,' Phoebe said. 'But you can't go yet, you're family too.'

'I'm sure I'm not needed so it's better if Kas and I leave now.'

'No, Rachel,' Adam intervened. 'Mr Fisher insists that we must all be here.'

'Kas too?'

'He's your husband, isn't he?' Belinda said sharply.

'Of course.'

'Well then?'

'I would much rather we didn't stay,' Rachel said. 'I feel positive there's nothing that involves me, and if there was Mr Fisher can always contact me later.'

'I have a letter your father expressly wishes me to read at this time,' Mr Fisher said. 'I have no knowledge of its contents but it is my duty to carry out Mr Hunter's requests.'

The solicitor was a small thin man. He was a pillar of the church and local community in Wickham but an unfriendly type. It was fairly evident that he didn't care for children or younger people and rumour had it that he had lost his job as a magistrate owing to the unwarranted harshness of his sentencing of young offenders.

The cottage seemed unnaturally cold and almost sinister after the other mourners had left. Phoebe sat with just her two daughters and sons-in-law, waiting with apprehension as Mr Fisher untied a sheaf of papers. He spread them out on the highly polished mahogany table and then looked from one to the other over the top of his spectacles.

'Most of Mr Hunter's estate goes to his wife, Phoebe Hunter. The property, Calder Cottage, which he purchased from Squire, and two cottages at Minstead in the New Forest which had recently come into his possession on the death of his own father are now yours, Mrs Hunter. All properties are to be bequeathed to your daughter, Belinda Taylor, to be equally shared between her and her offspring after your demise which I trust will be many years hence.' He paused to smile reassuringly at Phoebe before he went on, 'There is a bequest of three hundred pounds for you at this time, Belinda Taylor.'

Mr Fisher shuffled his feet nervously under the table as he then withdrew a sealed envelope.

'I will now read Wally's letter,' he said as if this might not be considered a truly legal document. 'It is specifically intended for his wife and daughters.' After coughing and taking a quick glance at the short letter in his hand his brow puckered in a frown. For a minute it seemed as if he couldn't go on and he visibly paled as he read aloud:

'My dears, anything I have been able to leave you has been obtained by sheer hard work. My life and love have gone into everything I have ever done for you both. Although I have become very fond of Adam Taylor as my son-in-law I would have wished for someone else for you, Belinda, after the scandal of his broken engagement with Rachel, but I trust he will be a good husband to you and will make you happy.'

Mr Fisher swallowed hard and tried to glance further along the page. 'Rachel, our wayward cuckoo in the nest, we took you in as a favour when you were just a few days old, doing all in our power to bring you up as a God-fearing, honest, hard-working young woman and look how you have repaid us. I was never able to love you as my own daughter though I did try for Phoebe's sake. Your mother did love and protect you, always loyal to the promise that she would treat you like Belinda's twin sister and she never thought of you as anything but her own child. Doing what you did and then disappearing for several days without a word caused your mother terrible anguish which I cannot forget. I hope someone will find you one day and pass this letter on so that you understand why you are not legally entitled to a legacy, and I cannot think of one good reason why I should make an exception.'

All eyes turned to Rachel. Phoebe gasped and cried into her handkerchief. Rachel's face went stiff, and turned the colour of stone.

226

Chapter Fifteen

No one heard the rest of the contents of Wally's letter. Even Mr Fisher was only vaguely aware of the words he read aloud as the painful silence seemed to drown his voice. Phoebe kept her head bowed as she continued to sob.

'How could Wally do such a thing?' she wailed after several minutes. 'We were never to tell anyone, least of all you girls.' She looked up with fear and pleading in her expression. 'What have you done?' she accused the solicitor. 'Why couldn't you have given me the letter first? There was no need for this to have come out – *ever* – let alone now. As if it isn't enough that Wally has gone . . .' She was inconsolable.

Rachel felt as if her brain had frozen. Even Belinda remained with her head lowered but Adam looked apologetically towards Kas.

'God!' he said. 'This is terrible. Kas, Wally was a good man, really he was. He probably wrote that letter in the heat of the moment when he was upset about Rachel running off. I'm sure he didn't mean to be so callous. It's so uncharacteristic of him.'

Suddenly Belinda ran from her chair and placed her arms round Rachel.

'We *are* sisters,' she exclaimed, 'we are! I can't believe this story. How can it be true?' She hugged Rachel as if she really meant what she was saying and kissed her cheek. 'Oh, my dear, *dear* Rachel, I'm so sorry for all the hurt we caused you. It was Adam's fault, he just couldn't wait. I'll share my legacy with you. Mother, I can, can't I? Dad was wrong, wasn't he?'

Mr Fisher stood up. 'I don't think there is any way in which I can be of further use to you, Mrs Hunter – not at this precise moment. I shall be available, of course, should you need any advice – any at all.'

Phoebe got to her feet and held on to the edge of the table. She felt weak and utterly weary. She and Wally thought they had put the past

227

behind them skilfully after the retirement of the Fletcher sisters who were the only people in the world who knew that Rachel wasn't their own child. Whatever had possessed him to do this terrible thing?

'No, Mr Fisher,' she said quietly. 'I don't think I shall need your services again. I suppose I can't blame you, you did what you were asked to do – and a right hornet's nest you've disturbed!' She ushered him to the front door. 'Poor Rachel, so upset when Adam jilted her and now to discover she's not really Belinda's sister. Not my true daughter. Somehow I must make her understand that I love her just as much as the day I agreed to pretend she was mine.'

Mr Fisher hovered on the door step. 'It sounds to me as if you may have been persuaded into making an unwise decision many years ago, Mrs Hunter. Now if Rachel had been legally adopted by you and your late husband, she could have contested the will.'

'I don't think what we did matters to anyone but our family. I shall see that Rachel gets her share, don't you worry, and please, not a word to anyone, especially local people.'

Mr Fisher leaned closer to Phoebe. 'May I be permitted to ask – if it isn't too impertinent – who was Rachel's father?'

Phoebe very nearly spat in his face with anger at his inference. 'No, you may not! I don't know who either of her parents were and if I did I wouldn't tell you. Because of her disfigurement she was unwanted. That's what we were told when she was brought to us under cover of darkness. I had just given birth to Belinda after fifteen years of hoping. We made an arrangement to bring Rachel up as Belinda's twin sister, which we did. Where we lived then in the New Forest no one ever questioned anything so there's no reason for you to either, Mr Fisher. I didn't give birth to her and Wally was not her father. Whether or not she was illegitimate I cannot tell you. A poor wee mite born with a blemish and rejected. Maybe if they'd realised that the strawberry mark would fade in time they'd have kept her, who knows? I know nothing of her background or circumstances, and I'll thank you to keep this whole matter in confidence. Good day to you, Mr Fisher.'

Phoebe almost pushed him out of the way as she closed the heavy oak door with a resounding thud. She stood with her back against it, the force of her rage having exhausted her. Several minutes passed before she could return to the parlour where Rachel was pacing the floor. The other three were trying to pacify her.

'I don't care who your parents were,' Kas was assuring her, 'it doesn't alter the fact that you're my wife and I love you. Isn't that enough?'

'My birth certificate, Mum,' Rachel demanded. 'I need it. The real one. I managed to get a copy from Somerset House when I got married but it was just a brief one. There must be some details on the genuine one.'

'Rachel, I'm sorry, my dear. First the shock of seeing your father in hospital, dying, and now this. I don't know anything about where you came from except that you were brought to us shortly after Belinda was born. The births were registered together and you became legally Belinda's twin sister. That's what it says on your birth certificate and you must accept it.' Phoebe sat down in the nearest chair. 'I can't understand how your father could so such a thing. He never talked even to me about his financial affairs so I had no idea that he'd even written this letter let alone altered his will. I can't imagine when he did it. He never said a word. Well, he wouldn't because he would have expected me to try to persuade him not to. I was always convinced you'd turn up again one day, Rachel.' She covered her face with her hands. 'Now I almost wish you hadn't.'

Kas placed a gentle hand on Phoebe's shoulder. 'Aren't we getting this out of all proportion, Mrs Hunter?' he said. 'Money isn't important. I work hard to keep Rachel and Carol as comfortable as I know how. I had some property left to me, down in Christchurch. I don't use the rental money, it goes into the bank and is kept for repairs. It's an investment for us and our children.'

'I never want children,' Rachel screamed. 'My childhood was wrecked by that awful birthmark. I always wondered why Belinda was so much prettier than me, and now I discover that I must have been born out of wedlock to some unknown woman. What was I thinking of to marry a gypsy? I never stopped to think of what the children would think of their heritage.'

'Rachel, please,' he begged. 'This isn't like you. What you've heard today makes no different to us.'

'Of course it does,' she said impatiently. 'I've got to find out where I came from and who my real parents are.'

Adam went to the sideboard and poured some spirits into a glass. 'Here,' he said, compelling Rachel to take the glass.

'What is it?' she asked, sniffing.

'Brandy, it'll calm your nerves. And you must calm down, Rachel. This has been a shock to everyone.' Not to me, he thought, and please God she'll never find out who her real father was. 'You must put it right out of your mind,' he went on. 'It happened years ago. No one can know the truth of the matter so it's best that you try to forget.'

'How can I? How would you feel if you suddenly discovered that the people you'd thought of as your parents weren't related at all?'

'I was in that very position,' Kas said. 'Josh and Merle were not my real parents, and I know very little about my mother or my father but

I'm grateful to Josh and Merle for all they did for me. How can it help you to know who they were, Rachel? Surely it's more important to be grateful to the folk who love you and gave you security and a home than to worry about your true parentage?'

'But they may still be alive,' she persisted. 'And if they are, I'd like to meet them.'

'And cause them as much of a shock as you've had?' Kas asked. 'I do understand how painful this has been for you, but what good will it do anyone to delve into the past?'

'I – I *need* to know, Kas,' she said with feeling.

'We're going home now,' he said abruptly. 'It's been a long and trying day for your mother. She needs a little peace.'

'I'm going to stay with her,' Rachel announced. 'I *will* find out who I am – I *will*!'

'Mum's coming back to Portsmouth with us,' Belinda said. 'We'll look after her.'

Phoebe held up her hand to silence them all.

'I want to be left on my own,' she said softly. 'I need some time to be quiet, and you would all do well to do the same. I'm sure dear Wally never meant to cause such a stir. He must have had his reasons and I want to read his letter in peace to try to understand. He was never a vindictive man. Maybe he was wise in his thinking and anticipated some future trouble for Rachel, being that we didn't know anything about her background.'

'But it's what we are, Mrs Hunter,' Adam said politely, 'not where we come from that counts. Rachel has never done anything wrong in her life to deserve this.'

'Hah!' she scoffed. 'Only desecrated God's house and then run away, which led my father – or the man I thought was my father – to write such a letter. He's not only hurt me but you, Belinda, and Adam and Kas.'

'It's only surprised us, Rachel,' Belinda said, 'not hurt us. As Kas says it doesn't make any difference to any of us. He is your husband and if it doesn't affect him then why should it worry you?'

Rachel stared at her sister. Now she knew that her childish jealousies had not been without foundation. Belinda, the pretty one with golden sunshine hair and baby blue eyes. The delicate one who was always had the best of everything and the most attention. The one who had stolen the heart of the man she loved. Rachel's gaze moved to Adam. He wasn't as handsome or strong-looking as Kas but there was a genuine warmth in his expression which she felt sure was for her alone. It wasn't pity. His cheeks flushed at her scrutiny.

'You'll help me find my parents, won't you, Adam?' Rachel asked in a low husky voice.

230

He averted his eyes and shook his head.

'No, Rachel. It would be like looking for a needle in a haystack. Where would you begin?'

'You must put such ideas right out of your head this minute!' Kas's voice was loud and clear. 'We're going home, Rachel. Bella needs feeding and it'll soon be dark. The roads are icy enough as it is.'

'But someone should stay with Mum,' Rachel said.

'We can stay,' Belinda offered. 'Our neighbour will understand.'

'No,' Phoebe said. 'Can't I make you understand I want to be by myself. Tonight, tomorrow, and probably for several days after that.'

Belinda went to fetch their coats from the bedroom and they sheepishly prepared to leave, not entirely certain that Phoebe was capable of knowing what she wanted or needed at that moment.

Rachel hugged her mother as she wept for the umpteenth time that day.

'When can I see you again, Mum?'

'Give me a few days, dear,' Phoebe said. 'Perhaps you could all come to tea on Sunday? We shall have had time to calm down by then.'

'I've got a better idea,' Belinda said. 'Why don't you all come to our house to tea? Your little girl can play with Billy. They're about the same age.'

'Carol is not my little girl and I shall make sure she grows up knowing that,' Rachel said adamantly.

'Thanks very much for the invitation,' Kas said. 'We'd be pleased to come. We'll be visiting Lemuel in hospital in the afternoon anyway.'

'Is he likely to be there much longer?' Phoebe asked.

'He's making good progress. The rest has done him good so hopefully in about a week they'll let him come home. Come along, Rachel. Carol will be missing us.'

She was reluctant to leave her mother, and it was hard for her to think of Phoebe as anything but that.

'Your parents are the people who rear you,' Kas said as explanations were made to Sybil on their return to camp. 'It doesn't matter who gave birth to you. Mr and Mrs Hunter looked after you almost from the day you were born, loved you, gave you all the things you needed, clothed and fed you. Isn't that enough, for God's sake?'

'I can understand what a shock you've had, Rachel,' Sybil said, 'and it'll take time to grow used to the idea. But whatever the circumstances, nothing can change the fact that your parents were good and kind to you. They gave you their name and shielded you from the stigma of being illegitimate – if you were. Maybe your real

231

mother died in childbirth. Who's to know the reason there was for you being given away. Think of the alternatives, my dearie. You might have ended up in an orphanage or in a home where there was no harmony – drunkenness, abuse, fighting for survival along with a dozen others. Maybe that's it, Rachel. Perhaps your real parents already had a large family and just couldn't make room for one more.'

She felt she had let Rachel down by not seeing some of this in her reading of the past. The plain truth was she had seen things she didn't want to see so had conveniently pulled a blind down on them.

Sybil had prepared a meal for them and although Rachel tried to show her appreciation she could only toy with the food on her plate and hardly spoke. Carol was as lively as ever and chattered non-stop. When she got no response from Rachel she leaned across and pulled Rachel's sleeve.

'Mummy, are you still unhappy?' she asked, gazing up into Rachel's face.

'I'm not your –'

'Careful,' Kas warned, and for the first time in her married life Rachel was afraid of the dark, angry expression in his eyes. 'Mummy has been feeling sad because her daddy was very ill,' he told Carol.

'I know – he's dead,' she said matter-of-factly.

'She asked lots of questions so t'was best the truth be told,' Sybil said. 'Children don't like being fobbed off with half truths.'

'But I was,' Rachel snapped. 'Why couldn't they have told me the truth when I was young? I always knew there was something. That horrible strawberry birthmark, and Belinda being so pretty.'

'Being pretty isn't everything,' Kas said. 'You have striking features – when you're your normal self.' He tried to smile, tried to cheer her up, but she was quick to retort:

'How can I be normal? What *is* normal? Evidently they didn't think I was normal when I was born or they wouldn't have got rid of me so quickly. Just two days old and my mother handed me over like some unwanted kitten.'

'You can't know that,' Sybil said in a firm low voice. 'It probably pained your mother a great deal to part with you.'

'Where is she now?' Rachel asked with a tremor in her voice. 'How can I find her? Please, Sybil, help me to find her?' she pleaded.

'You mustn't even think of trying to find her,' Kas said bluntly. 'Your parents lived in the New Forest at the time, so you could have been born in any one of a dozen places miles away. You can't think of them as anything but your real parents, Rachel.'

'Well, I mean to find out where I came from. I'll move heaven and earth to trace who I really am,' she said defiantly.

232

'Not with my help you won't,' he answered, equally defiantly. 'We've got our own little "cuckoo in the nest", as your father so delicately phrased it. We're going to see that Carol has everything in life that we were both given by substitute parents. I owe a lot to Josh and Merle just as you do Mr and Mrs Hunter.'

'But it isn't the same,' Rachel argued. 'At least you were told that your parents died.'

'And maybe yours did too.'

'I've got to know,' Rachel muttered.

Kas stood up and banged his fist hard down on the table, making the crockery jump. 'That is enough,' he shouted. 'I don't want to hear any more about it. Let's get home and put Carol to bed.'

Sybil pulled herself out of her chair too. 'Sleep on it,' she said. 'Don't let this come between you, Rachel. You've a good life with Kas. Knowing who your real parents were won't make any difference now, will it?'

'Yes, to me. Trust you to all stick together! At least let me have this legacy for myself. What sort of life have I had? Born with a birthmark, then loving a man who really wanted my sister, and now discovering that I'm not who I thought I was – oh, it's all too much!' She rushed out of Sybil's waggon, banging the door with wild fury.

She hurried away, darting between the trees just below Portsdown Hill where the group were sheltering from the cold weather. She unlocked their van door and inside lay on the bed, utterly worn out. Why did Lemuel have to be ill? Why did she have to bump into Adam of all people and what were they doing living in Portsmouth? He'd been an apprenticed carpenter before the war. She supposed there was more money to be earned as a hospital porter. It was regular work which was something to be thankful for in this day and age.

Rachel was full of remorse for the anguish she'd caused her parents. She had experienced regret many times before but not as deeply as she felt now. For her father to disinherit her she knew he must have been bitterly disappointed in her. Or had he been glad of the excuse to leave everything to Belinda eventually? Memories of her childhood came back to taunt Rachel. She remembered hearing him say, 'We won't let Rachel down,' when she'd been ill with fever. She had thought he meant he had some magic way of curing her measles but now she realised what he meant. That they were going to do their duty. Why had they agreed to take her in? she wondered. Who could the mystery couple be who had conceived her? Why? Why? Why?

She felt the draught from the open door as Kas brought Carol home.

233

'You might have stayed long enough to thank Sybil for her trouble,' he said. 'She's not a young woman to have the responsibility of a four year old.'

'I expect Precious or Charity helped,' Rachel said non-committally.

'Well now you can help – get up and see to Carol.'

She slid off the bed. The stove was kept alight during the cold weather and a kettle was already full of hot water. She poured some into the washing bowl and began to undress the little girl.

'We'll take you to meet Billy on Sunday,' she said as she bathed the child's face. 'What have you been doing today?'

'I played with the others.' As Rachel rubbed her dry Carol stretched out her arms and hugged her. 'You won't cry any more will you, Mummy? Lemuel will soon be better, won't he?'

Rachel hugged her back as she fought against more tears.

When she had settled Carol in the iron cot, covered her with warm knitted blankets and a patchwork quilt she'd made herself, Rachel drew the dividing curtains across the middle of the van and sat on the couch in silence. Kas was sitting close to the stove in a wooden rocking chair reading.

'Where d'you think the Smiths and Wellses went?' she asked suddenly.

Kas didn't move immediately and then with a pronounced sigh he put down his book and looked at Rachel.

'How would I know? Why d'you want to know?'

'You were clever enough to find Davey. I think we should take Carol back to her grandparents. She isn't related in any way to us, Kas. Isn't it her right to know her real family? What is she going to think of everyone when she grows up?'

'In most cases a child would probably never know that the people they call parents aren't their real ones. What you've heard today has stunned you. I'm full of sympathy for you, but Mr Hunter couldn't have been thinking rationally or he would have realised the terrible shock he was inflicting both on you and his beloved Belinda.'

'You don't like Belinda? Everyone likes Belinda,' Rachel said.

'I hardly know her but she doesn't seem as open as you are. Still, you can't judge people by their looks.'

'You don't like her,' Rachel repeated. 'You don't trust her.'

'Like I said, I don't know her so how can I trust her? After what she and Adam did, how can I trust either of them?'

'You think she had a hand in Adam changing his mind?'

'Well, don't you?'

'I've tried not to blame her,' Rachel said thoughtfully. 'Perhaps they poisoned Dad's mind against me?'

234

'You ran away – and I can't blame you for that, even though it was probably a foolish thing to do.'

'I lost my temper in the church – that's what Dad couldn't forgive. I wonder when he changed his will? When he wrote that awful letter? I felt sure he forgave me when he was in the hospital.'

Kas went back to his book. Rachel's eyes burned, her throat was dry and she ached everywhere while her tired brain chased a variety of thoughts round and round.

'Once we've found Carol's people and handed her back I'll travel all over the Forest to find my people,' she said.

Kas threw down his book and stood up.

'Shut up, Rachel!' he yelled angrily. 'Stop whining, for heaven's sake. I know it's been a hell of a day and what you need now is sleep so I suggest you go to bed.'

Rachel stood up to face him. 'How dare you shriek at me?' she said. 'It's my life, my background that's in question, so if I want to find out who I am, I will!'

'We both know who you are – my wife, Carol's substitute mother. And one day we'll have children of our own – a new family. The past is over and done with. I shall be glad when you can see Lemuel on Sunday. Maybe he can talk some sense into you.'

'I shouldn't have run away, I realise that now,' she said.

'No, you probably shouldn't, and then there would have been no need for your father to write that letter, but what's done is done. It all goes back to Adam jilting you. That wasn't a very noble thing to do and I daresay your sister had some part in it. I would have expected your parents to have been more sensitive to your feelings.'

'So everyone's to blame? But it still doesn't alter the fact that I want to know who my parents were – or are. They could still be alive and often wonder where I am and what became of me.'

Kas ran his hands through his hair in desperation. 'Rachel, Rachel,' he said. 'Stop tormenting yourself. Please – go to bed.'

'You don't want me to know. You're sorry I ever met up with my family again.'

'I'm sorry for your mother. She's the one who's most hurt by this, so you must try to be understanding to her. She's lost her husband, she's still in shock and grieving. If you carry on like you're doing now she'll wish you'd never turned up again.'

'But I love her – I always loved her more than Dad. I never want to be parted from her again, Kas.'

'Then try to be forgiving, darling. Be there when she needs you. Don't keep harping on about finding your real parents or you'll cause her untold pain. Can't you see that you'll make her feel she failed you?'

235

Rachel knew that she could never lay that at her mother's door. Her parents hadn't failed her, but she had them. She went behind the curtain and prepared for bed. Carol lay sleeping unperturbed, unaware of who her parents were or had been. In her circumstances Kas was right. She must never be told that her mother had hanged herself and that her father was a womaniser, and it was up to Rachel and Kas to see that she never knew. Ena had left her in their care, trusting them to do whatever was right. However she turned out, whatever she did, whether or not she disgraced the Romany group, she was Kas's and Rachel's responsibility and they must do the same for her as they would for their own children.

Rachel lay on the bed but couldn't sleep and when Kas joined her, placing loving, protecting arms around her, she moved away. She loved him, of course she did, but seeing Adam again had aroused old memories of their courting days when she hadn't a care in the world.

Lemuel was up and walking around the ward chatting to other patients when they visited the hospital on Sunday afternoon. The weather had changed again and frost had given way to mild damp days but he assured them that he would soon be back among them. Two visitors only were allowed at each bedside so as Kas and Rachel were visiting Belinda's home afterwards they went in first.

'You look so much better,' Rachel said as she kissed the elderly man. 'But you'll have to be extra careful when you get home not to catch a chill. You'll need special care to build you up so that you're fit again by spring.'

'And I've no doubt that you and Sybil will see to that,' Lemuel laughed. He shook hands with Kas, and then took Rachel's hands in his. 'My dear, you look quite wan. I wish I could offer you some comfort in the loss of your father but only time will soothe the pain. It was such a cold bleak day for the funeral. Was it a dreadful ordeal for you, my dear?'

'You could say that,' she said. 'It was strange being back in Wickham again and people stared as we knew they would, but the worse part was going to Calder Cottage without Dad there.'

'I'm sure your mother was quite relieved to have you there, and I trust everything is well between you now?'

'It was a strained reunion, Lemuel, and none of us were prepared for the will and letter Dad left.'

A nurse had insisted that Lemuel should get back into bed during visiting hours so Kas fetched chairs for them to sit one on either side of his bed. Rachel told Lemuel all that had transpired and he listened, hardly able to believe her story. Even though sleep had eluded her

236

she was calmer now, and determined to keep the trauma hidden from others.

'Life has treated you unkindly, my dear Rachel,' Lemuel said. 'It might have been better if we'd never come back to the mainland and I'm afraid I'm to blame for that.'

'No one's to blame,' Kas said. 'Naturally it seems that it was meant to be for Rachel to see her father before he died but no one can change events.'

'I'm pleased that you're going to spend some time with your mother and sister so I don't want to keep you this afternoon, Rachel dear,' Lemuel said. 'I expect the others are waiting to come in and after that I shall spend time considering what you've told me. It's quite a lot to take in for me so I can understand the effect the shock has had on you. As Kas says we can't change anything, but talking helps and I daresay you'll feel better when you've seen your family again today. As time passes the burden will get easier to bear, so go with peace in your heart, my dear.'

Rachel was eager to get to Adam and Belinda's home yet apprehensive too. If Kas wasn't going to support her in looking for her real family she hoped she could appeal to Adam. Didn't he owe her that much?

They joined the rest of the group outside the hospital grounds where the Sanders family were looking after Carol. Adam had told Kas how to find their house only a few minutes' walk away from the hospital so they were able to walk there, leaving Bella and the trap with Caleb.

The road seemed to stretch endlessly to the horizon but number seventeen, a well-kept terraced house, was only a few yards along and Adam opened the door almost before Rachel had let go of the wrought iron knocker. He was quickly joined by a small boy with fair hair and hazel-coloured eyes. At the sight of strangers he hid behind Adam but as soon as he saw Carol he forgot his shyness.

Rachel was surprised at the size of the house inside. It was clean and nicely decorated and in a corner of the square hall stood a tall jardiniere on which stood an aspidistra with shiny broad dark green leaves hanging over the sides. At a quick glance Rachel noticed the steep staircase with fine oak banisters, recently renewed, an example of Adam's craftsmanship, she guessed.

Adam showed them into the front sitting room where Belinda and Phoebe had been sitting by the fire.

'Take Carol up into the attic,' Belinda said. 'There are plenty of toys up there.' She smiled at her sister. 'That's one thing about a terraced house – it goes up three floors, and Adam has made the attic

237

into a good-sized playroom.' She greeted Rachel with a light kiss on her cheek.

Phoebe hugged Rachel warmly, kissed her and held her for several seconds. 'Come near to the fire, dear,' she said. 'You look pinched with the cold. And how was your friend today?'

'Up and about. He'll soon be able to leave hospital, I expect.'

Phoebe held out her hand to Kas. 'I hope we're going to have a chance to get to know you better. There's a few years of catching up to do. It's been a sad business but it's such a relief to see Rachel again.'

'Adam,' Belinda said, 'why don't you show Kas round the house while Mum and I have a chat to Rachel.'

Rachel felt herself bristle with annoyance. Trust Belinda to want to show off her home, she thought. But if she hoped to make Kas envious Rachel knew she would be unlucky. The Romany way of life suited him and he was unlikely to change even though he had property of his own.

'Are you feeling all right, Rachel?' Belinda asked after the men had left the room. 'The past week has been eventful to say the least. I can't begin to tell you how sorry I am that at Dad's funeral you had to learn you didn't really belong.'

'But she does belong to us, the same as she's always done,' Phoebe insisted. 'I've had time to think, Rachel, and although what your father did seems hard-hearted, it was because he was upset that he didn't know where you went. How could he have known that you were so close to us all the time or that you were going to turn up like that at the hospital?'

'I won't deny it was a shock,' Rachel said. 'But all I want to do now is to find out who my real parents were. Isn't there anything you can tell me, Mum? Any clue at all?'

'You're nearly twenty-four years old. All I can remember is the midwife bringing you all wrapped up in blankets and – well, I'm sorry – but you looked a poor little thing.'

'You mean with that awful birthmark?'

'Not so much that, although it was something of a shock, but we were assured that it would fade by the time you went to school. It didn't, it's true, but just look at you now, not a blemish – a bit too pale but I reckon that'll be the worry of all that's happened recently.' She smiled almost proudly at Rachel which brought a lump to her throat.

'What else can you remember? Didn't anyone say where the midwife got me from?'

'She was getting on then and seemed mighty agitated. She brought you to me and laid you beside Belinda. We were so grateful to have a daughter of our own at last, two was a blessing indeed.'

238

'But didn't you ask any questions? Surely you wanted to know something about me?'

'I suppose I was fairly weak. It wasn't an easy birth and we felt so sorry for you. Reckon at first it was touch and go whether you survived, but I remember the old midwife – Nurse Edwards her name was – a widow, everyone called her Teddy. Big woman, round rosy cheeks and a hearty laugh, but she was good at her job. Without her help I don't think you would have made it. Love was what you needed most, Teddy said. Yes, 'tis all coming back. Unwanted, unloved, she said, but she'd never tell us anything more.

"Course, as time passed we quite forgot you weren't really ours even though you and Belinda didn't look alike. Folk commented but so far as I know no one ever questioned it. T'was lucky we moved to Kingsmere then. The secret was between us and Teddy. We promised never to tell a soul and we kept our promise, which is why it's so out of character for Wally to have written that letter.' Phoebe put her arm round Rachel's shoulders as she directed her to a chair near the roaring log fire. 'You never wanted for love and protection, dear.'

'Oh, I know that, Mum. I do understand that, although I always felt Belinda was Dad's favourite. But now that I do know I'm not really a Hunter, I feel I want to know about my family.'

'It might be better not to know, Rachel,' Belinda said. 'Dad wasn't really capable of making the right decisions when he made his will and wrote that letter, so Adam agrees with me that you must share my legacy.'

'Thank you, but no, I couldn't take anything, Belinda. Not all gypsy people are poor. We work hard to earn a living but Kas has had property left him. He was away in the Army during the war so he learnt to be a blacksmith and can turn his hand to many jobs. He made our trap for my wedding present and bought Bella, the little miniature horse, especially for me and Carol.'

'What brought you back to the mainland?' Phoebe asked.

'Lemuel wanted to return here. They don't usually stay so long in one place but there was work on the island and we were all happy there.'

When Adam and Kas came back into the room Rachel was telling them about the book Lemuel was writing. She was anxious to bridge the years they'd spent apart and her face became flushed from the heat of the fire as she talked excitedly.

The children were brought down from the attic for tea and when Belinda called them all to go into the back living room Rachel stood up quickly. She felt her head begin to swim so promptly sat down again.

'Are you all right?' Kas asked anxiously.

Rachel laughed. 'Of course. It's just the heat from the fire.' But as she tried again her legs gave way beneath her and the light at the end of the long dark tunnel grew smaller and smaller. No matter how much she tried to keep it in sight it was slowly receding until everything around her became enveloped in the blackness.

When she recovered she found she had been placed on the couch and Kas was encouraging her to take a sip of brandy. Phoebe was loosening the neck of her dress and Belinda was waving a fan in front of her face.

'That's the second time,' Adam said, looking down at her with concern. 'And it wasn't the shock of seeing me this time.' He smiled, lovingly, warmly, and Rachel felt her heart flutter with the spark of affection she'd known of old. He still had the tender and gentle manner which had drawn him to her when she was younger. How could he have deserted her? What had she done to make him change his mind? She tried to sit up but they were all making a big fuss, so much so that she suddenly announced impatiently, 'It's all right – I'm expecting again. It's nothing.'

The news stunned them, in particular Kas. It was only six months since the last miscarriage and he thought he'd been too careful for this to happen. They had been advised to wait for a year before trying again but their love was strong and feelings uncontrollable, and now he felt guilty.

'That's marvellous,' Adam said.

'I am too,' Belinda cried. 'We'll have our babies more or less at the same time. How exciting!'

But Kas didn't seem pleased. 'Rachel has had three miscarriages already,' he said in a low voice. 'It's too soon, we should have waited.'

She held out her hand to him. 'I'm sorry,' she whispered. 'I know this wasn't the right time to tell you but I thought you'd be pleased. I'm not sure that I am.'

'Why ever not?' Belinda asked.

'I want to know about my background before I have a baby,' she said. 'It's only fair to the child.'

'But you weren't worried before when you thought you were Belinda's sister,' Kas said. 'All I'm concerned about is your health. This time you've got to put your feet up and rest. The doctors at Newport warned you – the first three months are important and you must rest.'

But Rachel was already making plans. She had a mission. She didn't care whether she had to travel all over the south of England, she was determined to find someone who knew where the midwife got her from.

Chapter Sixteen

The one thing Rachel didn't plan for was the way everyone cossetted her. Although she returned to the waggon with Kas and Carol, her mother and sister persuaded her to join the medical aid club and Belinda introduced her to the local doctor under whose care she herself was.

'Doctor King would like to see us both,' Rachel told Kas when she returned to the common where they were camped.

'We don't use doctors as you well know,' he replied sharply.

'Not as a general rule, Kas, but there are times when it's necessary, like when Carol was born for instance.'

'And he admitted that the job had been done when he arrived.'

'But he treated Ena after she'd lost such a lot of blood.'

'Our folks have their methods too and they've been well tried over centuries.'

'But you were as eager as anyone else to get Lemuel to hospital,' Rachel said. 'Otherwise we wouldn't be here now and I wouldn't have seen Dad before he died.'

'That was different. Lemuel's getting on and wasn't making the progress he should have been.'

'Perhaps you don't want me to have this baby?'

'You know that's not true, Rachel. But we were advised to wait a year before trying again.'

She sidled up to her husband and put her arms around his neck.

'That was asking a bit too much of both of us, though, wasn't it?' She inveigled him into kissing her but after a few moments he pushed her away. 'Kas,' she pursued, 'we both want a baby of our own. I agree now isn't such a good time, and although I had my suspicions I didn't think I could be pregnant again yet. With so much happening with Dad and everything I put it right out of my mind. I thought I felt ill because of Dad and then the shock of finding out that I'm sort of suspended in limbo.'

'Don't talk rot,' he said impatiently. 'You're not suspended anywhere, let alone in limbo. Things have only changed if you want them to change. As I've said a hundred or more times, Rachel, we can't change anything and now we can't alter the fact that you're expecting. I'm quite happy for this doctor to keep his eye on you but I can't see why he would want to see me.'

'But you've always looked after me.'

'It seems I've been relieved of that job as your mother and sister have taken over.'

'Kas,' she pleaded, 'it isn't like that at all. I want you to be as happy as I am that I've been reunited with the family again, and it'll be nice for Belinda and me to go through this together. I think her baby is due about a month before ours.'

'And what if we move on? The others have been talking about going down to the New Forest near Burley ready for the summer?'

'Oh.' Rachel's smiles changed to a frown. 'I didn't know. When was this decided?'

'It's not definite yet, but the others think it'll be better for Lemuel as soon as he's fit enough.'

'But probably not for us,' Rachel said thoughtfully.

'Why's that?' Kas asked.

'We-ell, Doctor King is going to get a report from the hospital in Newport, but from what I've told him he considers I should be spending the next few weeks in bed. I explained about us being travellers and he wants me to go and stay with Mum.'

Kas stared at Rachel darkly. Whereas he had always been so kind and caring, of late he seemed moody and quick-tempered. Rachel had tried to shrug off his moods as the effects of recent events. Now she realised that he was sorry she had found her family again.

'So that's it?' he said. 'They don't want anything to do with you if you're a gypsy?' He sighed. 'I suppose it's understandable but we don't have to stay around to embarrass them. As soon as Lemuel is well enough we'll move down to the New Forest.'

'I didn't want to tell you what the doctor said, Kas. I thought he could have explained it much better than me.'

'Doesn't matter who does the explaining, does it? I presume you'd like to go and stay with your mother? Where does that leave me and Carol?'

'You'd come as well, of course.'

'No, Rachel. I have a living to earn and we'll pay our own way.'

'Please go with me to see the doctor, Kas?' she pleaded. 'You heard what the one in Newport said and you were sympathetic then. Why are you so angry now?'

'Because I feel your mother and sister are making all the decisions.'

'But they didn't come in with me when I saw Doctor King. The consultation was between me and him.'

'So how come he suggested that you stay with your mother?'

'Belinda gave him some of the background when she introduced us. He'd like to see us in a week's time when he's had the report from Newport.'

'We shall have to see what the others think.'

'It's got nothing to do with them,' Rachel said.

'Forgotten all about community living so soon?' She could hardly believe that Kas could be so unfeeling. 'Can't you see, Rachel, they're trying to entice you back into their way of life and I'm not prepared to let that happen.'

'No, Kas. What's got into you? It's just to safeguard our baby, that's all. Three months and then I shall be over the danger period.'

'And by then you'll be so much under your mother's thumb you won't want to come and live free again.'

'Oh, dear Kas, of course I shall. That's what I want for my baby. Don't let's quarrel, please, I *do* want to keep this baby – for you.'

Kas turned and left the waggon. Rachel watched from the window expecting to see him make for Sybil's van to fetch Carol but he went to where the horses were tethered and in a few minutes she saw him astride Kitchener, galloping away.

She remained alone for a while wondering why this was happening to them. They hardly ever quarrelled and she hated it. When she felt composed enough she walked across and knocked on Sybil's door. There was no sound of Carol's voice as she expected.

'Come on in, me dearie,' Sybil called. 'Carol ain't 'ere, she's with Charity. Gone to the woods to look for snowdrops with some of the other young'uns.'

'She's been all right, Sybil? Not too much for you?'

'When 'as any of 'em been too much for me? More to the point, Rachel, how did you get on?'

'Don't ask.' She sat down wearily. 'The doctor Belinda's introduced me to is writing to the hospital in Newport to get my records. In view of what I've told him though he suggests I ought to remain in bed for the next few weeks, and thinks it would be a good idea if I stayed with Mum.'

She looked expectantly at Sybil for her reaction but her ageing features showed none as she waited for Rachel to continue.

'I thought Kas would understand. He's always been so thoughtful, but we quarrelled and he's ridden off on Kitchener.'

243

'I know, I saw him go. I've known Kas a long time, dearie, and it takes some'at to disturb 'im. I knew by the darkness of his frown that some'at was up and I was afraid t'was you and the baby.'

'It's hardly a baby yet. I must have started morning sickness almost as soon as it was conceived. Because of the shock of meeting Adam and Dad I thought it was that. I think Kas is upset that it's happened again so soon. We wanted to wait but there's no going back now.'

'And you – d'you want this child?'

'Yes, Sybil, of course I do. I want Kas's baby more than anything in the world but I too wish it had waited – waited until I've found out who I am.'

'You'm a child of the Lord. That should be enough to satisfy you.'

Rachel looked away, sad, uncertain about her future, her life, past and present.

'I thought if I stayed with Mum for a little while it would help her, and I'd try to make up to her for losing Dad as well as recompense for what I did.'

'You can't make up to her for your father's death, child. That was his destiny. It'll be hard for her for many months to come but with your love and support she'll weather that particular storm. You must put the past behind you, Rachel. We can't change what's gone – 'tis up to you to get on with your life. I understands about the need for rest and we've a month or two of winter to get through first. T'would be more comfortable with your mother although you knows everyone of us 'ere would see to it that you was properly looked after, Kas in particular.'

'I suggested he could come with me and Carol too.'

'She's at a busy age. Always on the go, always asking questions, so I daresay t'would be best if she stayed with us. And Kas has his work to do. Then there's Lemuel we'll have to look out for when he gets home.'

Rachel brightened. 'I popped in to the hospital to see him after I'd seen the doctor. It was quite close. He's looking so much better, more cheerful and a much healthier colour. He's been moving round the ward talking to the other men. Sister said they were reluctant to let him go, he's been such a comfort to the other patients. But that's our dear Lemuel, always thinking of other people.'

'Ah, 'tis a good man he is. Now why don't you have a talk to him about things.'

'I was going to, but visiting time was just ending.' Rachel made tea with the boiling water in the tin kettle on the stove. 'I need to talk to him and I hope he'll talk to Kas. I feel guilty about keeping Carol when she has grandparents who are her real family.'

244

'We don't know where Ena's folk went and I doubt that Davey will ever want to recognise that he had a daughter. He won't take responsibility for her. Ena made it quite clear what she wanted, and that was for you and Kas to be her ma and pa, and you'd be letting Ena down if you tried to push her back on her grandparents.'

'I wouldn't do that, Sybil. Surely you know me better than that?' Rachel sat down opposite her with a sigh. 'I love Carol and until recently I thought of her as ours, but now I'm confused and only want to do what's right.'

'Then carry on as if nothing has happened, dearie. You'm reconciled with your mother and that should be cause for rejoicing. Let bygones be bygones.'

'Sybil . . .' Rachel broached hesitantly. 'You won't like what I'm going to say but I must say it all the same.' She sipped her tea, avoiding looking directly at Rachel. 'Tell me honestly if you saw any of the recent events in my future?'

'I don't "see" no more – I've told you that before, Rachel.'

Rachel reached across the table and held the older woman's hand. She knew well enough that Sybil fought with her conscience over her gift but Rachel was keenly aware that she couldn't help herself at times. Hadn't she told them where to look for Ena? That was for good, Sybil had excused, so now Rachel hoped she could influence her to help her find out the truth.

'I told you that there would be happy times and sad times, child,' she said, dreamily, then pulled herself up smartly. 'Now that could apply to each and every one of us, so don't make nothing of that.'

'But just a little clue so that I know where to look for my real parents?' Rachel begged.

She covered Sybil's hand with her free one and she felt her enclosed hand grow warm and supple as Sybil smoothed gently over the ball of her thumb.

Rachel watched closely as Sybil's eyes narrowed then close.

'Sisters . . . sea . . .' Her voice became so soft Rachel held her breath for fear of not hearing what the gypsy was saying. 'Sisters . . . babies . . . nothing but good . . . all for the best . . .' Sybil jerked and opened her eyes. 'Rachel, you hoodwinked me.' She shook her head in disapproval.

'I need to know, Sybil dear,' Rachel said, 'and I'm sure you could guide me.'

Sybil withdrew her hand sharply. 'Lemuel's our guide, you talk to him.'

'You felt something though, didn't you?' Rachel said. 'Sisters, you said. Was that Belinda and myself? Babies – was that us too, meaning

245

that being brought up together was right? Nothing but good, all for the best. Please explain it, Sybil?'

'I talk a lot of rubbish, pay no attention, I ain't no good no more.' She stood up. 'Got to get me tea and then I need to rest, so you go home and do what's right for Kas and Carol. They'm your family now.'

'Come and have tea with us,' Rachel invited.

'So that you can cheat me into seeing again? No, Rachel. 'T'wouldn't be reliable anyway and I could send you off on some goose chase wasting everyone's time and energy. If Lemuel thinks I can help, he'll be the one to ask.'

Rachel knew it was no good trying to press Sybil so she left her and went to fetch Carol.

A large pot of scrag end of lamb with potatoes and onions had been simmering all day on the stove. It smelled good and Rachel felt quite hungry. When she had washed Carol's hands and face she sat her up to the table with her bib on. As she was cutting up the child's meat Kas came in.

'You must have smelled the dinner,' she said as light-heartedly as she could.

He came up to her and kissed her cheek.

'Yes, and I'm hungry. Nothing like a ride in the country to whip up an appetite.' He washed his hands in the bowl, dried them and sat down in his usual place. There was little opportunity for serious conversation when Carol was around. She chattered almost non-stop and her funny, appealing ways soon mended any rift.

When they went to bed that night Kas held Rachel close.

'I'm sorry if I seemed angry with you, my darling,' he said. 'The truth is, I can't bear the thought of losing you.'

'Losing me? Whatever d'you mean, Kas? I'm not going anywhere.'

'In a way you are. You're going back to your old home to live – and three months is a long time. Once you're settled in there will you ever want to come back to me?'

'Of course I will. You can come and spend time with us. Mum would like that, Kas. She wants to get to know you. Belinda and Adam do too. I've been part of your family for the past five years, now it's your turn to become part of mine.'

'I know that, but my main concern is for your health. You've lost three babies, Rachel, could you bear to lose a fourth?'

'Maybe this isn't such a good time to be expecting but if it's to be then everything will be all right. We must have faith, Kas. Isn't that what Lemuel will say?'

That was exactly what he did say when they visited him the following day.

'I've thought so much about all that you told me before, Rachel,' he said. 'Of course you want to know the truth about your birth but there's always the danger you won't like what you discover. Isn't that the reason your parents didn't tell you the truth earlier? Somehow I can't help thinking that your father didn't really mean to cause you such anguish. He was a sick man and when our bodies are unhealthy then our minds become confused too. Now you must decide what to do with this knowledge. How will it help you or your mother to discover who your real parents were? Have you thought about the emotional trauma you're going to cause Mrs Hunter as well as either or both your real parents should you find them and confront them?'

'I've tried to see it from everyone's point of view,' Rachel said solemnly. 'I know it may seem absurd to you, Kas and the others but I feel there's an urgency to seek out the truth. But for the moment I can't do anything as I'm supposed to be resting most of the time. There wasn't time to tell you yesterday but the doctor I saw suggested that I go to stay with Mum for the next three months.'

Lemuel stroked his beard while he took this in.

'And I daresay Kas doesn't agree with this idea?' he said slowly.

Kas shifted his feet uneasily. 'I know I'm being selfish, Lemuel,' he said. 'But I feel that Rachel is slipping away from me. Her family are taking over.'

'Then it's up to you to see that they don't. If Rachel doesn't go to her mother and loses your baby, I think you may well feel you're to blame, Kas. Rachel has been parted from her family for several years now. The Lord be praised that they've been reunited even if the circumstances were not entirely happy ones. Is three months too long to sacrifice for the sake of a baby? And to allow Rachel to spend this time with her mother?'

'It isn't as if we wouldn't see each other, is it? she said. 'You can always come to stay whenever you like?'

'We'll see what the doctor says when we see him next week. Then we'll discuss the matter with your mother,' Kas said. 'The others have been talking about moving down to the New Forest when you leave hospital, Lemuel. How d'you feel about it?'

'Whether she stays with her mother or not, the important thing is that every care is taken of Rachel this time. It might be sensible to stay within easy reach of the hospital.'

'Belinda did suggest that I stayed with them,' Rachel said. 'I declined the offer. She's being kind, I know, but underneath she dislikes my being a gypsy. I expect she'd like me to move away as far as possible. As Kas says, we don't want to embarrass them.'

'Then I think the better idea is for you to stay with your mother and we can move to Bere Forest so that we're all close. The time will soon pass, Kas. You must think of it as a time of reconciliation between Rachel and her family which I'm sure you wouldn't wish to deny her. There'll be plenty of time to go farther south by early summer.'

Rachel knew that Kas was not pleased about the decision but he recognised the wisdom of the elder of the group, and when he went with Rachel to see the doctor at the hospital he was assured that there was no reason for her not to carry the baby full term if they did as he advised.

Sybil made sure that Rachel spent most of every day resting in her van while Carol enjoyed being indulged by the other families and a week later, after Lemuel was discharged from hospital, the travellers moved in convoy towards Wickham. While the families made camp in a suitable copse on the western edge of the Forest of Bere, Kas drove Rachel in the trap to her old home at Kingsmere. She savoured every moment of renewing her acquaintance with the oak wood she had loved since childhood. After the Great War when so much timber had been felled, the newly formed Forestry Commission had taken over management of the forest and ordered that more conifers should be planted, but there was still a great variety of broadleaves left to be admired.

Phoebe was quickly at the door of Calder Cottage, obviously delighted at Rachel's decision to stay with her for the next three months.

'Adam helped me put up a bed in the front parlour,' she said. 'We thought it would be nicer for you to be near the window looking on to the road and the woods on the other side.' Kas carried in Rachel's belongings, noticing that the bed was a single one and assuming that he was not welcome to stay. Phoebe sensed his feelings. 'Now you feel free to come in at any time, Kas,' she said. 'My home is yours, and if you can stay overnight you can move up to Rachel's old bedroom with the bigger bed.'

'I'm sure this is putting you to a lot of trouble, Mrs Hunter,' he said.

'Nonsense. I can do with the company, and Rachel and I need to talk. We all want her to keep this baby. So sad to have lost three already. I know what it's like to want a baby. I thought I was never going to have a family at all. Belinda can't get here very often as it's too far to walk from the station at Wickham with young Billy, especially now she's expecting again. You can't always be sure a carter will be coming this way from the station, but Adam visits me when he comes to see his mother.'

'How is she?' Rachel asked. 'There's so much I want to ask and so many people I'd like to see. What about the Meads? Is Dick back with Nessie?'

'Yes, and they seem content to grow old together. Well, they're not old really. I think Nessie's about fiftyish and Dick'll be a few years older. They're enjoying their children and grandchildren and life's a good deal more peaceful than it used to be. Good job that Beth is out of the way. A real black sheep she was. As to Adam's mother, she's still a recluse and doesn't get out and about. But you must settle in gently and ask all your questions gradually.'

Phoebe made cocoa while Kas helped Rachel with her things.

'You will come to see me every day, won't you?' Rachel asked. 'Bring Sybil and Carol. The others are all welcome too.'

'You're looking flushed already, Rachel,' he said. 'I think the doctor really meant rest in every sense of the word. It isn't going to work unless you make the most of this opportunity.' He kissed the top of her dark head. 'Just remember that I love you very much indeed Strawberry Girl, and your health is what's most important.'

Rachel put her arms round Kas's neck and hugged him tightly. 'Thank you for everything,' she whispered. 'I love you too and we'll soon be back on the road together. I know this is a wrench for you. It's not so bad for me because I'm happy to have the chance to be with Mum for a while, and I think it'll help her so the sacrifice will be well worth it, I promise. We shall have time to talk, time to reflect on the past, and time to make up for lost time.' Rachel laughed happily. She had longed to be back in Calder Cottage, but her happiness was marred by the loss of her father and the knowledge that he had disowned her – her laughter died as she clung to Kas.

'Not too much talk, darling,' he said softly. 'I'm sure I shan't be able to sleep without you. Don't let the past come between us, please.'

'Dear Kas, as if I would. I shall sleep only because I'm weary.'

Phoebe came back in the room then with steaming cocoa and a plate of small cakes. She sat with them, listening to Rachel's chatter, observing the mental torment Kas was experiencing and wondering how a daughter of hers could have become involved with these travelling folk. But she had to admit Rachel appeared to be happy with such a lifestyle. She had done her best to give her a good start in life and Wally had been supportive. Phoebe still couldn't understand why Adam had behaved the way he had. He refused to enter into any dialogue on the matter, saying only that he had made a mistake. "T'would be too late once we'd been married,' she remembered him saying by way of an excuse. "Tis Belinda I want.' Want was one thing, love another, but they were happy enough, Phoebe thought.

Damp mild weather alternated with snow, ice and heavy frosts. The days were short, the nights long, but around teatime each day Phoebe

249

and Rachel talked at length about everything. Rachel plied her mother with questions about the time she was taken to them at Minstead but Phoebe insisted she knew nothing except that the midwife was anxious to find a good home for her. Rachel had to be content with that, and when on the Sunday Belinda, Adam and Billy visited for afternoon tea she had a different set of questions ready. She was alone with Adam as Belinda was helping her mother prepare tea.

'Why did you go to Portsmouth to live?' Rachel asked.

Adam sat forward in his chair and twisted his long fingers together nervously.

'There was gossip, Rachel,' he said. 'I didn't want Belinda to be hurt.'

'Hm,' she said shortly, 'never mind how much I was hurt.'

'Rachel, I know it was dreadful for you, and I'm sorry, but as I told your parents it was better it happened then than after we were married. I – well, I loved you both.' He ran his fingers through his hair. 'Nothing I can say or do can ever make things right, but believe me it had to be this way. We're happy, and I can see that you and Kas are too. Isn't that enough?'

Rachel looked long and hard at Adam. She wanted to despise him, hate him, but his pained expression made it impossible. He seemed to be troubled and hiding something.

'Everything is all right with your job though, isn't it?' she asked with genuine concern.

'Everything is fine, really, Rachel.' He sighed. 'It isn't easy living in Portsmouth when both our widowed mothers are hereabouts.'

'But your mother is well?'

'As well as she'll ever be. She's younger than your mother yet she's always been an old woman. If only she'd take an interest in what's going on in the village, but she prefers to remain housebound so the less she does, the less she can. Perhaps life hasn't been kind to her, and maybe I should do more.'

'I thought it was all settled that you were going to live with her when you and Belinda got married?'

'Yes, but work wasn't too easy after the war. We stayed with her for several months and then I heard about this job at the hospital. I used to go on the train every day to begin with but then it seemed sensible to sell that cottage I bought and use the money to buy a house in Portsmouth.'

'It's all very nice. You've evidently worked hard on it.'

'That's one thing I was trained to do and I enjoy working with wood so it was easy. Wally used to come and help us during the summer months when he was well enough. Oh, Rachel, and to think you were just across the water.'

'You must have thought I was in Portsmouth when I sent the postcard to Mum and Dad?'

'We . . . we guessed that you wouldn't stay there, but I always felt that there might be a possibility of seeing you there one day. It was just a gut feeling though I never expected to see you walk into the hospital, and with . . .'

'Gypsies?' she laughed. 'I saw Beth Cropper and Dick Mead on the island so I was sure they'd come home and tell everyone they'd seen me "dressed up like a bloomin' gypsy" as she said.'

Rachel told Adam how Beth had tried to entice Kas away from her, and how she'd taken Davey from Ena, and the subsequent events.

'Didn't you ever want to come home, Rachel?' Adam asked.

'Of course, quite often, especially at first, but Lemuel and Sybil were so kind to me that gradually I became one of them. I felt I had disgraced my family so I wouldn't be welcome back here, and I was right. Poor Dad, how he must have despised me.' Rachel's eyes were filled with tears when Belinda came into the room. She stopped short in the doorway just as Adam stretched out his hand to take Rachel's in his to console her.

'It wasn't really your fault, Rachel,' Adam said, not realising his wife was a witness to the scene. 'The circumstances were –'

'Were what?' Belinda challenged.

'Awkward,' Adam said, withdrawing his hand slowly. 'My mind was in such a turmoil after the war. You know, it wasn't easy to adjust – everything had changed.'

'And we'd all grown up,' Belinda said. 'At least now we know why Rachel and I don't look alike.' She studied her sister with steely blue eyes which slightly mocked as she added, 'Perhaps your mother was a –'

'Gypsy? You needn't be afraid of using that word.' Rachel stared directly at her. 'Yes, perhaps she was. Now why didn't I think of that? There were always gypsies in the forest.'

Phoebe came in carrying a silver teapot only used on Sundays.

'Mum?' Rachel said. 'Belinda's just suggested that my real mother might be a gypsy. There was a group in the New Forest, wasn't there?'

'Ouch!' Phoebe said as she scalded herself on the teapot which she almost dropped. 'I don't know much about them,' she said hurriedly. 'Travelling folk have been around for centuries. Like I've said, we weren't told anything, and we were so thankful to have Belinda safe and sound that it seemed only right to take you in.' She fussed about putting the teacosy on the teapot. 'I've made the tea. Kas and Carol are just taking their coats off.'

251

Conversation then centred around the two children who had become instant friends, and the two hours they were all together as a family passed very quickly. Kas was pleased to take the others to the station in the trap to catch the train from Wickham back to Portsmouth, and in the reverent silence of a winter Sunday evening Phoebe and Rachel watched pictures in the fire, each with their own memories.

After a few weeks the morning sickness which had plagued Rachel stopped. There were no more giddy turns and she began to feel extremely well, so much so that she persuaded Kas to take her mother into Wickham in the trap to buy wool and material to make things for the baby.

'I never got the chance to prepare much before,' Rachel said. 'But this time I feel different and it's such a waste of time lying here watching the world go by. I need to keep occupied otherwise the waiting will seem like an eternity.'

Rachel dozed for a while after dinner, then woke feeling restless for Phoebe and Kas's return. There had been method in her madness for although Phoebe kept her grief hidden for much of the time, Rachel felt that her mother too needed to something to fill the days apart from waiting on her hand and foot. Knitting or sewing would help her rest and relax.

Letters of condolence from people in neighbouring villages and towns continued to arrive each day as word was passed from place to place. Wally had been well thought of and respected wherever he went. Sometimes a letter would reopen the wound; another would bring Phoebe some much needed comfort. Quite a pile of such letters had accumulated, placed on a small table near Rachel's bed for her to read as and when she wanted to. Now she thumbed through them, knowing that to just take one out of its envelope would make her sad but would help pass the time. She looked first at the postmarks, villages she'd never heard of, and others from places like Romsey, Fareham, Winchester, Lyndhurst. And then Rachel looked and looked again. Minstead . . . Maybe the village where she'd been born even though her mother assured her that no other woman thereabouts had been expecting at the same time she was. The handwriting was neat, each letter perfectly formed on the thick parchment paper. Rachel glanced at the end to see who it was from and read a name she didn't remember – Grace Whitmarsh. The letter was fairly short, offering sympathy and adding that she hoped Phoebe would visit soon. 'I'm sure we can find some means of transport and you're welcome to stay a for as long as you wish. Your girls don't need you

252

now so you're free to take a much needed holiday and soon the forest will be at its best.'

Rachel read and re-read the letter. She searched her memory. Was there ever an Aunt Grace? No, she couldn't recall one. A relative or friend? Then her imagination flew in all directions. Supposing Grace Whitmarsh was her mother? Perhaps she'd been in service, let down by her lover so that she had to give her baby away in order to keep her job. Rachel watched eagerly for her mother's return. Was she about to discover the truth at last?

Chapter Seventeen

Rachel dozed off and was soon dreaming of a reunion with a woman, not so much faceless as unrecognisable, and then noises in the distance brought her back to reality. She felt rather hot and agitated until she remembered the letter from Grace Whitmarsh. It was lying on the bedcovers but before Kas and her mother entered the room Rachel put it back on the small table. She suddenly felt rather foolish for having such unwarranted flights of fancy. Why on earth should a woman named Grace Whitmarsh be her real mother?

Kas came in carrying a bag. He went at once to Rachel, kissed her and held her tightly.

'Have you been asleep? You smell all warm and cosy.'

'Yes, I dropped off while I was reading some of Mum's letters. Dad was a wonderful man, Kas. How could I have let him down like I did?'

'Hey, come on. No more feeling sorry, either for yourself or for what you did. The past is irretrievable. The future is ours. Don't read any more letters if they make you feel sad.'

'Some of them make me weep,' she said. 'Dear Dad, I wish he were here now.'

'Look what we've bought,' Kas said, opening the carrier bag to cheer her up. 'Balls of white wool, lace and fine lawn for petticoats, your mother said. At least she'll have something now to take her mind off her loss.'

Phoebe seemed quite excited by her purchases and after they'd eaten and Kas had left she showed Rachel some new knitting patterns she'd bought.

'I want to knit something for Billy as well as something new for Belinda's baby,' Rachel said, echoing her mother's enthusiasm.

'I think Belinda already has a good supply of baby clothes she kept from when Billy was small. Adam's mother has kept her well supplied with beautiful garments she makes herself, and she's very fond of young Billy.'

'Difficult to imagine Mrs Taylor being fond of any child,' Rachel sighed. 'Poor Adam, his home life couldn't have been very exciting. Not to be wondered at that he should behave so strangely having such odd parents.'

Phoebe went to the scullery to wash up. She didn't voice her opinion to Rachel for fear of upsetting her but she had observed the covetous looks Rachel gave Adam when she thought no-one was watching. Phoebe had to admit that Adam was a good son-in-law, kind and thoughtful, and he cared devotedly for his own mother, but now that Phoebe was getting to know Kas better she discovered he had many good qualities to his credit. He had the stronger character which she felt was right for Rachel and she was certain they were immensely happy together. She wished with all her heart that Wally was alive to meet Kas. Gypsy or no he was a likeable man with honourable principles.

The two women settled down on either side of the fire. At this time of day Rachel sat out of bed to make a change, and now they happily discussed which pattern to use for which type of wool. Stitches were cast on but the clicketty-click of needles was drowned when Rachel asked her mother, 'Who's Grace Whitmarsh, Mum?'

'You wouldn't know her, dear,' Phoebe said. 'But surely you remember letters arriving from abroad? You always wanted the stamps. Not that Grace wrote very often. Her Christmas card and letter usually arrived in time for Easter.' Phoebe laughed. 'We went to school together. Her father worked for the East India Company so when Grace was about fourteen she and her mother went out to Singapore to join him. Although her mother didn't want to go they had a good life, and Grace worked for the government out there, something to do with Customs and Excise.'

'She's back in Minstead now then and wants you to go to stay with her for a holiday?'

'Not back in Minstead. We went to school in Lee-on-Solent, remember that's where I was born. Grace retired a few years ago and just after your grandfather died wrote and said she was back in England and was thinking of settling down in the New Forest. Your father was looking for a new tenant for the cottage his parents had lived in and that's how she came to move to Minstead.'

'You need a holiday, Mum. Wouldn't you love to go and stay with her?'

'Too right I would, but how can I with you and Belinda both expecting babies?'

'That's not for ages, and once I can get about again our group is going to move down to somewhere near Burley. You could travel with us.'

'Oh, my goodness, whatever would your father have said to that?' Rachel lowered her head to hide her pink cheeks.

'I'm sorry, dear. I didn't mean to hurt your feelings but –'

'I know, nice people don't hobnob with gypsies,' Rachel said. 'But people criticise without really knowing them.' She went on to explain how she and Kas had first met in the wood just across the road from Calder Cottage, and how he had joined the group on the Isle of Wight.

'I have a lot to thank the gypsies for,' she said. 'I was quite ill after running away and being out all night in the rain. Sybil has the gift of seeing, but she tries not to use her gift. I know she can tell things about the past and future and I desperately wanted her to tell me what she could about my real mother. She went into a bit of a trance and said "sisters", which I suppose means Belinda and me, and "sea".'

Phoebe smiled gently at Rachel. 'Knowing doesn't always help, dear,' she said quietly. After a few minutes' silence she laughed. 'A gypsy came to the door before I knew I was going to have Belinda. I was a bit afraid of them, especially as Wally always told me to keep the doors locked when the gypsies were in the vicinity. Minstead as you know is a small village and our cottages were in an isolated spot in the forest. This woman had a basket of white heather and promised to tell my fortune if I bought some.' Phoebe put down her knitting and looked across at Rachel. 'I never did tell Wally I bought some, and in return this woman, whom I must admit was very pleasant, told me I was going to have a beautiful daughter . . .' Phoebe turned quite pale as she remembered. 'As she went out of the little wooden gate Wally had made she turned and gave me a lovely warm smile as she said, "Might even be two".'

'There you are,' Rachel said victoriously, 'she was right, wasn't she? Oh, Mum, I do wish you could remember more about me arriving.' Now it was her turn to laugh. 'D'you know, when I read Grace's letter I thought maybe she was my real mother.'

'I do assure you dear, it isn't anyone I know. Teddy brought you all rolled up in a blanket and said there was nothing we needed to know. I suppose we did ought to have asked a few questions, but there, that was all a long time ago, and it really doesn't matter now.'

Rachel had to be content with that. She felt she knew her mother well enough to know that she wasn't hiding anything, but there was always a flicker of doubt.

Early in March Rachel and Belinda celebrated their twenty-fourth birthdays. Doctor Barber from Wickham called in regularly to see how Rachel was and had pronounced her as fit and healthy as any other pregnant woman, but he agreed with the hospital doctor and advised caution until the first three months had passed.

Phoebe prepared a special tea for all the family and Kas took Bella and the trap to fetch Belinda, Adam and Billy. The evenings were drawing out at last and the weather was more spring-like.

Calder Cottage seemed hardly large enough for them all and the small kitchen was decidedly crowded when they arrived. Rachel insisted on getting up and dressed for the tea party. She had helped her mother with the preparations until Phoebe had made her go to sit by the fire with her feet up. The door opened and Adam was the first to enter.

'Ah, so you're up,' he greeted. 'Many happy returns of the day, Sister-in-law.' He went to her and kissed her cheek warmly. 'Are you sure you should be?'

'I couldn't spend my birthday in bed, now could I?' she said. 'And I'm not your sister-in-law. Stepsister-in-law maybe.'

He inclined his head. 'I hope you're not going to let this spoil the day, Rachel. You were brought up as Belinda's sister. Everyone accepted that so you must as well.'

The situation wasn't easy but she couldn't expect Adam to understand. Rachel wanted to despise him but when together they could still ignite the spark of attraction which had been so cruelly stamped out. In lonely moments during these inactive weeks she'd tried to cure herself of the 'what might have beens'. It was all fantasy, she had Kas now, but she knew deep down that Adam couldn't rid himself of his feelings either. Fortunately at that moment the children, freed from warm coats, hats, scarves and gloves, burst into the room and Carol fell on Rachel with great enthusiasm.

'Darling,' she said as she hugged the child and kissed her. 'Isn't this lovely, to come to Grandma's house for my birthday tea?' She felt vexed with herself for ever thinking that she would be able to part with Carol. The warmth of the child's love for her far outweighed any guilt at keeping her from her real family. Ena had wanted it this way. Kas and Sybil were right in honouring her wishes even if it meant that one day Carol might have to face the same truth that Rachel had. It was painful, it had stirred her emotions, unnerved her, and given her a mission even if no one else would help her find her real parents. In Carol's case it was different. Her mother had died and left instructions as to who she wanted her daughter to live with. One day she could be told the story if she wanted to know. But no one seemed to know anything about Rachel's parentage and it was the lack of identity which tormented her.

Kas and Belinda followed the children into the room bringing gifts for Rachel, and she stood up to kiss her sister and wish her a happy birthday. Between them Phoebe and Rachel had knitted a dainty bed-jacket for Belinda, also a pale blue jumper.

257

'Rather practical,' Rachel said. 'But the best we could do being stuck at home so much.'

Rachel noticed Belinda's response to her use of the word 'home'. Calder Cottage would always be her home as long as Phoebe continued to recognise her as her daughter, though now she could understand why Belinda might find her presence an intrusion.

'Kas took Mum into Wickham to buy the wool so we've been kept busy making things for the babies as well,' she added. 'I hope you like the colour.'

'It's lovely,' Belinda said, and then Adam pushed his way forward and handed small gift-wrapped presents to her and Rachel.

'But you've already given me my present,' Belinda said to him.

'Yes, I know, but this is a special occasion after all,' he said. 'My two special girls reunited,' he added with a broad smile.

Wife and sister, he thought and wished again that he could tell them all as much as he knew.

Rachel experienced acute embarrassment while Belinda's eyes showed her discomfiture. The presents were wrapped identically and inside the jeweller's boxes on a bed of cotton wool lay identical crystal necklaces.

'Adam,' Rachel exclaimed, 'you shouldn't have!'

'They must have cost the earth!' Belinda said sharply.

Adam held up his hands in surrender. 'It's all right, Belinda. You'll still get your housekeeping at the end of the week. I've been doing a carpentry job for an ex-patient in my spare time so I decided to treat you both to something special.'

'It's very nice,' Belinda said and shut the box decisively. 'Better get on with tea or it'll be time to go home before we've even sat down.'

'It's quite beautiful, Adam,' Rachel said. 'But you really shouldn't have included me.'

'I . . . I wanted to, let's leave it at that.' Then he turned to Kas with a worried frown. 'I hope you don't mind? I ought to have asked your permission first.'

Kas laughed. 'It's all right. I know it pleases Rachel. I think perhaps you should have asked your wife first, though.'

'I did it because I'm so thankful Rachel is back in the family circle. Grateful too that it was you who found her, and made her happy. We've all been grieving for Wally, but today I felt we should celebrate Belinda and Rachel's birthdays to make up for lost time.'

'I'm sure Wally is with us in spirit,' Phoebe said. 'He'd want both his girls to make the best life for themselves that they can and he'd be thrilled to have more grandchildren. We can't imagine what was in his mind to write the letter he did but now that Rachel is back he would want her and you, Belinda, to be best friends. He'd be glad for me that I've got you both, and two sons-in-law to care for us all.' She went back to the kitchen but in an instant returned carrying a vase full of beautiful flowers. 'It isn't *my* birthday as I've just told Kas but he's brought them for me for looking after you, Rachel. Such a kind and generous thought, thank you.'

Rachel reached out and took Kas's hand. 'That was a lovely idea, darling,' she said. 'Gosh, we are lucky, Belinda, to have such nice husbands.'

Belinda half laughed, half grunted and then went to the scullery to bring in the tea. Any awkwardness she had caused was quickly forgotten as the children enjoyed jelly and fruit and kept up a constant chatter.

'By the end of this month I shall be able to get about more,' Rachel said as Phoebe refused all offers of help.

'You're going to take it easy for the whole time,' Kas said.

'But I do feel it's going to be all right this time, and I'm looking forward to moving with the others down to the New Forest. Belinda, Mum's been invited to go to stay with an old friend in Minstead, did you know?'

Belinda looked across at her mother. 'You didn't tell me,' she said accusingly.

'I thought you'd read all the letters, dear,' Phoebe said.

'I didn't have time to go through all of them,' she replied. 'Not properly. How are you going to get to Minstead?'

'We're going to take her when we move on,' Rachel said.

'What a good idea,' Adam said. 'You need a change, Mother.'

'It isn't so much that,' Phoebe said. 'After all, I don't want to be away too long in case Belinda needs me, but there are matters to attend to with the cottages now that I'm the legal owner. Grace Whitmarsh is in the one Wally's parents lived in so I know she's a good tenant, but I'd like to see who's in the adjoining one. I fancy Wally was never too keen on the family. He thought they were rather destructive, but you know Wally, he was so careful and proud of anything he'd made.'

'How long d'you plan to stay away?' Belinda asked. 'And who will you be staying with?'

'Grace has invited me to stay with her. It'll be strange being back in the cottage where your grandparents lived but nice to see the few people in the area I know. It isn't all settled yet, though, we've got to see Rachel on her feet first, and if you'd rather I didn't go, Belinda
. . .'

'Of course you must go,' Adam said eagerly. 'Such a good idea to travel with Rachel and Kas.'

'You needn't worry about me,' Belinda said pointedly. 'Everything is ready for the baby and I've got good neighbours to help me.'

'I shall be back long before your baby is due,' Phoebe said. 'I shan't stay long.'

Belinda made no attempt to hide her irritation. Rachel recognised all the signs of jealousy. For the past few years Phoebe and Wally had been able to indulge her with Rachel out of the way. After all, they had always known that Rachel wasn't really theirs so it was probably quite a relief when she ran away. But Rachel had little doubt that her mother was glad to have her back. Phoebe demonstrated her love in every thought, word and deed.

Belinda and Adam lived too far away for Phoebe to visit often or them her. Belinda thought of herself as a town girl now with her fashionable friends. From little things Phoebe said Rachel guessed it was Adam who was the more frequent visitor.

A few days later when Rachel was in the house alone after Phoebe had gone in to Wickham to put fresh flowers on Wally's grave, she heard a knock on the back door and a male voice called, 'Hullo?' She scrambled out of bed and looking over the banisters saw Adam in the kitchen doorway.

'What are you doing here at this time of the morning?' she asked as she pulled her dressing-gown round her.

'Sorry to make you get out of bed,' he said. 'Where's your mother?'

'Gone into Wickham to the churchyard. There was a bit of shopping she wanted to do at the same time. I'm glad she's getting out as she needs to meet her old friends and she's used to walking.'

'I expect she's walking back by the river. I didn't see her. It's my day off so I cycled in to see Mum.'

'Didn't Belinda come with you?'

'No, Mum can't take too much of Billy – and you know, mother-in-law versus daughter-in-law.'

'Your mother always preferred Belinda to me,' Rachel reminded him.

'Mother didn't really know Belinda properly. No one could ever have lived with Mum.' Adam laughed. 'Not even you – especially not you.'

'Why especially not me?'

'Because you're quite quick-tempered. Mother really is impossible at times. I haven't said anything to her about your not being Belinda's real sister.' Adam sighed as he followed Rachel into the living room. 'Belinda and I had words about it. She seemed to think the whole world could be told but I've sworn her to secrecy.'

'It doesn't really matter, Adam,' Rachel said. 'I expect Belinda is pleased to think she was an only child, and the "cuckoo-in-the-nest" is not her real sister. I've got used to the idea now and it doesn't hurt quite so much, but we mustn't do or say anything to make it difficult for Mum.'

'Then don't you think you should stop wanting to find out where you came from? Don't you realise how hurtful that is to her? She couldn't have been a better mother to you if she had been your own. It's a bit like slapping her in the face to want to delve into the past in the hope of finding someone else you can call "Mother". It's all too long ago, Rachel. Besides, I doubt that the woman who gave birth to you then gave you away wants to be reminded, let alone have you turn up out of the blue.'

'I expect you're right,' Rachel agreed. 'But it's only natural for me to wonder. You know I wouldn't do anything to upset Mum. We were very close, and I love her very much. I loved Dad too but somehow he always kept me at arm's length. Now I know why.'

'But he was a good father, Rachel, and gave you a wonderful childhood, better than I had. Count your blessings, then, like Belinda says, we must get on with our lives.'

'Does she know you're here?'

'She knows I'm visiting Mum.' Adam sat down near the fire and twisted his cap between his fingers nervously.

'You are happy with Belinda aren't you, Adam?' Rachel asked as she curled up in the arm chair opposite him.

'Of course.' He didn't look up immediately. 'I never imagined it was possible to love two women at the same time,' he said sheepishly raising his head at last. 'I hope you really liked the necklace. S'pose it was a silly thing to do, or at least Belinda thinks it was.'

'What was she supposed to think, Adam? What was anyone supposed to think? Some kind of consolation prize?' On impulse Rachel slid off the chair and knelt on the floor in front of him. 'I never stopped loving you, you know. There were times I hated you for what you did, but I never ever stopped loving you.'

'But you love Kas, and you've got a good man there.'

'You don't have to tell me that, Kas is one of the best, but like you, I didn't think it was possible to love two people so desperately, and I do. Oh, Adam, I do still love you just as much as the day you fought Charlie Mead at the fair.'

He stood up so suddenly he knocked Rachel backwards.

'Then you'd best stop ever thinking about me because the love I feel for you is quite different from the passion I have for Belinda. I behaved badly and nothing can ever excuse that. I was weak, too weak to tell you when I came out of the Army that I preferred Belinda and it was her I wanted to marry. I've seen the look in your eyes,

261

Rachel, and so has Belinda and you're coming between us. Like she says, the sooner you pack up and move on the better t'will be for us all.' He stopped to help her up. 'I'm sorry. I've caused you enough pain but it had to be said. Don't hurt Kas by thinking that you still have feelings for me. Only you can cure yourself of those, and you must be strong enough to do it, Rachel.

'I wanted to do something to try to show you my regret at what happened. Now I realise that I let you think there could still be something special between us, but that's over, Rachel. I want you to regard the necklaces as a kind of bond between you and Belinda. You were brought up as sisters and you loved one another so much, don't let anything change that. But love between you and me?' Adam shook his head vigorously. 'No, Rachel. The past is over and done with. You're my sister-in-law and Belinda's twin sister – nothing in the world can change the way you were brought up.'

'And nothing can change the way I feel,' she said, standing to challenge him as she felt she had a right to. 'No one will ever erase the feeling I have inside me that things are not quite as I'm expected to believe.'

'You've been living with the gypsies long enough to think you've got second sight like your friend, I suppose,' Adam said. 'Forget it, Rachel. You're a grown woman now. You should know there's no truth in such rubbish. Go back to your travelling lifestyle, and make Kas and your unborn child happy and proud of you. I shan't call again, but tell your mother if there's anything she needs to send a postcard. I hope all goes well with you this time. Once you've got your own baby in your arms, believe me, Rachel, you'll forget all about us, but if ever you're Portsmouth way come and see us.'

He made for the door.

'Adam, please don't leave like this. There's still so much to say,' she pleaded.

'Too much has been said already. I made a mistake five years ago, I've made another one now and I'm sorry. I should have thought and spared you any further hurt, or caused Belinda to think badly of me. Like she says, the sooner you've gone the quicker we can get on with picking up the pieces.'

He hurried through the back door as if the house were on fire. Rachel ran through to the front window anxious to call him back but as she watched him pick up his bicycle from the hedge outside and jump on it the determination in his expression made her pause. She shivered. Someone walking over my grave again, she thought, and went back to the fire.

Adam had accused her of slapping her mother in the face but he had been equally as cruel. Rachel could just hear Belinda saying that it would be better for all concerned when she moved on. She tucked her feet beneath her warm winceyette nightdress and became engrossed in her troubled thoughts.

She had to admit that she had been revelling in this time back home at Calder Cottage. How many times during the past five years had she longed to be here, though not without her father? She couldn't rid herself of the feeling of guilt that she had driven him to his death and she had stupidly thought that being here with Phoebe would help compensate. Idiot, she reproached herself. Coming here to stay had caused even more trouble, and now between Adam and Belinda.

Belinda wasn't the same sweet delicate girl Rachel remembered. In spite of being cossetted she had proved to be the stronger after all. One son to her credit and another baby on the way and not so much as one day's sickness. It didn't seem fair but maybe this was Rachel's punishment. Already three babies lost; she couldn't bear to lose yet another one. Being with her mother had seemed as if it would consolidate the situation but Rachel knew there was no guarantee. It was time she returned to her chosen family of gypsies. She had caused inconvenience and distress to them at first, now she was blind to the upset she was causing her own family. But they weren't *her* family! All the more reason for leaving soon, she decided.

In her mind's eye she could still see Adam as he'd told her that he no longer loved her in the way she imagined. That wretched necklace was the real cause of this outburst. Rachel had told the truth when she said that she had never stopped loving Adam in spite of the agony. She had felt convinced that he felt the same, but now he was trying to excuse his expressions of affection as 'sisterly', a different kind of love. He had to say that to nip in the bud whatever was ripening between them.

'Only me, dear,' Phoebe called from the kitchen. Rachel didn't answer. She needed to be alone. She didn't want to have to tell her mother that Adam had even called but she supposed she'd have to. 'I'll pop the kettle on,' Phoebe called again.

Rachel heard her mother go into the hall to hang her coat on the hall stand, a fine peace of furniture crafted lovingly by Wally's gifted hands. Footsteps sounded on the stairs.

'I'm down here, Mum,' Rachel said dully.

'Oh, not dressed yet then?' Phoebe said coming into the living room and warming her hands by the fire. 'It's not a bad day out, getting warmer I think.' She looked into her daughter's face. 'You all right, Rachel? You look a bit pale.'

'I'm fine. You sit here, I'll make the cocoa.' Rachel got out of the chair and went into the kitchen. She put milk in the saucepan, got out two cups and stood looking out of the small window, down the garden, remembering how she had run away without really considering the consequences. As she mixed cocoa, sugar and milk together her thoughts were just as mixed. Regrets at her wilful actions but none at living with the gypsies and marrying Kas, and now all she wanted to do was to return to the safety of the group.

Phoebe sensed Rachel's reluctance to talk so for a while they sat on either side of the hearth drinking cocoa in silence. Then Phoebe said, 'Nice bit of spring weather without too much wind, and the flowers will keep better in the churchyard. Guess who I saw today?' She hurried on when she received no response. 'Nessie Mead. She offered her condolences and asked after you and Belinda. Can't believe the change in that woman. She's spruced herself up all nice and tidy and I do believe she's filling out a bit. Dick seems to have settled down at last since he left Beth and came back to Nessie. Think she's a brick for taking him back really, but he's the father of her children after all. Nessie was telling me about them all.

'Benjie's over thirty now, married with three boys, and all three of Nessie's girls, Kittie, Susy and June, are married too. Kittie and her husband moved to Winchester and bought a little grocer's shop. Doing very nicely, Nessie said, but no family. Susy and June both married local chaps who work on the estate and they've each got a little girl.' Rachel lifted her head and smiled but she wasn't taking in what her mother was saying. 'Nessie sent her best regards and hopes you'll have the baby all right this time.'

'I'm sure I will, Mum,' Rachel said softly. 'Adam came in while you were out. He said to tell you if you want anything doing to send them a postcard.'

'Oh, must be his day off then. Suppose he came to see his mother. Sounds as if they aren't intending to visit again for a bit.' Phoebe sniffed significantly, picked up the cups and went to he kitchen. Rachel realised that her mother was feeling the distance between Kingsmere and Portsmouth more acutely now that her father was gone, and wished there was more she could do to bridge the gap. She went upstairs, washed and dressed, and later as they sat down to eat their mid-day meal said, 'How soon can you be ready to leave for Minstead, Mum?'

Chapter Eighteen

It was a bright April day when Kas, Rachel and Carol pulled up outside Calder Cottage. Rachel had been back with the gypsy group for a couple of weeks since Doctor Barber had pronounced her fit and over the danger period, and as she was feeling so well the group had commenced their journey in the direction of the New Forest a few days earlier. To spare Phoebe's embarrassment Kas and Rachel decided to fetch her in the trap.

'Oh, you haven't got your pretty little miniature horse,' she said as she locked up the front door of Calder Cottage, and with her bag full to overflowing closed the front gate behind her.

'The others are already well ahead, Mum,' Rachel explained. 'With three adults and Carol the trap would have been a bit heavy for Bella to pull. She'll be happiest riding alongside our waggon with Strawberry Girl. We've borrowed Caleb's pony for today.'

Kas took Phoebe's small case and strapped it under the trap at the rear and then helped her up to her seat beside Carol and opposite Rachel. Phoebe didn't look back, she didn't dare as her memories of Wally were in every stick and stone of Calder Cottage and she felt guilty at going away. Yet she knew she needed this holiday and it would be lovely to see Minstead again and her old friend Grace. There were no neighbours either to wave her off and she questioned whether she would be able to continue living in such an isolated area. Loneliness had descended on her like a menacing cloud after Rachel had returned to Bere Forest with Kas and Carol. Adam and Belinda had called to see her the previous Sunday, staying for tea but making no promises to visit again before the holiday. Phoebe admitted if only to herself that they had no idea what loneliness was like. But she didn't feel sorry for herself long as every sign of a warm spring was evident in the countryside through which they travelled.

265

They caught up with the gypsy travellers just outside Botley where they were resting. Phoebe was introduced to all the families as well as Lemuel and Sybil.

'You could have visited Rachel at home,' Phoebe told them. 'It was nice for me to have her with me for three whole months, and I'm sure she missed you all.'

'It was good for Rachel,' Lemuel said. 'We felt she needed that time with you. But we've certainly missed her. She's been a great asset to our family, helping with the children when our group was larger and, most important, a Godsend to me with my work.'

Phoebe was amazed at the cleanliness of the brightly painted waggons, and the camaraderie which existed between the families. She thought she would have been viewed with suspicion. Instead, in no time at all she became one of them.

Once past Southampton where they stopped to rest the horses and enjoy some refreshment they entered the New Forest with its rich variety of woodland, open parkland, trees, bracken and thickets, the sun reflecting on the diverse shades of green. After several stops along the way they left the main Cadnam to Ringwood road to the pretty secluded village of Minstead.

The few residents from outlying cottages came out to see the gypsies arrive. Phoebe had sent word to Grace as to her anticipated arrival and suspected the news had been circulated as the welcome was particularly warm and friendly. One of the foresters directed them to a clearing among trees where they could camp and be sheltered from winds or storms.

'This is a charming place,' Lemuel said to the forester. 'To think we've travelled the nearby road many times but never found this little corner of God's earth.'

'How long will you be staying, sir?' the forester enquired.

'A few days at most, and I can assure you the site will look as clean and tidy when we leave as it is now.'

The forester touched his cap and returned to his home while the gypsies unpacked the things they needed to heat the water over open fires and prepare the evening meal. Rachel went with her mother to two adjoining cottages about half a mile on the other side of the clearing where a woman in a wide-brimmed hat was waiting at the gate.

'Is this Grace?' Rachel asked in a whisper.

'It must be but it's many years since we met,' Phoebe said.

The woman waved frantically. 'Phoebe, Phoebe – it's so good to see you again.' She came running down the track with arms outstretched and for both women the years spun round like a top out of

266

control. They hugged, laughed and cried together, while Rachel stood by to look on and appraise this old schoolfriend of her mother's. Grace Whitmarsh was elegantly tall and slim. Her face was elongated, but as Rachel looked into the woman's eyes she recognised at once that here was a woman of youthful exuberance and inner beauty.

'So this is Rachel,' she said, at last freeing Phoebe. She took Rachel's hands in her own and kissed her lightly on her cheek. 'I may not have seen your mother for several years but we have kept in touch. I'm so sorry about dear Wally. So very sad and it'll take time to realise he's gone, my dears. So the Romanies have adopted you, Rachel? I understand you've married into the clan. I hope I shall meet them and your husband. Come along into the house, tea's ready.'

'I'd better leave you then, Mum, and Kas and I will bring your things over later,' Rachel said.

'You come in whenever you like, my dear,' Grace said. She had a sharp turn of phrase which from anyone else might have sounded officious but from her exuded nothing but the warmest of invitations. Phoebe glanced round with a smile as Rachel left and Rachel felt instantly confident that her mother was in good hands.

Back in their own waggon where Kas had started to prepare the meal Rachel laughed merrily as she set the table.

'Grace is quite a character, I think,' she said. She went on to describe her, adding, 'By her size and tone of voice you'd think she was a school teacher but she has a lovely dimple in her left cheek and such a happy smile. She seems to sum you up with just a glance. I liked her at once.'

'That's really nice for your mother,' Kas said. 'She'll need a friend of her own age.'

'I hope she won't discard us though.'

'Never. Not your mother, Rachel. It's up to us to be there when she needs us, but we must remember not to intrude or take advantage of her. There'll be times when she'll seek company and others when she'll need solitude. I believe she's disappointed that Belinda and Adam live so far away. I got the impression that she doesn't see them often which is a shame. Children grow up so fast and once they go to school time is limited.'

'You're so sensitive to other people's feelings, Kas,' Rachel said, looking up into his face with admiration. 'It's lovely to all be back together again – and I did come back, didn't I?'

He leaned across and ruffled Rachel's hair, much to Carol's delight. 'There'd have been trouble if you hadn't,' he said in mock anger. Then, in more sombre mood, he added, 'I hope it helped your mother having you at home for a while. I know you think she wishes it had been Belinda but we must let nature take its course. One day Belinda may need your mother more than she realises. Maybe she hasn't experienced too many of life's disasters yet but you've been through troubled waters, and we've weathered our disappointments together, so we know what it's like not to have things all our own way.'

Rachel ate in silence. Life didn't stand still. It progressed, Lemuel said, and she was glad it did, but every now and then that last scene with Adam tormented her, washed over her, enveloping her in depression. Then she would find herself lying awake at night going over much of what had happened during their courtship and subsequent events. She'd never believe Adam didn't care for her. She remembered the railway cottage they were going to share and the gypsy woman who had warned them of some impending change in their plans. Adam had been quite rude to her but Rachel felt a certain respect and now recalled that the woman had said they'd never own the cottage. She'd said, 'Be kind to the woman', Rachel could remember that bit quite clearly. They'd thought it meant Adam's mother but now Rachel was left perplexed. Maybe her own mother? But there was no chance of them not being kind to Phoebe. The gypsy had warned that all was not as they believed. That bit had been proved right too – Rachel wasn't who she'd always thought she was! Adam had scoffed at any hint of fortune telling but Rachel knew better. She knew it didn't please Kas either to speak of finding out who her real parents were so she kept her thoughts private. Memories returned too of how she'd been taunted at school and called the Witch of Wickham because of the hideous birthmark. If for no other reason she desperately wanted to find her real mother to prove that she wasn't a freak and that the birthmark had faded. Rachel felt impatience growing but she had no idea where to start her search.

'We'd better hurry up,' she said while they were washing up. 'Or it'll be your bedtime, Carol, before we've taken Grandma's case and bag to her. I want to show you and Daddy where I lived when I was a little girl.'

It had been a long, tiring day and the light was beginning to fade as Rachel, Kas and Carol took the small path across the wood. No lights shone out from the cottage where Phoebe was staying with Grace, but next door a lamp was burning brightly in the window of the front room and distant voices could be heard.

'Oh that does bring back memories,' Rachel said as she stood still while she took in the scene. 'I was only seven when we left here but these cottages hold such precious recollections of our childhood.'

268

'And your grandparents lived in the adjoining one?' Kas asked.

'Yes. I believe my great-grandfather built them. Seems he had a bit of money. He was a builder, my father and grandfather both master carpenters. It was great fun having them live next door. If we got into trouble with Mum or Dad for any reason we would sneak next door and get given sweets.'

'What made your father want to move?'

'There wasn't enough work about, I think. Grandfather was too old to work and Dad heard about the Squire needing a carpenter at the Manor House at Wickham, with a tied cottage included. I remember the grandparents weeping when we left. At some time Dad must have been able to buy Calder Cottage but I don't remember exactly when. Maybe it was when Mum's parents died. We only visited Lee-on-Solent in the summer. Grandma was left on her own for several years but I think I remember something about some money being left to Mum when I was still at school. Maybe they bought Calder Cottage then.'

Behind the lace curtains Rachel could see movement as the lamp was lit and an eager hand waved them to come inside which they did.

'Can I take your case and bag upstairs, Mrs Hunter?' Kas enquired.

'I'll show you where,' Grace said. 'You can come too, Rachel. I expect you've forgotten about your grandparents' old home. I haven't had time to do much to the place except new wallpaper and a bit of varnish here and there. I love the fresh air so the garden takes precedence over housework. There's a tidy bit of garden too but I've got it all well planted with spuds and the rest. Hope we don't get any late frosts, I took a chance.'

Everywhere smelled either of carbolic soap or lavender polish. Rachel wondered if it was all for her mothers' benefit but considering Grace claimed to prefer the great outdoors she had certainly made her mark on the cottage. Downstairs was clean but more cluttered with Grace's memorabilia from abroad, and the time flew by as she related story after story about each item which intrigued her visitors.

'Now I want you to come every day for as long as you're staying in the woods,' Grace said when Rachel insisted it was past Carol's bedtime. 'Your mother and I are going to have fun catching up, and I do want to get to know you better before you go off travelling again.'

Even Kas had to agree that Grace seemed a kind person, and after all that had happened she just had to be the tonic Phoebe needed.

Carol too was much taken with Auntie Grace and eager to return to the cottage next day. The long garden was exciting to explore and as it was a lovely warm day Grace brought lemonade and a pot of tea outside.

'So what's Kas doing today then?' she asked.

'The men are out hawking round the houses. They take advantage of every opportunity,' Rachel said.

'D'you help too?'

'Of course. I have to help earn my keep the same as the others, but not just as the moment as we really want this baby.'

'Phoebe said both you and Belinda are expecting. Such a shame Wally won't be here to see his new grandchildren.' She poured the tea. 'I suppose you'd have liked these two cottages for the girls, Phoebe?' she said thoughtfully.

Phoebe glanced at Rachel quickly and she knew by her mother's look that Grace had been told nothing about her father's will and letter.

'If you haven't told Grace yet, Mum,' she said, meaning that she wasn't really Belinda's twin sister, 'you may as well.'

'Grace was the only person in the whole world who knew that I didn't give birth to twins, dear,' Phoebe said, slowly. 'When I got over Belinda's birth and grew stronger I realised what an enormous responsibility it was to take in someone else's baby, and Grace, being thousands of miles away in Singapore, was the best person to confide in.'

'Can you remember any details of what Mum told you, Grace?' Rachel asked eagerly.

'Heavens, no! How old are you now? Twenty-four? My memory isn't that good, I'm afraid, Rachel. I used to keep all the letters I received, but I wasn't very good at writing back, was I, Phoebe? The life was so exciting and hectic.' Grace paused and leaned forward in the whicker chair. 'But you know now, Rachel? I thought it was to be a never-to-be-discovered secret, Phoebe?'

She sighed. 'It was,' she said solemnly, 'and we didn't ever tell anyone but you. Moving to Kingsmere when the girls were seven it faded from our thoughts for much of the time, especially when the birthmark disappeared. Wally's death has been more tragic than you know, Grace.' She went on to tell her friend about the will and letter.

'Phew!' Grace exclaimed as she sat back in her chair again and sipped tea. 'That was a bit below the belt, wasn't it? You poor dear, Rachel. Such a revelation was enough to turn your brain.'

'It was a blow, but well deserved after what I did.' Rachel stretched out her hand and squeezed her mother's. 'It doesn't alter my love for Mum, and I do appreciate all she and Dad did for me. I was hurt that Dad disowned me, I can't deny that, but like Kas says, money isn't important, it's people that matter.'

'I'd like to buy this cottage, Phoebe,' Grace said. 'That's one of the reasons I wanted you to come to Minsted. I can afford it, and as I've

270

no relatives of my own I could leave it to Rachel.' She laughed. 'Won't be for a long time yet though, m'dear.'

'Wally left everything tied up in such a way that the cottages, all three of them, can't be sold until I die,' Phoebe explained. 'And then the proceeds have to be shared between Belinda and her offspring. If only we'd adopted Rachel legally she could have contested the will.'

'But could you have done that? Adopted Rachel, I mean?' Grace asked. 'I thought at the time you said you had no idea where the child came from?'

'That's true . . .' Phoebe began, but Rachel interrupted quickly.

'I mean to find out where I came from, and who my real parents are or were,' she said. 'Oh, I know everyone thinks I'm mad to rake up the past and I don't want to bring trouble to any family, but I *need* to know. Can you understand that, Grace?'

'But that's some task, dear, if Phoebe doesn't know anything.'

'I do wish Rachel could let the matter drop,' she said a trifle impatiently. 'I've told her all I know which is that Teddy, the midwife, brought her to us very early in the morning while it was still dark. No one in Minstead knew or suspected, not even Wally's parents. By the time we let them see the babies there were two, and when they saw Rachel's birthmark they assumed that was why they hadn't been allowed in. The truth was that Wally's mother was a bit of a ditherer and I couldn't take too much of her so Wally kept them away for the first few days.'

'And the midwife?' Grace asked. 'Where is she now? Dead, I suppose?'

'She and her sister retired during the war, I think. Nurse Fletcher was the elder, a spinster, and lived not at all that from the Calder Cottage strangely enough, but Teddy lived at Cadnam. She was a widow with three children and had to go back to work as a midwife after her husband died, to keep herself and her three children. I believe they went to live by the sea somewhere, Christchurch or Bournemouth it might have been.'

'Surely someone round here would know?' Rachel said, but her mother shrugged and remained silent.

After dinner Phoebe said that she wanted to visit the family next door. 'I expect you'd like to come, Rachel. After all, that's our old home. They're complaining that the roof leaks and a few other jobs need doing so I'd best get it over and done with.'

'How long have they lived there?' Grace asked.

'Ever since we left nineteen years ago,' Phoebe said. 'They had seven children so the cottage has taken a bit of a beating during the years. It used to grieve Wally to see the woodwork scratched and the windows broken but I suppose they're much like any other big family.'

Rachel listened eagerly. 'If they've lived there ever since we left,' she said, 'then surely the same midwife would have delivered some of the seven children?'

Grace laughed. 'I was thinking much the same thing, Rachel, but didn't dare say so. I expect your mother is right and it's better to let sleeping dogs lie, but I do understand how you feel. As if you don't belong – as if you don't have any identity – but your husband is right to say it doesn't really matter because you can't change anything now. If it wasn't a legal adoption you might be getting someone in trouble on top of everything else.'

'I wouldn't want to do that,' Rachel said, 'but I'd dearly love to talk to the midwife, if she's still alive.'

'There's not a lot I can do to help you, Rachel, but I'll ask around to see if anyone knows where the midwife went to live,' Grace offered.

But Rachel didn't want to accept help from anyone else and after she'd helped with the dishes went with her mother to the cottage next door.

From what Phoebe had said Rachel expected to find the woman of grubby appearance, but considering she had a family of seven children she looked surprisingly youthful and nicely dressed.

'Mrs Hunter,' Emily Young greeted. 'It's nice to meet you at last. And this must be . . . .?'

'My daughter, Rachel.'

'Yes, we heard a rumour that you were coming with the travellers.'

'I've come about the repairs that need doing,' Phoebe hurried on to hide her embarrassment about Rachel being a gypsy. 'I'll have a look round whenever it's convenient to you, Mrs Young, and then see what we can do.'

'It's convenient now, Mrs Hunter. I've only got Lucy at home today. Michael and Leslie are at school and the others are out at work. You've just missed my Alec, he's been in for his dinner and gone again. Come along in.'

Upstairs in the small bedroom a little white-faced girl lay in bed.

'I was sorry to hear about Mr Hunter,' Emily said quietly. 'Very sorry indeed. I know it's early days yet, but we was wondering, my Alec and me, if there'd be any changes?'

'None that I can think of, Mrs Young,' Phoebe said. 'As tenants you have certain rights, but of course without a man now I shall have to watch my expenses so I'd be grateful if you'd take as much care as you can of the house.'

'Well, we had a talk and we understand the situation so my Alec said I was to say that he and the boys will do what repairs they can themselves if you can provide the materials, same as before.'

'Hullo, you must be Lucy,' Rachel said to the little girl. 'How old are you?'

'Seven, Miss,' Lucy whispered.

'I lived here until I was seven,' Rachel said with a smile. 'Aren't you well?'

'A bit delicate, is Lucy,' Emily said. 'Picks up every germ that's going, she does. Doctor thinks she might have a heart murmur but I daresay she'll grow out of it and be as boisterous as the rest. She's the last of the brood so my Alec spoils her, I daresay.'

Rachel saw an opportunity not to be missed.

'Did you have all your children here in this cottage, Mrs Young?' she asked.

'Yes, came here soon after we was wed. Alec got a job on a farm near Cadnam and he's still there now. Had my Esme within the year, we did. Poor Nurse Edwards almost lived here for three or four days, my labour was so long.' Emily Young laughed heartily. 'Wasn't long about after that, though. More I had the quicker they came.'

'Don't suppose you happen to know where Nurse Edwards is now?' Rachel ventured.

'Retired a long time ago, but she remembers Esme's birthday even to this day. Thought she'd have to get the doctor to me for her, but Teddy wouldn't give up – and I couldn't.' She laughed again. 'My Esme's married now and living in Wiltshire. She'd have the address but I do know Teddy lives near the sea somewhere down Bournemouth way. In a home for retired nurses, I believe.'

'She delivered my – um, me too,' Phoebe said. 'She must know this cottage very well, though I only had Rachel and Belinda.'

'Reckon Teddy knows every stick and stone hereabouts. Couldn't have done without her, none of us.'

Lucy began to cough and her mother gave her a drink. After Phoebe had surveyed the damp patch on the ceilings of two of the bedrooms they went over the rest of the cottage while Mrs Young showed them where repairs were needed. Phoebe promised to do what she could, and as they left and returned to the cottage next door Rachel said, 'Wasn't in too bad a shape, Mum. What did you think?'

'They invited me in for a cup of tea the day I moved in,' Grace said, 'and I must say everywhere appeared to be clean and tidy. Quite a hard-working couple, I should say.'

'I daresay Wally coveted this place and saw damage where there wasn't any,' Phoebe said. 'Besides, the children are all growing up now. Not too much to do. I'll have to find a workman somewhere.'

'I'll speak to Kas, Mum,' Rachel offered. 'Travelling folk have to do their own repairs and most can turn their hand to anything. Grace, I've found out that the midwife who took me to Mum is living in a home for retired nurses somewhere on the coast.'

'She's still alive then?'

'Yes, so at least I know where to start looking.'

'Shouldn't be too difficult to find then, but whatever you do, Rachel, dear, don't rush into anything.'

'Kas won't let me,' she said dismally. 'I doubt very much that he'll agree to my searching for Nurse Edwards in Bournemouth or anywhere else.'

'If I were you I'd get your confinement over and done with before you continue with the search,' Grace said.

'But by then the sisters might be dead. They must be pretty old as it is,' Rachel said.

At the close of the day when Kas and Rachel were relaxing in their own van and Carol had been put to bed, Rachel told Kas what she had learned. As she had predicted the response was negative.

'Your health is what matters and after you've had the baby, Rachel, you'll have your work cut out looking after it. Should we ever find ourselves on the coast then you can make enquiries but we aren't making a special journey to Bournemouth where gypsies aren't received very cordially.'

Rachel knew that she had to accept his decision however difficult that was. But nothing could prevent her from thinking and planning. When they reached Burley the distance wouldn't be so great and it might prove to be her only chance. She would discuss the matter with Lemuel and Sybil and solicit their help.

As soon as she mentioned the repairs required by the tenants of the cottage, Kas offered to look into it at once.

'We didn't reckon on staying here more than a couple of days but if there's a job to be done we must see to it,' he said. 'If the others want to move on we'll stay here alone while I do the work.' He smiled, his dark eyes twinkling mischievously at Rachel. 'I know you'll find it very irksome to have to while away the days with your mother and her friend.'

Rachel tossed the nearest cushion at him. 'It's my guess,' she said, 'that the others will want to help too. I'd like Lemuel and Sybil to have time to get to know Mum and Grace better.' Rachel laughed. 'Poor Mum, it was quite obvious that she wasn't keen to be seen having anything to do with gypsies but I do believe she enjoyed travelling with us.'

Kas watched Rachel anxiously as the days passed. She blossomed in a way he couldn't describe and once the repairs to both cottages had been completed the group began to prepare to move on. He half expected Rachel to want to remain with her mother for longer but on the other hand he guessed that she was eager to move nearer the coast, while he planned to travel back towards Wickham once the time drew near for their baby to be born in late August. Although the gypsies were well experienced in childbirth he wanted what was best for Rachel, and knew that it would please her mother to be on hand, but he said nothing to his wife as he wanted it to be a surprise. After all that had happened with Ena he also felt he would be happier in close proximity to a doctor and hospital.

Their last evening at Minstead was a fine, dry, balmy one and with caravans packed and ready to move early next day a huge camp fire was lit. The forester had presented them with several rabbits as a token of his appreciation for not causing any undue noise and litter during their stay. In turn he and his family, along with Phoebe, Grace, the Youngs and any other neighbours who wanted to, were invited to join in the final gathering. Plenty to eat and drink, a joyous sing-song accompanied by Caleb's squeeze-box, and, to everyone's surprise, Grace's guitar, brought romanies and gorgios together in harmony for a feast they wouldn't easily forget.

Grace was a woman of the world, nothing shocked or surprised her, and she entered into the spirit of the happy occasion with gusto.

Rachel said her goodbyes after Lemuel had finished prayers.

'We'll see you again before too long, Mum,' she said emotionally. 'When August comes perhaps you can come to stay with us?' Then she turned to Grace. 'I can't tell you how pleased I am to have met you, and I know Mum is loving every minute of her holiday with you. You've been very kind.'

'Nonsense, Rachel,' Grace said. 'It's been my pleasure, and your mother and I are going to see a great deal of each other from now on. I'm hoping to go and stay at Calder Cottage so we'll meet again one of these days. Naturally I'm anxious to meet Belinda, Adam and Billy too.'

Rachel slept in Kas's arms that night full of contentment.

The dew had hardly dried on the grass verges when they set off southwards next morning, and when the first signpost to Bournemouth appeared at the roadside Rachel was filled with renewed hope.

Briar Hill near Burley was a good site, and they prospered financially by selling their wares among the local people who treated them kindly. Weeks passed in rapid succession, Rachel disappointed because no mention was made of travelling farther south to the coast

275

even though she had hesitantly suggested to Lemuel it might be good for him. Kas was just relieved that Rachel continued to keep well.

'I know I shouldn't worry,' he said one morning after he'd been to fetch water, 'but I shall feel more secure if we're near your mother and a doctor or hospital when the time comes.'

'It's ages yet before I'm due,' Rachel said, vying for time. 'It's nice here and I expect Lemuel would like to move nearer the sea. I thought perhaps one Sunday you and I could take him in the trap to Christchurch or Bournemouth.'

'Nice try,' Kas laughed. 'You can't fool me, you should know that, but it's quite a way and we don't want to travel out of our way in your condition.'

Rachel had been advised similarly by Sybil and Lemuel and was downhearted, but tried to keep her spirits up by promising herself that once she had her baby she would go to Bournemouth by herself on the train from Wickham. She might even persuade her mother to accompany her.

On a wet miserable June morning as Rachel and Carol sat inside the van doing a jig-saw puzzle while Kas was feeding the horses a strange noise distracted Carol.

'Oh, look, Mummy,' she called from her kneeling position on the window seat. 'A motor car – oh, and look, it's Grandma!'

With great excitement she ran to the door and looked out with Rachel, now rather too large to move quickly, hastily following.

'A car!' she exclaimed. 'It's Mum and Grace!'

The car chugged its way close to the van and Kas came running across the field greatly intrigued. He looked the shiny vehicle over enviously before helping Phoebe and Grace out.

'Come along in,' Rachel called. 'What a marvellous surprise.'

Phoebe and Grace ran in to avoid getting too wet. 'Just had to come to see how you all are,' Phoebe said. 'Oh, Rachel dear, I have missed you. That's the only thing I have against you living like this – we don't have any way of keeping in touch.'

'I assumed you would be back in Kingsmere,' Rachel said while Kas put the kettle on. 'And what's this – a borrowed car?'

'No, m'dear, 'tis all mine,' Grace said in her usual abrupt manner. 'I drove all the time in Singapore, well, everyone did, and now my finances are straightened out I decided to make life easier by being able to go where I want to, when I want to.'

'Grace came to stay at Calder Cottage,' Phoebe said. 'We had a lovely time and went to visit Belinda and Adam. He's talking about getting a little car one day.'

'I'd already made up my mind before that so we went to a reputable garage in Portsmouth, and here we are.'

276

'You haven't chosen a very nice day for travelling around,' Kas said.

Phoebe cast a cautious look towards Grace who said fearlessly,

'That's the whole point, Kas. I know you aren't too much in favour of Rachel pursuing her parentage, but Phoebe and I feel that she'll never settle until she knows. It's quite an intriguing story, after all. And as Rachel says, you do know a little about your roots but she knows nothing.'

'And what she doesn't know can't hurt her,' Kas said sternly.

'You have a valid point there, dear boy. But we thought as it is such a miserable day I could drive down to Bournemouth and take you all for a spin. It's June, after all, so it might buck up later on. Rain before seven, shine before eleven, isn't that right?'

Grace was not so much persuasive as coercive. Rachel couldn't believe her luck and for once was totally speechless. She could hardly bring herself to look at Kas but when she did his dark eyes melted her apprehension.

'OK, you win, I suppose,' he said with a lop-sided grin. 'I won't pretend I like the idea at all. I'm afraid of causing distress to some poor unsuspecting middle-aged couple. I don't want you to get hurt, darling. You must be prepared for disappointment. Even if you find the midwife it doesn't mean she'll be willing to betray a confidence.'

'Don't you think I've had time to think all this over a million times?' Rachel asked. 'I realise that I've only got a slim chance of finding out who my parents were but I feel compelled to try.'

'Grace and I have talked a lot about it too,' Phoebe said. 'It may be that after all these years Wally felt we'd done something not above board by taking you in without legal advice. He'd evidently given the matter considerable thought and it's possible he was of the opinion that he owed it to you, Rachel, to tell you the truth.' She pulled a scrap of paper from her bag. 'Mrs Young's daughter Esme sent her this address. I don't know that we'll be able to find the place though. It's on the outskirts of Bournemouth near a river.'

'We can stop off somewhere at a newsagents and get a map,' Grace said. 'Or we've got tongues in our heads, we can ask.'

'Well, I wish you the best of luck,' Kas said.

'But you're coming as well. I might need you to help me start her up,' Grace said, 'or change the wheel if we get a puncture.'

How could Kas rebel against such a command without appearing ungallant? Grace's Morris Oxford was a big attraction, and although with Rachel's extra bulk she and her mother had some difficulty squeezing in the rear seat with Carol, they managed comfortably, Kas riding in the front passenger seat as navigator. They journeyed

277

through country lanes to Bransgore and Christchurch before heading towards Bournemouth at over twenty miles per hour, Grace assuring them that they could travel fifty miles on one gallon of petrol.

By noon the clouds had scudded away and the roads were quickly drying in the June sunshine. They stopped near a small shop and received directions to some brick buildings enclosed in green-painted iron railings where a board near the gate announced that these were the homes for retired nurses and midwives.

'We've found it so easily,' Rachel said.

'Yes, and done it in good time,' Grace said proudly. 'In fact it may be a good thing we've got here before dinner time. Elderly people often have an afternoon nap so you might catch her now if she is still here. But I hope you'll agree with me, Kas, that it might be better for Rachel and Phoebe to go it alone from here?'

Kas agreed readily and they decided that he and Grace would take Carol for a walk along the river bank which was close by.

Phoebe led the way up the path, admiring the well-kept lawns and flower borders before entering a door marked 'Office'.

A grey-haired gentleman was sitting at a desk but stood up as they entered.

'Good afternoon,' he greeted politely. 'Can I be of help?'

Rachel opened her mouth but nothing came out. She felt as if she had been struck dumb and Phoebe looked at her with concern. Then she took the matter into her own hands.

'We've come to enquire about a lady named Mrs Edwards,' she said. 'She lived at Minstead in the New Forest where she was midwife for many years. We understand she came here to live with her sister Miss Fletcher – Minnie Fletcher. She was midwife in the Wickham area.'

The gentleman offered his hand to Phoebe has he introduced himself.

'Sydney Cox,' he said. 'I'm sorry to say dear Miss Fletcher died a few years back, but her sister, Mrs Edwards – yes, she's very much with us. Does she expect you?'

'No,' Phoebe said. 'We've come from Minstead and picked my daughter up near Burley. It wasn't arranged, you see, an unexpected opportunity – I don't want to upset Nurse Edwards.' Suddenly Phoebe had cold feet.

'I'm sure she will be delighted to have unexpected visitors. She's getting on, you know, well over eighty. Miss Fletcher was eighty-nine when she passed away but they enjoyed several years of happy retirement together, taking every opportunity to visit the seaside. Now if you take the path which leads to the rear of this building you'll

278

find the little dwellings all have numbers. Mrs Edwards lives in number twenty-three.'

He escorted them to the door and showed them which path to follow.

The solid doors were all painted green as were the small high windows but most looked attractive with frilled lace curtains. Rachel went ahead of her mother in her eagerness to find Teddy, but as they reached the door marked twenty-three she held back.

'What are we doing?' she whispered. 'Suddenly I'm afraid I won't like what I hear, or cause the old lady to have a heart attack or something.'

'She may not be prepared to tell us anything,' Phoebe whispered. 'We can't be sure what state of mind she's in so say we're just visiting my old midwife for old times' sake.'

Rachel knocked on the door and it was opened surprisingly quickly.

'Yes?' the elderly woman croaked, peering first at Rachel then at Phoebe. Then she threw her hands in the air and opened the door wider. 'Well, 'pon my soul, if it isn't Phoebe Hunter.'

'Hullo, Teddy,' Phoebe said, smiling broadly. 'I wasn't sure if you'd remember me.'

'Not remember you? 'Course I do – and that cottage at Minstead. Delivered another seven after yours. But don't stand out there, come along in. And let me see . . . is this your girl?'

As they went inside, carefully brushing their shoes on the doormat Phoebe said, 'One of them.'

'Ah, yes, there were two – 'tis all coming back.'

By the time they were all inside the living room Nurse Edwards' cheeks were rather flushed. She sat down in a high-backed chair near the window and Phoebe sat opposite. The old nurse appraised Rachel's condition.

'Long to go? Couple of months mebbe?'

'The end of August, Mrs Edwards,' she said. 'I've had three miscarriages though.'

'Mmm . . . 't'will be all right this time by the looks of things. Once you get over three months, should go full term. Well, fancy that, you coming to see me,' she mused as she stared hard at Phoebe.

'An old friend brought us in her car,' she explained. 'My husband Wally died at the beginning of the year.'

'I'm sorry, my dear. A good man was your husband, and such a wonder with wood. He couldn't have been all that old?'

'No, not even sixty-five, and his parents lived to well in their eighties.'

'Ah, well, that's one thing we can't arrange to suit ourselves.'

Phoebe went on to explain about Wally's illness, and then, looking down at her trembling hands, continued nervously, 'I'm sure dear Wally didn't mean to upset the apple cart, Teddy, but he left a letter explaining why he couldn't include Rachel in his will – because she isn't really Belinda's twin sister.'

'That wasn't the real reason though,' Rachel put in. 'I was jilted by my fiancé who then said he'd made a mistake and wanted to marry Belinda. I couldn't bear it so I ran away. Dad couldn't forgive that. I . . . I joined up with some gypsies. They're really nice people though.'

'I ain't got anything against gypsies, my dear. Helped a few of 'em out in me time when they had bad deliveries. It's always the few who give the rest a bad name. Mostly they're kind, clean and helpful.'

'I'm married to one,' Rachel said with a smile.

'Kas is an exceptionally good man,' Phoebe said. 'But he's not too happy about us bothering you. Neither am I if it comes to that.'

'But I *must* know, Mrs Edwards. I must find out who I am and where I came from. I hope you understand?' Rachel pleaded.

'You're Rachel Hunter as I recall,' Mrs Edwards said slowly, then pursed her lips and frowned. 'I could tell you that I don't know anything either. After all, t'was my sister who brought you to me – how do I know where you sprang from?'

'But you do, Mrs Edwards, don't you?' Rachel said in a soft persuasive voice.

'Let's have a cup of tea. You must be tired after your long journey and talking always makes me thirsty.'

'Can I help?' Phoebe offered. 'We don't want to put you to any trouble.'

Rachel was surprised at how spritely Teddy was for her age. She was keen-eyed and mentally alert, with no sign on senility.

'I don't get many visitors these days,' she said. 'Minnie and me wondered whether we'd done the right thing to move away from people we knew, but we love the sea and enjoyed our days together.'

'I'm sorry she passed away,' Phoebe said, following Teddy to the tiny kitchen. 'She was well-loved and remembered in her parish, just as you were and still are in yours.'

Teddy laughed heartily. '"Parish" is good,' she said. 'T'was like that for the both of us. We knew everyone for miles around and watched the children grow up, get married and have babies of their own. 'Tis the kind of job you miss, but Min and me, we had our memories to live with and we exchanged our stories – yes, and we often talked about you and your girls, Mrs Hunter.' She turned from

280

the table and put her arm round Phoebe's shoulder, whispering, 'D'you really want the girl to know the truth? I've kept Min's old records and I've read 'em through so knows 'tis all there. Remember it like it was yesterday – better'n what happened yesterday.'

'Do we have an option, Teddy? Doesn't she have the right to know, having been told this much now? We promised never to tell anyone and Wally and I kept that promise. I don't know what came over him to change his will and write the letter he did. It was pure chance that Rachel met up with Adam Taylor at Portsmouth hospital or she might not have seen her father before he died.' Phoebe found it difficult to talk about those unpleasant days, but she told Teddy the full story.

'Suppose in a way she blames herself for Wally's death then?'

Phoebe nodded. 'Poor Rachel, life wasn't very kind to her having to grow up with that horrible birthmark, but at last she does seem happy now, even if it is with gypsies. Wally's letter was a dreadful shock for her but she isn't going to let it rest until she knows the truth, Teddy.'

'But what does she plan to do if I tell her?'

'Best ask her,' Phoebe said.

The tea made, Phoebe carried the tray into the living room where Rachel sat patiently waiting, though inside she was churning with a mixture of excitement and fear.

'If we're keeping you from your dinner, Teddy, we could come back another time?' Phoebe suggested.

She nodded towards Rachel. 'That wouldn't please you now, would it?'

'I'm not here to cause trouble,' she said. 'I'm anxious to find the truth, even if I don't like it.'

'Oh, bless you, child, there's nothing you won't like. But I'll get Min's record book out and we'll see what it says.'

Rachel felt impatience growing as Teddy first poured a cup of tea each and offered them biscuits then went into the hallway where a huge oak blanket chest stood. She returned a few minutes later with a black notebook conspicuous by its red spine.

'Now I must warn you that once I've told you, Rachel, this book will be burnt. I should have done it after Min died, but something niggled in the back of me mind and I couldn't bring myself to. This isn't the official record book, you understand. Min had a feeling that one day someone might come asking questions. Once she'd died, o'course, no one need know anything, but now that you know a bit you might as well know the rest.'

'Oh, *please*,' Rachel urged.

Teddy put her spectacles on and turned the pages. 'Very meticulous was our Min over details of her work.' She paused, skipping

281

down the page, then read aloud, 'Because of the birthmark the man of the house, a man given to over indulgence in strong drink, threatened to kill this female infant. The mother had a difficult time, wasn't a strong woman after giving birth to five children previously. She had no interest in the sickly child and so in the interests of the baby the doctor present and myself decided to fake the infant's death.' Teddy glanced up to see how Rachel was accepting the story. 'We then colluded with my sister who was also a midwife and had recently delivered Phoebe Hunter of a female infant to give her the unwanted child and pass it off as a twin. They were duly registered officially as twin daughters of Phoebe and Walter Hunter of Minstead.'

'But the name of the woman – my mother,' Rachel asked anxiously.

Teddy's glance reverted to the top of the page. 'Case notes of Agnes Mead, wife of Richard Mead of Hundred Acres near Wickham.'

A deathly hush filled the small, stuffy room.

'*Nessie Mead*?' Phoebe cried, putting her hands to her throat. 'Heavens above! I can scarcely believe it. We took you back to within a couple of miles of where you were born, Rachel.'

Chapter Nineteen

Rachel sat white-faced with shock. Then she began to laugh.

'I'm Charlie Mead's sister!' she exclaimed. 'I've got another brother and three sisters. I'm one of a large family and Nessie is my real mother.' Her lips were dry and she drank almost greedily from her cup. It was almost too incredible to sink in. So many questions to ask Nessie and Dick, and perish the thought – Beth Cropper was her aunt!

'I would never have guessed in a hundred years,' she said. She stood up as discomfort compelled her to. A moment of giddiness possessed her.

Teddy and Phoebe fussed over her and gave her a drink of brandy. The colour returned to Rachel's cheeks and she blinked. 'I'm terribly sorry,' she said. 'Whatever came over me?'

'Quickening, I shouldn't wonder,' Teddy said. 'About five months, you say? Baby's turned all right then and it'll be plain sailing all the way now.'

'I don't know what to say.'

'You wanted to know, my dear, and now you do. Remember, this Mr and Mrs Mead think their baby died so it has to be your secret as it's been ours for this past twenty-four years. I never knew the Meads but Min told me all about them. I suppose she and the doctor could have been prosecuted for what they did, though as I told Min, with a good lawyer the authorities would have accepted that what was done was done in good faith for the sake of the child. Your parents gave you a good home, Rachel,' Teddy patted her hands. 'Now you be a good parent to your family, and may they all be healthy children.'

'Sisters – the sea,' Rachel muttered with a faraway look.

'What's that, dear?' Phoebe asked.'

'Oh, nothing. Something I remembered.' She recalled something else too, when she and Adam had been at the railway cottage. The gypsy there had said, 'Be kind to the woman.' Yes, Rachel thought, I've always had a warm feeling for Nessie Mead. I can understand why she didn't want me and I'll always be kind to her, just as I'll try to be extra kind to Mum.

They left Teddy and went to find the others. Kas and Grace listened with interest to Rachel's story while Carol announced with some impatience that she was hungry, so they travelled on to the cliff-top road and down to the promenade where they stopped for refreshment in the cafe there. Afterwards, while Rachel mused over what she knew and discussed it fully with Phoebe, Kas and Carol made a sandcastle on the beach and they allowed Carol to paddle in the water.

It was late afternoon when they returned to Mrs Edwards' home to present her with a bunch of pink carnations and a cake they'd thought she might like from a local bakery. From a fruit stall along the way they purchased a small basket of fresh strawberries for her. This time, Kas, Carol and Grace were introduced to her.

Teddy kissed Phoebe warmly as they made their goodbyes and then hugged Rachel. 'You've turned out a fine young woman, my dear. I hope all goes well when your time comes. Now, remember, that book never existed and there are no records left from my sister's work so the past is dead and buried too. Min wouldn't have wanted any recriminations, and when I'm dead and gone won't be any good anyone coming looking for evidence.' She tapped the side of her nose. 'What you know is your secret now.'

Rachel kissed Teddy warmly. 'You've been so helpful,' she said. 'I appreciate that you didn't have to tell us anything, but I'm so relieved and grateful that you did.' They waved goodbye, promising to visit if ever they were that way again. The journey back to Briar Hill seemed to be over as if by magic but only because Rachel couldn't stop talking.

There was an emotional goodbye between Rachel and Phoebe after they'd eaten together.

'You'll always be my real Mum,' Rachel said, giving her a hug. 'I'm glad it's turned out to be Nessie. It puts so much into place, like the friendship between me and Charlie. Not sure that I like the idea of Dick Mead being my dad, so I'm quite content to be a Hunter.'

'We shall be moving towards Wickham now, Mrs Hunter, during the next few weeks,' Kas told his mother-in-law.

'I shall be anxious for Rachel,' Phoebe said, 'and Belinda as well. I want to be on hand when my new grandchildren arrive.'

For the next few weeks of summer Rachel had much to brood over and discuss with Sybil and Lemuel. She wrote often to Phoebe, and even wrote to Belinda as well, hoping that she was well and saying that they would be seeing them fairly soon. She knew Phoebe planned to tell Belinda and Adam the true story in an effort to put an end to any speculation. It couldn't be the end for Rachel though. She desperately wanted to get back to Hundred Acres if only to see Nessie Mead from a distance. Kas, in his quiet, wise way, knew what Rachel hankered after and openly forebade any communication with the Meads except for polite greeting if they met by chance.

'The shock of discovering her baby didn't die, plus the fact of the doctor and midwife faking your death, might be very cruel to her,' he said.

'Yes, I know,' Rachel agreed. 'I've always felt so sad for her somehow, and I wouldn't ever do anything to hurt her, but I would like to see her – just to look at her and think, "You're my Mum".'

'It isn't likely that you'll ever meet up with people from that area again,' Kas said. 'After our baby is born we shall have to think seriously about the future, darling.'

'Why? Having a baby isn't going to change anything,' she said a trifle indignantly.

'Our group has split up a good deal since the war,' he said. 'We're a much smaller family now, and Lemuel and Sybil are not young travellers any more. I've been giving the matter some thought and I wondered how you'd feel about living in Christchurch?'

'Christchurch? Why Christchurch?' Rachel asked.

'Not for some while, but perhaps when our child gets to school age. As you know I own two cottages there. I thought we might take a trip down to see them before we move on. If they become vacant at any time we could live in one, and Sybil and Lemuel in the other.'

Rachel stared at Kas. 'It's a wonderful idea,' she said after thinking about it briefly. 'But would they want to? They've been travellers for many years. I'm sure it would be better for their health, but I'm not sure they'd approve of the idea.'

'Lemuel was talking about returning to the Isle of Wight. Sybil wasn't so keen, I felt. It's just an idea, Rachel, we must think carefully about it for the future.'

'How old are the people who live in the houses now?'

'An elderly couple live in one. They lost two sons in the war and I don't think the woman has ever recovered from the tragedy. A widow lives in the other one, but she's often away staying with her married daughter who lives in Poole. I can't turn them out, they're protected tenants, and I wouldn't want to, but we must be prepared for the houses to become empty one of these days.'

'It might not happen for years,' Rachel said. 'But I like the idea, Kas. It would be good to be more settled if we're to have a family.'

He wrapped his arms round her. 'Let's bring this one into the world safely to start with,' he said, cuddling her and their unborn child.

A month later and the travelling gypsies had regrouped in the Forest of Bere. It was pleasant for Rachel to be able to spend time with her mother as Kas, Caleb and some of the younger men found temporary work on local farms. The strawberry season had all but ended, and the fields needed to be cleared and ploughed ready for the following year. Rachel felt happier than she had done for a long while, and with the bloom of motherhood came contentment as she entered into the final phase of waiting.

'I'd feel easier in my mind if you'd let a doctor give you a check-up,' Kas persuaded her. 'I know nature takes its course but Doctor Barber knows the situation and would be glad to confirm that everything's all right. Bring the trap to the farm at 5 o'clock and we'll go into Wickham – please, Rachel, time is getting short.'

She laughed at Kas's concern but eventually agreed to do as he wished. She knew he was taking precautions for her sake and she appreciated the care he took of her, but doubted that any doctor could offer any better advice than Sybil and Precious. All the same, in spite of her well-being she had many moments of apprehension. Everyone was a tower of strength and did their best to reassure her, but too much had happened to Rachel since the day she had walked out of Calder Cottage and into a completely different lifestyle not to feel that fate might be waiting round the corner with some unexpected bombshell. At times she felt there must be some kind of jinx on her. First the strawberry birthmark. What had Nessie and Dick Mead done to cause such a blemish, she wondered? None of the other Meads had such a mark. Then Adam jilting her, and much later her father disowning her. She was afraid of what else there might be in store for her and tried hard to press Sybil into seeing into the future, but all she would say was, 'Happy times and sad times Rachel, and we all 'as to accept those.'

There was an early autumn feel to the late afternoon when Rachel set off alone in the trap drawn by Bella. Rachel and Carol had been to Calder Cottage to have dinner with Phoebe. Carol and her grandma were the best of friends so Phoebe was pleased to have the child's company while Rachel went to meet Kas.

'I've picked some of the best of the gladioli and roses,' Phoebe said. 'Perhaps you could take them to your father's grave before you come home?'

286

Wally would have been proud of his garden. Phoebe had worked hard to keep everything just as he'd always done, and the flowers had been particularly colourful and plenteous this year.

Rachel took the Wickham road towards the farm where Kas and the others were working, and when she reached the open fields pulled in at the side of the track. Her back ached from the bumpy ride so she climbed down and looked about her. Huge black rooks their glossy plumage shot with purple and green, tumbled in the sky before descending on the ground to scavenge whatever was going, making a noisy pantomime. She decided to walk about to try to ease the pain low in her back. In the near distance she could see the neat brick houses of Hundred Acres. I was born in one of those, she thought, and with her own confinement so close now tried to imagine the scene on the day she opened her eyes to the Mead household. There was no sign of Kas or any of the other workers yet. The church clock struck five and she guessed that Kas was washing up in the outhouse at the farm in readiness to take her to the doctor's. Rachel turned to go back to Bella and saw a woman coming along the track by the hedge. It was Nessie Mead.

As Nessie approached Rachel felt her bosom swell with admiration for this woman who she now knew was her mother. She'd had a hard life, Rachel knew, but Nessie looked younger than she remembered, still slim but somewhat more rounded. Her well-brushed chestnut coloured hair shone in the sunlight and her pretty green eyes sparkled with happy recognition.

'Hullo, dear,' Nessie said.

Rachel wanted to speak, there was so much to say but the words wouldn't come. 'I'm your daughter,' she wanted to shout from the rooftops, but how could she cause Nessie such a shock?

It seemed they stood and regarded each other for ages and then Nessie said in a low voice, 'I know what's in your heart, Rachel, dear. I think I always knew there was something special between you and me.'

'You . . . you . . . know?' she gasped.

Nessie nodded, and her eyes filled with sad tears. 'Adam came to see me.'

'He had no right,' Rachel said, suddenly angry. 'It's none of his business. The last thing I wanted was for you to be hurt, Mrs Mead.'

'It's as much Adam's business as anyone else's dear,' Nessie said. 'I'm not hurt – rather glad – to think that the baby I felt was a curse on me survived, and had such a good home with wonderful parents.'

'How long have you known?' Rachel asked, perplexed.

'Looking back I realise there was always some doubt about my baby. I wanted it to die, God forgive me, and afterwards when I thought it had, oh, I longed to have it back again to love, blemish and all. I've only known the truth of the matter since Adam came to see me a couple of weeks ago. After you'd discovered I was your real mother, and Adam was told, he was afraid you wouldn't be able to help yourself but come to see me or blurt it out if we met. He felt I should be warned.'

'It must have come as a dreadful shock, Mrs Mead. Adam didn't have the right to interfere though. He's Belinda's husband, my brother-in-law. He shouldn't have taken matters into his own hands.'

'I'm glad he did. It's best for the truth to come out and be done with. Rachel, his father was yours too!'

'Mr Taylor, my father?' she was stunned. 'And Adam knew all the time?'

'Don't you see? That's why he couldn't marry you,' Nessie went on. 'If you'd gone through with marriage, it would have been against the law. It was fate intervening that brought Doctor Grant back to Wickham after the war in time to prevent such a terrible mistake.' She placed her hand on Rachel's arm. 'It was a terrible shock for Adam then and he couldn't share it with anyone. He thought he'd have to live with the secret for the rest of his life. He had a notion that I might be your mother from rumours he'd heard. He was devastated when he had to treat you so cruelly.' She looked into Rachel's face anxiously. 'I think you'd best sit up in the trap, dear. I'm sorry if this is all too much for you.' Nessie got up to sit beside Rachel and took her hand in hers.

'Why ever couldn't Mum or Adam have told me the rest of the story once they knew that I knew who my mother was?' Rachel asked.

'Mrs Hunter doesn't know that Jake was your father. She and Belinda think you're Dick's child. Adam hasn't told anyone else. He doesn't want his mother upset. Being that you're in the family way and not living in the district, he felt I should know, but asked that we keep our secret.'

'Another brother,' Rachel said slowly as the truth finally dawned and everything became so much clearer. How could she ever forget the fight between Dick Mead and Jake Taylor which caused – her father's death? And all over her, she supposed.

'*Half*-brother, just as Charlie and Benjie are, and my girls are your half-sisters,' Nessie explained.

'But . . . but how . . .' Rachel shook her head. Perhaps this was one question she shouldn't be asking.

'How did Adam's father come to be your father too?' Nessie asked the question for her, then looked away, her lips twisting in a wry smile. 'Rivalry,' she said bluntly. 'Jake wanted me to marry him.' Nessie sighed. 'All our lives might have been very different if I had, but Dick was a bit wild and made sure a shot gun wedding was necessary. I suppose Jake never forgave him for that. He married Lily on the rebound. Life was hard for me with Dick being too fond of the drink and I couldn't always pay the rent, so when Jake became rent collector for the Manor he suggested I could pick strawberries during the season to help out.'

Nessie put her workworn hands to her face at the hurtful memories.

'He forced himself on me,' she said with trembling lips. 'I was used to rough treatment, but after five children I was thin and weak so had no strength to deal him the blow he deserved. It all happened so quickly, here in this very field,' she said softly. 'Doctor Grant found me. He wanted me to prosecute Jake, but I didn't want Dick to know for fear of what he'd do.' She turned and looked at Rachel with alarm in her eyes. 'He found out from Beth eventually. That's what the fight was about all those years later. He was furious that Jake got me in the end, but he knows nothing of your being that baby. There's no reason for him to know.'

She put her arms round Rachel and hugged her. 'I'm so grateful to Doctor Grant and Minnie Fletcher – glad that your life was spared. And I'm sure you're all the stronger for having had to endure the taunts over that strawberry mark. You're such a beautiful woman now, Rachel. I'm proud that you're my daughter, and Jake would have been too.' She laughed. ''Tis no wonder you thought you were in love with Adam – but now that you know you're half-brother and sister, both you and Belinda will be able to understand and accept the situation better.'

'I could never understand why I felt sorry for you, and for Charlie too,' Rachel said. 'I think I must always have loved you.'

'But think what you owe Mrs Hunter – never forget that she brought you up and gave you more than I ever could.'

'Be kind to the woman,' the gypsy's warning echoed in Rachel's ears, and when she saw Kas coming across the field she got down from the trap and went eagerly to share the story with him.

The flock of rooks took off on their flight of fancy to weather storms, mate, nest and prepare for the next strawberry season.

Epilogue

Through the window of the van Rachel marvelled at the enormous orange harvest moon. Another season over; a new and very special one just beginning for her and Kas. She looked down at the month-old baby girl she was cradling in her arms with its mass of rich black hair, navy blue eyes, round and trusting, which Rachel knew would be almost black in a few weeks time. A tiny eager tongue, still milky-white from the last feed, peeped through a dainty rosebud mouth. Rachel glanced back at the moon and offered up a silent prayer for the perfect infant entrusted to her and Kas, though she wished she could have borne him the son he longed for.

'Next time,' she promised with a warm smile. Three times Kas had stood up to go to settle the horses for the night but he hadn't been able to pull himself away from watching Rachel with his baby daughter at her breast.

'The important thing is that you're all right,' he said softly.

'I was beginning to think I'd never be able to give you a baby,' she said. 'And then to have such an easy birth.' Rachel crooned lovingly to her baby. 'She's so beautiful – not the tiniest blemish anywhere. No one will ever be able to call her names, will they?'

'Blemish or no, she'd still be perfect in our eyes,' Kas said. 'Just as I'm sure you were to your parents. But just think, darling, without that strawberry mark Mrs Mead might never have been convinced that you were the baby girl she had.'

Rachel gently touched little Mary's pink cheek. 'I wonder who she'll take after? The Mead girls are all nice-looking, and Adam is too.'

'She's *ours*, and we aren't that bad, are we?'

Rachel laughed. 'I s'pose not. I hope life will be kind to her. We'll try to be good parents, little Mary.' She pulled the exquisite knitted shawl up round the baby's head, wrapped the two ends across in front

290

and laid her in the crib. 'It's a lovely idea to have little Mary and Douglas christened at the same time,' she said after she'd pulled the dividing curtains across the van. Kas already had the kettle on.

'I thought you were going to see to the horses?' she said.

'I'll make us a cup of tea first.' Kas poked the boiler until the coals showed red and then stood with his arm round her. 'Your mother is so proud of both new babies. Now we have two daughters and Belinda and Adam have two sons.'

'She's so pleased that the group has decided to stay on here in the Forest of Bere for the winter.'

'And she'd not the only one,' Kas said, kissing the top of her head.

'Suddenly everything in the world has come right. No more wondering why Adam behaved the way he did. I understand now how awful such a discovery was for him, though I can't imagine how he managed not to tell anyone. Perhaps it made it easier, when I ran away. At last I feel much more contented now that I know the real truth, and it's lovely to be back on friendly, easy terms with Belinda again. We're special to each other – chosen sisters.'

'As Lemuel says, you must regard the past twenty-four years as an era, one which has ended satisfactorily. And as Sybil says we can look forward to the happy times now. No more jealousies, no more misunderstandings.'

Rachel sighed. 'I just wish Dad had lived long enough to know all the answers.'

'You might never have known the truth of your parentage if your father had lived, Rachel. I'm sure wherever he is he knows, and he'll be your guardian angel. Belinda's as well. He'll also know that his letter was meant to be written, and his blessing is on us all, I'm sure.'

While Carol and little Mary slept Kas and Rachel sat outside on the steps of the van, watching the moon rise in all its majesty amidst a myriad of stars.

You have been reading a novel published by Piatkus Books. We hope you have enjoyed it and that you would like to read more of our titles. Please ask for them in your local library or bookshop.

If you would like to be put on our mailing list to receive details of new publications, please send a large stamped addressed envelope (UK only) to:

Piatkus Books: 5 Windmill Street
London W1P 1HF

PIATKUS

The sign of a good book